TINKER, TAILOR, SOLDIER, SPY

TINKER, TAILOR, SOLDIER, SPY

John le Carré

ALFRED A. KNOPF: New York
1974

This Is a Borzoi Book
Published by Alfred A. Knopf, Inc.

Copyright © 1974 by le Carré Productions

Library of Congress Cataloging in Publication Data
- - - - - - - - - - - - - -
Tinker, tailor, soldier, spy.
I. Title.
PZ4.C819Ti3   [PR6053.074]   823'.9'14   74–5084
ISBN 0-394-49219-6

Grateful acknowledgment is made to The Clarendon
Press for permission to reprint the eight-line rhyme
and descriptive paragraph from page 404 of the *Oxford
Dictionary of Nursery Rhymes*, edited by Iona and
Peter Opie (1951).

Manufactured in the United States of America

Published June 17, 1974
Reprinted four times
Sixth Printing, November 1974

For James Bennett
and Dusty Rhodes,
in memory

TINKER,
TAILOR,
SOLDIER,
SAILOR,
RICH MAN,
POOR MAN,
BEGGARMAN,
THIEF.

Small children's fortune-telling rhyme
used when counting cherry stones,
waistcoat buttons, daisy petals,
or the seeds of the Timothy grass.

—from the *Oxford Dictionary*
of Nursery Rhymes

PART I

1

The truth is, if old Major Dover hadn't dropped dead at
Taunton races Jim would never have come to Thursgood's at
all. He came in mid-term without an interview—late May, it
was, though no one would have thought it from the weather—
employed through one of the shiftier agencies specialising in
supply teachers for prep schools, to hold down old Dover's
teaching till someone suitable could be found. "A linguist,"
Thursgood told the common-room, "a temporary measure,"
and brushed away his forelock in self-defence. "Priddo." He
gave the spelling, "P-r-i-d"—French was not Thursgood's
subject so he consulted the slip of paper—"e-a-u-x, first name
James. I think he'll do us very well till July." The staff had no
difficulty in reading the signals. Jim Prideaux was a poor
white of the teaching community. He belonged to the same
sad bunch as the late Mrs. Loveday, who had a Persian-
lamb coat and stood in for junior divinity until her
cheques bounced, or the late Mr. Maltby, the pianist who had
been called from choir practice to help the police with their
enquiries, and as far as anyone knew was helping them to this
day, for Maltby's trunk still lay in the cellar awaiting instructions. Several of the staff, but chiefly Marjoribanks, were in
favour of opening that trunk. They said it contained notori-
ous missing treasures: Aprahamian's silver-framed picture of
his Lebanese mother, for instance; Best-Ingram's Swiss army
penknife and Matron's watch. But Thursgood set his crease-
less face resolutely against their entreaties. Only five years
had passed since he had inherited the school from his father,
but they had taught him already that some things are best
locked away.

Jim Prideaux arrived on a Friday in a rainstorm. The rain rolled like gun-smoke down the brown combes of the Quantocks, then raced across the empty cricket fields into the sandstone of the crumbling façades. He arrived just after lunch, driving an old red Alvis and towing a second-hand trailer that had once been blue. Early afternoons at Thursgood's are tranquil, a brief truce in the running fight of each school day. The boys are sent to rest in their dormitories, the staff sit in the common-room over coffee reading newspapers or correcting boys' work. Thursgood reads a novel to his mother. Of the whole school, therefore, only little Bill Roach actually saw Jim arrive, saw the steam belching from the Alvis's bonnet as it wheezed its way down the pitted drive, windscreen wipers going full pelt and the trailer shuddering through the puddles in pursuit.

Roach was a new boy in those days and graded dull, if not actually deficient. Thursgood's was his second prep school in two terms. He was a fat round child with asthma, and he spent large parts of his rest kneeling on the end of his bed, gazing through the window. His mother lived grandly in Bath; his father was agreed to be the richest in the school, a distinction which cost the son dear. Coming from a broken home, Roach was also a natural watcher. In Roach's observation Jim did not stop at the school buildings but continued across the sweep to the stable yard. He knew the layout of the place already. Roach decided later that he must have made a reconnaissance or studied maps. Even when he reached the yard, he didn't stop but drove straight onto the wet grass, travelling at speed to keep the momentum. Then over the hummock into the Dip, head-first and out of sight. Roach half expected the trailer to jackknife on the brink, Jim took it over so fast, but instead it just lifted its tail and disappeared like a giant rabbit into its hole.

The Dip is a piece of Thursgood folklore. It lies in a patch of wasteland between the orchard, the fruit house, and the stable yard. To look at, it is no more than a depression in the ground, grass covered, with hummocks on the northern side, each about boy height and covered in tufted thickets which in summer grow spongy. It is these hummocks that give the Dip its special virtue as a playground and also its reputation, which varies with the fantasy of each new generation of boys. They are the traces of an open-cast silver mine, says one year, and digs enthusiastically for wealth. They are a Romano-British fort, says another, and stages battles with sticks and clay missiles. To others the Dip is a bomb-crater from the war and the hummocks are seated bodies buried in the blast. The truth is more prosaic. Six years ago, and not long before his abrupt elopement with a receptionist from the Castle Hotel, Thursgood's father had launched an appeal for a swimming pool and persuaded the boys to dig a large hole with a deep and a shallow end. But the money that came in was never quite enough to finance the ambition, so it was frittered away on other schemes, such as a new projector for the art school, and a plan to grow mushrooms in the school cellars. And even, said the cruel ones, to feather a nest for certain illicit lovers when they eventually took flight to Germany, the lady's native home.

Jim was unaware of these associations. The fact remains that by sheer luck he had chosen the one corner of Thursgood's academy which, as far as Roach was concerned, was endowed with supernatural properties.

Roach waited at the window but saw nothing more. Both the Alvis and the trailer were in dead ground, and if it hadn't been for the wet red tracks across the grass he might have wondered whether he had dreamed the whole thing. But the tracks were real, so when the bell went for the end of rest he put on his rubber boots and trudged through the rain to the top of the Dip and peered down, and there was Jim dressed in an army raincoat and a quite extraordinary hat, broad-brimmed like a safari hat but hairy, with one side pinned up in a rakish piratical curl and the water running off it like a gutter.

The Alvis was in the stable yard; Roach never knew how Jim spirited it out of the Dip, but the trailer was right down there, at what should have been the deep end, bedded on platforms of weathered brick, and Jim was sitting on the step drinking from a green plastic beaker, and rubbing his right shoulder as if he had banged it on something, while the rain poured off his hat. Then the hat lifted and Roach found himself staring at an extremely fierce red face, made still fiercer by the shadow of the brim and by a brown moustache washed into fangs by the rain. The rest of the face was criss-crossed with jagged cracks, so deep and crooked that Roach concluded in another of his flashes of imaginative genius that Jim had once been very hungry in a tropical place and filled up again since. The left arm still lay across his chest, the right shoulder was still drawn high against his neck. But the whole tangled shape of him was stock-still, he was like an animal frozen against its background: a stag, thought Roach, on a hopeful impulse; something noble.

"Who the hell are you?" asked a very military voice.

"Sir, Roach, sir. I'm a new boy."

For a moment longer, the brick face surveyed Roach from the shadow of the hat. Then, to his intense relief, its features relaxed into a wolfish grin, the left hand, still clapped over the right shoulder, resumed its slow massage while at the same time he managed a long pull from the plastic beaker.

"New boy, eh?" Jim repeated into the beaker, still grinning. "Well, that's a lucky break, I will say."

Rising now, and turning his crooked back on Roach, Jim set to work on what appeared to be a detailed study of the trailer's four legs, a very critical study that involved much rocking of the suspension, and much tilting of the strangely garbed head, and the emplacement of several bricks at different angles and points. Meanwhile the spring rain was clattering down on everything: his coat, his hat, and the roof of the old trailer. And Roach noticed that throughout these manoeuvres Jim's right shoulder had not budged at all but stayed wedged high against his neck like a rock under the mackintosh. Therefore he wondered whether Jim was a sort of giant hunchback and whether all hunch backs hurt as Jim's did. And he noticed as a generality, a thing to store away, that people with bad backs take long strides; it was something to do with balance.

"New boy, eh? Well, *I'm* not a new boy," Jim went on, in altogether a much more friendly tone, as he pulled at a leg of the trailer. "I'm an old boy. Old as Rip van Winkle, if you want to know. Older. Got any friends?"

"No, sir," said Roach simply, in the listless tone that schoolboys always use for saying "no," leaving all positive response to their interrogators. Jim, however, made no response at all, so that Roach felt an odd stirring of kinship suddenly, and of hope.

"My other name's Bill," he said. "I was christened Bill but Mr. Thursgood calls me William."

"Bill, eh. The unpaid Bill. Anyone ever call you that?"

"No, sir."

"Good name, anyway."

"Yes, sir."

"Known a lot of Bills. They've all been good'uns."

With that, in a manner of speaking, the introduction was made. Jim did not tell Roach to go away, so Roach stayed on the brow peering downward through his rain-smeared spectacles. The bricks, he noticed with awe, were pinched from the cucumber frame. Several had been loose already and Jim must have loosened them a bit more. It seemed a wonderful thing to Roach that anyone just arrived at Thursgood's should be so self-possessed as to pinch the actual fabric of the school for his own purposes, and doubly wonderful that Jim had run a lead off the hydrant for his water, for that hydrant was the subject of a special school rule: to touch it at all was a beatable offence.

"Hey, you, Bill. You wouldn't have such a thing as a marble on you, by any chance?"

"A, sir, what, sir?" Roach asked, patting his pockets in a dazed way.

"Marble, old boy. Round glass marble, little ball. Don't boys play marbles any more? We did when I was at school."

Roach had no marble, but Aprahamian had had a whole collection flown in from Beirut. It took Roach about fifty seconds to race back to the school, secure one against the wildest undertakings, and return panting to the Dip. There he hesitated, for in his mind the Dip was already Jim's and Roach required leave to descend it. But Jim had disappeared into the trailer, so, having waited a moment, Roach stepped gingerly down the bank and offered the marble through the doorway. Jim didn't spot him at once. He was sipping from the beaker and staring out the window at the black clouds as they tore this way and that over the Quantocks. This sipping movement, Roach noticed, was actually quite difficult, for Jim could not easily swallow standing up straight; he had to tilt his whole twisted trunk backward to achieve the angle. Meanwhile the rain came on really hard again, rattling against the trailer like gravel.

"Sir," said Roach, but Jim made no move.

"Trouble with an Alvis is, no damn springs," said Jim at last, more to the window than to his visitor. "You drive along with your rump on the white line, eh? Cripple anybody." And, tilting his trunk again, he drank.

"Yes, sir," said Roach, much surprised that Jim should assume he was a driver.

Jim had taken off his hat. His sandy hair was close-cropped; there were patches where someone had gone too low with the scissors. These patches were mainly on one side, so that Roach guessed that Jim had cut the hair himself with his good arm, which made him even more lopsided.

"I brought you a marble," said Roach.

"Very good of you. Thanks, old boy." Taking the marble, he slowly rolled it round his hard, powdery palm, and Roach knew at once that he was very skillful at all sorts of things;

that he was the kind of man who lived on terms with tools and objects generally. "Not level, you see, Bill," he confided, still intent upon the marble. "Skewy. Like me. Watch," and turned purposefully to the larger window. A strip of aluminium beading ran along the bottom, put there to catch the condensation. Laying the marble in it, Jim watched it roll to the end and fall on the floor.

"Skewy," he repeated. "Listing in the stern. Can't have that, can we? Hey, hey, where d'you get to, you little brute?"

The trailer was not a homey place, Roach noticed, stooping to retrieve the marble. It might have belonged to anyone, though it was scrupulously clean. A bunk, a kitchen chair, a ship's stove, a calor gas cylinder. Not even a picture of his wife, thought Roach, who had not yet met a bachelor, with the exception of Mr. Thursgood. The only personal things he could find were a webbing kit-bag hanging from the door, a set of sewing things stored beside the bunk, and a homemade shower made from a perforated biscuit tin and neatly welded to the roof. And on the table one bottle of colourless drink, gin or vodka, because that was what his father drank when Roach went to his flat for weekends in the holidays.

"East-west looks okay, but north-south is undoubtedly skewy," Jim declared, testing the other window ledge. "What are you good at, Bill?"

"I don't know, sir," said Roach woodenly.

"Got to be good at something, surely; everyone is. How about football? Are you good at football, Bill?"

"No, sir," said Roach.

"Are you a grind, then?" Jim asked carelessly, as he lowered himself with a short grunt onto the bed and took a pull from the beaker. "You don't look a grind, I must say," he added politely. "Although you're a loner."

"I don't know," Roach repeated, and moved half a pace towards the open door.

"What's your best thing, then?" He took another long sip.

"Must be good at something, Bill; everyone is. My best thing was ducks and drakes. Cheers."

Now this was an unfortunate question to ask of Roach just then, for it occupied most of his waking hours. Indeed he had recently come to doubt whether he had any purpose on earth at all. In work and play he considered himself seriously inadequate; even the daily routine of the school, such as making his bed and tidying his clothes, seemed to be beyond his reach. Also he lacked piety: old Mrs. Thursgood had told him so; he screwed up his face too much at chapel. He blamed himself very much for these shortcomings, but most of all he blamed himself for the break-up of his parents' marriage, which he should have seen coming and taken steps to prevent. He even wondered whether he was more directly responsible; whether, for instance, he was abnormally wicked or divisive or slothful, and that his bad character had wrought the rift. At his last school he had tried to explain this by screaming, and feigning fits of cerebral palsy, which his aunt had. His parents conferred, as they frequently did in their reasonable way, and changed his school. Therefore this chance question, levelled at him in the cramped trailer by a creature at least halfway to divinity—a fellow solitary, at that—brought him suddenly very near disaster. He felt the heat charging to his face; he watched his spectacles mist over and the trailer begin to dissolve into a sea of grief. Whether Jim noticed this, Roach never knew, for suddenly he had turned his crooked back on him, moved away to the table, and was helping himself from the plastic beaker while he threw out saving phrases.

"You're a good watcher, anyway, I'll tell you that for nothing, old boy. Us singles always are—no one to rely on, what? Nobody else spotted me. Gave me a real turn up there, parked on the horizon. Thought you were a juju man. Best watcher in the unit, Bill Roach is, I'll bet. Long as he's got his specs on. What?"

"Yes," Roach agreed gratefully, "I am."

"Well, you stay here and watch, then," Jim commanded,

clapping the safari hat back on his head, "and I'll slip outside and trim the legs. Do that?"

"Yes, sir."

"Where's damn marble?"

"Here, sir."

"Call out when she moves, right? North, south, whichever way she rolls. Understand?"

"Yes, sir."

"Know which way's north?"

"That way," said Roach promptly, and struck out his arm at random.

"Right. Well, you call when she rolls," Jim repeated, and disappeared into the rain. A moment later, Roach felt the ground swaying under his feet and heard another roar either of pain or anger, as Jim wrestled with a recalcitrant leg.

In the course of that same summer term, the boys paid Jim the compliment of a nickname. They had several shots before they were happy. They tried "Trooper," which caught the bit of military in him, his occasional, quite harmless cursing, and his solitary rambles in the Quantocks. All the same, "Trooper" didn't stick, so they tried "Pirate" and for a while "Goulash." "Goulash" because of his taste for hot food, the smell of curries and onions and paprika that greeted them in warm puffs as they filed past the Dip on their way to evensong. "Goulash" for his perfect French, which was held to have a slushy quality. Spikely, of Five B, could imitate it to a hair: "You heard the question, Berger. What is Emile looking at?"—a convulsive jerk of the right hand—"Don't gawp at me, old boy, I'm not a juju man. *Qu'est-ce qu'il regarde, Emile dans le tableau que tu as sous le nez? Mon cher Berger,* if you do not very soon summon one lucid sentence of French, *je te mettrai tout de suite à la porte, tu comprends,* you beastly toad?"

But these terrible threats were never carried out, either in

French or in English. In a quaint way, they actually added to the aura of gentleness which quickly surrounded him, a gentleness only possible in big men seen through the eyes of boys.

Yet "Goulash" did not satisfy them, either. It lacked the hint of strength contained. It took no account of Jim's passionate Englishness, which was the only subject where he could be relied on to waste time. Toad Spikely had only to venture one disparaging comment on the monarchy, extol the joys of some foreign country, preferably a hot one, for Jim to colour sharply and snap out a good three minutes' worth on the privilege of being born an Englishman. He knew they were teasing him but he was unable not to rise. Often he ended his homily with a rueful grin, and muttered references to red herrings, and red faces too, when certain people would have to come in for extra work and miss their football. But England was his love; when it came down to it, no one suffered for her.

"Best place in the whole damn world!" he bellowed once. "Know why? Know why, toad?"

Spikely did not, so Jim seized a crayon and drew a globe. To the west, America, he said, full of greedy fools fouling up their inheritance. To the east, China-Russia; he drew no distinction: boiler suits, prison camps, and a damn long march to nowhere. In the middle . . .

Finally they hit on "Rhino."

Partly this was a play on "Prideaux," partly a reference to his taste for living off the land and his appetite for physical exercise, which they noted constantly. Shivering in the shower queue first thing in the morning, they would see the Rhino pounding down Combe Lane with a rucksack on his crooked back as he returned from his morning march. Going to bed, they could glimpse his lonely shadow through the plastic roof of the fives court as the Rhino tirelessly attacked the concrete wall. And sometimes, on warm evenings, from their dormitory windows they would covertly watch him at golf, which he played with a dreadful old iron, zigzagging across the playing fields, often after reading to them from an extremely English adventure book: Biggles, Percy Westerman, or Jeffrey Farnol, grabbed haphazard from the dingy library. At each stroke they waited for the grunt as he started his back-swing, and they were seldom disappointed. They kept a meticulous score. At the staff cricket match he made twenty-five before dismissing himself with a ball deliberately lofted to Spikely at square leg. "Catch, toad, catch it—go on. Well done, Spikely, good lad—that's what you're there for."

He was also credited, despite his taste for tolerance, with a sound understanding of the criminal mind. There were several examples of this, but the most telling occurred a few days before the end of term, when Spikely discovered in Jim's waste-basket a draft of the next day's examination paper, and rented it to candidates at five new pence a time. Several boys paid their shilling and spent an agonised night memorising answers by torchlight in their dormitories. But when the exam came round Jim presented a quite different paper.

"You can look at this one for nothing," he bellowed as he sat down. And, having hauled open his *Daily Telegraph,* he calmly gave himself over to the latest counsels of the juju men, which they understood to mean almost anyone with intellectual pretension, even if he wrote in the Queen's cause.

There was lastly the incident of the owl, which had a separate place in their opinion of him, since it involved death, a phenomenon to which children react variously. The weather continuing cold, Jim brought a bucket of coal to his classroom and one Wednesday lit it in the grate, and sat there with his back to the warmth, reading a *dictée*. First some soot fell, which he ignored; then the owl came down, a full-sized barn owl which had nested up there, no doubt, through many unswept winters and summers of Dover's rule, and was now smoked out, dazed and black from beating itself to exhaustion in the flue. It fell over the coals and collapsed in a heap on the wooden floorboard with a clatter and a scuffle, then lay like an emissary of the devil, hunched but breathing, wings stretched, staring straight out at the boys through the soot that caked its eyes. There was no one who was not frightened; even Spikely, a hero, was frightened. Except for Jim, who had in a second folded the beast together and taken it out the door without a word. They heard nothing, though they listened like stowaways, till the sound of running water from down the corridor as Jim evidently washed his hands. "He's having a pee," said Spikely, which earned a nervous laugh. But as they filed out of the classroom they discovered the owl still folded, neatly dead and awaiting burial, on top of the compost heap beside the Dip. Its neck, as the braver ones established, was snapped. Only a gamekeeper, declared Sudeley, who had one, would know how to kill an owl so well.

Among the rest of the Thursgood community, opinion regarding Jim was less unanimous. The ghost of Mr. Maltby, the pianist, died hard. Matron, siding with Bill Roach, pronounced him heroic and in need of care: it was a miracle he managed with that back. Marjoribanks said he had been run over by a bus when he was drunk. It was Marjoribanks also, at the staff match where Jim so excelled, who pointed out the sweater. Marjoribanks was not a cricketer but he had strolled down to watch with Thursgood.

"Do you think that sweater's kosher," he asked in a high, jokey voice, "or do you think he pinched it?"

"Leonard, that's very unfair," Thursgood scolded, hammering at the flanks of his Labrador. "Bite him, Ginny, bite the bad man."

By the time he reached his study, however, Thursgood's laughter had quite worn off and he became extremely nervous. Bogus Oxford men he could deal with, just as in his time he had known classics masters who had no Greek and parsons who had no divinity. Such men, confronted with proof of their deception, broke down and wept and left, or stayed on half-pay. But men who withheld genuine accomplishment—these were a breed he had not met but he knew already that he did not like them. Having consulted the university calendar, he telephoned the agency—a Mr. Stroll, of the house of Stroll & Medley.

"What precisely do you want to know?" Mr. Stroll asked with a dreadful sigh.

"Well, nothing *precisely*." Thursgood's mother was sewing at a sampler and seemed not to hear. "Merely that if one asks for a written *curriculum vitae* one likes it to be complete. One doesn't like gaps. Not if one pays one's fee."

At this point Thursgood found himself wondering rather wildly whether he had woken Mr. Stroll from a deep sleep to which he had now returned.

"Very patriotic bloke," Mr. Stroll observed finally.

"I did not employ him for his patriotism."

"He's been in dock," Mr. Stroll whispered on, as if through frightful draughts of cigarette smoke. "Laid up. Spinal."

"Quite so. But I assume he has not been in hospital for the whole of the last twenty-five years. *Touché*," he murmured to his mother, his hand over the mouthpiece, and once more it crossed his mind that Mr. Stroll had dropped off to sleep.

"You've only got him till the end of term," Mr. Stroll breathed. "If you don't fancy him, chuck him out. You asked for temporary, temporary's what you've got. You said cheap, you've got cheap."

"That's as may be," Thursgood retorted gamely. "But I've paid you a twenty-guinea fee; my father dealt with you for many years and I'm entitled to certain assurances. You've put here—may I read it to you?—you've put here: 'Before his injury, various overseas appointments of a commercial and prospecting nature.' Now that is hardly an enlightening description of a lifetime's employment, is it?"

At her sewing his mother nodded her agreement. "It is *not*," she echoed aloud.

"That's my first point. Let me go on a little."

"Not too much, darling," warned his mother.

"I happen to know he was up at Oxford in 1938. Why didn't he finish? What went wrong?"

"I seem to recall there was an interlude round about then," said Mr. Stroll after another age. "But I expect you're too young to remember it."

"He can't have been in prison *all* the time," said his mother after a very long silence, still without looking up from her sewing.

"He's been somewhere," said Thursgood morosely, staring across the windswept gardens towards the Dip.

All through the summer holidays, as he moved uncomfortably between one household and another, embracing and rejecting, Bill Roach fretted about Jim: whether his back was hurting; what he was doing for money now that he had no one to teach and only half a term's pay to live on; worst of all, whether he would be there when the new term began, for Bill had a feeling he could not describe that Jim lived so precariously on the world's surface that he might at any time fall off it into a void; he feared that Jim was like himself, without a natural gravity to hold him on. He rehearsed the circumstances of their first meeting, and in particular Jim's enquiry regarding friendship, and he had a holy terror that just as he had failed his parents in love, so he had failed Jim, largely owing to the disparity in their ages. And that therefore Jim had moved on and was already looking somewhere else for a companion, scanning other schools with his pale eyes. He imagined also that, like himself, Jim had had a great attachment that had failed him and that he longed to replace. But here Bill Roach's speculation met a dead end: he had no idea how adults loved each other.

There was so little he could do that was practical. He consulted a medical book and interrogated his mother about hunchbacks and he longed but did not dare to steal a bottle of his father's vodka and take it back to Thursgood's as a lure. And when at last his mother's chauffeur dropped him at the hated steps, he did not pause to say goodbye but ran for all he was worth to the top of the Dip, and there to his immeasurable joy was Jim's trailer in its same spot at the bottom, a shade dirtier than before, and a fresh patch of earth beside it, he supposed for winter vegetables. And Jim sitting on the step, grinning up at him as if he had heard Bill coming and got the grin of welcome ready before he appeared at the brink.

That same term, Jim invented a nickname for Roach. He dropped "Bill" and called him "Jumbo" instead. He gave no reason for this and Roach, as is common in the case of christenings, was in no position to object. In return, Roach appointed himself Jim's guardian; a regent-guardian was how he thought of the appointment; a stand-in replacing Jim's departed friend, whoever that friend might be.

2

Unlike Jim Prideaux, Mr. George Smiley was not naturally equipped for hurrying in the rain, least of all at dead of night. Indeed, he might have been the final form for which Bill Roach was the prototype. Small, podgy, and at best middle-aged, he was by appearance one of London's meek who do not inherit the earth. His legs were short, his gait anything but agile, his dress costly, ill-fitting, and extremely wet. His overcoat, which had a hint of widowhood about it, was of that black loose weave which is designed to retain moisture. Either the sleeves were too long or his arms were too short, for, as with Roach, when he wore his mackintosh, the cuffs all but concealed the fingers. For reasons of vanity he wore no hat, believing rightly that hats made him ridiculous. "Like an egg-cosy," his beautiful wife had remarked not long before the last occasion on which she left him, and her criticism, as so often, had endured. Therefore the rain had formed in fat, unbanishable drops on the thick lenses of his spectacles, forcing him alternately to lower or throw back his head as he scuttled along the pavement that skirted the blackened arcades of Victoria Station. He was proceeding west, to the sanctuary of Chelsea, where he lived. His step, for whatever reason, was a fraction uncertain, and if Jim Prideaux had risen out of the shadows demanding to know whether he had any friends, he would probably have answered that he preferred to settle for a taxi.

"Roddy's such a windbag," he muttered to himself as a fresh deluge dashed itself against his ample cheeks, then trickled downward to his sodden shirt. "Why didn't I just get up and leave?"

Ruefully, Smiley once more rehearsed the reasons for his present misery, and concluded with a dispassion inseparable from the humble part of his nature that they were of his own making.

It had been from the start a day of travail. He had risen too late after working too late the night before, a practice that had crept up on him since retirement last year. Discovering he had run out of coffee, he queued at the grocer's till he ran out of patience also, then haughtily decided to attend to his personal administration. His bank statement, which had arrived with the morning's post, revealed that his wife had drawn the lion's share of his monthly pension: very well, he decreed, he would sell something. The response was irrational, for he was quite decently off and the obscure City bank responsible for his pension paid it with regularity. Wrapping up an early edition of Grimmelshausen, nevertheless, a modest treasure from his Oxford days, he solemnly set off for Heywood Hill's bookshop in Curzon Street, where he occasionally contracted friendly bargains with the proprietor. On the way he became even more irritable, and from a call-box sought an appointment with his solicitor for that afternoon.

"George, how can you be so vulgar? Nobody divorces Ann. Send her flowers and come to lunch."

This advice bucked him up and he approached Heywood Hill with a merry heart only to walk slap into the arms of Roddy Martindale emerging from Trumper's after his weekly haircut.

Martindale had no valid claim on Smiley either professionally or socially. He worked on the fleshy side of the Foreign Office and his job consisted of lunching visiting dignitaries whom no one else would have entertained in his woodshed. He was a floating bachelor with a grey mane and that nimbleness which only fat men have. He affected buttonholes and pale suits, and he pretended on the flimsiest grounds to an intimate familiarity with the large back rooms of Whitehall. Some years ago, before it was disbanded, he had adorned a Whitehall working party to co-ordinate intelligence. In the war, having a certain mathematical facility, he had also haunted the fringes of the secret world; and once, as he never tired of telling, he had worked with John Landsbury on a Circus coding operation of transient delicacy. But the war, as Smiley sometimes had to remind himself, was thirty years ago.

"Hullo, Roddy," said Smiley. "Nice to see you."

Martindale spoke in a confiding upper-class bellow of the sort that, on foreign holidays, had more than once caused Smiley to sign out of his hotel and run for cover.

"My dear boy, if it isn't the maestro himself! They told me you were locked up with the monks in Saint Gallen or somewhere, poring over manuscripts! Confess to me at once. I want to know all you've been doing, every little bit. Are you well? Do you love England still? How's the delicious Ann?" His restless gaze flicked up and down the street before lighting on the wrapped volume of Grimmelshausen under

Smiley's arm. "Pound to a penny that's a present for her. They tell me you spoil her outrageously." His voice dropped to a mountainous murmur: "I say, you're not back on the beat, are you? Don't tell me it's all cover, George, *cover?*" His sharp tongue explored the moist edges of his little mouth, then, like a snake, vanished between its folds.

So, fool that he was, Smiley bought his escape by agreeing to dine that same evening at a club in Manchester Square to which they both belonged but which Smiley avoided like the pest, not least because Roddy Martindale was a member. When evening came, he was still full of luncheon at the White Tower, where his solicitor, a very self-indulgent man, had decided that only a great meal would recover George from his doldrums. Martindale, by a different route, had reached the same conclusion, and for four long hours over food Smiley did not want they had bandied names as if they were forgotten footballers. Jebedee, who was Smiley's old tutor: "*Such* a loss to us, bless him," murmured Martindale, who so far as Smiley knew had never clapped eyes on Jebedee. "And what a talent for the game, eh? One of the real greats, I always say." Then Fielding, the French mediaevalist from Cambridge: "Oh, but what a *lovely* sense of humour. Sharp mind, sharp!" Then Sparke from the School of Oriental Languages, and lastly Steed-Asprey, who had founded that very club in order to escape from bores like Roddy Martindale.

"I knew his poor brother, you know. Half the mind and twice the brawn, bless him. Brain went all the other way."

And Smiley through a fog of drink had listened to this nonsense, saying "yes" and "no" and "what a pity" and "no, they never found him," and once, to his abiding shame, "oh, come, you flatter me," till with lugubrious inevitability Martindale came to more recent things—the change of power and Smiley's withdrawal from the service.

Predictably, he started with the last days of Control: "Your old boss, George, bless him, the only one who ever kept his name a secret. Not from you, of course, he never had *any*

secrets from you, George, did he? Close as thieves, Smiley and
Control were, so they say, right to the end."

"They're very complimentary."

"Don't flirt, George; I'm an old trooper, you forget. You
and Control were just like that." Briefly the plump hands
made a token marriage. "That's why you were thrown out—
don't deceive me, that's why Bill Haydon got your job.
That's why he's Percy Alleline's cup-bearer and you're not."

"If you say so, Roddy."

"I do. I say more than that. *Far* more."

As Martindale drew closer, Smiley caught the odour of one
of Trumper's most sensitive creations.

"I say something else: Control never died at all. He's been
seen." With a fluttering gesture he silenced Smiley's protests.
"Let me finish. Willy Andrewartha walked straight into him
in Jo'burg airport, in the waiting-room. Not a ghost. Flesh.
Willy was at the bar buying a soda for the heat; you haven't
seen Willy recently but he's a balloon. He turned round, and
there was Control beside him dressed up like a ghastly Boer.
The moment he saw Willy he bolted. How's that? So now we
know. Control never died at all. He was driven out by Percy
Alleline and his three-piece band, so he went to ground in
South Africa, bless him. Well, you can't blame him, can you?
You can't blame a man for wanting a drop of peace in the
evening of his life. I can't."

The monstrosity of this, reaching Smiley through a
thickening wall of spiritual exhaustion, left him momentarily
speechless.

"That's ridiculous! That's the most idiotic story I ever
heard! Control is dead. He died of a heart attack after a long
illness. Besides, he hated South Africa. He hated everywhere
except Surrey, the Circus, and Lords Cricket Ground. Really,
Roddy, you mustn't tell stories like that." He might have
added: I buried him myself at a hateful crematorium in the
East End, last Christmas Eve, alone. The parson had a speech
impediment.

"Willy Andrewartha was always the most God-awful liar,"

Martindale reflected, quite unruffled. "I said the same to him myself: 'The sheerest nonsense, Willy; you should be ashamed of yourself.' " And straight on, as if never by thought or word had he subscribed to that silly view: "It was the Czech scandal that put the final nail into Control's coffin, I suppose. That poor fellow who was shot in the back and got himself into the newspapers, the one who was so thick with Bill Haydon always, so we hear. *Ellis*, we're to call him, and we still do, don't we, even if we know his real name as well as we know our own."

Shrewdly Martindale waited for Smiley to cap this, but Smiley had no intention of capping anything, so Martindale tried a third tack.

"Somehow I can never quite believe in Percy Alleline as Chief, can you? Is it age, George, or is it just my natural cynicism? Do tell me, you're so good at people. I suppose power sits poorly on those we've grown up with. Is that a clue? There are so few who can carry it off for me these days and poor Percy's such an *obvious* person, I always think, specially after that little serpent, Control. That heavy good fellowship—how can one take him seriously? One has only to think of him in the old days lolling in the bar of the Travellers', sucking away on that log pipe of his and buying drinks for the moguls; well, really, one does like one's perfidy to be subtle, don't you agree? Or don't you care as long as it's successful? What's his knack, George, what's his secret recipe?" He was speaking most intently, leaning forward, his eyes greedy and excited. Only food could otherwise move him so deeply. "Living off the wits of his subordinates—well, maybe that's leadership these days."

"Really, Roddy, I can't help you," said Smiley weakly. "I never knew Percy as a force, you see. Only as a—" He lost the word.

"A striver," Martindale suggested, eyes glistening. "With his sights on Control's purple, day and night. Now he's wearing it and the mob loves him. So who's his strong left arm,

George? Who's earning him his reputation? Wonderfully well he's doing, we hear it from all sides. Little reading rooms at the Admiralty, little committees popping up with funny names, red carpet for Percy wherever he goes in the White-hall corridors, junior ministers receiving special words of congratulation from on high, people one's never heard of getting grand medals for nothing. I've seen it all before, you know."

"Roddy, I can't help you," Smiley insisted, making to get up. "You're out of my depth, truly." But Martindale was physically restraining him, holding him at the table with one damp hand while he talked still faster.

"So who's the cleverboots? Not Percy, that's for sure. And don't tell me the Americans have started trusting us again, either." The grip tightened. "Dashing Bill Haydon, our latter-day Lawrence of Arabia, bless him; there you are—it's Bill, your old rival." Martindale's tongue poked out its head again, reconnoitred and withdrew, leaving a thin smile like a trail. "I'm told that you and Bill shared *everything* once upon a time," he said. "Still, he never was orthodox, was he? Genius never is."

"Anything further you require, Mr. Smiley?" the waiter asked.

"Then it's Bland: the shop-soiled white hope, the redbrick don." Still he would not release him. "And if those two aren't providing the speed, it's someone in retirement, isn't it? I mean someone pretending to be in retirement, don't I? And if Control's dead, who is there left? Apart from you."

They were putting on their coats. The porters had gone home; they had to fetch them for themselves from the empty brown racks.

"Roy Bland's not redbrick," Smiley said loudly. "He was at Saint Antony's College, Oxford, if you want to know."

Heaven help me, it was the best I could do, thought Smiley.

"Don't be silly, dear," Martindale snapped. Smiley had bored him: he looked sulky and cheated; distressing downward folds had formed on the lower contours of his cheeks.

"Of course Saint Antony's is redbrick; it makes no difference there's a little bit of sandstone in the same street, even if he was your protégé. I expect he's Bill Haydon's now—don't tip him, it's my party, not yours. Father to them all, Bill is— always was. Draws them like bees. Well, he has the glamour, hasn't he; not like some of us. Star quality I call it, one of the few. I'm told the women literally bow down before him, if that's what women do."

"Good night, Roddy."

"Love to Ann, mind."

"I won't forget."

"Well, don't."

And now it was pouring with rain, Smiley was soaked to the skin, and God as a punishment had removed all taxis from the face of London.

3

"Sheer lack of will-power," he told himself as he courteously declined the suggestions of a lady in a doorway. "One calls it politeness, whereas in fact it is nothing but weakness. You *featherhead*, Martindale. You pompous, bogus, effeminate, non-productive—" He stepped widely to avoid an unseen obstacle. "Weakness," he resumed, "and an inability to live a self-sufficient life independent of institutions"—a puddle emptied itself neatly into his shoe—"and emotional attachments that have long outlived their purpose. *Viz.*, my wife; *viz.*, the Circus; *viz.*, living in London. Taxi!"

Smiley lurched forward but was already too late. Two girls, giggling under one umbrella, clambered aboard in a flurry of arms and legs. Uselessly pulling up the collar of his black overcoat, he continued his solitary march. "Shop-soiled white hope," he muttered furiously. "Little bit of sandstone in the street. You bombastic, inquisitive, impertinent—"

And then, of course, he remembered far too late that he had left the Grimmelshausen at his club.

"Oh, damn!" he cried *sopra voce*, halting in his tracks for greater emphasis. "Oh, damn—oh, *damn*—oh, damn."

He would sell his London house: he had decided. Back there under the awning, crouching beside the cigarette machine, waiting for the cloudburst to end, he had taken this grave decision. Property values in London had risen out of proportion; he had heard it from every side. Good. He would sell and with a part of the proceeds buy a cottage in the Cotswolds. Burford? Too much traffic. Steeple Aston—that was a place. He would set up as a mild eccentric, discursive, withdrawn, but possessing one or two lovable habits such as muttering to himself as he bumbled along pavements. Out of date, perhaps, but who wasn't these days? Out of date, but loyal to his own time. At a certain moment, after all, every man chooses: will he go forward, will he go back? There was nothing dishonourable in not being blown about by every little modern wind. Better to have worth, to entrench, to be an oak of one's own generation. And if Ann wanted to return—well, he would show her the door.

Or not show her the door, according to—well, how much she wanted to return.

Consoled by these visions, Smiley arrived at the King's Road, where he paused on the pavement as if waiting to cross. To either side, festive boutiques. Before him, his own Bywater Street, a cul-de-sac exactly 117 of his own paces long. When he had first come to live here, these Georgian cottages had a modest, down-at-heel charm, with young couples making do on fifteen pounds a week and a tax-free lodger hidden in the basement. Now steel screens protected their lower windows, and for each house three cars jammed the curb. From long habit, Smiley passed these in review, checking which were familiar, which were not; of the unfamiliar, which had aerials and extra mirrors, which were the closed vans that watchers like. Partly he did this as a test of memory to preserve his mind from the atrophy of retirement, just as on other days he learnt the names of the shops along his bus route to the British Museum; just as he knew how many stairs there were to each flight of his own house and which way each of the twelve doors opened.

But Smiley had a second reason, which was fear, the secret fear that follows every professional to his grave. Namely, that one day, out of a past so complex that he himself could not remember all the enemies he might have made, one of them would find him and demand the reckoning.

At the bottom of the street, a neighbour was exercising her dog; seeing him, she lifted her head to say something, but he ignored her, knowing it would be about Ann. He crossed the road. His house was in darkness; the curtains were as he had left them. He climbed the six steps to the front door. Since Ann's departure, his cleaning woman had also left: no one but Ann had a key. There were two locks, a Banham deadlock and a Chubb Pipekey, and two splinters of his own manufacture, splits of oak each the size of a thumbnail, wedged into the lintel above and below the Banham. They were a hangover from his days in the field. Recently, without quite knowing why, he had started using them again; perhaps he didn't want her to take him by surprise. With the tips of his fingers he discovered each in turn. The routine over, he unlocked the door, pushed it open, and felt the midday mail slithering over the carpet.

What was due? he wondered. *German Life and Letters? Philology? Philology*, he decided; it was already overdue. Putting on the hall light, he stooped and peered through his post. One "account rendered" from his tailor for a suit he had not ordered but that he suspected was one of those presently adorning Ann's lover; one bill from a garage in Henley for her petrol (what, pray, were they doing in Henley, broke, on the ninth of October?); one letter from the bank regarding a local cashing facility in favour of the Lady Ann Smiley at a branch of the Midland Bank in Immingham.

And what the devil, he demanded of this document, are they doing in Immingham? Who ever had a love affair in Immingham, for goodness' sake? Where *was* Immingham?

He was still pondering the question when his gaze fell upon an unfamiliar umbrella in the stand, a silk one with a stitched leather handle and a gold ring with no initial. And it passed through his mind with a speed which has no place in time that since the umbrella was dry it must have arrived there before six-fifteen when the rain began, for there was no moisture in the stand either. Also that it was an elegant umbrella and the ferrule was barely scratched, though it was not new. And that therefore the umbrella belonged to someone agile—even young, like Ann's latest swain. But that since its owner had known about the wedges and known how to put them back once he was inside the house, and had the wit to lay the mail against the door after disturbing and no doubt reading it, then most likely he knew Smiley, too; and was not a lover but a professional like himself, who had at some time worked closely with him and knew his handwriting, as it is called in the jargon.

The drawing-room door was ajar. Softly he pushed it further open.

"Peter?" he said.

Through the gap he saw by the light of the street two suède shoes, lazily folded, protruding from one end of the sofa.

"I'd leave that coat on if I were you, George, old boy," said an amiable voice. "We've got a long way to go."

Five minutes later, dressed in a vast brown travelling coat, a gift from Ann and the only one he had that was dry, George Smiley was sitting crossly in the passenger seat of Peter Guillam's extremely draughty sports car, which he had parked in an adjoining square. Their destination was Ascot, a place famous for women and horses. And less famous, perhaps, as the residence of Mr. Oliver Lacon, of the Cabinet Office, a senior adviser to various mixed committees and a watchdog of intelligence affairs. Or, as Guillam had it less reverentially, Whitehall's head prefect.

While, at Thursgood's school, wakefully in bed, Bill Roach was contemplating the latest wonders that had befallen him in the course of his daily vigil over Jim's welfare. Yesterday Jim had amazed Latzy. Thursday he had stolen Miss Aaronson's mail. Miss Aaronson taught violin and scripture; Roach courted her for her tenderness. Latzy, the assistant gardener, was a D.P., said Matron, and D.P.s spoke no English, or very little. D.P. meant Different Person, said Matron, or anyway, foreign from the war. But yesterday Jim had spoken to Latzy, seeking his assistance with the car club, and he had spoken to him in D.P., or whatever D.P.s speak, and Latzy had grown a foot taller on the spot.

The matter of Miss Aaronson's mail was more complex. There were two envelopes on the staffroom sideboard Thursday morning after chapel when Roach called for his form's exercise books, one addressed to Jim and one to Miss Aaronson. Jim's was typewritten. Miss Aaronson's was handwritten, in a hand not unlike Jim's own. The staffroom, while Roach made these observations, was empty. He helped himself to the exercise books and was quietly taking his leave when Jim walked in by the other door, red and blowing from his early walk.

"On your way, Jumbo, bell's gone," stooping over the sideboard.

"Yes, sir."

"Foxy weather, eh, Jumbo?"

"Yes, sir."

"On your way, then."

At the door, Roach looked round. Jim was standing again, leaning back to open the morning's *Daily Telegraph*. The sideboard was empty. Both envelopes had gone.

Had Jim written to Miss Aaronson and changed his mind? Proposing marriage, perhaps? Another thought came to Bill Roach. Recently, Jim had acquired an old typewriter, a wrecked Remington that he had put right with his own hands. Had he typed his own letter on it? Was he so lonely that he wrote himself letters, and stole other people's as well? Roach fell asleep.

4

Guillam drove languidly but fast. Smells of autumn filled the car, a full moon was shining, strands of mist hung over open fields, and the cold was irresistible. Smiley wondered how old Guillam was and guessed forty, but in that light he could have been an undergraduate sculling on the river; he moved the gear lever with a long flowing movement as if he were passing it through water. In any case, Smiley reflected irritably, the car was far too young for Smiley. They had raced through Runny-mede and begun the run up Egham Hill. They had been driving for twenty minutes and Smiley had asked a dozen questions and received no answer worth a penny, and now a nagging fear was waking in him that he refused to name.

"I'm surprised they didn't throw you out with the rest of us," he said, not very pleasantly, as he hauled the skirts of his coat more tightly round him. "You had all the qualifications: good at your work, loyal, discreet."

"They put me in charge of scalp-hunters."

"Oh, my Lord," said Smiley with a shudder, and, pulling up his collar round his ample chins, he abandoned himself to that memory in place of others more disturbing: Brixton, and the grim flint schoolhouse that served the scalp-hunters as their headquarters. The scalp-hunters' official name was

Travel. They had been formed by Control on Bill Haydon's suggestion in the pioneer days of the cold war, when murder and kidnapping and crash blackmail were common currency, and their first commandant was Haydon's nominee. They were a small outfit, about a dozen men, and they were there to handle the hit-and-run jobs that were too dirty or too risky for the residents abroad. Good intelligence work, Control had always preached, was gradual and rested on a kind of gentleness. The scalp-hunters were the exception to his own rule. They weren't gradual and they weren't gentle either, thus reflecting Haydon's temperament rather than Control's. And they worked solo, which was why they were stabled out of sight behind a flint wall with broken glass and barbed wire on the top.

"I asked whether 'lateralism' was a word to you."

"It most certainly is not."

"It's the 'in' doctrine. We used to go up and down. Now we go along."

"What's that supposed to mean?"

"In your day, the Circus ran itself by regions. Africa, satellites, Russia, China, South East Asia, you name it: each region was commanded by its own juju man; Control sat in heaven and held the strings. Remember?"

"It strikes a distant chord."

"Well, today everything operational is under one hat. It's called London Station. Regions are out, lateralism is in. Bill Haydon's Commander London Station, Roy Bland's his number two, Toby Esterhase runs between them like a poodle. They're a service within a service. They share their own secrets and don't mix with the proles. It makes us more secure."

"It sounds a very good idea," said Smiley, studiously ignoring the innuendo.

As the memories once more began seething upward into his conscious mind, an extraordinary feeling passed over him: that he was living the day twice, first with Martindale in the club, now again with Guillam in a dream. They passed a plantation of young pine trees. The moonlight lay in strips between them.

Smiley began, "Is there any word of—" Then he asked, in a more tentative tone, "What's the news of Ellis?"

"In quarantine," said Guillam tersely.

"Oh, I'm sure. Of course. I don't mean to pry. Merely, can he get around and so on? He did recover; he can walk? Backs can be terribly tricky, I understand."

"The word says he manages pretty well. How's Ann, I didn't ask."

"Fine. Just fine."

It was pitch dark inside the car. They had turned off the road and were passing over gravel. Black walls of foliage rose to either side, lights appeared, then a high porch, and the steepled outline of a rambling house lifted above the treetops. The rain had stopped, but as Smiley stepped into the fresh air he heard all round him the restless ticking of wet leaves.

Yes, he thought, it was raining when I came here before, when the name Jim Ellis was headline news.

They had washed and, in the lofty cloakroom, inspected Lacon's climbing kit mawkishly dumped on the Sheraton chest of drawers. Now they sat in a half-circle facing one empty chair. It was the ugliest house for miles around and Lacon had picked it up for a song. "A Berkshire Camelot," he had once called it, explaining it away to Smiley, "built by a teetotal millionaire." The drawing-room was a great hall with stained-glass windows twenty feet high and a pine gallery over the entrance. Smiley counted off the familiar things: an upright piano littered with musical scores, old portraits of clerics in gowns, a wad of printed invitations. He looked for the Cambridge University oar and found it slung over the fireplace. The same fire was burning, too mean for the enormous grate. An air of need prevailing over wealth.

"Are you enjoying retirement, George?" Lacon asked, as if blurting into the ear trumpet of a deaf aunt. "You don't miss the warmth of human contact? I rather would, I think. One's work, one's old buddies."

He was a string bean of a man, graceless and boyish: church and spy establishment, said Haydon, the Circus wit. His father was a dignitary of the Scottish church and his mother something noble. Occasionally the smarter Sundays wrote about him, calling him "new-style" because he was young. The skin of his face was clawed from hasty shaving.

"Oh, I think I manage very well, really, thank you," said Smiley politely. And to draw it out: "Yes. Yes, I'm sure I do. And you? All goes well with you?"

"No big changes, no. All very smooth. Charlotte got her scholarship to Roedean, which was nice."

"Oh, good."

"And your wife, she's in the pink and so on?"

His expressions were also boyish.

"Very bonny, thank you," said Smiley, trying gallantly to respond in kind.

They were watching the double doors. From far off they heard the jangle of footsteps on a ceramic floor. Smiley guessed two people, both men. The doors opened and a tall figure appeared half in silhouette. For the fraction of a moment, Smiley glimpsed a second man behind him, dark, small, and attentive; but only the one man stepped into the room before the doors were closed by unseen hands.

"Lock us in, please," Lacon called, and they heard the snap of the key. "You know Smiley, don't you?"

"Yes, I think I do," said the figure as he began the long walk towards them out of the far gloom. "I think he once gave me a job, didn't you, Mr. Smiley?"

His voice was as soft as a southerner's drawl, but there was no mistaking the colonial accent. "Tarr, sir. Ricki Tarr from Penang."

A fragment of firelight illuminated one side of the stark

smile and made a hollow of one eye. "The lawyer's boy, remember? Come on, Mr. Smiley, you changed my first nappies."

And then, absurdly, they were all four standing, and Guillam and Lacon looked on like godparents while Tarr shook Smiley's hand once, then again, then once more for the photographs.

"How are you, Mr. Smiley? It's real nice to see you, sir."

Relinquishing Smiley's hand at last, he swung away in the direction of his appointed chair, while Smiley thought, Yes, with Ricki Tarr it could have happened. With Tarr, anything could have happened. My God, he thought; two hours ago I was telling myself I would take refuge in the past. He felt thirsty, and supposed it was fear.

Ten? Twelve years ago? It was not his night for understanding time. Among Smiley's jobs in those days was the vetting of recruits: no one taken on without his nod, no one trained without his signature on the schedule. The cold war was running high, scalp-hunters were in demand, the Circus's residencies abroad had been ordered by Haydon to look out for likely material. Steve Mackelvore from Djakarta came up with Tarr. Mackelvore was an old pro with cover as a shipping agent, and he had found Tarr angry drunk, kicking round the docks looking for a girl called Rose, who had walked out on him.

According to Tarr's story, he was mixed up with a bunch of Belgians running guns between the islands and up-coast. He disliked Belgians and he was bored with gunrunning and he was angry because they'd stolen Rose. Mackelvore reckoned he would respond to discipline and was young enough to train for the type of mailfist operation that the scalp-hunters undertook from behind the walls of their glum Brixton schoolhouse. After the usual searches, Tarr was forwarded to Singapore for a second look, then to the Nursery at Sarratt for a third. At that point Smiley came into the act as moderator at a succession of interviews, some hostile. Sarratt Nursery was the training compound, but it had space for other uses.

Tarr's father was an Australian solicitor living in Penang, it seemed. The mother was a small-time actress from Bradford who came East with a British drama group before the war. The father, Smiley recalled, had an evangelical streak and preached in local gospel halls. The mother had a small criminal record in England, but Tarr's father either didn't know or didn't care. When the war came, the couple evacuated to Singapore for the sake of their young son. A few months later, Singapore fell and Ricki Tarr began his education in Changi jail under Japanese supervision. In Changi the father preached God's charity to everyone in sight, and if the Japs hadn't persecuted him his fellow prisoners would have done the job for them. With Liberation, the three of them went back to Penang. Ricki tried to read for the law but more often broke it, and the father turned some rough preachers loose on him to beat the sin out of his soul. Tarr flew the coop to Borneo. At eighteen he was a fully paid-up gunrunner playing all seven ends against the middle around the Indonesian islands, and that was how Mackelvore stumbled on him.

By the time he had graduated from the Nursery, the Malayan emergency had broken. Tarr was played back into gunrunning. Almost the first people he bumped into were his old Belgian friends. They were too busy supplying guns to the Communists to bother where he had been, and they were shorthanded. Tarr ran a few shipments for them in order to blow their contacts, then one night got them drunk, shot four of them, including Rose, and set fire to their boat. He hung around Malaya and did a couple more jobs before being called back to Brixton and refitted for special operations in Kenya— or, in less sophisticated language, hunting Mau Mau for bounty.

After Kenya, Smiley pretty much lost sight of him, but a couple of incidents stuck in his memory because they might have become scandals and Control had to be informed. In 1964, Tarr was sent to Brazil to make a crash offer of a bribe to an armaments minister known to be in deep water. Tarr was too rough; the minister panicked and told the press. Tarr had Dutch cover and no one was wiser except Netherlands intelligence, who were furious. In Spain a year later, acting on a tip-off supplied by Bill Haydon, Tarr blackmailed—or burned, as the scalp-hunters would say—a Polish diplomat who had lost his heart to a dancer. The first yield was good; Tarr won a commendation and a bonus. But when he went back for a second helping the Pole wrote a confession to his ambassador and threw himself, with or without encouragement, from a high window.

In Brixton, they used to call him accident-prone. Guillam, by the expression on his immature but aging face, as they sat in their half-circle round the meagre fire, called him a lot worse than that.

"Well, I guess I'd better make my pitch," Tarr said pleasantly as he settled his easy body into the chair.

5

"It happened around six months ago," Tarr began.

"April," Guillam snapped. "Just keep it precise, shall we, all the way along?"

"April, then," Tarr said equably. "Things were pretty quiet in Brixton. I guess there must have been half a dozen of us on stand-by. Pete Sembrini, he was in from Rome; Cy Vanhofer had just made a hit in Budapest"—he gave a mischievous smile—"Ping-Pong and snooker in the Brixton waiting room. Right, Mr. Guillam?"

"It was the silly season."

When out of the blue, said Tarr, came a flash requisition from Hong Kong residency.

"They had a low-grade Soviet trade delegation in town, chasing up electrical goods for the Moscow market. One of the delegates was stepping wide in the nightclubs. Name of Boris; Mr. Guillam has the details. No previous record. They'd had the tabs on him for five days, and the delegation was booked in for fourteen more. Politically it was too hot for the local boys to handle but they reckoned a crash approach might do the trick. The yield didn't look that special, but so what? Maybe we'd just buy him for stock—right, Mr. Guillam?"

Stock meant sale or exchange with another intelligence service: a commerce in small-time defectors handled by the scalp-hunters.

Ignoring Tarr, Guillam said, "South East Asia was Tarr's parish. He was sitting around with nothing to do, so I ordered him to make a site inspection and report back by cable."

Each time someone else spoke, Tarr sank into a dream. His gaze settled upon the speaker, a mistiness entered his eyes, and there was a pause like a coming back before he began again.

"So I did what Mr. Guillam ordered," he said. "I always do, don't I, Mr. Guillam? I'm a good boy really, even if I am impulsive."

He flew the next night—Saturday, March 31st—with an Australian passport describing him as a car salesman and with two virgin Swiss escape passports hidden in the lining of his suitcase. These were contingency documents to be filled in as circumstances demanded: one for Boris, one for himself. He made a car rendezvous with the Hong Kong resident not far from his hotel, the Golden Gate on Kowloon.

Here Guillam leaned over to Smiley and murmured, "Tufty Thesinger, buffoon. Ex-major, King's African Rifles. Percy Alleline's appointment."

Thesinger produced a report on Boris's movements based on one week's surveillance.

"Boris was a real oddball," Tarr said. "I couldn't make him out. He'd been boozing every night without a break. He hadn't slept for a week and Thesinger's watchers were folding at the knees. All day he trailed round after the delegation, inspecting factories, chiming in at discussions, and being the bright young Soviet official."

"How young?" Smiley asked.

Guillam threw in: "His visa application gave him born Minsk 1946."

"Evening time, he'd go back to the Alexandra Lodge, an old shanty house out on North Point where the delegation had holed out. He'd eat with the crew; then around nine he'd ease out the side entrance, grab a taxi, and belt down to the mainline night spots around Pedder Street. His favourite haunt was the Cat's Cradle in Queen's Road, where he bought drinks for local businessmen and acted like Mr. Personality. He might stay there till midnight. From the Cradle he cut right down to Aberdeen Harbour, a place called Angelika's, where the drink was cheaper. Alone. It's mainly floating restaurants and the big spenders down there, but Angelika's is a landbound café with a hellhole in the basement. He'd have three or four drinks and keep the receipts. Mainly he drank brandy but now and then he'd have a vodka to vary his diet. He'd had one tangle with a Eurasian girl along the way, and Thesinger's watchers got after her and bought the story. She said he was lonely and sat on the bed moaning about his wife for not appreciating his genius. That was a real breakthrough," he added sarcastically as Lacon noisily swooped on the little fire and stirred it, one coal against the other, into life. "That night I went down to the Cradle and took a look at him. Thesinger's watchers had been sent to bed with a glass of milk. They didn't want to know."

Sometimes as Tarr spoke, an extraordinary stillness came over his body, as if he were hearing his own voice played back to him.

"He arrived ten minutes after me and he brought his own

company, a big blond Swede with a Chinese broad in tow. It was dark, so I moved into a table nearby. They ordered Scotch, Boris paid, and I sat six feet away watching the lousy band and listening to their conversation. The Chinese kid kept her mouth shut and the Swede was doing most of the running. They talked English. The Swede asked Boris where he was staying, and Boris said the Excelsior, which was a damn lie because he was staying at the Alexandra Lodge with the rest of the church outing. All right, the Alexandra is down the list; the Excelsior sounds better. About midnight the party breaks up. Boris says he's got to go home and tomorrow's a busy day. That was the second lie, because he was no more going home than—what's the one, Jekyll and Hyde, right!— the regular doctor who dressed up and went on the razzle. So Boris was who?"

For a moment no one helped him.

"Hyde," said Lacon to his scrubbed red hands. Sitting again, he had clasped them on his lap.

"Hyde," Tarr repeated. "Thank you, Mr. Lacon; I always saw you as a literary man. So they settle the bill and I traipse down to Aberdeen to be there ahead of him when he hits Angelika's. By this time I'm pretty sure I'm in the wrong ball game."

On dry long fingers, Tarr studiously counted off the reasons: first, he never knew a Soviet delegation that didn't carry a couple of security gorillas whose job was to keep the boys out of the fleshpots. So how did Boris slip the leash night after night? Second, he didn't like the way Boris pushed his foreign currency around. For a Soviet official, that was against nature, he insisted: "He just doesn't have any damn currency. If he does, he buys beads for his squaw. And three, I didn't like the way he lied. He was a sight too glib for decency."

So Tarr waited at the Angelika, and sure enough half an hour later his Mr. Hyde turned up all on his own. "He sits down and calls for a drink. That's all he does. Sits and drinks like a damn wallflower!"

Once more it was Smiley's turn to receive the heat of Tarr's charm: "So what's it all about, Mr. Smiley? See what I mean? It's *little* things I'm noticing," he confided, still to Smiley. "Just take the way he sat. Believe me, sir, if we'd been in that place ourselves we couldn't have sat better than Boris. He had the pick of the exits and the stairway; he had a fine view of the main entrance and the action; he was right-handed and he was covered by a left-hand wall. Boris was a professional, Mr. Smiley; there was no doubt of it whatsoever. He was waiting for a connect, working a letter-box, maybe, or trailing his coat and looking for a pass from a mug like me. Well, now listen: it's one thing to burn a small-time trade delegate. It's quite a different ball game to swing your legs at a Centre-trained hood—right, Mr. Guillam?"

Guillam said, "Since the reorganisation, scalp-hunters have no brief to trawl for double agents. They must be turned over to London Station on sight. The boys have a standing order, over Bill Haydon's own signature. If there's even a smell of the opposition, abandon." He added, for Smiley's special ear, "Under lateralism our autonomy is cut to the bone."

"And I've been in double-double games before," Tarr confessed in a tone of injured virtue. "Believe me, Mr. Smiley, they are a can of worms."

"I'm sure they are," said Smiley, and gave a prim tug at his spectacles.

Tarr cabled Guillam "no sale," booked a flight home, and went shopping. However, since his flight didn't leave till Thursday, he thought that before he left, just to pay his fare, he might as well burgle Boris's room.

"The Alexandra's a real ramshackle old place, Mr. Smiley, off Marble Road, with a stack of wooden balconies. As for the locks—why, sir, they give up when they see you coming."

In a very short time, therefore, Tarr was standing inside Boris's room with his back against the door, waiting for his eyes to grow accustomed to the dark. He was still standing there when a woman spoke to him in Russian drowsily from the bed.

"It was Boris's wife," Tarr explained. "She was crying. Look, I'll call her Irina, right? Mr. Guillam has the details."

Smiley was already objecting: wife was impossible, he said. Centre would never let them both out of Russia at the same time; they'd keep one and send the other—

"Common-law marriage," Guillam said dryly. "Unofficial but permanent."

"There's a lot that are the other way round these days," said Tarr with a sharp grin at no one, least of all Smiley, and Guillam shot him another foul look.

6

From the outset of this meeting, Smiley had assumed for the main a Buddha-like inscrutability from which neither Tarr's story nor the rare interjections of Lacon and Guillam could rouse him. He sat leaning back with his short legs bent, head forward, and plump hands linked across his generous stomach. His hooded eyes had closed behind the thick lenses. His only fidget was to polish his glasses on the silk lining of his tie, and when he did this his eyes had a soaked, naked look that was embarrassing to those who caught him at it. His interjection, however, and the donnish, inane sound that followed Guillam's explanation, now acted like a signal upon the rest of the gathering, bringing a shuffling of chairs and a clearing of throats.

Lacon was foremost: "George, what are your drinking habits? Can I get you a Scotch or anything?" He offered drink solicitously, like aspirin for a headache. "I forgot to say it earlier," he explained. "George, a bracer: come. It's winter, after all. A nip of something?"

"I'm fine, thank you," Smiley said.

He would have liked a little coffee from the percolator but somehow he didn't feel able to ask. Also he remembered it was terrible.

"Guillam?" Lacon proceeded. No; Guillam also found it impossible to accept alcohol from Lacon.

He didn't offer anything to Tarr, who went straight on with his narrative.

Tarr took Irina's presence calmly, he said. He had worked up his fallback before he entered the building, and now he went straight into his act. He didn't pull a gun or slap his hand over her mouth or any of that tripe, as he put it, but he said he had come to speak to Boris on a private matter; he was sorry and he was damn well going to sit there till Boris showed up. In good Australian, as became an outraged car salesman from down under, he explained that while he didn't want to barge into anyone's business he was damned if he was going to have his girl and his money stolen in a single night by a lousy Russian who couldn't pay for his pleasures. He worked up a lot of outrage but managed to keep his voice down, and then he waited to see what she did.

And that, said Tarr, was how it all began.

It was eleven-thirty when he made Boris's room. He left at one-thirty with a promise of a meeting next night. By then the situation was all the other way: "We weren't doing anything improper, mind. Just pen friends—right, Mr. Smiley?"

For a moment, that bland sneer seemed to lay claim to Smiley's most precious secrets.

"Right," he assented vapidly.

There was nothing exotic about Irina's presence in Hong Kong and no reason why Thesinger should have known of it, Tarr explained. Irina was a member of the delegation in her own right. She was a trained textile buyer: "Come to think of it, she was a sight better qualified than her old man, if I can call him that. She was a plain kid, a bit blue-stocking for my taste, but she was young and she had one hell of a pretty smile when she stopped crying." Tarr coloured quaintly. "She was good company," he insisted, as if arguing against a trend. "When Mr. Thomas from Adelaide came into her life, she was at the end of the line from worrying what to do about the demon Boris. She thought I was the Angel Gabriel. Who could she talk to about her husband who wouldn't turn the dogs on him? She'd no chums on the delegation; she'd no one she trusted even back in Moscow, she said. Nobody who hadn't been through it would ever know what it was like trying to keep a ruined relationship going while all the time you're on the move." Smiley was once more in a deep trance. "Hotel after hotel, city after city, not even allowed to speak to the natives in a natural way or get a smile from a stranger—that's how she described her life. She reckoned it was a pretty miserable state of affairs, Mr. Smiley, and there was a lot of God-thumping and an empty vodka bottle beside the bed to show for it. Why couldn't she be like normal people? she kept saying. Why couldn't she enjoy the Lord's sunshine like the rest of us? She loved sightseeing, she loved foreign kids; why couldn't she have a kid of her own? A kid born free, not in captivity. She kept saying that: born in captivity, born free. 'I'm a jolly person, Thomas. I'm a normal, sociable girl. I like people: why should I deceive them when I like them?' And then she said, the trouble was that long ago she had been chosen for work that made her frozen like an old woman and cut her off from God. So that's why she'd had a drink and why she was having a cry. She'd kind of forgotten her husband by then; she was apologising for having a fling, more." Again he faltered. "I could scent it, Mr. Smiley. There was gold in her. I could scent it from the start. Knowledge is power, they say, sir, and Irina had the power, same as she had the quality. She was hellbent maybe, but she could still give her all. I can sense generosity in a woman where I meet it, Mr. Smiley. I have a talent for it. And this lady was generous. Jesus, how do you describe a hunch? Some people can smell water under the ground . . ."

He seemed to expect some show of sympathy, so Smiley said, "I understand," and plucked at the lobe of his ear.

Watching him with a strange dependence in his expression, Tarr kept silent a stretch longer. "First thing next morning, I cancelled my flight and changed my hotel," he said finally.

Abruptly Smiley opened his eyes wide. "What did you tell London?"

"Nothing."

"Why not?"

"Because he's a devious fool," said Guillam.

"Maybe I thought Mr. Guillam would say, 'Come home, Tarr,' " he replied, with a knowing glance at Guillam that was not returned. "You see, long ago when I was a little boy I made a mistake and walked into a honey trap."

"He made an ass of himself with a Polish girl," said Guillam. "He sensed her generosity, too."

"I knew Irina was no honey trap, but how could I expect Mr. Guillam to believe me? No way."

"Did you tell Thesinger?"

"Hell, no."

"What reason did you give London for postponing your flight?"

"I was due to fly Thursday. I reckoned no one back home would miss me till Tuesday. Specially with Boris being a dead duck."

"He didn't give a reason and the housekeepers posted him absent without leave on the Monday," said Guillam. "He broke every rule in the book. And some that aren't. By the middle of that week, even Bill Haydon was beating his war drums. And I was having to listen," he added tartly.

However that was, Tarr and Irina met next evening. They met again the evening after that. The first meeting was in a café and it limped. They took a lot of care not to be seen, because Irina was frightened stiff not just of her husband but of the security guards attached to the delegation—the gorillas, as Tarr called them. She refused a drink and she was shaking. The second evening Tarr was still waiting on her generosity. They took the tram up to Victoria Peak, jammed between American matrons in white socks and eyeshades. The third he hired a car and drove her round the New Territories till she suddenly got the heebies about being so close to the Chinese border, so they had to run for harbour. Nevertheless she loved that trip, and often spoke of the tidy beauty of it, the fish ponds and the paddy fields. Tarr also liked the trip because it proved to both of them that they weren't being watched. But Irina had still not unpacked, as he put it.

"Now I'll tell you a damn odd thing about this stage of the game. At the start, I worked Thomas the Aussie to death. I fed her a lot of smoke about a sheep station outside Adelaide and a big property in the high street with a glass front and 'Thomas' in lights. She didn't believe me. She nodded and fooled around and waited till I'd said my piece; then she said, 'Yes, Thomas,' 'No, Thomas,' and changed the subject."

On the fourth evening, he drove her into the hills overlooking North Shore, and Irina told Tarr that she had fallen in love with him and that she was employed by Moscow Centre, she and her husband both, and that she knew Tarr was in the trade, too; she could tell by his alertness and the way he listened with his eyes.

"She'd decided I was an English colonel of intelligence," said Tarr with no smile at all. "She was crying one minute and laughing the next, and in my opinion she was three-quarters of the way to being a basket case. Half, she talked like a pocket-book loony heroine, half like a nice up-and-down suburban kid. The English were her favourite people. Gentlemen, she kept saying. I'd brought her a bottle of vodka and she drank half of it in about fifteen seconds flat. Hooray for English gentlemen. Boris was the lead and Irina was the backup girl. It was a his-and-hers act, and one day she'd talk to Percy Alleline and tell him a great secret all for himself. Boris was on a trawl for Hong Kong businessmen and had a post-box job on the side for the local Soviet residency. Irina ran courier, boiled down the microdots, and played radio for him on a high-speed squirt to beat the listeners. That was how it read on paper, see? The two nightclubs were rendezvous and fallback for his local connect, in that order. But all Boris really wanted to do was drink and chase the dancing girls and have depressions. Or else go for five-hour walks because he couldn't stand being in the same room with his wife. All Irina did was wait around crying and getting plastered, and fancy herself sitting alone at Percy's fireside, telling him all she knew. I kept her there talking, up on the hill, sitting in the car. I didn't move because I didn't want to break the spell. We watched the dusk fall on the harbour and the lovely moon come up there, and the peasants slipping by with their long poles and kerosene lamps. All we needed was Humphrey Bogart in a tuxedo. I kept my foot on the vodka bottle and let her talk. I didn't move a muscle. Fact, Mr. Smiley. Fact," he declared, with the defencelessness of a man longing to be believed, but Smiley's eyes were closed and he was deaf to all appeal.

"She just completely let go," Tarr explained, as if it were suddenly an accident, a thing he had had no part in. "She told me her whole life story, from birth to Colonel Thomas; that's me. Mummy, Daddy, early loves, recruitment, training, her lousy half-marriage, the lot. How her and Boris were teamed at training and had been together ever since: one of the great unbreakable relationships. She told me her real name, her workname, and the cover names she'd travelled and transmitted by; then she hauled out her handbag and started showing me her conjuring set: recessed fountain pen, signal plan folded up inside; concealed camera—the works. 'Wait till Percy sees that,' I tell her—playing her along, like. It was production-line stuff, mind, nothing coach-built, but grade-one material all the same. To round it off, she starts barking the dirt about the Soviet Hong Kong set-up: legmen, safe houses, letter-boxes, the lot. I was going crazy trying to remember it all."

"But you did," said Guillam shortly.

Yes, Tarr agreed; near on, he did. He knew she hadn't told him the whole truth, but he knew truth came hard to a girl who'd been a hood since puberty, and he reckoned that for a beginner she was doing pretty nice.

"I kind of felt for her," he said with another flash of that false confessiveness. "I felt we were on the same wave-length, no messing."

"Quite so," said Lacon in a rare interjection. He was very pale, but whether that was anger or the effect of the grey light of early morning creeping through the shutters, there was no way to tell.

7

"Now I was in a queer situation. I saw her next day and the day after, and I reckoned that if she wasn't already schizoid she was going to be that way damn soon. One minute talking about Percy giving her a top job in the Circus working for Colonel Thomas, and arguing the hell with me about whether she should be a lieutenant or a major. Next minute saying she wouldn't spy for anybody ever again and she was going to grow flowers and rut in the hay with Thomas. Then she had a convent kick: Baptist nuns were going to wash her soul. I nearly died. Who the hell ever heard of Baptist nuns, I ask her. Never mind, she says, Baptists are the greatest; her mother was a peasant and knew. That was the second biggest secret she would ever tell me. 'What's the biggest, then?' I ask. No dice. All she's saying is, we're in mortal danger, bigger than I could possibly know: there's no hope for either of us unless she has that special chat with Brother Percy. 'What danger, for Christ's sake? What do you know that

I don't?' She was vain as a cat but when I pressed her she clammed up, and I was frightened to death she'd belt home and sing the lot to Boris. I was running out of time, too. Then it was Wednesday already and the delegation was due to fly home to Moscow Friday. Her tradecraft wasn't all lousy but how could I trust a nut like her? You know how women are when they fall in love, Mr. Smiley. They can't hardly—"

Guillam had already cut him off. "You just keep your head down, right?" he ordered, and Tarr sulked for a space.

"All I knew was Irina wanted to defect—talk to Percy, as she called it. She had three days left, and the sooner she jumped the better for everybody. If I waited much longer, she was going to talk herself out of it. So I took the plunge and walked in on Thesinger, first thing while he was opening up the shop."

"Wednesday, the eleventh," Smiley murmured. "In London the early hours of the morning."

"I guess Thesinger thought I was a ghost," Tarr said. " 'I'm talking to London, personal for Head of London Station,' I said. He argued like hell but he let me do it. I sat at his desk and coded up the message myself from a one-time pad while Thesinger watched me like a sick dog. We had to top and tail it like trade code because Thesinger has export cover. That took me an extra half hour. I was nervy, I really was. Then I burnt the whole damn pad and typed out the message on the ticker machine. At that point, there wasn't a soul on earth but me who knew what the numbers meant on that sheet of paper—not Thesinger, nobody but me. I applied for full defector treatment for Irina on emergency procedure. I held out for all the goodies she'd never even talked about: cash, nationality, a new identity, no limelight, and a place to live. After all, I was her business representative in a manner of speaking, wasn't I, Mr. Smiley?"

Smiley glanced up as if surprised to be addressed. "Yes," he said quite kindly. "Yes, I suppose in a manner of speaking that's what you were."

"He also had a piece of the action, if I know him," said Guillam under his breath.

Catching this or guessing the meaning of it, Tarr was furious.

"That's a damn lie!" he shouted, colouring deeply. "That's a—" After glaring at Guillam a moment longer, he went back to his story.

"I outlined her career to date and her access, including jobs she'd had at Centre. I asked for inquisitors and an Air Force plane. She thought I was asking for a personal meeting with Percy Alleline on neutral ground, but I reckoned we'd cross that bridge when we were past it. I suggested they should send out a couple of Esterhase's lamplighters to take charge of her, maybe a tame doctor as well."

"Why lamplighters?" Smiley asked sharply. "They're not allowed to handle defectors."

The lamplighters were Toby Esterhase's pack, based not in Brixton but in Acton. Their job was to provide the support services for mainline operations: watching, listening, transport, and safe houses.

"Ah, well, Toby's come up in the world since your day, Mr. Smiley," Tarr explained. "They tell me even his pavement artists ride around in Cadillacs. Steal the scalp-hunters' bread out of their mouths, too, if they get the chance—right, Mr. Guillam?"

"They've become the general footpads for London Station," Guillam said shortly. "Part of lateralism."

"I reckoned it would take half a year for the inquisitors to clean her out, and for some reason she was crazy about Scotland. She had a great wish to spend the rest of her life there, in fact. With Thomas. Raising our babies in the heather. I gave it the London Station address group; I graded it flash and by hand of officer only."

Guillam put in: "That's the new formula for maximum limit. It's supposed to cut out handling in the coding rooms."

"But not in London Station?" said Smiley.

"That's their affair."

"You heard Bill Haydon got that job, I suppose?" said Lacon, jerking round on Smiley. "Head of London Station? He's effectively their chief of operations, just as Percy used to be when Control was there. They've changed all the names, that's the thing. You know how your old buddies are about names. You ought to fill him in, Guillam, bring him up to date."

"Oh, I think I have the picture, thank you," Smiley said politely. Of Tarr, with a deceptive dreaminess, he asked, "She spoke of a great secret, you said?"

"Yes, sir."

"Did you give any hint of this in your cable to London?"

He had touched something, there was no doubt of it; he had found a spot where touching hurt, for Tarr winced, and darted a suspicious glance at Lacon, then at Guillam.

Guessing his meaning, Lacon at once sang out a disclaimer: "Smiley knows nothing beyond what you have so far told him in this room," he said. "Correct, Guillam?" Guillam nodded yes, watching Smiley.

"I told London the same as she'd told me," Tarr conceded grumpily, like someone who has been robbed of a good story.

"What form of words, precisely?" Smiley asked. "I wonder whether you remember that."

" 'Claims to have further information crucial to the well-being of the Circus, but not yet disclosed.' Near enough, anyhow."

"Thank you. Thank you very much."

They waited for Tarr to continue.

"I also requested Head of London Station to inform Mr. Guillam here that I'd landed on my feet and wasn't playing hookey for the hell of it."

"Did that happen?" Smiley asked.

"Nobody said anything to me," said Guillam dryly.

"I hung around all day for an answer, but by evening it still hadn't come. Irina was doing a normal day's work. I insisted on that, you see. She wanted to stage a light dose of fever to keep her in bed but I wouldn't hear of it. The delegation had factories to visit on Kowloon and I told her to tag along and look intelligent. I made her swear to keep off the bottle. I didn't want her involved in amateur dramatics at the last moment. I wanted it normal right up to when she jumped. I waited till evening, then cabled a flash follow-up."

Smiley's shrouded gaze fixed upon the pale face before him. "You had an acknowledgement, of course?" he asked.

" 'We read you.' That's all. I sweated out the whole damn night. By dawn I still didn't have an answer. I thought, Maybe that R.A.F. plane is already on its way. London's playing it long, I thought, tying all the knots before they bring me in. I mean when you're that far away from them you *have* to believe they're good. Whatever you think of them, you *have* to believe that. And I mean now and then they are—right, Mr. Guillam?"

No one helped him.

"I was worried about Irina, see? I was damn certain that if she had to wait another day she would crack. Finally the answer did come. It wasn't an answer at all. It was a stall: 'Tell us what sections she worked in, names of former contacts and acquaintances inside Moscow Centre, name of her present boss, date of intake into Centre.' Jesus, I don't know what else. I drafted a reply fast because I had a three o'clock date with her down by the church—"

"What church?" Smiley again.

"English Baptist." To everyone's astonishment, Tarr was once again blushing. "She liked to visit there. Not for services, just to sniff around. I hung around the entrance looking natural but she didn't show. It was the first time she'd broken a date. Our fallback was for three hours later on the hilltop, then a one-minute-fifty descending scale back at the church till we met up. If she was in trouble, she was going to leave her bathing suit on her window-sill. She was a swimming nut, swam every day. I shot round to the Alexandra: no bathing suit. I had two and a half hours to kill. There was nothing I could do any more except wait."

Smiley said, "What was the priority of London Station's telegram to you?"

"Immediate."

"But yours was flash?"

"Both of mine were flash."

"Was London's telegram signed?"

Guillam put in: "They're not any more. Outsiders deal with London Station as a unit."

"Was it decypher yourself?"

"No," said Guillam.

They waited for Tarr to go on.

"I kicked around Thesinger's office but I wasn't too popular there; he doesn't approve of scalp-hunters and he has a big thing going on the Chinese mainland that he seemed to think I was going to blow for him. So I sat in a café and I had this idea I just might go down to the airport. It was an idea: like you might say, "Maybe I'll go to a movie." I took the Star Ferry, hired a cab, and told the driver to go like hell. It got like a panic. I barged the Information queue and asked for all departures to Russia, or connections in. I nearly went mad going through the flight lists, yelling at the Chinese clerks, but there wasn't a plane since yesterday and none till six tonight. But now I had this hunch. I had to know. What about charters, what about the unscheduled flights, freight, casual transit? Had nothing, but *really* nothing, been routed for Moscow since yesterday morning? Then this little girl comes through with the answer, one of the Chinese hostesses. She fancies me, see. She's doing me a favour. An unscheduled Soviet plane had taken off two hours ago. Only four passengers boarded. The centre of attraction was a woman invalid. A lady. In a coma. They had to cart her to the plane on a stretcher, and her face was wrapped in bandages. Two male nurses went with her and one doctor—that was the party. I called the Alexandra as a last hope. Neither Irina nor her so-called husband had checked out of their room, but there was no reply. The lousy hotel didn't even know they'd left."

Perhaps the music had been going on a long time and Smiley only noticed it now. He heard it in imperfect fragments from different parts of the house: a scale on a flute, a child's tune on a recorder, a violin piece more confidently played. The many Lacon daughters were waking up.

8

"Perhaps she *was* ill," said Smiley stolidly, speaking more to Guillam than anyone else. "Perhaps she *was* in a coma. Perhaps they were real nurses who took her away. By the sound of her, she was a pretty good mess, at best." He added, with half a glance at Tarr: "After all, only twenty-four hours had elapsed between your first telegram and Irina's departure. You can hardly lay it at London's door on that timing."

"You can *just*," said Guillam, looking at the floor. "It's extremely fast, but it does just work, if somebody in London—" They were all waiting. "If somebody in London had very good footwork. And in Moscow, too, of course."

"Now, that's exactly what I told myself, sir," said Tarr proudly, taking up Smiley's point and ignoring Guillam's. "My very words, Mr. Smiley. 'Relax, Ricki,' I said; 'you'll be shooting at shadows if you're not damn careful.' "

"Or the Russians tumbled to her," Smiley said. "The security guards found out about your affair and removed her. It would be a wonder if they *hadn't* found out, the way you two carried on."

"Or she told her husband," Tarr suggested. "I understand

psychology as well as the next man, sir. I know what can happen between a husband and wife when they have fallen out. She wishes to annoy him. To goad him, to obtain a reaction, I thought. 'Want to hear what I've been doing while you've been out boozing and cutting the rug?'—like that. Boris peels off and tells the gorillas; they sandbag her and take her home. I went through all those possibilities, Mr. Smiley, believe me. I really worked on them, truth. Same as any man does whose woman walks out on him."

"Let's just have the story, shall we?" Guillam whispered, furious.

Well, now, said Tarr, he would agree that for twenty-four hours he went a bit berserk: "Now, I don't often get that way—right, Mr. Guillam?"

"Often enough."

"I was feeling pretty physical. Frustrated, you could almost say."

His conviction that a considerable prize had been brutally snatched away from him drove him to a distracted fury that found expression in a rampage through old haunts. He went to the Cat's Cradle, then to Angelika's, and by dawn he had taken in half a dozen other places besides, not to mention a few girls along the way. At some point he crossed town and raised a spot of dust around the Alexandra. He was hoping to have a couple of words with those security gorillas. When he sobered down, he got thinking about Irina and their time together, and he decided before he flew back to London to go round their dead letter-boxes to check whether by any chance she had written to him before she left.

Partly it was something to do. "Partly, I guess, I couldn't bear to think of a letter of hers kicking around in a hole in a wall while she sweated it out in the hot seat," he added, the ever-redeemable boy.

They had two places where they dropped mail for one another. The first was not far from the hotel on a building site.

"Ever seen that bamboo scaffolding they use? Fantastic.
I've seen it twenty storeys high and the coolies swarming over
it with slabs of precast concrete." A bit of discarded piping,
he said, handy at shoulder height. It seemed most likely, if
Irina was in a hurry, that the piping was the letter-box she
would use, but when Tarr went there it was empty. The
second was back by the church, "in under where they stow
the pamphlets," as he put it. "This stand was part of an old
wardrobe, see. If you kneel in the back pew and grope
around, there's a loose board. Behind the board there's a
recess full of rubbish and rat's mess. I tell you, it made a real
lovely drop, the best ever."

There was a short pause, illuminated by the vision of Ricki
Tarr and his Moscow Centre mistress kneeling side by side in
the rear pew of a Baptist church in Hong Kong.

In this dead letter-box, Tarr said, he found not a letter but
a whole damn diary. The writing was fine and done on both
sides of the paper, so that quite often the black ink came
through. It was fast urgent writing with no erasures. He
knew at a glance that she had maintained it in her lucid
periods.

"This isn't it, mind. This is only my copy."

Slipping a long hand inside his shirt, he had drawn out a
leather purse attached to a broad thong of hide. From it he
took a grimy wad of paper.

"I guess she dropped the diary just before they hit her," he
said. "Maybe she was having a last pray at the same time. I
made the translation myself."

"I didn't know you spoke Russian," said Smiley—a comment lost to everyone but Tarr, who at once grinned.

"Ah, now, a man needs a qualification in this profession,
Mr. Smiley," he explained as he separated the pages. "I may
not have been too great at law but a further language can be
decisive. You know what the poets say, I expect?" He looked
up from his labours and his grin widened. " 'To possess
another language is to possess another soul.' A great king

wrote that, sir, Charles the Fifth. My father never forgot a quotation, I'll say that for him, though the funny thing is he couldn't speak a damn thing but English. I'll read the diary aloud to you, if you don't mind."

"He hasn't a word of Russian to his name," said Guillam. "They spoke English all the time. Irina had done a three-year English course."

Guillam had chosen the ceiling to look at, Lacon his hands. Only Smiley was watching Tarr, who was laughing quietly at his own little joke.

"All set?" he enquired. "Right, then, I'll begin. 'Thomas, listen, I am talking to you.' She called me by my surname," he explained. "I told her I was Tony, but it was always Thomas, right? 'This diary is my gift for you in case they take me away before I speak to Alleline. I would prefer to give you my life, Thomas, and naturally my body, but I think it more likely that this wretched secret will be all I have to make you happy. Use it well!' " Tarr glanced up. "It's marked Monday. She wrote the diary over the four days." His voice had become flat, almost bored. " 'In Moscow Centre there is more gossip than our superiors would wish. Especially the little fellows like to make themselves grand by appearing to be in the know. For two years before I was attached to the Trade Ministry, I worked as a supervisor in the filing department of our headquarters in Dzerzhinsky Square. The work was so dull, Thomas, the atmosphere was not happy, and I was unmarried. We were encouraged to be suspicious of one another; it is such a strain never to give your heart, not once. Under me was a clerk named Ivlov. Though Ivlov was not socially or in rank my equal, the oppressive atmosphere brought out a mutuality in our temperaments. Forgive me, sometimes only the body can speak for us—you should have appeared earlier, Thomas! Several times Ivlov and I worked night shifts together, and eventually we agreed to defy regulations and meet outside the building. He was blond, Thomas, like you, and I wanted him. We met in a café in a poor district of Moscow.

In Russia we are taught that Moscow has no poor districts, but this is a lie. Ivlov told me that his real name was Brod but he was not a Jew. He brought me some coffee sent to him illicitly by a comrade in Teheran—he was very sweet—also some stockings. Ivlov told me that he admired me greatly and that he had once worked in a section responsible for recording the particulars of all the foreign agents employed by Centre. I laughed and told him that no such record existed; it was an idea of dreamers to suppose so many secrets would be in one place. Well, we were both dreamers I suppose.' "

Again Tarr broke off. "We get a new day," he announced. "She kicks off with a lot of 'good morning Thomas's,' prayers, and a bit of love-talk. A woman can't write to the air, she says, so she's writing to Thomas. Her old man's gone out early; she's got an hour to herself. Okay?"

Smiley grunted.

" 'On the second occasion with Ivlov, I met him in the room of a cousin of Ivlov's wife, a teacher at Moscow State University. No one else was present. The meeting, which was extremely secret, involved what in a report we would call an incriminating act. I think, Thomas, you yourself once or twice committed such an act! Also at this meeting Ivlov told me the following story to bind us in even closer friendship. Thomas, you must take care. Have you heard of Karla? He is an old fox, the most cunning in the Centre, the most secret; even his name is not a name that Russians understand. Ivlov was extremely frightened to tell me this story, which according to Ivlov concerned a great conspiracy, perhaps the greatest we have. The story of Ivlov is as follows. You should tell it only to *most trustworthy people*, Thomas, because of its extremely conspiratorial nature. You must tell no one in the Circus, for no one can be trusted until the riddle is solved. Ivlov said it was not true that he once worked on agent records. He had invented this story only to show me the great depth of his knowledge concerning the Centre's affairs and to assure me that I was not in love with a nobody. The truth was he had worked for Karla as a helper in one of Karla's great conspiracies and he had actually been stationed in England in a conspiratorial capacity, under the cover of being a driver and assistant coding clerk at the Embassy. For this task he was provided with the workname Lapin. Thus Brod became Ivlov and Ivlov became Lapin: of this poor Ivlov was extremely proud. (I did not tell him what Lapin means in French.) That a man's wealth should be counted by the number of his names! Ivlov's task was to service a mole. A mole is a deep-penetration agent so called because he burrows deep into the fabric of Western imperialism, in this case an Englishman. Moles are very precious to the Centre because of the many years it takes to place them, often fifteen or twenty. Most of the English moles were recruited by Karla before the war and came from the higher bourgeoisie, even aristocrats and nobles who were disgusted with their origins, and became secretly fanatic, much more fanatic than their working-class English comrades, who are slothful. Several were applying to join the Party when Karla stopped them in time and directed them to special work. Some fought in Spain against Franco Fascism, and Karla's talent-spotters found them there and turned them over to Karla for recruitment. Others were recruited in the war during the alliance of expediency between Soviet Russia and Britain. Others afterwards, disappointed that the war did not bring Socialism to the West . . .' It kind of dries up here," Tarr announced without looking anywhere but at his own manuscript. "I wrote down, 'dries up.' I guess her old man came back earlier than she expected. The ink's all blotted. God knows where she stowed the damn thing. Under the mattress maybe."

If this was meant as a joke, it failed.

" 'The mole whom Lapin serviced in London was known by the code name Gerald. He had been recruited by Karla and was the object of extreme conspiracy. The servicing of moles is performed only by comrades with a very high stand-ard of ability, said Ivlov. Thus while in appearance Ivlov-

Lapin was at the Embassy a mere nobody, subjected to many humiliations on account of his apparent insignificance, such as standing with women behind the bar at functions, by right he was a great man, the secret assistant to Colonel Gregor Viktorov, whose workname at the Embassy is Polyakov.' "

Here Smiley made his one interjection, asking for the spelling. Like an actor disturbed in midflow, Tarr answered rudely, "P-o-l-y-a-k-o-v, got it?"

"Thank you," said Smiley with unshakeable courtesy, in a manner which conveyed conclusively that the name had no significance for him whatever. Tarr resumed.

" 'Viktorov is himself an old professional of great cunning, said Ivlov. His cover job is cultural attaché and that is how he speaks to Karla. As Cultural Attaché Polyakov, he organises lectures to British universities and societies concerning cultural matters in the Soviet Union, but his nightwork as Colonel Gregor Viktorov is briefing and debriefing the mole Gerald on instruction from Karla at Centre. For this purpose, Colonel Viktorov-Polyakov uses legmen and poor Ivlov was for a while one. Nevertheless it is Karla in Moscow who is the real controller of the mole Gerald.' "

"Now it really changes," said Tarr. "She's writing at night and she's either plastered or scared out of her pants, because she's going all over the damn page. There's talk about footsteps in the corridor and the dirty looks she's getting from the gorillas. Not transcribed—right, Mr. Smiley?" And, receiving a small nod, he went on: " 'The measures for the mole's security were remarkable. Written reports from London to Karla at Moscow Centre even after coding were cut in two and sent by separate couriers, others in secret inks underneath orthodox Embassy correspondence. Ivlov told me that the mole Gerald produced at times more conspiratorial material than Viktorov-Polyakov could conveniently handle. Much was on undeveloped film, often thirty reels in a week. Anyone opening the container in the wrong fashion at once exposed the film. Other material was given by the mole in speeches, at extremely con-

spiratorial meetings, and recorded on special tape that could
only be played through complicated machines. This tape was
also wiped clean by exposure to light or to the wrong machine.
The meetings were of the crash type, always different, always
sudden, that is all I know except that it was the time when the
Fascist aggression in Vietnam was at its worst; in England the
extreme reactionaries had again taken the power. Also that
according to Ivlov-Lapin, the mole Gerald was a high func-
tionary in the Circus. Thomas, I tell you this because, since I
love you, I have decided to admire all English, you most of
all. I do not wish to think of an English gentleman behaving
as a traitor, though naturally I believe he was right to join the
workers' cause. Also I fear for the safety of anyone employed
by the Circus in a conspiracy. Thomas, I love you; take care
with this knowledge—it could hurt you also. Ivlov was a man
like you, even if they called him Lapin . . .'" Tarr paused
diffidently. "There's a bit at the end which . . ."

"Read it," Guillam murmured.

Lifting the wad of paper slightly sideways, Tarr read in the
same flat drawl: " 'Thomas, I am telling you this also because
I am afraid. This morning when I woke, he was sitting on
the bed, staring at me like a madman. When I went downstairs for coffee, the guards Trepov and Novikov watched me
like animals, eating very carelessly. I am sure they had been
there hours; also from the Residency, Avilov sat with them,
a boy. Have you been indiscreet, Thomas? Did you tell
more than you let me think? Now you see why only Alleline
would do. You need not blame yourself; I can guess what you
have told them. In my heart I am free. You have seen only the
bad things in me—the drink, the fear, the lies we live. But deep
inside me burns a new and blessed light. I used to think that
the secret world was a separate place and that I was banished
for ever to an island of half-people. But, Thomas, it is not
separate. God has shown me that it is here, right in the middle
of the real world, all round us, and we have only to open the
door and step outside to be free. Thomas, you must always

long for the light which I have found. It is called love. Now I shall take this to our secret place and leave it there while there is still time. Dear God, I hope there is. God give me sanctuary in His Church. Remember it: I loved you there also.'" Tarr was extremely pale, and his hands, as he pulled open his shirt to return the diary to its purse, were trembling and moist. "There's a last bit," he said. "It goes: 'Thomas, why could you remember so few prayers from your boyhood? Your father was a great and good man.' Like I told you," he explained, "she was crazy."

Lacon had opened the blinds and now the full white light of day was pouring into the room. The windows looked onto a small paddock where Jackie Lacon, a fat little girl in plaits and a riding hat, was cautiously cantering her pony.

9

Before Tarr left, Smiley asked a number of questions of him. He was gazing not at Tarr but myopically into the middle distance, his pouchy face despondent from the tragedy.

"Where is the original of that diary?"

"I put it straight back in the dead letter-box. Figure it this way, Mr. Smiley: by the time I found the diary, Irina had been in Moscow twenty-four hours. I guessed she wouldn't have a lot of breath when it came to the interrogation. Most likely they'd sweated her on the plane, then a second going over when she touched down, then question one as soon as the big boys had finished their breakfast. That's the way they do it to the timid ones: the arm first and the questions after, right? So it might be only a matter of a day or two before Centre sent along a footpad to take a peek round the back of

the church, okay?" Primly again: "Also I had my own welfare to consider."

"He means that Moscow Centre would be less interested in
cutting his throat if they thought he hadn't read the diary,"
said Guillam.

"Did you photograph it?"

"I don't carry a camera. I bought a dollar notebook. I
copied the diary into the notebook. The original I put back.
The whole job took me four hours flat." He glanced at
Guillam, then away from him. In the fresh daylight, a deep
inner fear was suddenly apparent in Tarr's face. "When I got
back to the hotel, my room was a wreck; they'd even stripped
the paper off the walls. The manager told me, 'Get the hell
out.' He didn't want to know."

"He's carrying a gun," said Guillam. "He won't part with
it."

"You're damn right I won't."

Smiley offered a dyspeptic grunt of sympathy. "These
meetings you had with Irina: the dead letter-boxes, the safety
signals, and fallbacks. Who proposed the tradecraft, you or
she?"

"She did."

"What were the safety signals?"

"Body-talk. If I wore my collar open, she knew I'd had a
look around and I reckoned the coast was clear. If I wore it
closed, scrub the meeting till the fallback."

"And Irina?"

"Handbag. Left hand, right hand. I got there first and
waited up somewhere she could see me. That gave her the
choice: whether to go ahead or split."

"All this happened more than six months ago. What have
you been doing since?"

"Resting," said Tarr rudely.

Guillam said, "He panicked and went native. He bolted to
Kuala Lumpur, then lay up in one of the hill villages. That's
his story. He has a daughter called Danny."

"Danny's my little kid."

"He shacked up with Danny and her mother," said Guillam, talking, as was his habit, clean across anything Tarr said. "He's got wives scattered across the globe, but she seems to lead the pack just now."

"Why did you choose this particular moment to come to us?"

Tarr said nothing.

"Don't you want to spend Christmas with Danny?"

"Sure."

"So what happened? Did something scare you?"

"There was rumours," said Tarr sullenly.

"What sort of rumours?"

"Some Frenchman turned up in K.L. telling them all I owed him money. Wanted to get some lawyer hounding me. I don't owe anybody money."

Smiley returned to Guillam. "At the Circus he's still posted as a defector?"

"Presumed."

"What have they done about it so far?"

"It's out of my hands. I heard on the grapevine that London Station held a couple of war parties over him a while back, but they didn't invite me and I don't know what came of them. Nothing, I should think, as usual."

"What passport's he been using?"

Tarr had his answer ready: "I threw away Thomas the day I hit Malaya. I reckoned Thomas wasn't exactly the flavour of the month in Moscow and I'd do better to kill him off right there. In K.L. I had them run me up a British." He handed it to Smiley. "Name of Poole. It's not bad for the money."

"Why didn't you use one of your Swiss escapes?"

Another wary pause.

"Or did you lose them when your hotel room was searched?"

Guillam said, "He cached them as soon as he arrived in Hong Kong. Standard practice."

"So why didn't you use them?"

"They were numbered, Mr. Smiley. They may have been blank but they were numbered. I was feeling a mite windy, frankly. If London had the numbers, maybe Moscow did, too, if you take my meaning."

"So what did you do with your Swiss escapes?" Smiley repeated pleasantly.

"He says he threw them away," said Guillam. "He sold them, more likely. Or swapped them for that one."

"How? Threw them away how? Did you burn them?"

"That's right, I burned them," said Tarr with a nervy ring to his voice, half a threat, half fear.

"So when you say this Frenchman was enquiring for you—"

"He was looking for Poole."

"But who else ever heard of Poole, except the man who faked this passport?" Smiley asked, turning the pages. Tarr said nothing. "Tell me how you travelled to England," Smiley suggested.

"Soft route from Dublin. No problem." Tarr lied badly under pressure. Perhaps his parents were to blame. He was too fast when he had no answer ready, too aggressive when he had one up his sleeve.

"How did you get to Dublin?" Smiley asked, checking the border stamps on the middle page.

"Roses." He had recovered his confidence. "Roses all the way. I've got a girl who's an air hostess with South African. A pal of mine flew me cargo to the Cape; at the Cape my girl took care of me, then hitched me a free ride to Dublin with one of the pilots. As far as anyone back East knows, I never left the peninsula."

"I'm doing what I can to check," said Guillam to the ceiling.

"Well, you be damn careful, baby," Tarr snapped down the line to Guillam. "Because I don't want the wrong people on my back."

"Why did you come to Mr. Guillam?" Smiley enquired, still deep in Poole's passport. It had a used, well-thumbed look, neither too full nor too empty. "Apart from the fact that you were frightened, of course."

"Mr. Guillam's my boss," said Tarr virtuously.

"Did it cross your mind he might just turn you straight over to Alleline? After all, you're something of a wanted man as far as the Circus top brass is concerned, aren't you?"

"Sure. But I don't figure Mr. Guillam's any fonder of the new arrangement than you are, Mr. Smiley."

"He also loves England," Guillam explained with mordant sarcasm.

"Sure. I got homesick."

"Did you ever consider going to anyone else but Mr. Guillam? Why not one of the overseas residencies, for instance, where you were in less danger? Is Mackelvore still headman in Paris?" Guillam nodded. "There you are, then: you could have gone to Mr. Mackelvore. He recruited you, you can trust him: he's old Circus. You could have sat safely in Paris instead of risking your neck over here. Oh, dear God. Lacon, quick!"

Smiley had risen to his feet, the back of one hand pressed to his mouth as he stared out the window. In the paddock Jackie Lacon was lying on her stomach screaming while a riderless pony careered between the trees. They were still watching as Lacon's wife, a pretty woman with long hair and thick winter stockings, bounded over the fence and gathered the child up.

"They're often taking tumbles," Lacon remarked, quite cross. "They don't hurt themselves at that age." And scarcely more graciously: "You're not responsible for everyone, you know, George."

Slowly they settled again.

"And if you had been making for Paris," Smiley resumed, "which route would you have taken?"

"The same till Ireland, then Dublin-Orly, I guess. What do you expect me to do—walk on the damn water?"

At this Lacon coloured and Guillam with an angry exclamation rose to his feet. But Smiley seemed quite unbothered. Taking up the passport again, he turned slowly back to the beginning.

"And how did you get in touch with Mr. Guillam?"

Guillam answered for him, speaking fast: "He knew where I garage my car. He left a note on it saying he wanted to buy it and signed it with his workname Trench. He suggested a place to meet and put in a veiled plea for privacy before I took my trade elsewhere. I brought Fawn along to baby-sit—"

Smiley interrupted: "That was Fawn at the door just now?"

"He watched my back while we talked," Guillam said. "I've kept him with us ever since. As soon as I'd heard Tarr's story, I rang Lacon from a call-box and asked for an interview . . . George, why don't we talk this over among ourselves?"

"Rang Lacon down here or in London?"

"Down here," said Lacon.

There was a pause till Guillam explained. "I happened to remember the name of a girl in Lacon's office. I mentioned her name and said she had asked me to speak to him urgently on an intimate matter. It wasn't perfect but it was the best I could think of on the spur of the moment." He added, filling the silence, "Well, damn it, there was no *reason* to suppose the phone was tapped."

"There was every reason."

Smiley had closed the passport and was examining the binding by the light of a tattered reading lamp at his side. "This is rather good, isn't it?" he remarked lightly. "Really very good indeed. I'd say that was a professional product. I can't find a blemish."

"Don't worry, Mr. Smiley," Tarr retorted, taking it back; "it's not made in Russia." By the time he reached the door, his smile had returned. "You know something?" he said, addressing all three of them down the aisle of the long room. "If Irina is right, you boys are going to need a whole new Circus. So if we all stick together I guess we could be in on the ground floor." He gave the door a playful tap. "Come on, darling, it's me. Ricki."

"Thank you! It's all right now! Open up, please," Lacon shouted, and a moment later the key was turned, the dark figure of Fawn the baby-sitter flitted into view, and then the footsteps faded into the big hollows of the house, to the distant accompaniment of Jackie Lacon's crying.

10

On another side of the house, away from the pony paddock, a grass tennis court was hidden among the trees. It was not a good tennis court; it was mown seldom. In spring the grass was sodden from the winter and no sun got in to dry it, in summer the balls disappeared into the foliage, and this morning it was ankle deep in frosted leaves that had collected from all over the garden. But round the outside, roughly following the wire rectangle, a footpath wandered between some beech trees and here Smiley and Lacon wandered also. Smiley had fetched his travelling coat but Lacon wore only his threadbare suit. For this reason, perhaps, he chose a brisk, if unco-ordinated, pace which with each stride took him well ahead of Smiley, so that he had constantly to hover, shoulders and elbows lifted, waiting till the shorter man caught up. Then he promptly bounded off again, gaining ground. They completed two laps in this way before Lacon broke the silence.

"When you came to me a year ago with a similar suggestion, I'm afraid I threw you out. I suppose I should apologise. I was remiss." There was a suitable silence while he pondered his dereliction. "I instructed you to abandon your enquiries."

"You told me they were unconstitutional," Smiley said mournfully, as if he were recalling the same sad error.

"Was that the word I used? Good Lord, how very pompous of me!"

From the direction of the house came the sound of Jackie's continued crying.

"You never had any, did you?" Lacon piped at once, his head lifted to the sound.

"I'm sorry?"

"Children. You and Ann."

"No."

"Nephews, nieces?"

"One nephew."

"On your side?"

"Hers."

Perhaps I never left the place, Smiley thought, peering around him at the tangled roses, the broken swings and sodden sandpits, the raw red house so shrill in the morning light. Perhaps we're still here from last time.

Lacon was apologising again: "Dare I say I didn't absolutely trust your motives? It rather crossed my mind that Control had put you up to it, you see. As a way of hanging on to power and keeping Alleline out"—swirling away again, long strides, wrists outward.

"Oh, no, I assure you Control knew nothing about it at all."

"I realise that now. I didn't at the time. It's a little difficult to know when to trust you people and when not. You do live by rather different standards, don't you? I mean you have to. I accept that. I'm not being judgemental. Our aims are the same, after all, even if our methods are different"—bounding over a cattle ditch. "I once heard someone say morality was method. Do you hold with that? I suppose you wouldn't. You would say that morality was vested in the aim, I expect. Difficult to know what one's aims *are*, that's the trouble, specially if you're British. We can't expect you people to determine our *policy* for us, can we? We can only ask you to further it. Correct? Tricky one, that."

Rather than chase after him, Smiley sat on a rusted swing seat and huddled himself more tightly in his coat, till finally Lacon stalked back and perched beside him. For a while they rocked together to the rhythm of the groaning springs.

"Why the devil did she choose Tarr?" Lacon muttered at last, fiddling his long fingers. "Of all the people in the world to choose for a confessor, I can imagine none more miserably unsuitable."

"I'm afraid you'll have to ask a woman that question, not us," said Smiley, wondering again where Immingham was.

"Oh, indeed," Lacon agreed lavishly. "All that's a complete mystery. I'm seeing the Minister at eleven," he confided, in a lower tone. "I have to put him in the picture. Your parliamentary cousin," he added, forcing an intimate joke.

"Ann's cousin, actually," Smiley corrected him, in the same absent tone. "Far removed I may add, but cousin for all that."

"And Bill Haydon is also Ann's cousin? Our distinguished Head of London Station." They had played this game before as well.

"By a different route, yes, Bill is also her cousin." He added quite uselessly: "She comes from an old family with a strong political tradition. With time it's rather spread."

"The tradition?"—Lacon loved to nail an ambiguity.

"The family."

Beyond the trees, Smiley thought, cars are passing. Beyond the trees lies a whole world, but Lacon has this red castle and a sense of Christian ethic that promises him no reward except a knighthood, the respect of his peers, a fat pension, and a couple of charitable directorships in the City.

"Anyway I'm seeing him at eleven." Lacon had jerked to his feet and they were walking again. Smiley caught the name "Ellis" floating backward to him on the leafy morning air. For a moment, as in the car with Guillam, an odd nervousness overcame him.

"After all," Lacon was saying, "we both held perfectly honourable positions. You felt that Ellis had been betrayed and you wanted a witch-hunt. My Minister and I felt there had been gross incompetence on the part of Control—a view which to put it mildly the Foreign Office shared—and we wanted a new broom."

"Oh, I quite understood *your* dilemma," said Smiley, more to himself than to Lacon.

"I'm glad. And don't forget, George: you were Control's man. Control preferred you to Haydon, and when he lost his grip towards the end—and launched that whole extraordinary adventure—it was you who fronted for him. No one but you, George. It's not everyday that the head of one's secret service embarks on a private war against the Czechs." It was clear that the memory still smarted. "In other circumstances, I suppose, Haydon might have gone to the wall, but you were in the hot seat and—"

"And Percy Alleline was the Minister's man," said Smiley, mildly enough for Lacon to slow himself and listen.

"It wasn't as if you had a suspect, you know! You didn't point the finger at anyone! A directionless enquiry can be extraordinarily destructive!"

"Whereas a new broom sweeps cleaner."

"Percy Alleline has produced intelligence instead of scandals, he has stuck to the letter of his charter and won the trust of the customers. And he has not, to my knowledge, invaded Czechoslovak territory. All in all he has done extremely well."

"With Bill Haydon to field for him, who wouldn't?"

"Control, for one," said Lacon, with punch.

They had drawn up at an empty swimming pool and now stood staring into the deep end. From its grimy depths Smiley fancied he heard again the insinuating tones of Roddy Martindale: "Little reading rooms at the Admiralty, little committees popping up with funny names . . ."

"Is that special source of Percy's still running?" Smiley enquired. "The Witchcraft material, or whatever it's called these days?"

"I didn't know you were on the list," Lacon said, not at all pleased. "Since you ask, yes. Source Merlin's our mainstay and Witchcraft is still the name of his product. The Circus hasn't turned in such good material for years. Since I can remember, in fact."

"And still subject to all that special handling?"

"Certainly, and now that this has happened I've no doubt that we shall take even more rigorous precautions."

"I wouldn't do that if I were you. Gerald might smell a rat."

"That's the point, isn't it?" Lacon observed quickly. His strength was improbable, Smiley reflected. One minute he was like a thin, drooping boxer whose gloves were too big for his wrists; the next he had reached out and rocked you against the ropes, and was surveying you with Christian compassion. "We can't move. We can't investigate because all the instruments of enquiry are in the Circus's hands, perhaps in the mole Gerald's. We can't watch, or listen, or open mail. To do any one of those things would require the resources of Esterhase's lamplighters, and Esterhase like anyone else must be suspect. We can't interrogate; we can't take steps to limit a particular person's access to delicate secrets. To do any of these things would be to run the risk of alarming the mole. It's the oldest question of all, George. Who can spy on the spies? Who can smell out the fox without running with him?" He made an awful stab at humour: "Mole, rather," he said, in a confiding aside.

In a fit of energy Smiley had broken away and was pounding ahead of Lacon down the path that led towards the paddock.

"Then go to the competition," he called. "Go to the security people. They're the experts; they'll do you a job."

"The Minister won't have that. You know perfectly well how he and Alleline feel about the competition. Rightly, too, if I may say so. A lot of ex-colonial administrators ploughing through Circus papers: you might as well bring in the army to investigate the navy!"

"That's no comparison at all," Smiley objected.

But Lacon as a good civil servant had his second metaphor ready: "Very well, the Minister would rather live with a damp roof than see his castle pulled down by outsiders. Does that satisfy you? He has a perfectly good point, George. We do have agents in the field, and I wouldn't give much for their chances once the security gentlemen barge in."

Now it was Smiley's turn to slow down. "How many?"

"Six hundred, give or take a few."

"And behind the Curtain?"

"We budget for a hundred and twenty." With numbers, with facts òf all sorts, Lacon never faltered. They were the gold he worked with, wrested from the grey bureaucratic earth. "So far as I can make out from the financial returns, almost all of them are presently active." He took a long bound. "So I can tell him you'll do it, can I?" he sang quite casually, as if the question were mere formality, check the appropriate box. "You'll take the job, clean the stables? Go backwards, go forwards, do whatever is necessary? It's your generation, after all. Your legacy."

Smiley had pushed open the paddock gate and slammed it behind him. They were facing each other over its rickety frame. Lacon, slightly pink, wore a dependent smile.

"Why do I say Ellis?" he asked conversationally. "Why do I talk about the Ellis affair when the poor man's name was Prideaux?"

"Ellis was his workname."

"Of course. So many scandals in those days, one forgets the details." Hiatus. Swinging of the right forearm. Lunge. "And he was Haydon's friend, not yours?" Lacon enquired.

"They were at Oxford together before the war."

"And stablemates in the Circus during and after. The famous Haydon-Prideaux partnership. My predecessor spoke of it interminably." He repeated, "But you were never close to him?"

"To Prideaux? No."

"Not a cousin, I mean?"

"For heaven's sake," Smiley breathed.

Lacon grew suddenly awkward again, but a dogged purpose kept his gaze on Smiley. "And there's no emotional or other reason which you feel might debar you from the assignment? You must speak up, George," he insisted anxiously, as if speaking up were the last thing he wanted. He waited a fraction, then threw it all away: "Though I see no real case. There's always a part of us that belongs to the public domain, isn't there? The social contract cuts both ways; you always knew that, I'm sure. So did Prideaux."

"What does that mean?"

"Well, good Lord, he was shot, George. A bullet in the back is held to be quite a sacrifice, isn't it, even in your world?"

Alone, Smiley stood at the further end of the paddock, under the dripping trees, trying to make sense of his emotions while he reached for breath. Like an old illness, his anger had taken him by surprise. Ever since his retirement, he had been denying its existence, steering clear of anything that could touch it off: newspapers, former colleagues, gossip of the Martindale sort. After a lifetime of living by his wits and his considerable memory, he had given himself full time to the profession of forgetting. He had forced himself to pursue scholarly interests which had served him well enough as a distraction while he was at the Circus, but which now that he was unemployed were nothing, absolutely nothing. He could have shouted: Nothing!

"Burn the lot," Ann had suggested helpfully, referring to his books. "Set fire to the house. But don't rot."

If by rot, she meant conform, she was right to read that as his aim. He had tried, really tried, as he approached what the insurance advertisements were pleased to call the evening of his life, to be all that a model *rentier* should be; though no one, least of all Ann, thanked him for the effort. Each morning as he got out of bed, each evening as he went back to it, usually alone, he had reminded himself that he never was and never had been indispensable. He had schooled himself to admit that in those last wretched months of Control's career, when disasters followed one another with heady speed, he had been guilty of seeing things out of proportion. And if the old professional Adam rebelled in him now and then and said: You *know* the place went bad, you *know* Jim Prideaux was betrayed—and what more eloquent testimony is there than a bullet, two bullets, in the back? Well, he had replied, suppose he did? And suppose he was right? "It is sheer vanity to believe that one fat middle-aged spy is the only person capable of holding the world together," he would tell himself. And other times: "I never heard of anyone yet who left the Circus without some unfinished business."

Only Ann, though she could not read his workings, refused to accept his findings. She was quite passionate, in fact, as only women can be on matters of business, really driving him to go back, take up where he had left off, never to veer aside in favour of the easy arguments. Not of course that she knew anything, but what woman was ever stopped by a want of information? She felt. And despised him for not acting in accordance with her feelings.

And now, at the very moment when he was near enough beginning to believe his own dogma, a feat made no easier by Ann's infatuation for an out-of-work actor, what happens but that the assembled ghosts of his past—Lacon, Control, Karla, Alleline, Esterhase, Bland, and finally Bill Haydon himself— barge into his cell and cheerfully inform him, as they drag him back to this same garden, that everything he had been calling vanity is truth?

"Haydon," he repeated to himself, no longer able to stem the tides of memory. Even the name was like a jolt. "I'm told that you and Bill shared *everything* once upon a time," said Martindale. He stared at his chubby hands, watching them shake. Too old? Impotent? Afraid of the chase? Or afraid of what he might unearth at the end of it? "There are always a dozen reasons for doing nothing," Ann liked to say—it was a favourite apologia, indeed, for many of her misdemeanours. "There is only one reason for doing *something*. And that's because you want to." Or have to? Ann would furiously deny it: coercion, she would say, is just another word for doing what you want; or for not doing what you are afraid of.

Middle children weep longer than their brothers and sisters. Over her mother's shoulder, stilling her pains and her injured pride, Jackie Lacon watched the party leave. First, two men she had not seen before: one tall, one short and dark. They drove off in a small green van. No one waved to them, she noticed, or even said goodbye. Next, her father left in his own car; lastly a blond, good-looking man and a short fat one in an enormous overcoat like a pony blanket made their way to a sports car parked under the beech trees. For a moment she really thought there must be something wrong with the fat one, he followed so slowly and so painfully. Then, seeing the handsome man hold the car door for him, he seemed to wake, and hurried forward with a lumpy skip. Unaccountably, this gesture upset her afresh. A storm of sorrow seized her and her mother could not console her.

11

Peter Guillam was a chivalrous fellow whose conscious loyalties were determined by his affections. The others had been made over long ago to the Circus. His father, a French businessman, had spied for a Circus *réseau* in the war while his mother, an Englishwoman, did mysterious things with codes. Until eight years ago, under the cover of a shipping clerk, Guillam himself had run his own agents in French North Africa, which was considered a murderous assignment. He was blown, his agents were hanged, and he entered the long middle age of the grounded pro. He did hackwork in London, sometimes for Smiley, ran a few home-based operations, including a network of girlfriends who were not, as the jargon has it, inter-conscious, and when Alleline's crowd took over he was shoved out to grass in Brixton—he supposed because he had the wrong connections, among them Smiley. That, resolutely, was how until last Friday he would have told the story of his life. Of his relationship with Smiley he would have dwelt principally upon the end.

Guillam was living mainly in London docks in those days, where he was putting together low-grade Marine networks from whatever odd Polish, Russian, and Chinese seamen he and a bunch of talent-spotters occasionally managed to get their hands on. Betweenwhiles he sat in a small room on the first floor of the Circus and consoled a pretty secretary called Mary, and he was quite happy except that no one in authority would answer his minutes. When he used the phone, he got "engaged" or no answer. He had heard vaguely there was trouble, but there was always trouble. It was common knowledge, for instance, that Alleline and Control had locked horns, but they had been doing little else for years. He also knew, like everyone else, that a big operation had aborted in Czechoslovakia, that the Foreign Office and the Defence Ministry had jointly blown a gasket, and that Jim Prideaux—head of scalp-hunters, the oldest Czecho hand, and Bill Haydon's lifelong stringer—had been shot up and put in the bag. Hence, he assumed, the loud silence and the glum faces. Hence also Bill Haydon's manic anger, of which the news spread like a nervous thrill through all the building: like God's wrath, said Mary, who loved a full-scale passion. Later he heard the catastrophe called Testify. Testify, Haydon told him much later, was the most incompetent bloody operation ever launched by an old man for his dying glory, and Jim Prideaux was the price of it. Bits made the newspapers, there were parliamentary questions, and even rumours, never officially confirmed, that British troops in Germany had been put on full alert.

Eventually, by sauntering in and out of other people's offices, he began to realise what everyone else had realised some weeks before. The Circus wasn't just silent, it was frozen. Nothing was coming in, nothing was going out; not at the level on which Guillam moved, anyhow. Inside the building, people in authority had gone to earth, and when pay day came round there were no buff envelopes in the pigeon-holes because, according to Mary, the housekeepers had not received the usual monthly authority to issue them. Now and then somebody would say they had seen Alleline leaving his club and he looked furious. Or Control getting into his car and he looked sunny. Or that Bill Haydon had resigned, on the grounds that he had been overruled or undercut, but Bill was always resigning. This time, said the rumour, the grounds were somewhat different, however: Haydon was furious that the Circus would not pay the Czech price for Jim Prideaux's repatriation; it was said to be too high in agents, or prestige. And that Bill had broken out in one of his fits of chauvinism and declared that any price was fair to get one loyal Englishman home: give them everything, only get Jim back.

Then, one evening, Smiley peered round Guillam's door and suggested a drink. Mary didn't realise who he was and just said "Hullo" in her stylish classless drawl. As they walked out of the Circus side by side, Smiley wished the janitors good night with unusual terseness, and in the pub in Wardour Street he said, "I've been sacked," and that was all.

From the pub they went to a wine bar off Charing Cross, a cellar with music playing and no one there. "Did they give any reason?" Guillam enquired. "Or is it just because you've lost your figure?"

It was the word "reason" that Smiley fixed on. He was by then politely but thoroughly drunk, but reason, as they walked unsteadily along the Thames embankment, reason got through to him.

"Reason as logic, or reason as motive?" he demanded, sounding less like himself than Bill Haydon, whose pre-war, Oxford Union style of polemic seemed in those days to be in everybody's ears. "Or reason as a way of life?" They sat on a bench. "They don't have to give *me* reasons. I can write my own damn reasons. And that is not the same," he insisted as Guillam guided him carefully into a cab, gave the driver the money and the address, "that is not the same as the half-baked tolerance that comes from no longer caring."

"Amen," said Guillam, fully realising as he watched the cab pull into the distance that by the rules of the Circus their friendship, such as it was, had that minute ended. Next day Guillam learned that more heads had rolled and that Percy Alleline was to stand in as night watchman with the title of acting chief, and that Bill Haydon, to everyone's astonishment, but most likely out of persisting anger with Control, would serve under him; or, as the wise ones said, over him.

By Christmas, Control was dead. "They'll get you next," said Mary, who saw these events as a second storming of the Winter Palace, and she wept when Guillam departed for the siberias of Brixton, ironically to fill Jim Prideaux's slot.

Climbing the four steps to the Circus that wet Monday afternoon, his mind bright with the prospect of felony, Guillam passed these events in review and decided that today was the beginning of the road back.

He had spent the previous night at his spacious flat in Eaton Place in the company of Camilla, a music student with a long body and a sad, beautiful face. Though she was not more than twenty, her black hair was streaked with grey, as if from a shock she never talked about. As another effect, perhaps, of the same undescribed trauma, she ate no meat, wore no leather, and drank nothing alcoholic; only in love, it seemed to Guillam, was she free of these mysterious restraints.

He had spent the morning alone in his extremely dingy room in Brixton photographing Circus documents, having first drawn a subminiature camera from his own operational stores, a thing he did quite often to keep his hand in. "Daylight or electric?" the storeman asked, and they had a friendly discussion about film grain. He told his secretary he didn't want to be disturbed, closed his door, and set to work according to Smiley's precise instructions. The windows were high in the wall. Even sitting, he could see only the sky and the tip of the new school up the road.

He began with works of reference from his personal safe. Smiley had given him priorities. First the staff directory, on issue to senior officers only, which supplied the home addresses, telephone numbers, names, and worknames of all home-based Circus personnel. Second, the handbook on staff duties, including the fold-in diagram of the Circus's reorganisation under Alleline. At its centre lay Bill Haydon's London Station, like a giant spider in its own web. "After the Prideaux fiasco," Bill had reputedly fumed, "we'll have no more damned private armies, no more left hand not knowing what the left hand is doing." Alleline, he noticed, was billed twice: once as Chief, once as Director Special Sources. According to rumour, it was those sources that kept the Circus in business. Nothing else, in Guillam's view, could account for the Circus's inertia at working level and the esteem it enjoyed in Whitehall. To these documents, at Smiley's insistence, he added the scalp-hunters' revised charter, in the form of an Alleline letter beginning "Dear Guillam," and setting out in detail the diminution of his powers. In several cases, the winner was Toby Esterhase, head of Acton lamplighters, the one outstation that had actually grown fatter under lateralism.

Next he moved to his desk and photographed, also on
Smiley's instruction, a handful of routine circulars that might
be useful as background reading. These included a belly-ache
from Admin., on the state of safe houses in the London area
(*"Kindly* treat them as if they were your *own"*), and another
about the misuse of unlisted Circus telephones for private
calls. Lastly a very rude personal letter from documents
warning him "for the last time of asking" that his workname
driving licence was out of date, and that unless he took the
trouble to renew it "his name would be forwarded to the
housekeepers for appropriate disciplinary action."

He put away the camera and returned to his safe. On the
bottom shelf lay a stack of lamplighter reports issued over
Toby Esterhase's signature and stamped with the code word
"Hatchet." These supplied the names and cover jobs of the
two or three hundred identified Soviet intelligence officers
operating in London under legal or semi-legal cover: trade,
Tass, Aeroflot, Radio Moscow, consular, and diplomatic.
Where appropriate, they also gave the dates of lamplighter
investigations and names of branch lines, which is jargon for
contacts thrown up in the course of surveillance and not
necessarily run to earth. The reports came in a main annual
volume and monthly supplements. He consulted the main
volume first, then the supplements. At eleven-twenty he
locked his safe, rang London Station on the direct line, and
asked for Lauder Strickland, of Banking Section.

"Lauder, this is Peter from Brixton; how's trade?"

"Yes, Peter, what can we do for you?"

Brisk and blank. We of London Station have more important friends, said the tone.

It was a question of washing some dirty money, Guillam
explained, to finance a ploy against a French diplomatic
courier who seemed to be for sale. In his meekest voice, he
wondered whether Lauder could possibly find the time for
them to meet and discuss it. Was the project cleared with
London Station, Lauder demanded. No, but Guillam had

already sent the papers to Bill by shuttle. Lauder Strickland came down a peg. Guillam pressed his cause: "There are one or two tricky aspects, Lauder; I think we need your sort of brain."

Lauder said he could spare him half an hour.

On his way to the West End, he dropped his films at the meagre premises of a chemist called Lark, in the Charing Cross Road. Lark, if it was he, was a very fat man with tremendous fists. The shop was empty.

"Mr. Lampton's films, to be developed," said Guillam. Lark took the package to the back room, and when he returned he said "All done" in a gravel voice, then blew out a lot of air at once, as if he were smoking, which he wasn't. He saw Guillam to the door and closed it behind him with a clatter. Where on God's earth does George find them, Guillam wondered. He had bought some throat pastilles. Every move must be accountable, Smiley had warned him: assume that the Circus has the dogs on you twenty-four hours a day. So what's new about that, Guillam thought; Toby Esterhase would put the dogs on his own mother if it bought him a pat on the back from Alleline.

From Charing Cross he walked up to Chez Victor for lunch with his head man, Cy Vanhofer, and a thug calling himself Lorimer, who claimed to be sharing his mistress with the East German ambassador in Stockholm. Lorimer said the girl was ready to play ball but she needed British citizenship and a lot of money on delivery of the first take. She would do anything, he said: spike the ambassador's mail, bug his rooms, or "put broken glass in his bath," which was supposed to be a joke. Guillam reckoned Lorimer was lying, and he was inclined to wonder whether Vanhofer was too, but he was wise enough to realise that he was in no state to say which way anyone was leaning just then. He liked Chez Victor but had no recollection of what he ate, and now as he entered the lobby of the Circus he knew the reason was excitement.

"Hullo, Bryant."

"Nice to see you, sir. Take a seat, sir, please, just for a moment, sir, thank you," said Bryant, all in one breath, and Guillam perched on the wooden settle thinking of dentists and Camilla. She was a recent and somewhat mercurial acquisition; it was a while since things had moved quite so fast for him. They met at a party and she talked about truth, alone in a corner over a carrot juice. Guillam, taking a long chance, said he wasn't too good at ethics, so why didn't they just go to bed together? She considered for a while, gravely; then fetched her coat. She'd been hanging around ever since, cooking nut rissoles and playing the flute.

The lobby looked dingier than ever. Three old lifts, a wooden barrier, a poster for Mazawattee tea, Bryant's glass-fronted sentry box with a "Scenes of England" calendar, and a line of mossy telephones.

"Mr. Strickland *is* expecting you, sir," said Bryant as he emerged, and in slow motion stamped a pink chit with the time of day: "14:55, P. Bryant, Janitor." The grille of the centre lift rattled like a bunch of dry sticks.

"Time you oiled this thing, isn't it?" Guillam called as he waited for the mechanism to mesh.

"We keep asking," said Bryant, embarking on a favourite lament. "They never do a thing about it. You can ask till you're blue in the face. How's the family, sir?"

"Fine," said Guillam, who had none.

"That's right," said Bryant. Looking down, Guillam saw the creamy head vanish between his feet. Mary called him strawberry and vanilla, he remembered: red face, white hair, and mushy.

In the lift he examined his pass. "Permit to enter L.S.," ran the headline. "Purpose of visit: Banking Section. This document to be handed back on leaving." And a space, marked "host's signature," blank.

"Well met, Peter. Greetings. You're a trifle late, I think, but never mind."

Lauder was waiting at the barrier—all five foot nothing of

him, white collared and secretly on tiptoe—to be visited. In Control's day this floor had been a thoroughfare of busy people. Today a barrier closed the entrance and a rat-faced janitor scrutinised his pass.

"Good God, how long have you had that monster?" Guillam asked, slowing down before a shiny new coffee machine. A couple of girls, filling beakers, glanced round and said "Hullo, Lauder," looking at Guillam. The tall one reminded him of Camilla: the same slow-burning eyes, censuring male insufficiency.

"Ah, but you've no notion how many man-hours it saves!" Lauder cried at once. "Fantastic. Quite fantastic," and all but knocked over Bill Haydon in his enthusiasm.

He was emerging from his room, an hexagonal pepper pot overlooking New Compton Street and the Charing Cross Road. He was moving in the same direction as they were but at about half a mile an hour, which for Bill indoors was full throttle. Outdoors was a different matter; Guillam had seen that, too—on training games at Sarratt, and once on a night drop in Greece. Outdoors he was swift and eager; his keen face, in this clammy corridor shadowed and withdrawn, seemed in the free air to be fashioned by the outlandish places where he had served. There was no end to them: no operational theatre, in Guillam's admiring eyes, that did not bear the Haydon imprint somewhere. Over and again in his own career, he had made the same eerie encounter with Bill's exotic progress. A year or two back, still working on Marine intelligence and having as one of his targets the assembly of a team of coast-watchers for the Chinese ports of Wenchow and Amoy, Guillam discovered to his amazement that there were actually Chinese stay-behind agents living in those very towns, recruited by Bill Haydon in the course of some forgotten wartime exploit, rigged out with cached radios and equipment, with whom contact might be made. Another time, raking through war records of Circus strong-arm men, more out of nostalgia for the period than present professional optimism, Guillam stumbled twice on Haydon's workname in as many minutes: in 1941 he was running French fishing smacks out of the Helford Estuary; in the same year, with Jim Prideaux as his stringer, he was laying down courier lines across southern Europe from the Balkans to Madrid. To Guillam, Haydon was of that unrepeatable, fading Circus generation, to which his parents and George Smiley also belonged—exclusive and, in Haydon's case, blue-blooded—which had lived a dozen leisured lives to his own hasty one, and still, thirty years later, gave the Circus its dying flavour of adventure.

Seeing them both, Haydon stood rock-still. It was a month since Guillam had spoken to him; he had probably been away on unexplained business. Now, against the light of his own open doorway, he looked strangely black and tall. He was carrying something—Guillam could not make out what it was—a magazine, a file, or a report; his room, split by his own shadow, was an undergraduate mayhem, monkish and chaotic. Reports, flimsies, and dossiers lay heaped everywhere; on the wall a baize noticeboard jammed with postcards and press cuttings; beside it, askew and unframed, one of Bill's old paintings, a rounded abstract in the hard flat colours of the desert.

"Hullo, Bill," said Guillam.

Leaving his door open—a breach of housekeeper regulations—Haydon fell in ahead of them, still without a word. He was dressed with his customary dottiness. The leather patches of his jacket were stitched on like diamonds, not squares, which from behind gave him a harlequin look. His spectacles were jammed up into his hair like goggles. For a moment they followed him uncertainly, till, without warning, he suddenly turned himself round, all of him at once like a statue being slowly swivelled on its plinth, and fixed his gaze on Guillam. Then he grinned, so that his crescent eyebrows went straight up like a clown's, and his face became handsome and absurdly young.

"What the hell are you doing here, you pariah?" he enquired pleasantly.

Taking the question seriously, Lauder started to explain about the Frenchman and the dirty money.

"Well, mind you lock up the spoons," said Bill, talking straight through him. "Those bloody scalp-hunters will steal the gold out of your teeth. Lock up the girls, too," he added as an afterthought, his eyes still on Guillam, "if they'll let you. Since when did scalp-hunters wash their own money? That's our job."

"Lauder's doing the washing. We're just spending the stuff."

"Papers to me," Haydon said to Strickland, with sudden curtness. "I'm not crossing any more bloody wires."

"They're already routed to you," said Guillam. "They're probably in your in-tray now."

A last nod sent them on ahead, so that Guillam felt Haydon's pale blue gaze boring into his back all the way to the next dark turning.

"Fantastic fellow," Lauder declared, as if Guillam had never met him. "London Station could not be in better hands. Incredible ability. Incredible record. Brilliant."

Whereas you, thought Guillam savagely, are brilliant by association. With Bill, with the coffee machine, with banks. His meditations were interrupted by Roy Bland's caustic cockney voice, issuing from a doorway ahead of them.

"Hey, Lauder, hold on a minute: have you seen Bloody Bill anywhere? He's wanted urgently."

Followed at once by Toby Esterhase's faithful mid-European echo from the same direction: "Immediately, Lauder; actually, we have put out an alert for him."

They had entered the last cramped corridor. Lauder was perhaps three paces on and was already composing his answer to this question as Guillam arrived at the open doorway and looked in. Bland was sprawled massively at his desk. He had thrown off his jacket and was clutching a paper. Arcs of sweat ringed his armpits. Tiny Toby Esterhase was stooped over him like a headwaiter, a stiff-backed miniature ambassador with silvery hair and a crisp unfriendly jaw, and he had stretched out one hand towards the paper as if to recommend a speciality. They had evidently been reading the same document when Bland caught sight of Lauder Strickland passing.

"Indeed I have seen Bill Haydon," said Lauder, who had a trick of rephrasing questions to make them sound more seemly. "I suspect Bill is on his way to you this moment. He's a way back there down the corridor; we were having a brief word about a couple of things."

Bland's gaze moved slowly to Guillam and settled there; its chilly appraisal was uncomfortably reminiscent of Haydon's. "Hullo, Pete," he said. At this, Tiny Toby straightened up and turned his eyes also directly towards Guillam; brown and quiet like a pointer's.

"Hi," said Guillam, "what's the joke?"

Their greeting was not merely frosty; it was downright hostile. Guillam had lived cheek by jowl with Toby Esterhase for three months on a very dodgy operation in Switzerland and Toby had never smiled once, so his stare came as no surprise. But Roy Bland was one of Smiley's discoveries, a warmhearted and impulsive fellow for that world, red-haired and burly, an intellectual primitive whose idea of a good evening was talking Wittgenstein in the pubs round Kentish Town. He'd spent ten years as a Party hack, plodding the academic circuit in Eastern Europe, and now, like Guillam, he was grounded, which was even something of a bond. His usual style was a big grin, a slap on the shoulder, and a blast of last night's beer; but not today.

"No joke, Peter, old boy," said Roy, mustering a belated smile. "Just surprised to see you, that's all. We're used to having this floor to ourselves."

"Here's Bill," said Lauder, very pleased to have his prognostication so promptly confirmed. In a strip of light, as he entered it, Guillam noticed the queer colour of Haydon's cheeks. A blushing red, daubed high on the bones, but deep, made up of tiny broken veins. It gave him, thought Guillam in his heightened state of nervousness, a slightly Dorian Gray look.

His meeting with Lauder Strickland lasted an hour and twenty minutes; Guillam spun it out that long, and throughout it his mind went back to Bland and Esterhase and he wondered what the hell was eating them.

"Well, I suppose I'd better go and clear all this with the Dolphin," he said at last. "We all know how she is about Swiss banks." The housekeepers lived two doors down from Banking. "I'll leave this here," he added and tossed the pass on to Lauder's desk.

Diana Dolphin's room smelt of fresh deodorant; her chain-mail handbag lay on the safe beside a copy of the *Financial Times*. She was one of those groomed Circus brides whom no one ever marries. Yes, he said wearily, the operational papers were already on submission to London Station. Yes, he understood that freewheeling with dirty money was a thing of the past.

"Then we shall look into it and let you know," she announced, which meant she would go and ask Phil Porteous, who sat next door.

"I'll tell Lauder, then," said Guillam, and left.

Move, he thought.

In the men's room he waited thirty seconds at the basins, watching the door in the mirror and listening. A curious quiet had descended over the whole floor. Come on, he thought, you're getting old; move. He crossed the corridor, stepped boldly into the duty officers' room, closed the door with a slam, and looked round. He reckoned he had ten minutes, and he reckoned that a slammed door made less noise in that silence than a door surreptitiously closed. Move.

He had brought the camera but the light was awful. The

net-curtained window looked onto a courtyard full of black-ened pipes. He couldn't have risked a brighter bulb even if he'd had one with him, so he used his memory. Nothing much seemed to have changed since the takeover. In the daytime the place was used as a restroom for girls with the vapours, and to judge by the smell of cheap scent it still was. Along one wall lay the imitation-leather divan, which at night made into a rotten bed; beside it the first-aid chest with the red cross peeling off the front, and a clapped-out television. The steel cupboard stood in its same place between the switchboard and the locked telephones, and he made a beeline for it. It was an old cupboard and he could have opened it with a tin opener. He had brought his picks and a couple of light alloy tools. Then he remembered that the combination used to be 31-22-11 and he tried it, four anti, three clock, two anti, clockwise till she springs. The dial was so jaded it knew the way. When he opened the door, dust rolled out of the bottom in a cloud, crawled a distance, then slowly lifted towards the dark win-dow. At the same moment, he heard what sounded like a single note played on a flute: it came from a car, most likely, braking in the street outside; or the wheel of a file trolley squeaking on linoleum. But for that moment it was one of those long, mournful notes which made up Camilla's practice scales. She played exactly when she felt like it. At midnight, in the early morning, or whenever. She didn't give a damn about the neighbours; she seemed quite nerveless altogether. He remembered her that first evening: "Which is your side of the bed? Where shall I put my clothes?" He prided himself on his delicate touch in such things, but Camilla had no use for it; technique was already a compromise, a compromise with reality—she would say an escape from it. All right, so get me out of this lot.

The duty logbooks were on the top shelf, in bound vol-umes with the dates pasted on the spines. They looked like family account books. He took down the volume for April and studied the list of names on the inside cover, wondering whether anyone could see him from the dupe-room across the courtyard, and if they could, would they care? He began working through the entries, searching for the night of the tenth and eleventh, when the signals traffic between London Station and Tarr was supposed to have taken place. Hong Kong was eight hours ahead, Smiley had pointed out: Tarr's telegram and London's first answer had both happened out of hours.

From the corridor came a sudden swell of voices, and for a second he even fancied he could pick out Alleline's growling border brogue lifted in humourless banter, but fancies were two a penny just now. He had a cover story and a part of him believed it already. If he was caught, the whole of him would believe it; and if the Sarratt inquisitors sweated him, he had a fallback—he never travelled without one. All the same, he was terrified. The voices died, and the ghost of Percy Alleline with them. Sweat was running over his ribs. A girl tripped past humming a tune from *Hair*. If Bill hears you, he'll murder you, he thought; if there's one thing that sends Bill spare it's humming. "What are you doing here, you pariah?"

Then, to his fleeting amusement, he actually heard Bill's infuriated roar, echoing from God knows what distance: "Stop that moaning. Who *is* the fool?"

Move. Once you stop, you never start again: there is a special stage-fright that can make you dry up and walk away, that burns your fingers when you touch the goods and turns your stomach to water. Move. He put back the April volume and drew four others at random: February, June, September, and October. He flicked through them fast, looking for comparisons, returned them to the shelf, and dropped into a crouch. He wished to God the dust would settle; there seemed to be no end to it. Why didn't someone complain? Always the same when a lot of people use one place: no one's responsible, no one gives a hoot. He was looking for the night janitors' attendance lists. He found them on the bottom shelf, jammed in with the tea-bags and the condensed milk: sheafs

of them in envelope-type folders. The janitors filled them in
and brought them to you twice in your twelve-hour tour of
duty: at midnight and again at 6 A.M. You vouched for their
correctness—God knows how, since the night staff were
scattered all over the building—signed them off, kept the
third copy, and chucked it in the cupboard, no one knew
why. That was the procedure before the Flood, and it seemed
to be the procedure now.

Dust and tea-bags on one shelf, he thought. How long since
anyone made tea?

Once again he fixed his sights on April 10th-11th. His shirt
was clinging to his ribs. What's happened to me? Christ, I'm
over the hill. He turned forward and back, forward again,
twice, three times, then closed the cupboard on the lot. He
waited, listened, took a last worried look at the dust, then
stepped boldly across the corridor, back to the safety of the
men's room. On the way the clatter hit him: coding machines,
the ringing of the telephones, a girl's voice calling "Where's
that damn float—I had it in my hand," and that mysterious
piping again, but no longer like Camilla's in the small hours.
Next time I'll get her to do the job, he thought savagely;
without compromise, face to face, the way life should be.

In the men's room he found Spike Kaspar and Nick de
Silsky standing at the hand basins and murmuring at each
other into the mirror: legmen for Haydon's Soviet networks,
they'd been around for years, known simply as "the Russians." Seeing Guillam, they at once stopped talking.

"Hullo, you two. Christ, you really *are* inseparable."

They were blond and squat and they looked more like
Russians than the real ones. He waited till they'd gone, rinsed
the dust off his fingers, then drifted back to Lauder Strickland's room.

"Lord save us, that Dolphin does talk," he said carelessly.

"Very able officer. Nearest thing to indispensable we have
around here. Extremely competent, you can take my word
for it," said Lauder. He looked closely at his watch before he

signed the chit, then led Guillam back to the lifts. Toby Esterhase was at the barrier, talking to an unfriendly young janitor.

"You are going back to Brixton, Peter?" His tone was casual, his expression as usual impenetrable.

"Why?"

"I have a car outside, actually. I thought maybe I could run you. We have some business out that way."

Run you: Tiny Toby spoke no known language perfectly, but he spoke them all. In Switzerland, Guillam had heard his French and it had a German accent; his German had a Slav accent and his English was full of stray flaws and stops and false vowel sounds.

"It's all right, Tobe, I think I'll just go home. Night."

"Straight home? I would run you, that's all."

"Thanks, I've got shopping to do. All those bloody godchildren."

"Sure," said Toby as if he hadn't any, and stuck in his little granite jaw in disappointment.

What the hell does he want, Guillam thought. Tiny Toby and Big Roy, both: why were they giving me the eye? Was it something they were reading or something they ate?

Out in the street he sauntered down the Charing Cross Road peering at the windows of the bookshops while his other mind checked both sides of the pavement. It had turned much colder, a wind was getting up, and there was a promise to people's faces as they bustled by. He felt elated. Till now he had been living too much in the past, he decided. Time to get my eye in again. In Zwemmer's he examined a coffee-table book called *Musical Instruments Down the Ages* and remembered that Camilla had a late lesson with Dr. Sand, her flute-teacher. He walked back as far as Foyle's, glancing down bus queues as he went. Think of it as abroad, Smiley had said. Remembering the duty room and Roy Bland's fishy stare, Guillam had no difficulty. And Bill, too: was Haydon party to their same suspicion? No. Bill was his own category, Guil-

lam decided, unable to resist a surge of loyalty to Haydon.
Bill would share nothing that was not his own in the first
place. Set beside Bill, those other two were pygmies.

In Soho he hailed a cab and asked for Waterloo Station. At
Waterloo, from a reeking phone box, he telephoned a number
in Mitcham, Surrey, and spoke to an Inspector Mendel, formerly of Special Branch, known to both Guillam and Smiley
from other lives. When Mendel came on the line, Guillam
asked for Jenny and heard Mendel tell him tersely that no
Jenny lived there. He apologised and rang off. He dialled the
time and feigned a pleasant conversation with the automatic
announcer because there was an old lady outside waiting for
him to finish. By now he should be there, he thought. He rang
off and dialled a second number in Mitcham, this time a call-
box at the end of Mendel's avenue.

"This is Will," said Guillam.

"And this is Arthur," said Mendel cheerfully. "How's
Will?" He was a quirkish, loping tracker of a man, sharp-
faced and sharp-eyed, and Guillam had a very precise picture
of him just then, leaning over his policeman's notebook with
his pencil poised.

"I want to give you the headlines now in case I go under a
bus."

"That's right, Will," said Mendel consolingly. "Can't be
too careful."

He gave his message slowly, using the scholastic cover they
had agreed on as a last protection against random intercep-
tion: exams, students, stolen papers. Each time he paused, he
heard nothing but a faint scratching. He imagined Mendel
writing slowly and legibly and not speaking till he had it all
down.

"I got those happy snaps from the chemist, by the by," said
Mendel finally, when he had checked it all back. "Come out a
treat. Not a miss among them."

"Thanks. I'm glad."

But Mendel had already rung off.

I'll say one thing for moles, thought Guillam: it's a long dark tunnel all the way. As he held open the door for the old lady, he noticed the telephone receiver lying on its cradle, how the sweat crawled over it in drips. He considered his message to Mendel; he thought again of Roy Bland and Toby Esterhase staring at him through the doorway; he wondered quite urgently where Smiley was, and whether he was taking care. He returned to Eaton Place needing Camilla badly, and a little afraid of his reasons. Was it really age that was against him suddenly? Somehow, for the first time in his life, he had sinned against his own notions of nobility. He had a sense of dirtiness, even of self-disgust.

12

There are old men who go back to Oxford and find their youth beckoning to them from the stones. Smiley was not one of them. Ten years ago he might have felt a pull. Not now. Passing the Bodleian, he vaguely thought, I worked there. Seeing the house of his old tutor in Parks Road, he remembered that before the war in its long garden Jebedee had first suggested he might care to talk to "one or two people I know in London." And hearing Tom Tower strike the evening six, he found himself thinking of Bill Haydon and Jim Prideaux, who must have arrived here the year that he went down, and were then gathered up by the war; and he wondered idly how they must have looked together then; Bill, the painter, polemicist, and socialite; Jim, the athlete, hanging on his words. In their heyday together in the Circus, he reflected, that distinction had all but evened out: Jim grew nimble at the brainwork and Bill in the field was no man's fool. Only at the end, the old polarity asserted itself: the workhorse went back to his stable, the thinker to his desk.

Spots of rain were falling but he couldn't see them. He had travelled by rail and walked from the station, making detours all the way: Blackwell's, his old college, anywhere, then north. Dusk had come here early because of the trees.

Reaching a cul-de-sac, he once more dawdled, once more took stock. A woman in a shawl rode past him on a push-bike, gliding through the beams of the streetlamps where they pierced the swathes of mist. Dismounting, she pulled open a gate and vanished. Across the road a muffled figure was walking a dog—man or woman, he couldn't tell. Otherwise the road was empty, so was the phone box. Then abruptly two men passed him, talking loudly about God and war. The younger one did most of the talking. Hearing the older one agree, Smiley supposed he was the don.

He was following a high paling that bulged with shrubs. The gate of number 15 was soft on its hinges, a double gate but only one side used. When he pushed it, the latch was broken. The house stood a long way back; most of the windows were lit. In one, high up, a young man stooped over a desk. At another, two girls seemed to be arguing; at a third, a very pale woman was playing the viola but he couldn't hear the sound. The ground-floor windows were also lit but the curtains were drawn. The porch was tiled, the front door panelled with stained glass; on the jamb was pinned an old notice: "After 11 P.M. use side door only." Over the bells, more notices: "Prince, three rings," "Lumby, two rings," "Buzz: out all evening, see you, Janet." The bottom bell said "Sachs" and he pressed it. At once dogs barked and a woman started yelling.

"Flush, you *stupid* boy, it's only a dunderhead. Flush, shut up, you fool. Flush!"

The door opened part way, held on a chain; a body swelled into the opening. While Smiley in the same instant gave his whole effort to seeing who else was inside the house, two shrewd eyes, wet like a baby's, appraised him, noted his brief-case and his spattered shoes, flickered upward to peer past his shoulder down the drive, then once more looked him over. Finally the white face broke into a charming smile, and

Miss Connie Sachs, formerly queen of research at the Circus, registered her spontaneous joy.

"George Smiley," she cried, with a shy trailing laugh as she drew him into the house. "Why, you lovely darling man, I thought you were selling me a Hoover, bless you, and all the time it's George!"

She closed the door after him, fast.

She was a big woman, bigger than Smiley by a head. A tangle of white hair framed her sprawling face. She wore a brown jacket like a blazer and trousers with elastic at the waist and she had a low belly like an old man's. A coke fire smouldered in the grate. Cats lay before it and a mangy grey spaniel, too fat to move, lounged on the divan. On a trolley were the tins she ate from and the bottles she drank from. From the same adapter she drew power for her radio, her electric ring, and her curling tongs. A boy with shoulder-length hair lay on the floor, making toast. Seeing Smiley, he put down his brass trident.

"Oh, Jingle, darling, *could* it be tomorrow?" Connie implored. "It's not often my oldest, oldest lover comes to see me." He had forgotten her voice. She played with it constantly, pitching it at all odd levels. "I'll give you a whole free hour, dear, all to himself: will you? One of my dunderheads," she explained to Smiley, long before the boy was out of earshot. "I still teach, I don't know why. *George*," she murmured, watching him proudly across the room as he took the sherry bottle from his briefcase and filled two glasses. "Of all the lovely darling men I ever knew. *He walked*," she explained to the spaniel. "Look at his boots. Walked all the way from London, didn't you, George? Oh, *bless*, God bless."

It was hard for her to drink. Her arthritic fingers were turned downward, as if they had all been broken in the same accident, and her arm was stiff. "Did you walk alone, George?" she asked, fishing a loose cigarette from her blazer pocket. "Not accompanied, were we?"

He lit the cigarette for her and she held it like a peashooter, fingers along the top, then watched him down the line of it with her shrewd, pinkish eyes. "So what does he want from Connie, you bad boy?"

"Her memory."

"What part?"

"We're going back over some old ground."

"Hear that, Flush?" she yelled to the spaniel. "First they chuck us out with an old bone, then they come begging to us. Which *ground*, George?"

"I've brought a letter for you from Lacon. He'll be at his club this evening at seven. If you're worried, you're to call him from the phone box down the road. I'd prefer you not to do that, but if you must he'll make the necessary impressive noises."

She had been holding him, but now her hands flopped to her sides and for a good while she floated round the room, knowing the places to rest and the holds to steady her, and cursing, "Oh, damn George Smiley and all who sail in him." At the window, perhaps out of habit, she parted the edge of the curtain but there seemed to be nothing to distract her.

"Oh, George, damn you so," she muttered. "How could you let a *Lacon* in? Might as well let in the competition, while you're about it."

On the table lay a copy of the day's *Times*, crossword uppermost. Each square was inked in laboured letters. There were no blanks.

"Went to the soccer today," she sang from the dark under the stairs as she cheered herself up from the trolley. "Lovely Will took me. My favourite dunderhead, wasn't that super of him?" Her little-girl voice; it went with an outrageous pout: "Connie got *cold*, George. Froze solid, Connie did, toes an' all."

He guessed she was crying, so he fetched her from the dark and led her to the sofa. Her glass was empty and he filled it half. Side by side on the sofa, they drank while Connie's tears ran down her blazer onto his hands.

"Oh, George," she said. "Do you know what she told me when they threw me out? That personnel cow?" She was holding one point of Smiley's collar, working it between her finger and thumb while she cheered up. "You know what the cow said?" Her sergeant-major voice: " 'You're losing your sense of proportion, Connie. It's time you got out into the real world.' I *hate* the real world, George. I like the Circus and all my lovely boys." She took his hands, trying to interlace her fingers with his.

"Polyakov," he said quietly, pronouncing it in accordance with Tarr's instruction. "Aleksey Aleksandrovich Polyakov, cultural attaché, Soviet Embassy, London. He's come alive again, just as you predicted."

A car was drawing up in the road; he heard only the sound of the wheels, the engine was already switched off. Then footsteps, very lightly.

"Janet, smuggling in her boyfriend," Connie whispered, her pink-rimmed eyes fixed on his while she shared his distraction. "She thinks I don't know. Hear that? Metal quarters on his heels. Now, wait." The footsteps stopped, there was a small scuffle. "She's giving him the key. He thinks he works it more quietly than she can. He can't." The lock turned with a heavy snap. "Oh, you men," Connie breathed with a hopeless smile. "Oh, George. Why do you have to drag up Aleks?" And for a while she wept for Aleks Polyakov.

Her brothers were dons, Smiley remembered; her father was a professor of something. Control had met her at bridge and invented a job for her.

She began her story like a fairy-tale: "Once upon a time, there was a defector called Stanley, way back in 1963," and she applied to it the same spurious logic—part inspiration, part intellectual opportunism—born of a wonderful mind that had never grown up. Her formless white face took on the grandmother's glow of enchanted reminiscence. Her memory was as compendious as her body and surely she loved it more, for she had put everything aside to listen to it: her drink, her cigarette, even for a while Smiley's passive hand. She sat no longer slouched but strictly, her big head to one side as she dreamily plucked the white wool of her hair. He had assumed she would begin at once with Polyakov, but she began with Stanley; he had forgotten her passion for family trees. Stanley, she said; the inquisitors' cover name for a fifth-rate defector from Moscow Centre. March, 1963. The scalphunters bought him secondhand from the Dutch and shipped him to Sarratt, and probably if it hadn't been the silly season and if the inquisitors hadn't happened to have time on their hands—well, who knows whether any of it would ever have come to light? As it was, Brother Stanley had a speck of gold on him, one teeny speck, and they found it. The Dutch missed it but the inquisitors found it, and a copy of their report came to Connie, "which was a whole *other* miracle in itself," Connie bellowed huffily, "considering that everyone, and *specially* Sarratt, made an absolute *principle* of leaving research off their distribution lists."

Patiently Smiley waited for the speck of gold, for Connie was of an age where the only thing a man could give her was time.

Now, Stanley had defected while he was on a mailfist job in The Hague, she explained. He was by profession an assassin of some sort and had been sent to Holland to murder a Russian émigré who was getting on Centre's nerves. Instead, he decided to give himself up. "Some *girl* had made a fool of him," said Connie with great contempt. "The Dutch set him a honey trap, my dear, and he barged in with his eyes wide shut."

To prepare him for the mission, Centre had posted him to one of their training camps outside Moscow for a brush-up in the black arts: sabotage and silent killing. The Dutch, when they had him, were shocked by this and made it the focal point of their interrogation. They put his picture in the newspapers and had him drawing pictures of cyanide bullets and all the other dreary weaponry Centre so adored. But at the Nursery the inquisitors knew that stuff by heart, so they concentrated on the camp itself, which was a new one, not much known: "Sort of a millionaires' Sarratt," she explained. They made a sketch-plan of the compound, which covered several hundred acres of forest and lakeland, and put in all the buildings Stanley could remember: laundries, canteens, lecture huts, ranges, all the dross. Stanley had been there several times and remembered a lot. They thought they were about finished when Stanley went very quiet. He took a pencil and in the north west corner he drew five more huts and a double fence round them for the guard dogs, bless him. These huts were new, said Stanley, built in the last few months. You reached them by a private road; he had seen them from a hilltop when he was out walking with his instructor, Milos. According to Milos (who was Stanley's *friend*, said Connie with much innuendo), they housed a special school recently founded by Karla for training military officers in conspiracy.

"So, my dear, there we were," Connie cried. "For *years* we'd been hearing rumours that Karla was trying to build a private army of his own inside Moscow Centre but, poor lamb, he hadn't the power. We knew he had agents scattered round the globe, and *naturally* he was worried that as he grew older and more senior he wouldn't be able to manage them alone. We knew that, like everyone else, he was *dreadfully* jealous of them and couldn't bear the idea of handing them over to the legal residencies in the target countries. Well, *naturally* he wouldn't: you know how he hated residencies— overstaffed, insecure. Same as he hated the old guard. 'Flat-earthers,' he called them. Quite right. Well, now he had the power and he was doing something about it, as any real man would. March, 1963," she repeated, in case Smiley had missed the date.

Then nothing, of course. "The usual game: sit on your thumbs, get on with other work, whistle for a wind." She sat on them for three years, until Major Mikhail Fedorovich Komarov, assistant military attaché in the Soviet Embassy in Tokyo, was caught *in flagrante* taking delivery of six reels of top-secret intelligence procured by a senior official in the Japanese Defence Ministry. Komarov was the hero of her second fairy-tale: not a defector but a soldier with the shoulder boards of the artillery.

"And medals, my dear! Medals galore!"

Komarov himself had to leave Tokyo so fast that his dog got locked in his flat and was later found starved to death, which was something Connie could *not* forgive him for. Whereas Komarov's Japanese agent was, of course, duly interrogated and by a happy chance the Circus was able to buy the report from the Toka.

"Why, George, come to think of it, it was you who arranged the deal!"

With a quaint pout of professional vanity, Smiley conceded that it might well have been.

The essence of the report was simple. The Japanese defence official was a mole. He had been recruited before the war in the shadow of the Japanese invasion of Manchuria, by one Martin Brandt, a German journalist who seemed to be connected with the Comintern. Brandt, said Connie, was one of Karla's names in the nineteen-thirties. Komarov himself had never been a member of the official Tokyo residency inside the Embassy; he'd worked solo, with one legman and a direct line to Karla, whose brother officer he had been in the war. Better still, before he arrived in Tokyo he had attended a special training course at a new school outside Moscow set up specially for Karla's handpicked pupils. "Conclusion," Connie sang. "Brother Komarov was our first and, alas, *not* very distinguished graduate of the Karla training school. He was shot, poor lamb," she added, with a dramatic fall of her voice. "They never *hang*, do they: too impatient, the little horrors."

Now Connie had felt able to go to town, she said. Knowing what signs to look for, she tracked back through Karla's file.

She spent three weeks in Whitehall with the army's Moscow-gazers combing Soviet Army posting bulletins for disguised entries until, from a host of suspects, she reckoned she had three new, identifiable Karla trainees. All were military men, all were personally acquainted with Karla, all were ten to fifteen years his junior. She gave their names as Bardin, Stokovsky, and Viktorov—all colonels.

At the mention of this third name, Smiley's eyes turned very tired, as if he were staving off boredom.

"So what became of them all," he asked.

"Bardin changed to Sokolov, then Rusakov. Joined the Soviet Delegation to the United Nations in New York. No overt connection with the local residency, no involvement in bread-and-butter operations, no coat-trailing, no talent-spotting—a good solid cover job. Still there, for all I know."

"Stokovsky?"

"Went illegal, set up a photographic business in Paris as Grodescu, French Rumanian. Formed an affiliate in Bonn, believed to be running one of Karla's West German sources from across the border."

"And the third? Viktorov?"

"Sunk without trace."

"Oh, dear," said Smiley, and his boredom seemed to deepen.

"Trained and disappeared off the face of the earth. May have died, of course. One does *tend* to forget the natural causes."

"Oh, indeed," Smiley agreed; "oh, quite."

He had that art, from miles and miles of secret life, of listening at the front of his mind; of letting the primary incidents unroll directly before him while another, quite separate faculty wrestled with their historical connection. The connection ran through Tarr to Irina, through Irina to her poor lover who was so proud of being called Lapin, and of serving one Colonel Gregor Viktorov "whose workname at the Embassy is Polyakov." In his memory, these things were like part of a childhood: he would never forget them.

"Were there photographs, Connie?" he asked glumly. "Did you land physical descriptions at all?"

"Of Bardin at the United Nations, naturally. Of Stokovsky, perhaps. We had an old press picture from his soldiering days, but we could never quite nail the verification."

"And of Viktorov, who sank without trace?" Still, it might have been any name. "No pretty picture of him, either?" Smiley asked, going down the room to fetch more drink.

"Viktorov, Colonel Gregor," Connie repeated with a fond distracted smile. "Fought like a terrier at Stalingrad. No, we never had a photograph. Pity. They said he was yards the best." She perked up: "Though, of course, we don't *know* about the others. Five huts and a two-year course: well, my dear, that adds up to a sight more than three graduates after all these years!"

With a tiny sigh of disappointment, as if to say there was nothing so far in that whole narrative, let alone in the person of Colonel Gregor Viktorov, to advance him in his laborious quest, Smiley suggested they should pass to the wholly unrelated phenomenon of Polyakov, Aleksey Aleksandrovich, of the Soviet Embassy in London, better known to Connie as dear Aleks Polyakov, and establish just where he fitted into Karla's scheme of things and why it was that she had been forbidden to investigate him further.

13

She was much more animated now. Polyakov was not a fairy-tale hero; he was her lover Aleks, though she had never spoken to him, probably never seen him in the flesh. She had moved to another seat closer to the reading lamp, a rocking-chair that relieved certain pains: she could sit nowhere for long. She had tilted her head back so that Smiley was looking at the white billows of her neck and she dangled one stiff hand coquettishly, recalling indiscretions she did not regret; while to Smiley's tidy mind her speculations, in terms of the acceptable arithmetic of intelligence, seemed even wilder than before.

"*Oh*, he was so good," she said. "Seven long years Aleks had been here before we even had an inkling. Seven years, my dear, and not so much as a *tickle!* Imagine!"

She quoted his original visa application, those nine years ago: Polyakov, Aleksey Aleksandrovich, graduate of Leningrad State University, cultural attaché with second-secretary rank, married but not accompanied by wife, born March 3, 1922, in the Ukraine, son of a transporter, early education not supplied. She ran straight on, a smile in her voice as she gave the lamplighters' first routine description: "Height, five foot eleven; heavy build; colour of eyes, green; colour of hair, black; no other visible distinguishing marks. Jolly giant of a bloke," she declared with a laugh. "Tremendous joker. Black tuft of hair, here, over the right eye. I'm sure he was a bottom pincher, though we never caught him at it. I'd have offered him one or two bottoms of our own if Toby had played ball, which he wouldn't. Not that Aleksey Aleksandrovich would have fallen for *that*, mind. Aleks was *far* too artful," she said proudly. "Lovely voice. Mellow like yours. I often used to play the tapes twice, just to listen to him speaking. Is he really still around, George? I don't even like to ask, you see. I'm afraid they'll all change and I won't know them any more."

He was still there, Smiley assured her. The same cover, the same rank.

"And still occupying that dreadful little suburban house in Highgate that Toby's watchers hated so? Forty Meadow Close, top floor. Oh, it was a *pest* of a place. I love a man who really lives his cover, and Aleks did. He was the busiest cul-

ture vulture that Embassy ever had. If you wanted something done fast—lecturer, musician, you name it—Aleks cut
through the red tape faster than any man."

"How did he manage that, Connie?"

"Not how *you* think, George Smiley," she sang as the
blood shot to her face. "*Oh,* no. Aleksey Aleksandrovich was
nothing but what he said he was—so there; you ask Toby
Esterhase or Percy Alleline. Pure as the driven snow, he was.
Unbesmirched in any shape or form—Toby will put you
right on that!"

"Hey," Smiley murmured, filling her glass. "Hey, steady,
Connie. Come down."

"*Fooey,*" she shouted, quite unmollified. "Sheer unadulter-
ated *fooey.* Aleksey Aleksandrovich Polyakov was a six-
cylinder Karla-trained hood if ever I saw one, and they
wouldn't even listen to me! 'You're seeing spies under the
bed,' says Toby. 'Lamplighters are fully extended,' says
Percy"—her Scottish brogue—" 'We've no place for luxuries
here.' Luxuries my foot!" She was crying again. "Poor
George," she kept saying. "Poor George. You tried to help
but what could you do? You were on the down staircase
yourself. Oh, George, don't go hunting with the Lacons.
Please don't."

Gently he guided her back to Polyakov, and why she was
so sure he was Karla's hood, a graduate of Karla's special
school.

"It was Remembrance Day," she sobbed. "We photographed his medals—'course we did."

Year one again, year one of her seven-year love affair
with Aleks Polyakov. The curious thing was, she said, that
she had her eye on him from the moment he arrived:

"Hullo, I thought. I'm going to have a bit of fun with you."

Quite why she thought that she didn't know. Perhaps it
was his self-sufficiency, perhaps it was his poker walk, straight

off the parade-ground: "Tough as a button. Army written all over him." Or perhaps it was the way he lived: "He chose the one house in London those lamplighters couldn't get within fifty yards of." Or perhaps it was his work: "There were three cultural attachés already: two of them were hoods and the only thing the third did was cart the flowers up to High-gate Cemetery for poor Karl Marx."

She was a little dazed, so he walked her again, taking the whole weight of her when she stumbled. Well, she said, at first Toby Esterhase agreed to put Aleks on the A list and have his Acton lamplighters cover him for random days, twelve out of every thirty, and each time they followed him he was as pure as the driven snow.

"My dear, you'd have thought I'd rung him up and told him, 'Aleks Aleksandrovich, mind your "p"s and "q"s be-cause I'm putting Tiny Toby's dogs on you. So just you live your cover and no monkey business.'"

He went to functions, lectures, strolled in the park, played a little tennis, and short of giving sweets to the kids he couldn't have been more respectable. Connie fought for con-tinued coverage but it was a losing battle. The machinery ground on and Polyakov was transferred to the B list: to be topped up every six months or as resources allowed. The six-monthly top-ups produced nothing at all, and after three years he was graded Persil: investigated in depth and found to be of no intelligence interest. There was nothing Connie could do, and really she had almost begun to live with the assessment when one gorgeous November day lovely Teddy Hankie telephoned her rather breathlessly from the Laundry at Acton to say Aleks Polyakov had blown his cover and run up his true colours at last. They were splashed all over the masthead.

"Teddy was an old *old* chum. Old Circus and a perfect pet; I don't care if he's ninety. He'd finished for the day and was on his way home when the Soviet Ambassador's Volga drove past going to the wreath-laying ceremony, carrying the three service attachés. Three others were following in a second car. One was Polyakov and he was wearing more medals than a Christmas tree. Teddy shot down to Whitehall with his camera and photographed them across the street. My dear, *everything* was on our side: the weather was perfect, a bit of rain and then some lovely afternoon sunshine; he could have got the smile on a fly's backside at three hundred yards. We blew up the photographs and there they were: two gallantry and four campaign. Aleks Polyakov was a war veteran and he'd never told a soul in seven years. Oh, I was excited! I didn't even need to plot the campaigns. 'Toby,' I said—I rang him straight away—'You just listen to me for a moment, you Hungarian poison dwarf. This is one of the occasions when ego has finally got the better of cover. I want you to turn Aleks Aleksandrovich *inside out* for me, no "if"'s or "but"'s. Connie's little hunch has come home trumps.' "

"And what did Toby say?"

The grey spaniel let out a dismal sigh, and dropped off to sleep again.

"Toby?" Connie was suddenly very lonely. "Oh, Tiny Toby gave me his dead-fish voice and said Percy Alleline was now head of operations, didn't he? It was Percy's job, not his, to allocate resources. I knew straight away something was wrong but I thought it was Toby." She fell silent. "Damn fire," she muttered morosely. "You only have to turn your back and it goes out." She had lost interest. "You know the rest. Report went to Percy. 'So what?' Percy says. 'Polyakov used to be in the Russian Army. It was a biggish army and not everybody who fought in it was Karla's agent.' Very funny. Accused me of unscientific deduction. 'Whose expression is that?' I said to him. 'It's not *de*duction at all,' he says, 'it's *in*duction.' 'My dear Percy, wherever have you been learning words like that; you sound just like a beastly doctor or someone.' My *dear*, he was cross! As a sop, Toby puts the dogs on Aleks and nothing happens. 'Spike his house,' I said. 'His car, everything! Rig a mugging, turn him inside out, put the listeners on him! Fake a mistaken identity, search him. Anything, but for God's *sake* do something, because it's a pound to a rouble Aleks Polyakov is running an English mole!' So Percy sends for me, all lofty,"—the brogue again: " 'You're to leave Polyakov alone. You're to put him out of your silly woman's mind, do you understand? You and your blasted Polly what's-'is-name are becoming a damned nuisance, so lay off him.' Follows it up with a rude letter. 'We spoke and you agreed,' copy to head cow. I wrote, 'yes repeat no' on the bottom and sent it back to him." She switched to her sergeant-major voice: " 'You're losing your sense of proportion, Connie. Time you got out into the real world.' "

Connie was having a hangover. She was sitting again, slumped over her glass. Her eyes had closed and her head kept falling to one side.

"Oh, God," she whispered, waking up again. "Oh, my Lordy be."

"Did Polyakov have a legman?" Smiley asked.

"Why should he? He's a culture vulture. Culture vultures don't need legmen."

"Komarov had one in Tokyo. You said so."

"Komarov was military," she said sullenly.

"So was Polyakov. You saw his medals."

He held her hand, waiting. Lapin the rabbit, she said, clerk driver at the Embassy, twerp. At first she couldn't work him out. She suspected him of being one Ivlov, but she couldn't prove it and no one would help her anyway. Lapin the rabbit spent most of his day padding round London looking at girls and not daring to talk to them. But gradually she began to pick up the connection. Polyakov gave a reception, Lapin helped pour the drinks. Polyakov was called in late at night, and half an hour later Lapin turned up presumably to unbutton a telegram. And when Polyakov flew to Moscow, Lapin the rabbit actually moved into the Embassy and slept there till he came back. "He was doubling up," said Connie firmly. "Stuck out a mile."

"So you reported that, too?"

" 'Course I did."

"And what happened?"

"Connie was sacked and Lapin went home," Connie said with a giggle. "Couple of weeks later, Jimmy Prideaux got shot in the bot, George Smiley was pensioned off, and Control . . ." She yawned. "Hey, ho," she said. "Halcyon days. Landslide. Did I start it, George?"

The fire was quite dead. From somewhere above them came a thud; perhaps it was Janet and her lover. Gradually, Connie began humming, then swaying to her own music.

He stayed, trying to cheer her up. He gave her more drink and finally it brightened her.

"Come on," she said, "I'll show you *my* bloody medals."

Dormitory feasts again. She had them in a scuffed attaché case, which Smiley had to pull out from under the bed. First a real medal in a box and a typed citation calling her by her workname Constance Salinger and putting her on the Prime Minister's list.

" 'Cause Connie was a good girl," she explained, her cheek against his. "And loved all her gorgeous boys."

Then photographs of past members of the Circus: Connie in Wren's uniform in the war, standing between Jebedee and old Bill Magnus, the wrangler, taken somewhere in England; Connie with Bill Haydon one side and Jim Prideaux the other, the men in cricket gear and all three looking very-nicely-thank-you, as Connie put it, on a summer course at Sarratt, the grounds stretching out behind them, mown and sunlit, and the sight screens glistening. Next an enormous magnifying glass with signatures engraved on the lens: from Roy, from Percy, from Toby and lots of others, "To Connie with love and never say goodbye!"

Lastly, Bill's own special contribution: a caricature of Connie lying across the whole expanse of Kensington Palace Gardens while she peered at the Soviet Embassy through a telescope: "With love and fond memories, dear, dear Connie."

"They still remember him here, you know," she said. "The

golden boy. Christ Church common-room has a couple of his paintings. They take them out quite often. Giles Langley stopped me in the High only the other day: did I ever hear from Haydon? Don't know what I said: Yes. No. Does Giles's sister still do safe houses, do you know?" Smiley did not. " 'We miss his flair,' says Giles, 'they don't breed them like him any more.' Giles must be a hundred and eight in the shade. Says he taught Bill modern history, in the days before 'Empire' became a dirty word. Asked after Jim, too. 'His alter ego, we might say, hem hem, hem hem.' You never liked Bill, did you?" Connie ran on vaguely, as she packed it all away again in plastic bags and bits of cloth. "I never knew whether you were jealous of him or he was jealous of you. Too glamorous, I suppose. You always distrusted looks. Only in men, mind."

"My dear Connie, don't be absurd," Smiley retorted, off guard for once. "Bill and I were perfectly good friends. What on earth makes you say that?"

"Nothing." She had almost forgotten it. "I heard once he had a run round the park with Ann, that's all. Isn't he a cousin of hers, or something? I always thought you'd have been so good together, you and Bill, if it could have worked. You'd have brought back the old spirit. Instead of that Scottish twerp. Bill rebuilding Camelot"—her fairy-tale smile again— "and George—"

"George picking up the bits," said Smiley, vamping for her, and they laughed, Smiley falsely.

"Give me a kiss, George. Give Connie a kiss."

She showed him through the kitchen garden, the route her lodgers used; she said he would prefer it to the view of the filthy new bungalows the Harrison pigs had flung up in the next door garden. A thin rain was falling, a few stars glowed big and pale in the mist; on the road lorries rumbled north-ward through the night. Clasping him, Connie grew suddenly frightened.

"You're very naughty, George. Do you hear? Look at me.

Don't look that way, it's all neon lights and Sodom. Kiss me.
All over the world, beastly people are making our time into
nothing; why do you help them? Why?"

"I'm not helping them, Connie."

" 'Course you are. Look at me. It was a good time, do you
hear? A real time. Englishmen could be proud then. Let them
be proud now."

"That's not quite up to me, Connie."

She was pulling his face onto her own, so he kissed her full
on the lips.

"Poor loves." She was breathing heavily, not perhaps from
any one emotion but from a whole mess of them, washed
around in her like mixed drinks. "Poor loves. Trained to
Empire, trained to rule the waves. All gone. All taken away.
Bye-bye, world. You're the last, George, you and Bill. And
filthy Percy a bit." He had known it would end like this; but
not quite so awfully. He had had the same story from her
every Christmas at the little drinking parties that went on in
corners round the Circus. "You don't know Millponds, do
you?" she was asking.

"What's Millponds?"

"My brother's place. Beautiful Palladian house, lovely
grounds, near Newbury. One day a road came. Crash. Bang.
Motorway. Took all the grounds away. I grew up there, you
see. They haven't sold Sarratt, have they? I was afraid they
might."

"I'm sure they haven't."

He longed to be free of her but she was clutching him more
fiercely; he could feel her heart thumping against him.

"If it's bad, don't come back. Promise? I'm an old leopard
and I'm too old to change my spots. I want to remember you
all as you were. Lovely, lovely boys."

He did not like to leave her there in the dark, swaying
under the trees, so he walked her halfway back to the house,
neither of them talking. As he went down the road, he heard
her humming again, so loud it was like a scream. But it was

nothing to the mayhem inside him just then, the currents of alarm and anger and disgust at this blind night walk, with God knew what bodies at the end.

He caught a stopping train to Slough, where Mendel was waiting for him with a hired car. As they drove slowly towards the orange glow of the city, he listened to the sum of Peter Guillam's researches. The duty officers' ledger contained no record of the night of April 10th-11th, said Mendel. The pages had been excised with a razor blade. The janitors' returns for the same night were also missing, as were the signals' returns.

"Peter thinks it was done recently. There's a note scribbled on the next page, saying, 'All enquiries to Head of London Station.' It's in Esterhase's handwriting and dated Friday."

"*Last* Friday?" said Smiley, turning so fast that his seat belt let out a whine of complaint. "That's the day Tarr arrived in England."

"It's all according to Peter," Mendel replied stolidly.

And finally, concerning Lapin alias Ivlov, and Cultural Attaché Aleksey Aleksandrovich Polyakov, both of the Soviet Embassy in London, Toby Esterhase's lamplighter reports carried no adverse trace whatever. Both had been investigated, both were graded Persil: the cleanest category available. Lapin had been posted back to Moscow a year ago.

In a briefcase, Mendel had also brought Guillam's photographs, the result of his foray at Brixton, developed and blown up to full-plate size. Close to Paddington Station, Smiley got out and Mendel held the case out to him through the doorway.

"Sure you don't want me to come with you?" Mendel asked.

"Thank you. It's only a hundred yards."

"Lucky for you there's twenty-four hours in the day, then."

"Yes, it is."

"Some people sleep."

"Good night."

Mendel was still holding onto the briefcase. "I may have found the school," he said. "Place called Thursgood's, near Taunton. He did half a term's supply work in Berkshire first, then seems to have hoofed it to Somerset. Got a trailer, I hear. Want me to check?"

"How will you do that?"

"Bang on his door. Sell him a magazine, get to know him socially."

"I'm sorry," said Smiley, suddenly worried. "I'm afraid I'm jumping at shadows. I'm sorry, that was rude of me."

"Young Guillam's jumping at shadows, too," said Mendel firmly. "Says he's getting funny looks around the place. Says there's something up and they're all in it. I told him to have a stiff drink."

"Yes," said Smiley after further thought. "Yes, that's the thing to do. Jim's a pro," he explained. "A fieldman of the old school. He's good, whatever they did to him."

Camilla had come back late. Guillam had understood her flute lesson with Sand ended at nine, yet it was eleven by the time she let herself in, and he was accordingly short with her; he couldn't help it. Now she lay in bed, with her grey-black hair spread over the pillow, watching him as he stood at the unlit window staring into the square.

"Have you eaten?" he said.

"Dr. Sand fed me."

"What on?"

Sand was a Persian, she had told him.

No answer. Dreams, perhaps? Nut steak? Love? In bed she never stirred except to embrace him. When she slept, she barely breathed; sometimes he would wake and watch her, wondering how he would feel if she were dead.

"Are you fond of Sand?" he asked.

"Sometimes."

"Is he your lover?"

"Sometimes."

"Maybe you should move in with him instead of me."

"It's not like that," said Camilla. "You don't understand."

No. He didn't. First there had been a loving couple necking in the back of a Rover, then a lonely queer in a trilby exercising his Sealyham; then a girl made an hour-long call from the phone box outside his front door. There need be nothing to any of it, except that the events were consecutive, like a changing of the guard. Now a van had parked and no one got out. More lovers, or a lamplighters' night team? The van had been there ten minutes when the Rover drove away.

Camilla was asleep. He lay awake beside her, waiting for tomorrow when, at Smiley's request, he intended to steal the file on the Prideaux affair, otherwise known as the Ellis scandal or—more locally—Operation Testify.

14

It had been, till that moment, the second happiest day of Bill Roach's short life. The happiest was shortly before the dissolution of his household, when his father discovered a wasps' nest in the roof and recruited Bill to help him smoke them out. His father was not an outdoor man—not even handy—but after Bill had looked up wasps in his encyclopaedia they drove to the chemist together and bought sulphur, which they burned on a charger under the eave, and did the wasps to death.

Whereas today had seen the formal opening of Jim Prideaux's car-club rally. Till now they had only stripped the Alvis down, refurbished her, and put her together again, but today, as the reward, they had laid out—with the help of Latzy, the D.P.—a slalom of straw bales on the stony side of the drive. Then each in turn had taken the wheel and, with Jim as time-keeper, puffed and shunted through the gates to the tumult of their supporters. "Best car England ever made" was how Jim had introduced his car. "Out of production, thanks to Socialism." She was now repainted, she had a racing Union Jack on the bonnet, and she was undoubtedly the finest, fastest car on earth. In the first round, Roach had come third out of fourteen, and now in the second he had reached the chestnut trees without once stalling, and was all set for the home lap and a record time. He had never imagined that anything could give him so much pleasure. He loved the car, he loved Jim, and he even loved the school, and for the first time in his life he loved trying to win. He could hear Jim yelling, "Easy, Jumbo," and he could see Latzy leaping up and down with the improvised chequered flag; but as he clattered past the post he already knew that Jim wasn't watching him any more but glaring down the course towards the beech trees.

"Sir, how long, sir?" he asked breathlessly, and there was a small hush.

"Timekeeper!" sang Spikely, chancing his luck. "Time, please, Rhino."

"Was very good, Jumbo," Latzy said, also looking at Jim.

For once, Spikely's impertinence, like Roach's entreaty, found no response. Jim was staring across the field, towards the lane that formed the eastern border. Beside him stood a boy named Coleshaw, whose nickname was Cole Slaw. He was a lag from Three B, and famous for sucking up to staff. The ground lay very flat just there before lifting to the hills; often after a few days' rain it flooded. For this reason there was no good hedge beside the lane but a post-and-wire fence; and no trees, either—just the fence, the flats, and sometimes the Quantocks behind, which today had vanished in the general whiteness. The flats could have been a marsh leading to a lake, or simply to the white infinity. Against this washed-out background strolled a single figure, a trim, inconspicuous pedestrian, male and thin-faced, in a trilby hat and grey raincoat, carrying a walking stick that he barely used. Watching him also, Roach decided that the man wanted to walk faster but was going slowly for a purpose.

"Got your specs on, Jumbo?" asked Jim, staring after the man, who was about to draw level with the next post.

"Yes, sir."

"Who is he, then? Looks like Solomon Grundy."

"Don't know, sir."

"Never seen him before?"

"No, sir."

"Not staff, not village. So who is he? Beggarman? Thief? Why doesn't he look this way, Jumbo? What's wrong with us? Wouldn't you, if you saw a bunch of boys flogging a car round a field? Doesn't he like cars? Doesn't he like boys?"

Roach was still thinking up an answer to all these questions when Jim started speaking to Latzy in D.P., using a murmured, level sort of tone, which at once suggested to Roach that there was a complicity between them, a special foreign bond. The impression was strengthened by Latzy's reply, plainly negative, which had the same unstartled quietness.

"Sir, please, sir, I think he's to do with the church, sir," said Cole Slaw. "I saw him talking to Wells Fargo, sir, after chapel."

The vicar's name was Spargo and he was very old. It was Thursgood legend that he was in fact the great Wells Fargo in retirement. At this intelligence, Jim thought awhile and Roach, furious, told himself that Coleshaw was making the story up.

"Hear what they talked about, Cole Slaw?"

"Sir, no, sir. They were looking at pew lists, sir. But I could ask Wells Fargo, sir."

"*Our* pew lists? Thursgood pew lists?"

"Yes, sir. School pew lists. Thursgood's. With all the names, sir, where we sit."

And where the staff sit, too, thought Roach sickly.

"Anybody sees him again, let me know. Or any other sinister bodies, understand?" Jim was addressing them all, making light of it now. "Don't hold with odd bods hanging about the school. Last place I was at, we had a whole damn gang. Cleared the place out. Silver, money, boys' watches, radios—God knows what they didn't pinch. He'll pinch the Alvis next. Best car England ever made, and out of production. Colour of hair, Jumbo?"

"Black, sir."

"Height, Cole Slaw?"

"Sir, six foot, sir."

"Everybody looks six foot to Cole Slaw, sir," said a wit, for Coleshaw was a midget, reputedly fed on gin as a baby.

"Age, Spikely, you toad?"

"Ninety-one, sir."

The moment dissolved in laughter; Roach was awarded a redrive and did badly, and the same night lay in an anguish of jealousy that the entire car club, not to mention Latzy, had been recruited wholesale to the select rank of watcher. It was poor consolation to assure himself that their vigilance would never match his own; that Jim's order would not outlive the day; or that from now on he must increase his efforts to meet what was clearly an advancing threat.

The thin-faced stranger disappeared, but next day Jim paid a rare visit to the churchyard; Roach saw him talking to Wells Fargo before an open grave. Thereafter Bill Roach noticed a steady darkening of Jim's face, and an alertness which at times was like an anger in him, as he stalked through the twilight every evening, or sat on the hummocks outside his trailer, indifferent to the cold or wet, smoking his tiny cigar and sipping his vodka as the dusk closed on him.

PART II

15

The Hotel Islay in Sussex Gardens—where, on the day after his visit to Ascot, George Smiley under the name of Barraclough had set up his operational headquarters—was a very quiet place, considering its position, and perfectly suited to his needs. It lay a hundred yards south of Paddington Station, one of a terrace of elderly mansions cut off from the main avenue by a line of plane trees and a parking patch. The traffic roared past it all night. But the inside, though it was a fire-bowl of clashing wallpapers and copper lampshades, was a place of extraordinary calm. Not only was there nothing going on in the hotel, there was nothing going on in the world, either, and this impression was strengthened by Mrs. Pope Graham, the proprietor, a major's widow with a terribly langorous voice that imparted a sense of deep fatigue to Mr. Barraclough or anyone else who sought her hospitality. Inspector Mendel, whose informant she had been for many years, insisted that her name was plain Graham. The Pope had been added for grandeur or out of deference to Rome.

"Your father wasn't a Green Jacket, was he, dear?" she enquired, with a yawn, as she read Barraclough in the register. Smiley paid her fifty pounds' advance for a two-week stay, and she gave him Room 8 because he wanted to work. He asked for a desk and she gave him a rickety card table; Norman, the boy, brought it. "It's Georgian," she said with a sigh, supervising its delivery. "So you will love it for me, won't you, dear? I shouldn't lend it to you, really; it was the Major's."

To the fifty, Mendel privately had added a further twenty

on account, from his own wallet—"dirty oncers," as he called them—which he later recovered from Smiley. "No smell to nothing, is there?" he said.

"You could say so," Mrs. Pope Graham agreed, demurely stowing the notes among her nether garments.

"I'll want every scrap," Mendel warned, seated in her basement apartment over a bottle of the one she liked. "Times of entry and exit, contacts, life-style, and most of all," he said, lifting an emphatic finger, "most of all—and more important than you can possibly know, this is—I'll want suspicious persons taking an interest or putting questions to your staff under a pretext." He gave her his state-of-the-nation look. "Even if they say they're the Guards Armoured and Sherlock Holmes rolled into one."

"There's only me and Norman," said Mrs. Pope Graham, indicating a shivery boy in a black overcoat to which had been stitched a velvet collar of beige. "And they'll not get far with Norman—will they, dear; you're too sensitive."

"Same with his incoming letters," said the Inspector. "I'll want postmarks and times posted where legible, but no tampering or holding back. Same with his objects." He allowed a hush to fall as he eyed the substantial safe that formed such a feature of the furnishings. "Now and then, he's going to ask for objects to be lodged. Mainly they'll be papers, sometimes books. There's only one person allowed to look at those objects apart from him." He pulled a sudden piratical grin: "Me. Understand? No one else can even know you've got them. And don't fiddle with them, or he'll know because he's sharp. It's got to be expert fiddling. I'm not saying any more," Mendel concluded. Though he did remark to Smiley, soon after returning from Somerset, that if twenty quid was all it cost them, Norman and his protectress were the cheapest baby-sitting service in the business.

In which boast he was pardonably mistaken, for he could hardly be expected to know of Jim's recruitment of the entire car club; or the means by which Jim was able subsequently to trace the path of Mendel's wary investigations. Nor could Mendel, or anyone else, have guessed the state of electric alertness to which anger, and the strain of waiting, and perhaps a little madness, had seemingly brought Jim.

Room 8 was on the top floor. Its window looked onto the parapet. Beyond the parapet lay a side street with a shady bookshop and a travel agency called Wide World. The hand towel was embroidered "Swan Hotel Marlow." Lacon stalked in that evening carrying a fat briefcase containing the first consignment of papers from his office. To talk, the two men sat side by side on the bed while Smiley played a transistor wireless to drown the sound of their voices. Lacon took this mawkishly; he seemed somehow too old for the picnic. Next morning on his way to work, Lacon reclaimed the papers and returned the books that Smiley had given him to pad out his briefcase. In this role Lacon was at his worst. His manner was offended and off-hand; he made it clear he detested the irregularity. In the cold weather, he seemed to have developed a permanent blush. But Smiley could not have read the files by day, because they were on call to Lacon's staff and their absence would have caused an uproar. Nor did he want to. He knew better than anyone that he was desperately short of time. Over the next three days this procedure varied very little. Each evening on his way to take the train from Paddington, Lacon dropped in his papers, and each night Mrs. Pope Graham furtively reported to Mendel that the sour gangly one had called again—the one who looked down his nose at Norman. Each morning, after three hours' sleep and a disgusting breakfast of undercooked sausage and overcooked tomato—there was no other menu—Smiley waited for Lacon to arrive, then slipped gratefully into the cold winter's day to take his place among his fellow men.

They were extraordinary nights for Smiley, alone up there on the top floor. Thinking of them afterwards—though his

days between were just as fraught, and on the surface more
eventful—he recalled them as a single journey, almost a single
night. "And you'll do it," Lacon had piped shamelessly in the
garden. "Go forwards, go backwards?" As Smiley retraced
path after path into his own past, there was no longer any
difference between the two: forwards or backwards, it was
the same journey and its destination lay ahead of him. There
was nothing in that room, no object among that whole
magpie collection of tattered hotel junk, that separated him
from the rooms of his recollection. He was back on the top
floor of the Circus, in his own plain office with the Oxford
prints, just as he had left it a year ago. Beyond his door lay
the low-ceilinged anteroom where Control's grey-haired
ladies, the mothers, softly typed and answered telephones;
while here in the hotel an undiscovered genius along the
corridor night and day tapped patiently at an old machine. At
the anteroom's far end—in Mrs. Pope Graham's world there
was a bathroom there, and a warning not to use it—stood the
blank door that led to Control's sanctuary: an alley of a place,
with old steel cupboards and old red books, a smell of sweet
dust and jasmine tea. Behind the desk Control himself, a
carcass of a man by then, with his lank grey forelock and his
smile as warm as a skull.

This mental transposition was so complete in Smiley that
when his phone rang—the extension was an extra, payable in
cash—he had to give himself time to remember where he was.
Other sounds had an equally confusing effect on him, such as
the rustle of pigeons on the parapet, the scraping of the television mast in the wind, and—in rain—the sudden river gur-
gling in the roof valley. For these sounds also belonged to his
past, and in Cambridge Circus were heard by the fifth floor
only. His ear selected them, no doubt, for that very reason:
they were the background jingle of his past. Once in the early
morning, hearing a footfall in the corridor outside his room,
Smiley actually went to the bedroom door expecting to let in
the Circus night coding clerk. He was immersed in Guillam's

photographs at the time, puzzling out, from far too little information, the likely Circus procedure under lateralism for handling an incoming telegram from Hong Kong. But instead of the clerk he found Norman, barefooted in pyjamas. Confetti was strewn over the carpet and two pairs of shoes stood outside the opposite door, a man's and a girl's, though no one at the Islay—least of all Norman—would ever clean them.

"Stop prying and go to bed," said Smiley. And when Norman only stared: "Oh, do go away, will you?"—And nearly, but he stopped himself in time, "You grubby little man."

"Operation Witchcraft," read the title on the first volume Lacon had brought to him that first night. "Policy regarding distribution of Special Product." The rest of the cover was obliterated by warning labels and handling instructions, including one that quaintly advised the accidental finder to "return the file UNREAD" to the Chief Registrar at the Cabinet Office. "Operation Witchcraft," read the second. "Supplementary estimates to the Treasury, special accommodation in London, special financing arrangements, bounty, etc." "Source Merlin," read the third, bound to the first with pink ribbon. "Customer Evaluations, cost effectiveness, wider exploitation; see also Secret Annexe." But the secret annexe was not attached, and when Smiley asked for it there was a coldness.

"The Minister keeps it in his personal safe," Lacon snapped.

"Do you know the combination?"

"Certainly not," he retorted, now furious.

"What is the title of it?"

"It can be of no possible concern to you. I entirely fail to see why you should waste your time chasing after this material in the first place. It's highly secret and we have done everything humanly possible to keep the readership to the minimum."

"Even a secret annexe has to have a title," said Smiley mildly.

"This has none."

"Does it give the identity of Merlin?"

"Don't be ridiculous. The Minister would not want to know, and Alleline would not want to tell him."

"What does 'wider exploitation' mean?"

"I refuse to be interrogated, George. You're not family any more, you know. By rights, I should have you specially cleared, as it is."

"Witchcraft-cleared?"

"Yes."

"Do we have a list of people who have been cleared in that way?"

It was in the policy file, Lacon retorted, and all but slammed the door on him before coming back, to the slow chant of "Where Have All the Flowers Gone?" introduced by an Australian disc-jockey. "The Minister—" He stopped, and began again. "He doesn't like devious explanations. He has a saying: he'll only believe what can be written on a postcard. He's very impatient to be given something he can get his hands on."

Smiley said, "You won't forget Prideaux, will you? Just anything you have on him at all; even scraps are better than nothing."

With that, Smiley left Lacon to glare awhile, then make a second exit: "You're not going fey, are you, George? You realise that Prideaux had most likely never even *heard* of Witchcraft before he was shot? I really do fail to see why you can't stick with the primary problem instead of rootling around in . . ." But by this time he had talked himself out of the room.

Smiley turned to the last of the batch: "Operation Witchcraft, correspondence with Department." "Department" being one of Whitehall's many euphemisms for the Circus. This volume was conducted in the form of official minutes between the Minister on the one side, and on the other—recognisable at once by his laborious schoolboy hand—Percy Alleline, at that time still consigned to the bottom rungs of Control's ladder of beings.

A very dull monument, Smiley reflected, surveying these much-handled files, to such a long and cruel war.

16

It was this long and cruel war that in its main battles Smiley now relived as he embarked upon his reading. The files contained only the thinnest record of it; his memory contained far more. Its protagonists were Alleline and Control, its origins misty. Bill Haydon—a keen, if saddened, follower of those events—maintained that the two men learned to hate each other at Cambridge during Control's brief spell as a don and Alleline's as an undergraduate. According to Bill, Alleline was Control's pupil and a bad one, and Control taunted him, which he certainly might have.

The story was grotesque enough for Control to play it up: "Percy and I are blood brothers, I hear. We romped together in punts, imagine!" He never said whether it was true.

To half-legend of that sort, Smiley could add a few hard facts from his knowledge of the two men's early lives. While Control was no man's child, Percy Alleline was a lowland Scot and a son of the Manse; his father was a Presbyterian hammer, and if Percy did not have his faith, he had surely inherited the faculty of bullish persuasion. He missed the war by a year or two and joined the Circus from a City company. At Cambridge he had been a bit of a politician (somewhat to the right of Genghis Khan, said Haydon who was himself,

Lord knows, no milk-and-water liberal) and a bit of an athlete. He was recruited by a figure of no account called Maston, who for a short time contrived to build himself a corner in counter-intelligence. Maston saw a great future in Alleline and, having peddled his name furiously, fell from grace. Finding Alleline an embarrassment, Circus personnel packed him off to South America, where he did two full tours under consular cover without returning to England.

Even Control later admitted that Percy did extremely well there, Smiley recalled. The Argentinians, liking his tennis and the way he rode, took him for a gentleman—Control speaking—and assumed he was stupid, which Percy never quite was. By the time he handed over to his successor, he had put together a string of agents along both seaboards and was spreading his wings northward as well. After home leave and a couple of weeks' briefing, he was moved to India, where his agents seemed to regard him as the reincarnation of the British Raj. He preached loyalty to them, paid them next to nothing, and—when it suited him—sold them down the river. From India he went to Cairo. That posting should have been difficult for Alleline, if not impossible, for the Middle East till then had been Haydon's favourite stamping-ground. The Cairo networks looked on Bill quite literally in the terms which Martindale had used of him that fateful night in his anonymous dining-club: as a latter-day Lawrence of Arabia. They were all set to make life hell for his successor. Yet somehow Percy bulldozed his way through and, if he had only steered clear of the Americans, might have gone down in memory as a better man than Haydon. Instead there was a scandal and an open row between Percy and Control.

The circumstances were still obscure: the incident occurred long before Smiley's elevation as Control's high chamberlain. With no authority from London, it appeared, Alleline had involved himself in a silly American plot to replace a local potentate with one of their own. Alleline had always had a fatal reverence for the Americans. From Argentina he had observed with admiration their rout of left-wing politicians around the hemisphere; in India he had delighted in their skill at dividing the forces of centralisation. Whereas Control, like most of the Circus, despised them and all their works, which he frequently sought to undermine.

The plot aborted, the British oil companies were furious, and Alleline, as the jargon happily puts it, had to leave in his socks. Later, Alleline claimed that Control had urged him on, then pulled the rug out from under; even that he had deliberately blown the plot to Moscow. However it was, Alleline reached London to find a posting order directing him to the Nursery, where he was to take over the training of greenhorn probationers. It was a slot normally reserved for rundown contract men with a couple of years to go before their pension. There were just so few jobs left in London those days for a man of Percy's seniority and talents, explained Bill Haydon, then head of personnel.

"Then you'll damn well have to invent me one," said Percy. He was right. As Bill frankly confessed to Smiley some while later, he had reckoned without the power of the Alleline lobby.

"But who are these people?" Smiley used to ask. "How can they force a man on you when you don't want him?"

"Golfers," Control snapped. Golfers and conservatives, for Alleline in those days was flirting with the opposition and was received with open arms, not least by Miles Sercombe, Ann's lamentably unremoved cousin and now Lacon's Minister. Yet Control had little power to resist. The Circus was in the doldrums and there was loose talk of scrapping the existing outfit entirely and starting elsewhere with a new one. Failures in that world occur traditionally in series, but this had been an exceptionally long run. Product had slumped; more and more of it had turned out to be suspect. In the places where it mattered, Control's hand was none too strong.

This temporary incapacity did not mar Control's joy in the drafting of Percy Alleline's personal charter as Operational Director. He called it Percy's Fool's Cap.

There was nothing Smiley could do. Bill Haydon was in

Washington by then, trying to renegotiate an intelligence treaty with what he called the Fascist puritans of the American agency. But Smiley had risen to the fifth floor, and one of his tasks was to keep petitioners off Control's back. So it was to Smiley that Alleline came to ask "Why?" Would call on him in his office when Control was out, invite him to that dismal flat of his, having first sent his paramour to the cinema, and interrogate him in his plaintive brogue. "Why?" He even invested in a bottle of a malt whisky, which he forced on Smiley liberally while sticking to the cheaper brand himself.

"What have I done to him, George, that's so damn special? We'd a brush or two—what's so unusual to that, if you'll tell me? Why does he pick on me? All I want is a place at the top table. God knows my record entitles me to that!"

By top table, he meant the fifth floor.

The charter which Control had drafted for him, and which at a glance had a most impressive shape, gave Alleline the right to examine all operations before they were launched. The small print made this right conditional upon the consent of the operational sections, and Control made sure that this was not forthcoming. The charter invited him to "co-ordinate resources and break down regional jealousies," a concept Alleline had since achieved with the establishment of London Station. But the resources sections, such as the lamplighters, the forgers, the listeners, and the wranglers, declined to open their books to him and he lacked the powers to force them. So Alleline starved; his trays were empty from lunchtime onwards.

"I'm mediocre, is that it? We've all to be geniuses these days, prima donnas and no damn chorus; old men, at that." For Alleline, though it was easily forgettable in him, was still a young man to be at the top table, with eight or ten years to brandish over Haydon and Smiley, and more over Control.

Control was immovable: "Percy Alleline would sell his mother for a knighthood and this service for a seat in the House of Lords." And later, as his hateful illness began creeping over him: "I refuse to bequeath my life's work to a parade horse. I'm too vain to be flattered, too old to be ambitious, and I'm ugly as a crab. Percy's quite the other way and there are enough witty men in Whitehall to prefer his sort to mine."

Which was how, indirectly, Control might be said to have brought Witchcraft upon his own head.

"George, come in here," Control snapped one day over the buzzer. "Brother Percy's trying to twist my tail. Come in here or there'll be bloodshed."

It was a time, Smiley remembered, when unsuccessful warriors were returning from foreign parts. Roy Bland had just flown in from Belgrade, where with Toby Esterhase's help he had been trying to save the wreck of a dying network; Paul Skordeno, at that time head German, had just buried his best Soviet agent in East Berlin; and as to Bill, after another fruitless trip he was back in his pepper pot room fuming about Pentagon arrogance, Pentagon idiocy, Pentagon duplicity, and claiming that "the time had come to do a deal with the bloody Russians instead."

And in the Islay it was after midnight; a late guest was ringing the bell. Which will cost him ten bob to Norman, thought Smiley, for whom the revised British coinage was still something of a puzzle. With a sigh, he drew towards him the first of the Witchcraft files, and, having vouchsafed a gingerly lick to his right finger and thumb, set to work matching the official memory with his own.

"We spoke," wrote Alleline, only a couple of months after that interview, in a slightly hysterical personal letter addressed to Ann's distinguished cousin the Minister and entered on Lacon's file. "Witchcraft reports derive from a source of extreme sensitivity. To my mind, no existing method of Whitehall distribution meets the case. The dispatch-box system which we used for GADFLY fell down when keys were lost by Whitehall customers, or in one disgraceful case when an overworked Under-Secretary gave his key to his personal assistant. I have already spoken to Lilley, of naval intelligence, who is prepared to put at our disposal a special reading-room in the Admiralty main building where the material is made available to customers and watched over by a senior janitor of this service. The reading-room will be known, for cover purposes, as the conference room of the Adriatic Working Party, or the A.W.P. room for short. Customers with reading rights will not have passes, since these also are open to abuse. Instead they will identify themselves personally to my janitor"—Smiley noted the pronoun—"who will be equipped with an indoctrination list illustrated with customers' photographs."

Lacon, not yet convinced, to the Treasury through his odious master, the Minister, on whose behalf his submissions were invariably made:

> Even allowing that this is necessary, the reading-room will have to be extensively rebuilt.
> 1. Will you authorise cost?
> 2. If so, the cost should seem to be borne by the Admiralty. Department will covertly reimburse.
> 3. There is also the question of extra janitors, a further expense . . .

And there is the question of Alleline's greater glory, Smiley commented as he slowly turned the pages. It shone already like a beacon everywhere: Percy is heading for the top table and Control might already be dead.

From the stairwell came the sound of rather beautiful singing. A Welsh guest, very drunk, was wishing everyone good night.

Witchcraft, Smiley recalled—his memory again, the files knew nothing so plainly human—Witchcraft was by no means Percy Alleline's first attempt, in his new post, at launching his own operation; but since his charter bound him to obtain Control's approval, its predecessors had been stillborn. For a while, for instance, he had concentrated on tunnelling. The Americans had built audio tunnels in Berlin and Belgrade; the French had managed something similar against the Americans. Very well, under Percy's banner the Circus would get in on the market. Control looked on benignly, an inter-services committee was formed (known as the Alleline Committee), and a team of boffins from nuts and bolts made a survey of the foundations of the Soviet Embassy in Athens, where Alleline counted on the unstinted support of the latest military régime which, like its predecessors, he greatly admired. Then, very gently, Control knocked over Percy's bricks and waited for him to come up with something new. Which, after several shots between, was exactly what Percy was doing that grey morning when Control peremptorily summoned Smiley to the feast.

Control was sitting at his desk, Alleline was standing at the window; between them lay a plain folder, bright yellow and closed.

"Sit over there and take a look at this nonsense."

Smiley sat in the easy chair and Alleline stayed at the window resting his big elbows on the sill, staring over the rooftops to Nelson's Column and the spires of Whitehall beyond.

Inside the folder was a photograph of what purported to be a high-level Soviet naval dispatch fifteen pages long.

"Who made the translation?" Smiley asked, thinking that it looked good enough to be Roy Bland's work.

"God," Control replied. "God made it, didn't he, Percy? Don't ask him anything, George, he won't tell you."

It was Control's time for looking exceptionally youthful. Smiley remembered how Control had lost weight, how his cheeks were pink, and how those who knew him little tended to congratulate him on his good appearance. Only Smiley, perhaps, ever noticed the tiny beads of sweat that in those days habitually followed his hairline.

Precisely, the document was an appreciation, allegedly prepared for the Soviet High Command, of a recent Soviet naval exercise in the Mediterranean and Black Sea. In Lacon's file it was entered simply as Report No. 1, under the title "Naval." For months the Admiralty had been screaming at the Circus for anything relating to this exercise. It therefore had an impressive topicality, which at once, in Smiley's eyes, made it suspect. It was detailed but it dealt with matters that Smiley did not understand even at a distance: shore-to-sea strike power, radio activation of enemy alert procedures, the higher mathematics of the balance of terror. If it was genuine it was gold-dust, but there was no earthly reason to suppose it was genuine. Every week the Circus processed dozens of unsolicited so-called Soviet documents. Most were straight pedlar material. A few were deliberate plants by allies with an axe to grind; a few more were Russian chicken-feed. Very rarely, one turned out to be sound, but usually after it had been rejected.

"Whose initials are these?" Smiley asked, referring to some annotations pencilled in Russian in the margin. "Does anyone know?"

Control tilted his head at Alleline. "Ask the authority. Don't ask me."

"Zharov," said Alleline. "Admiral, Black Sea Fleet."

"It's not dated," Smiley objected.

"It's a draft," Alleline replied complacently, his brogue richer than usual. "Zharov signed it Thursday. The finished dispatch with those amendments went out on circulation Monday, dated accordingly."

Today was Tuesday.

"Where does it come from?" Smiley asked, still lost.

"Percy doesn't feel able to tell," said Control.

"What do our own evaluators say?"

"They've not seen it," said Alleline, "and what's more they're not going to."

Control said icily, "My brother in Christ, Lilley, of naval intelligence, has passed a preliminary opinion, however, has he not, Percy? Percy showed it to him last night—over a pink gin, was it, Percy, at the Travellers'?"

"At the Admiralty."

"Brother Lilley, being a fellow Caledonian of Percy's, is as a rule sparing in his praise. However, when he telephoned me half an hour ago he was positively fulsome. He even congratulated me. He regards the document as genuine and is seeking our permission—Percy's, I suppose I should say—to apprise his fellow sea-lords of its conclusions."

"Quite impossible," said Alleline. "It's for his eyes only, at least for a couple more weeks."

"The stuff is so hot," Control explained, "that it has to be cooled off before it can be distributed."

"But where does it come from?" Smiley insisted.

"Oh, Percy's dreamed up a cover name, don't you worry. Never been slow on cover names, have we, Percy?"

"But what's the access? Who's the case officer?"

"You'll enjoy this," Control promised, aside. He was extraordinarily angry. In their long association Smiley could not remember him so angry. His slim, freckled hands were shaking and his normally lifeless eyes were sparkling with fury.

"Source Merlin," Alleline said, prefacing the announcement with a slight but very Scottish sucking of the teeth, "is a highly placed source with access to the most sensitive levels of Soviet policy-making." And, as if he were royalty: "We have dubbed his product 'Witchcraft.'"

He had used the identical form of words, Smiley noticed, in a top-secret and personal letter to a fan at the Treasury, requesting for himself greater discretion in *ad hoc* payments to agents.

"He'll be saying he won him at the football pool next," Control warned, who despite his second youth had an old man's inaccuracy when it came to popular idiom. "Now get him to tell you why he won't tell you."

Alleline was undeterred. He, too, was flushed, but with triumph, not disease. He filled his big chest for a long speech, which he delivered entirely to Smiley, tonelessly, rather as a Scottish police sergeant might give evidence before the courts.

"The identity of Source Merlin is a secret which is not mine to divulge. He's the fruit of a long cultivation by certain people in this service. People who are bound to me, as I am to them. People who are not at all entertained, either, by the failure rate around this place. There's been too much blown. Too much lost, wasted, too many scandals. I've said so many times, but I might as well have spoken to the wind for all the damn care he paid me."

"He's referring to me," Control explained from the sidelines. "I am *he* in this speech—you follow, George?"

"The ordinary principles of tradecraft and security have gone to the wall in this service. Need to know: where is it? Compartmentation at all levels: where is it, George? There's too much regional backbiting, stimulated from the top."

"Another reference to myself," Control put in.

"Divide and rule, that's the principle at work these days. Personalities who should be helping to fight Communism are all at one another's throats. We're losing our top partners."

"He means the Americans," Control explained.

"We're losing our livelihood. Our self-respect. We've had enough." He took back the report and jammed it under his arm. "We've had a bellyful, in fact."

"And like everyone who's had enough," said Control as Alleline noisily left the room, "he wants more."

Now for a while Lacon's files, instead of Smiley's memory, once more took up the story. It was typical of the atmosphere of those last months that, having been brought in on the affair at the beginning, Smiley should have received no subsequent word of how it had developed. Control detested failure as he detested illness, and his own failures most. He knew that to recognise failure was to live with it; that a service that did not struggle did not survive. He detested the silk-shirt agents, who hogged large chunks of the budget to the detriment of the bread-and-butter networks in which he put his faith. He loved success, but he detested miracles if they put the rest of his endeavour out of focus. He detested weakness as he detested sentiment and religion, and he detested Percy Alleline, who had a dash of most of them. His way of dealing with them was literally to close the door: to withdraw into the dingy solitude of his upper rooms, receive no visitors, and have all his phone calls fed to him by the mothers. The same quiet ladies fed him jasmine tea and the countless office files that he sent for and returned in heaps. Smiley would see them piled before the door as he went about his own business of trying to keep the rest of the Circus afloat. Many were old, from the days before Control led the pack. Some were personal, the biographies of past and present members of the service.

Control never said what he was doing. If Smiley asked the mothers, or if Bill Haydon sauntered in, favourite boy, and made the same enquiry, they only shook their heads or silently raised their eyebrows towards paradise: "A terminal case," said these gentle glances. "We are humouring a great man at the end of his career." But Smiley—as he now patiently leafed through file after file, and in a corner of his complex mind rehearsed Irina's diary to Ricki Tarr—Smiley knew, and in a quite real way took comfort from the knowledge, that he was not after all the first to make this journey of exploration; that Control's ghost was his companion into all but the furthest reaches; and might even have stayed the whole distance if Operation Testify, at the eleventh hour, had not stopped him dead.

Breakfast again, and a much-subdued Welshman not drawn by undercooked sausage and overcooked tomato.

"Do you want these back," Lacon demanded, "or have you done with them? They can't be very enlightening, since they don't even contain the reports."

"Tonight, please, if you don't mind."

"I suppose you realise you look a wreck."

He didn't realise, but at Bywater Street, when he returned there, Ann's pretty gilt mirror showed his eyes red-rimmed and his plump cheeks clawed with fatigue. He slept a little, then went his mysterious ways. When evening came, Lacon was actually waiting for him. Smiley went straight on with his reading.

For six weeks, according to the files, the naval dispatch had no successor. Other sections of the Ministry of Defence echoed the Admiralty's enthusiasm for the original dispatch; the Foreign Office remarked that "this document sheds an extraordinary sidelight on Soviet aggressive thinking," whatever that meant; Alleline persisted in his demands for special handling of the material, but he was like a general with no army. Lacon referred frostily to "the somewhat delayed follow-up," and suggested to his Minister that he should "defuse the situation with the Admiralty." From Control, according to the file, nothing. Perhaps he was lying low and praying it would blow over. In the lull, a Treasury Moscow-gazer sourly pointed out that Whitehall had seen plenty of this in recent years: an encouraging first report, then silence or, worse, a scandal.

He was wrong. In the seventh week, Alleline announced publication of three new Witchcraft reports all on the same day. All took the form of secret Soviet interdepartmental correspondence, though the topics differed widely.

Witchcraft No. 2, according to Lacon's summary, described tensions inside Comecon and spoke of the degenerative effect of Western trade deals on its weaker members. In Circus terms, this was a classic report from Roy Bland territory, covering the very target that the Hungarian-based Aggravate network had been attacking in vain for years. "Excellent *tour d'horizon*," wrote a Foreign Office customer, "and backed by good collateral."

Witchcraft No. 3 discussed revisionism in Hungary and Kadar's renewed purges in political and academic life: the best way to end loose talk in Hungary, said the author of the paper, borrowing a phrase coined by Khrushchev long before, would be to shoot some more intellectuals. Once again this was Roy Bland territory. "A salutary warning," wrote the same Foreign Office commentator, "to all those who like to think the Soviet Union is going soft on satellites."

These two reports were both in essence background, but Witchcraft No. 4 was sixty pages long and held by the customers to be unique. It was an immensely technical Soviet Foreign Service appreciation of the advantages and disadvantages of negotiating with a weakened American President. The conclusion, on balance, was that by throwing the President a bone for his own electorate, the Soviet Union could buy useful concessions in forthcoming discussions on multiple nuclear warheads. But it seriously questioned the desirability of allowing the United States to feel too much the loser, since this could tempt the Pentagon into a retributive or preemptive strike. The report was from the very heart of Bill Haydon territory. But, as Haydon himself wrote in a touching minute to Alleline (promptly copied, without Haydon's knowledge, to the Minister and entered on the Cabinet Office file), in twenty-five years of attacking the Soviet nuclear target he had not laid his hands on anything of this quality.

"Nor," he concluded, "unless I am extremely mistaken, have our American brothers-in-arms. I know that these are early days, but it does occur to me that anyone taking this material to Washington could drive a very hard bargain in return. Indeed, if Merlin maintains the standard, I would venture to predict that we could buy anything there is to have in the American agency's shop."

Percy Alleline had his reading-room; and George Smiley made himself a coffee on the derelict burner beside the washstand. Midway the meter ran out, and in a temper he called for Norman and ordered five pounds' worth of shillings.

17

With mounting interest, Smiley continued his journey through Lacon's meagre records from that first meeting of protagonists until the present day. At the time, such a mood of suspicion had gripped the Circus that even between Smiley and Control the subject of Source Merlin became taboo. Alleline brought up the Witchcraft reports and waited in the anteroom while the mothers took them to Control, who signed them at once in order to demonstrate that he had not read them. Alleline took back the file, poked his head round Smiley's door, grunted a greeting, and clumped down the staircase. Bland kept his distance, and even Bill Haydon's breezy visits—traditionally a part of the life up there, of the "talking shop" that Control in the old days had liked to foster among his senior lieutenants—became fewer and shorter, then ceased entirely.

"Control's going potty," Haydon told Smiley with contempt. "And if I'm not mistaken he's also dying. It's just a question of which gets him first."

The customary Tuesday meetings were discontinued, and Smiley found himself constantly harassed by Control either to go abroad on some blurred errand or to visit the domestic outstations—Sarratt, Brixton, Acton, and the rest—as his personal envoy. He had a growing feeling that Control wanted him out of the way. When they talked, he felt the heavy strain of suspicion between them, so that even Smiley seriously wondered whether Bill was right and Control was unfit for his job.

The Cabinet Office files made it clear that those next three months saw a steady flowering of the Witchcraft operation, without any help from Control. Reports came in at the rate of two or even three a month, and the standard, according to the customers, continued excellent, but Control's name was seldom mentioned and he was never invited to comment. Occasionally the evaluators produced quibbles. More often they complained that corroboration was not possible, since Merlin took them into uncharted areas: could we not ask the Americans to check? We could not, said the Minister. Not yet, said Alleline; who in a confidential minute seen by no one, added, "When the time is ripe we shall do more than barter our material for theirs. We are not interested in a one-time deal. Our task is to establish Merlin's track record beyond all doubt. When that is done, Haydon can go to market . . ."

There was no longer any question of it. Among the chosen few who were admitted to the chambers of the Adriatic Working Party, Merlin was already a winner. His material was accurate; often other sources confirmed it retrospectively. A Witchcraft committee formed, with the Minister in the chair. Alleline was vice-chairman. Merlin had become an industry, and Control was not even employed. Which was why in desperation he had sent out Smiley with his beggar's bowl: "There are three of them and Alleline," he said. "Sweat them, George. Tempt them, bully them, give them whatever they eat."

Of those meetings also, the files were blessedly ignorant, for they belonged in the worst rooms of Smiley's memory. He had known already that there was nothing left in Control's larder that would satisfy their hunger.

It was April. Smiley had come back from Portugal, where he had been burying a scandal, to find Control living under siege. Files lay strewn over the floor; new locks had been fitted to the windows. He had put the tea-cosy over his one telephone and from the ceiling hung a baffler against electronic eavesdropping—a thing like an electric fan, which constantly varied its pitch. In the three weeks Smiley had been away, Control had become an old man.

"Tell them they're buying their way in with counterfeit

money," he ordered, barely looking up from his files. "Tell them any damn thing. I need time."

"There are three of them and Alleline," Smiley now repeated to himself, seated at the Major's card table and studying Lacon's list of those who had been Witchcraft-cleared. Today there were sixty-eight licensed visitors to the Adriatic Working Party's reading-room. Each, like a member of the Communist Party, was numbered according to the date of his admission. The list had been retyped since Control's death; Smiley was not included. But the same four founding fathers still headed the list: Alleline, Bland, Esterhase, and Bill Haydon. Three of them and Alleline, Control had said.

Suddenly Smiley's mind, open as he read to every inference, every oblique connection, was assailed by a quite extraneous vision: of himself and Ann walking the Cornish cliffs. It was the time immediately after Control's death, the worst time Smiley could remember in their long, puzzled marriage. They were high on the coast, somewhere between Lamorna and Porthcurno; they had gone there out of season ostensibly for Ann to take the sea air for her cough. They had been following the coast path, each lost in his thoughts: she to Haydon, he supposed; he to Control, to Jim Prideaux and Testify, and the whole mess he had left behind him on retirement. They shared no harmony. They had lost all calmness in one another's company; they were a mystery to each other, and the most banal conversation could take strange, uncontrollable directions. In London, Ann had been living quite wildly, taking anyone who would have her. He knew she was trying to bury something that hurt or worried her very much; but he knew no way to reach her.

"If *I* had died," she demanded suddenly, "rather than Control, say, how would you feel towards Bill?"

Smiley was still pondering his answer when she threw in: "I sometimes think I safeguard your opinion of him. Is that possible? That I somehow keep the two of you together. Is that possible?"

"It's possible." He added, "Yes, I suppose I'm dependent on him, too, in a way."

"Is Bill still important in the Circus?"

"More than he was, probably."

"And he still goes to Washington, wheels and deals with them, turns them upside down?"

"I expect so. I hear so."

"Is he as important as you were?"

"I suppose."

"I suppose," she repeated. "I expect. I hear. Is he *better*, then? A better performer than you, better at the arithmetic? Tell me. Please tell me. You must."

She was strangely excited. Her eyes, tearful from the wind, shone desperately upon him; she had both hands on his arm and, like a child, was dragging on him for an answer.

"You've always told me that men aren't to be compared," he replied awkwardly. "You've always said you didn't think in that category of comparison."

"Tell me!"

"All right: no, he's not better."

"As good?"

"No."

"And if I wasn't there, what would you think of him then? If Bill were not my cousin, not my anything? Tell me, would you think more of him, or less?"

"Less, I suppose."

"Then think less *now*. I divorce him from the family, from our lives, from everything. Here and now. I throw him into the sea. There. Do you understand?"

He understood only: go back to the Circus, finish your business. It was one of a dozen ways she had of saying the same thing.

Still disturbed by this intrusion on his memory, Smiley stood up in rather a flurry and went to the window, his habitual look-out when he was distracted. A line of sea-gulls, a half dozen of them, had settled on the parapet. He must have heard them calling, and remembered that walk to Lamorna.

"I cough when there are things I can't say," Ann had told him once. What couldn't she say then, he asked glumly of the chimney-pots across the street. Connie could say it, Martindale could say it; so why couldn't Ann?

"Three of them and Alleline," Smiley muttered aloud. The sea-gulls had gone, all at once, as if they had spotted a better place. "Tell them they're buying their way in with counterfeit money." And if the banks accept the money? If the experts pronounce it genuine, and Bill Haydon praises it to the skies? And the Cabinet Office files are full of plaudits for the brave new men of Cambridge Circus, who have finally broken the jinx?

He had chosen Esterhase first because Toby owed Smiley his career. Smiley had recruited him in Vienna, a starving student living in the ruins of a museum of which his dead uncle had been curator. He drove down to Acton and bearded him at the Laundry across his walnut desk with its row of ivory telephones. On the wall, kneeling Magi, questionable Italian seventeenth century. Through the window, a closed courtyard crammed with cars and vans and motorbikes, and rest-huts where the teams of lamplighters killed time between shifts. First Smiley asked Toby about his family: there was a son who went to Westminster and a daughter at medical school, first year. Then he put it to Toby that the lamplighters were two months behind on their worksheets, and when Toby hedged he asked him outright whether his boys had been doing any special jobs recently, either at home or abroad, which for good reasons of security Toby didn't feel able to mention in his returns.

"Who would I do that for, George?" Toby had asked, dead-eyed. "You know in my book that's completely illegal." And idiom, in Toby's book, had a way of being ludicrous.

"Well, I can see you doing it for Percy Alleline, for one," Smiley suggested, feeding him the excuse: "After all, if Percy *ordered* you to do something and not to record it, you'd be in a very difficult position."

"What sort of something, though, George, I wonder?"

"Clear a foreign letter-box, prime a safe house, watch someone's back, spike an embassy. Percy's Director of Operations, after all. You might think he was acting on instructions from the fifth floor. I can see that happening quite reasonably."

Toby looked carefully at Smiley. He was holding a cigarette, but apart from lighting it he hadn't smoked it at all. It was a hand-rolled affair, taken from a silver box, but once lit, it never went into his mouth. It swung around, along the line or away to the side; sometimes it was poised to take the plunge, but it never did. Meanwhile Toby made his speech: one of Toby's personal statements, supposedly definitive about where he stood at this point in his life.

Toby liked the service, he said. He would prefer to remain in it. He felt sentimental about it. He had other interests and at any time they could claim him altogether, but he liked the service best. His trouble was, he said, promotion. Not that he wanted it for any greedy reason. He would say his reasons were social.

"You know, George, I have so many years' seniority I feel actually quite embarrassed when these young fellows ask me to take orders from them. You know what I mean? Acton, even—just the name of Acton for them is ridiculous."

"Oh," said Smiley mildly. "Which young fellows are these?"

But Esterhase had lost interest. His statement completed, his face settled again into its familiar blank expression, his doll's eyes fixed on a point in the middle distance.

"Do you mean Roy Bland?" Smiley asked. "Or Percy? Is Percy young? Who, Toby?"

It was no good, Toby regretted: "George, when you are overdue for promotion and working your fingers to the bones, anyone looks young who's above you on the ladder."

"Perhaps Control could move you up a few rungs," Smiley suggested, not much caring for himself in this role.

Esterhase's reply struck a chill. "Well, actually, you know, George, I am not too sure he is able these days. Look here"—opening a drawer—"I give Ann something. When I heard you were coming, I phone a couple of friends of mine; something beautiful, I say, something for a faultless woman; you know I never forget her since we met once at Bill Haydon's cocktail?"

So Smiley carried off the consolation prize—a costly scent, smuggled, he assumed, by one of Toby's homing lamplighters—and took his beggar bowl to Bland, knowing as he did so that he was coming one step nearer to Haydon.

Returning to the Major's table, Smiley searched through Lacon's files till he came to a slim volume marked "Operation Witchcraft, direct subsidies," which recorded the earliest expenses incurred through the running of Source Merlin. "For reasons of security it is proposed," wrote Alleline in yet another personal memo to the Minister, this one dated almost two years ago, "to keep the Witchcraft financing *absolutely separate* from all other Circus imprests. Until some proper cover can be found, I am asking you for *direct subventions from Treasury funds* rather than mere supplementaries to the Secret Vote, which in due course *are certain to find their way into the mainstream of Circus accounting.* I shall then account to you personally."

"Approved," wrote the Minister a week later, "provided always . . ."

There were no provisions. A glance at the first row of figures showed Smiley all he needed to know: already by May of that year, when that interview at Acton took place, Toby Esterhase had personally made no fewer than eight trips on the Witchcraft budget, two to Paris, two to The Hague, one to Helsinki, and three to Berlin. In each case the purpose of the journey was curtly described as "Collecting product."

Between May and November, when Control faded from the scene, he made a further nineteen. One of these took him to Sofia, another to Istanbul. None required him to be absent for more than three full days. Most took place at weekends. On several such journeys, he was accompanied by Bland.

Not to put too fine an edge on it, Toby Esterhase, as Smiley had never seriously doubted, had lied in his teeth. It was nice to find the record confirming his impression.

Smiley's feelings towards Roy Bland had at that time been ambivalent. Recalling them now, he decided they still were. A don had spotted him, Smiley had recruited him; the combination was oddly akin to the one that had brought Smiley himself into the Circus net. But this time there was no German monster to fan the patriotic flame, and Smiley had always been a little embarrassed by protestations of anti-Communism. Like Smiley, Bland had no real childhood. His father was a docker, a passionate trade-unionist, and a Party member. His mother died when Bland was a boy. His father hated education as he hated authority, and when Bland grew clever the father took it into his head that he had lost his son to the ruling class and beat the life out of him. Bland fought his way to grammar school and in the holidays worked his fingers, as Toby would say, to the bones, in order to raise the extra fee. When Smiley met him in his tutor's rooms at Oxford, he had the battered look of someone just arrived from a bad journey.

Smiley took him up, and over several months edged closer to a proposition, which Bland accepted—largely, Smiley assumed, out of animosity towards his father. After that he passed out of Smiley's care. Subsisting on odd grants undescribed, Bland toiled in the Marx Memorial Library and wrote leftish papers for tiny magazines that would have died long ago had the Circus not subsidized them. In the evenings he disputed loud and long at smoky meetings in pubs and school halls. In the vacations he went to the Nursery, where a fanatic called Thatch ran a charm school for outward-bound penetration agents, one pupil at a time. Thatch trained Bland in tradecraft and carefully nudged his progressive opinions nearer to his father's Marxist camp. Three years to the day after his recruitment, partly thanks to his proletarian pedigree, and his father's influence at King Street, Bland won a year's appointment as assistant lector in economics at the University of Poznan. He was launched.

From Poland he applied successfully for a post at the Budapest Academy of Sciences, and for the next eight years he lived the nomadic life of a minor left-wing intellectual in search of light, often liked but never trusted. He staged in Prague, returned to Poland, did a hellish two semesters in Sofia and six in Kiev, where he had a nervous breakdown, his second in as many months. Once more the Nursery took charge of him, this time to dry him out. He was passed as clean, his networks were given to other fieldmen, and Roy himself was brought into the Circus to manage, mainly from a desk, the networks he had recruited in the field. Recently, it had seemed to Smiley, Bland had become very much Haydon's colleague. If Smiley chanced to call on Roy for a chat, like as not Bill was lounging in his armchair surrounded by papers, charts, and cigarette smoke; if he dropped in on Bill, it was no surprise to find Bland, in a sweat-soaked shirt, padding heavily back and forth across the carpet. Bill had Russia, Bland the satellites; but already in those early days of Witchcraft, the distinction had all but vanished.

They met at a pub in St. John's Wood—still May—half past five on a dull day and the garden empty. Roy brought a child, a boy of five or so, a tiny Bland, fair, burly, and pink-faced. He didn't explain the boy, but sometimes as they talked he shut off and watched him where he sat on a bench away from them, eating nuts. Nervous breakdowns or not, Bland still bore the imprimatur of the Thatch philosophy for agents in the enemy camp: self-faith, positive participation, Pied Piper appeal, and all those other uncomfortable phrases which in the high day of the cold-war culture had turned the Nursery into something close to a moral-rearmament centre.

"So what's the deal?" Bland asked affably.

"There isn't one really, Roy. Control feels that the present situation is unhealthy. He doesn't like to see you getting mixed up in a cabal. Nor do I."

"Great. So what's the deal?"

"What do you want?"

On the table, soaked from the earlier rain fall, was a cruet set left over from lunchtime, with a bunch of paper-wrapped cellulose toothpicks in the centre compartment. Taking one, Bland spat the paper onto the grass and began working his back teeth with the fat end.

"Well, how about a five-thousand-quid backhander out the reptile fund?"

"And a house and a car?" said Smiley, making a joke of it.

"And the kid to Eton," Bland added, and winked across the concrete paving to the boy while he went on working with the toothpick. "I've paid, see, George. You know that. I don't know what I've bought with it but I've paid a hell of a lot. I want some back. Ten years' solitary for the fifth floor; that's big money at any age. Even yours. There must have been a reason why I fell for all that spiel, but I can't quite remember what it was. Must be your magnetic personality."

Smiley's glass was still going, so Bland fetched himself another from the bar, and something for the boy as well.

"You're an educated sort of swine," he announced easily as he sat down again. "An artist is a bloke who can hold two fundamentally opposing views and still function: who dreamed that one up?"

"Scott Fitzgerald," Smiley replied, thinking for a moment that Bland was proposing to say something about Bill Haydon.

"Well, Fitzgerald knew a thing or two," Bland affirmed. As he drank, his bulging eyes slid sideways toward the fence, as if in search of someone. "And I'm definitely functioning, George. As a good Socialist, I'm going for the money. As a good capitalist, I'm sticking with the revolution, because if

you can't beat it spy on it. Don't look like that, George. It's
the name of the game these days: you scratch my conscience,
I'll drive your Jag, right?" He was already lifting an arm as
he said this. "With you in a minute!" he called across the
lawn. "Set one up for me!"

Two girls were hovering on the other side of the wire
fence.

"Is that Bill's joke?" Smiley asked, suddenly quite angry.

"Is what?"

"Is that one of Bill's jokes about materialist England, the
pigs-in-clover society?"

"Could be," said Bland, and finished his drink. "Don't you
like it?"

"Not too much, no. I never knew Bill before as a radical
reformer. What's come over him all of a sudden?"

"That's not radical," Bland retorted, resenting any devalua-
tion of his Socialism, or of Haydon. "That's just looking out
the bloody window. That's just England now, man. Nobody
wants that, do they?"

"So how do you propose," Smiley demanded, hearing himself at his pompous worst, "to destroy the acquisitive and
competitive instincts in Western society without also destroy-
ing . . ."

Bland had finished his drink; and the meeting, too. "Why
should you be bothered? You've got Bill's job. What more do
you want? Long as it lasts."

And Bill's got my wife, Smiley thought as Bland rose to go;
and, damn him, he's told you.

The boy had invented a game. He had laid a table on its
side and was rolling an empty bottle onto the gravel. Each
time, he started the bottle higher up the table-top. Smiley left
before it smashed.

Unlike Esterhase, Bland had not even bothered to lie.
Lacon's files made no pretence of his involvement with the
Witchcraft operation:

"Source Merlin," wrote Alleline, in a minute dated soon after Control's departure, "is in every sense a committee operation . . . I cannot honestly say which of my three assistants deserves most praise. The energy of Bland has been an inspiration to us all . . ." He was replying to the Minister's suggestion that those responsible for Witchcraft should be honoured in the New Year's list. "While Haydon's operational ingenuity is at times little short of Merlin's own," he added. The medals went to all three; Alleline's appointment as Chief was confirmed, and with it his beloved knighthood.

18

Which left me Bill, thought Smiley.

In the course of most London nights, there is one respite from alarm. Ten, twenty minutes, thirty, even an hour, and not a drunk groans or a child cries or a car's tyres whine into a collision. In Sussex Gardens it happens around three. That night it came early, at one, as Smiley stood once more at his dormer window peering down like a prisoner at Mrs. Pope Graham's sand patch, where a Bedford van had recently parked. Its roof was daubed with slogans: "Sydney 90 Days," "Athens Non-Stop," "Mary Lou Here We Come." A light glowed inside, and he presumed some children were sleeping there in unmarried bliss. "Kids," he was supposed to call them. Curtains covered the windows.

Which left me Bill, he thought, still staring at the closed curtains of the van and its flamboyant globe-trotting proclamations; which left me Bill, and our friendly little chat in Bywater Street—just the two of us, old friends, old comrades-at-arms, "sharing everything," as Martindale had it so elegantly, but Ann sent out for the evening so that the men could be alone. "Which left me Bill," he repeated hopelessly, and felt the blood rise, and the colours of his vision heighten, and his sense of moderation begin its dangerous slide.

Who was he? Smiley had no focus on him any more. Each time he thought of him, he drew him too large, and different. Until Ann's affair with him, he thought he knew Bill pretty well, his brilliance and its limitations. He was of that pre-war set that seemed to have vanished for good, which managed to be disreputable and high-minded at the same time. His father was a high court judge, two of his several beautiful sisters had married into the aristocracy; at Oxford he favoured the unfashionable right rather than the fashionable left, but never to the point of strain. From his late teens he had been a keen explorer and amateur painter of brave, if over-ambitious, stamp; several of his paintings now hung in Miles Sercombe's fatuous palace in Carlton Gardens. He had connections in every embassy and consulate across the Middle East and he used them ruthlessly. He took up remote languages with ease, and when 1939 came, the Circus snapped him up; they had had their eye on him for years. He had a dazzling war. He was ubiquitous and charming; he was unorthodox and occasionally outrageous. He was probably heroic. The comparison with Lawrence was inevitable.

And it was true, Smiley conceded, that Bill in his time had fiddled with substantial pieces of history; had proposed all sorts of grand designs for restoring England to influence and greatness—like Rupert Brooke, he seldom spoke of Britain. But Smiley, in his rare moments of objectivity, could remember few that ever got off the ground.

It was the other side of Haydon's nature, by contrast, that as a colleague he had found easier to respect: the slow-burning skills of the natural agent runner; his rare sense of balance in the playing back of double agents and the mounting of deception operations; his art of fostering affection, even love, though it ran against the grain of other loyalties.

As witness, thank you, my wife.

Perhaps Bill really *is* out of scale, Smiley thought hopelessly, still grappling for a sense of proportion. Picturing him now, and putting him beside Bland, Esterhase, even Alleline, it did truthfully seem to Smiley that all of them were, to a great or small extent, imperfect imitations of that one original, Haydon. That their affectations were like steps towards the same unobtainable ideal of the rounded man, even if the ideal was itself misconceived, or misplaced; even if Bill was utterly unworthy of it. Bland in his blunt impertinence, Esterhase in his lofty artificial Englishness, Alleline with his shallow gift of leadership—without Bill they were a disarray. Smiley also knew, or thought he knew—the idea came to him now as a mild enlightenment—that Bill in turn was also very little by himself: that while his admirers (Bland, Prideaux, Alleline, Esterhase, and all the rest of the supporters' club) might find in him completeness, Bill's real trick was to use them, to live through them to complete himself, here a piece, there a piece, from their passive identities, thus disguising the fact that he was less, far less, than the sum of his apparent qualities . . . and finally submerging this dependence beneath an artist's arrogance, calling them the creatures of his mind . . .

"That's quite enough," said Smiley aloud.

Withdrawing abruptly from this insight, dismissing it irritably as yet another theory about Bill, he cooled his overheated mind with the recollection of their last meeting.

"I suppose you want to grill me about bloody Merlin," Bill began. He looked tired and nervy; it was his time for commuting to Washington. In the old days he would have brought an unsuitable girl and sent her to sit with Ann upstairs while they talked their business; expecting Ann to bolster his genius to her, thought Smiley cruelly. They were all of the same sort: half his age, bedraggled art school, clinging, surly; Ann used to say he had a supplier. And once, to shock, he brought a ghastly youth called Steggie, an assistant barman from one of the Chelsea pubs, with an open shirt and a gold chain round his midriff.

"Well, they do say you write the reports," Smiley explained.

"I thought that was Bland's job," said Bill with his foxy grin.

"Roy makes the translations," said Smiley. "You draft the covering reports; they're typed on your machine. The material's not cleared for typists at all."

Bill listened carefully, brows lifted, as if at any moment he might interrupt with an objection or a more congenial topic, then hoisted himself from the deep armchair and ambled to the bookcase, where he stood a full shelf higher than Smiley. Fishing out a volume with his long fingers, he peered into it, grinning.

"Percy Alleline won't do," he announced, turning a page. "Is that the premise?"

"Pretty well."

"Which means that Merlin won't do, either. Merlin would do if he were *my* source, wouldn't he? What would happen if Bloody Bill here pottered along to Control and said he'd hooked a big fish and wanted to play him alone? 'That's very nifty of you, Bill, boy,' Control would say. 'You do it just the way you want, Bill, boy—'course you do. Have some filthy tea.' He'd be giving me a medal by now, instead of sending you snooping round the corridors. We used to be rather a classy bunch. Why are we so vulgar these days?"

"He thinks Percy's on the make," Smiley said.

"So he is. So am I. I want to be head boy. Did you know that? Time I made something of myself, George. Half a painter, half a spy—time I was *all* something. Since when was ambition a sin in our beastly outfit?"

"Who runs him, Bill?"

"Percy? Karla does—who else? Lower-class bloke with upper-class sources, must be a bounder. Percy's sold out to Karla; it's the only explanation." He had developed the art, long ago, of deliberately misunderstanding. "Percy's our house mole," he said.

"I meant who runs Merlin? Who *is* Merlin? What's going on?"

Leaving the bookcase, Haydon took himself on a tour of Smiley's drawings. "This is a Callot, isn't it," unhooking a small gilt frame and holding it to the light. "It's nice." He tilted his spectacles to make them magnify. Smiley was certain he had looked at it a dozen times before. "It's *very* nice. Doesn't anyone think *my* nose should be out of joint? I am supposed to be in charge of the Russian target, you know. Given it my best years, set up networks, talent-spotters, all mod cons. You chaps on the fifth floor have forgotten what it's like to run an operation where it takes you three days to post a letter and you don't even get an answer for your trouble."

Smiley, dutifully: Yes, I have forgotten. Yes, I sympathise. No, Ann is nowhere in my thoughts. We are colleagues, after all, and men of the world; we are here to talk about Merlin and Control.

"Along comes this upstart Percy, damn Caledonian street-merchant, no shadow of class, shoving a whole wagonload of Russian goodies. Bloody annoying, don't you think?"

"Very."

"Trouble is, my networks aren't very good. Much easier to spy on Percy than—" He broke off, tired of his own thesis. His attention had settled on a tiny van Mieris head in chalk. "And I fancy this *very* much," he said.

"Ann gave it me."

"Amends?"

"Probably."

"Must have been quite a sin. How long have you had it?"

Even now, Smiley remembered noticing how silent it was in the street. Tuesday? Wednesday? And he remembered thinking: No, Bill. For you I have so far received no consolation prize at all. As of this evening, you don't even rate a pair of bedroom slippers . . . Thinking but not saying.

"Is Control dead yet?" Haydon asked.

"Just busy."

"What does he do all day? He's like a hermit with the clap, scratching around all on his own in that cave up there. All those bloody files he reads—what's he about, for God's sake? Sentimental tour of his unlovely past, I'll bet. He looks sick as a cat. I suppose that's Merlin's fault, too, is it?"

Again Smiley said nothing.

"Why doesn't he eat with the cooks? Why doesn't he join us instead of grubbing around for truffles up there? What's he after?"

"I didn't know he was after anything," said Smiley.

"Ah, stop flirting around. Of course he is. I've got a source up there—one of the mothers, didn't you know? Tells me indiscretions for chocolate. Control's been toiling through personal dossiers of old Circus folk heroes, sniffing out the dirt, who was pink, who was a queen. Half of them are under the earth already. Making a study of all our failures. Can you imagine? And for why? Because we've got a success on our hands. He's mad, George. He's got the big itch: senile paranoia, take my word for it. Ann ever tell you about wicked Uncle Fry? Thought the servants were bugging the roses to find out where he'd hidden his money. Get away from him, George. Death's a bore. Cut the cord, move down a few floors. Join the proles."

Ann had still not returned, so they sauntered side by side down the King's Road looking for a cab while Bill enunciated his latest vision of politics, and Smiley said "Yes, Bill," "No, Bill," and wondered how he was going to break it to Control. He forgot now which particular vision it was. The year before, Bill had been a great hawk. He had wanted to run down conventional forces in Europe and replace them outright with nuclear weapons. He was about the only person left in Whitehall who believed in Britain's independent deterrent. This year, if Smiley remembered rightly, Bill was an aggressive English pacifist and wanted the Sweden solution but without the Swedes.

No cab came; it was a beautiful night, and like old friends they went on walking, side by side.

"By the by, if you ever want to sell that Mieris, let me know, will you? I'll give you a bloody decent price for it."

Thinking Bill was making another bad joke, Smiley rounded on him, at last prepared to be angry. Haydon was not even conscious of his interest. He was gazing down the street, his long arm raised at an approaching cab.

"Oh, Christ, look at them," he shouted irritably. "Full of bloody Jews going to Quag's."

"Bill's backside must look like a damn gridiron," Control muttered next day, barely looking up from his reading. "The years he's spent sitting on the fence."

For a moment he stared at Smiley in an unfocused way, as if looking through him to some different, less fleshy prospect; then ducked his eyes and seemed to resume his reading. "I'm glad he's not *my* cousin," he said.

The following Monday, the mothers had surprising news for Smiley. Control had flown to Belfast for discussions with the army. Later, checking the travel imprests, Smiley nailed the lie. No one in the Circus had flown to Belfast that month, but there was a charge for a first-class return to Vienna and the issuing authority was given as G. Smiley.

Haydon, also looking for Control, was cross: "So now what's the pitch? Dragging Ireland into the net, creating an organisational diversion, I suppose. Jesus, your man's a bore!"

The light in the van went out, but Smiley continued to gaze at its garish roof. How do they live? he wondered. What do they do for water, money? He tried to fathom the logistics of a troglodyte life in Sussex Gardens: water, drains, light. Ann would work them out all right; so would Bill.

Facts. What were the facts?

Facts were that one balmy pre-Witchcraft summer evening, I returned unexpectedly from Berlin to find Bill

Haydon stretched on the drawing-room floor and Ann playing Liszt on the gramophone. Ann was sitting across the room from him in her dressing gown, wearing no make-up. There was no scene; everyone behaved with painful naturalness. According to Bill, he had dropped by on his way from the airport, having just flown in from Washington; Ann had been in bed but insisted on getting up to receive him. We agreed it was a pity we hadn't shared a car from Heathrow. Bill left; I asked "What did he want?" And Ann said: "A shoulder to cry on." Bill was having girl trouble, wanted to pour out his heart, she said.

"There's Felicity in Washington, who wants a baby, and Jan in London, who's having one."

"Bill's?"

"God knows. I'm sure Bill doesn't."

Next morning, without even wishing to, Smiley established that Bill had been back in London two days, not one. Following the episode, Bill showed an uncharacteristic deference towards Smiley, and Smiley reciprocated with acts of courtesy which normally belong to a newer friendship. In due course Smiley noticed that the secret was out, and he was still mystified by the speed with which that had happened. He supposed Bill had boasted to someone, perhaps Bland. If the word was correct, Ann had broken three of her own rules. Bill was Circus and he was Set—her word for family and ramifications. On either count he would be out of bounds. Thirdly, she had received him at Bywater Street, an agreed violation of territorial decencies.

Withdrawing once more into his own lonely life, Smiley waited for Ann to say something. He moved into the spare room and arranged for himself plenty of evening engagements in order that he would not be too aware of her comings and goings. Gradually it dawned on him that she was deeply unhappy. She lost weight, she lost her sense of play, and if he didn't know her better he would have sworn she was having a bad bout of the guilts, even of self-disgust. When he was gentle with her, she fended him off; she showed no interest in Christmas shopping and developed a wasting cough, which he knew was her signal of distress. If it had not been for Operation Testify, they would have left for Cornwall earlier. As it was, they had to postpone the trip till January, by which time Control was dead, Smiley was unemployed, the scale had tipped; and Ann, to his mortification, was covering the Haydon card with as many others as she could pull from the pack.

So what happened? Did she break off the affair? Did Haydon? Why did she never speak of it? Did it matter, anyway—one among so many? He gave up. Like the Cheshire cat, the face of Bill Haydon seemed to recede as soon as he advanced upon it, leaving only the smile behind. But he knew that somehow Bill had hurt her deeply, which was the sin of sins.

19

Returning with a grunt of distaste to the unlovable table, Smiley resumed his reading of Merlin's progress since his own enforced retirement from the Circus. The new regime of Percy Alleline, he at once noticed, had immediately produced several favourable changes in Merlin's life-style. It was like a maturing, a settling down. The night dashes to European capitals ceased; the flow of intelligence became more regular and less nervy. There were headaches, certainly. Merlin's demands for money—requirements, never threats—continued, and with the steady decline in the value of the pound these large payments in foreign currency caused the Treasury much agony. There was even a suggestion at one point, never pursued, that "since we are the country of Merlin's choice, he should be

ready to shoulder his portion of our financial vicissitudes."
Haydon and Bland exploded, apparently: "I have not the
face," wrote Alleline with rare frankness to the Minister, "to
mention this subject to my staff again."

There was also a row about a new camera, which at great
expense was broken into tubular components by nuts and
bolts section and fitted into a standard lamp of Soviet manufacture. The lamp, after screams of pain—this time from the
Foreign Office—was spirited to Moscow by diplomatic bag.
The problem was then the drop. The residency could not be
informed of Merlin's identity, nor did it know the contents of
the lamp. The lamp was unwieldy, and would not fit the boot
of the resident's car. After several shots, an untidy handover
was achieved, but the camera never worked and there was bad
blood between the Circus and its Moscow residency as a
result. A less ambitious model was taken by Esterhase to
Helsinki, where it was handed—thus Alleline's memo to the
Minister—to "a trusted intermediary whose frontier crossings
would go unchallenged."

Suddenly, Smiley sat up with a jolt.

"We spoke," wrote Alleline to the Minister, in a minute
dated February 27th this year. "You agreed to submit a
supplementary estimate to the Treasury for a London house
to be carried on the Witchcraft budget."

He read it once, then again more slowly. The Treasury had
sanctioned sixty thousand pounds for the freehold and another ten for furniture and fittings. To cut costs, it wanted its
own lawyers to handle the conveyance. Alleline refused to
reveal the address. For the same reason there was an argument
about who should keep the deeds. This time the Treasury put
its foot down and its lawyers drew up instruments to get the
house back from Alleline should he die or go bankrupt. But
he still kept the address to himself, as also the justification for
this remarkable, and costly, adjunct to an operation that was
supposedly taking place abroad.

Smiley searched eagerly for an explanation. The financial

files, he quickly confirmed, were scrupulous to offer none. They contained only one veiled reference to the London house, and that was when the rates were doubled: Minister to Alleline: "I assume the London end is still necessary?" Alleline to Minister: "Eminently. I would say more than ever. I would add that the circle of knowledge has not widened since our conversation." What knowledge?

It was not till he went back to the files which appraised the Witchcraft product that he came on the solution. The house was paid for in late March. Occupancy followed immediately. From the same date exactly, Merlin began to acquire a personality, and it was shaped here in the customers' comments. Till now, to Smiley's suspicious eye, Merlin had been a machine: faultless in tradecraft, eerie in access, free of the strains that make most agents such hard going. Now, suddenly, he was having a tantrum.

"We put to Merlin your follow-up question about the prevailing Kremlin view on the sale of Russian oil surpluses to the United States. We suggested to him, at your request, that this was at odds with his report last month that the Kremlin is presently flirting with the Tanaka government for a contract to sell Siberian oil on the Japanese market. Merlin saw no contradiction in the two reports and declined to forecast which market might ultimately be favoured."

Whitehall regretted its temerity.

"Merlin will not, repeat not, add to his report on the repression of Georgian nationalism and the rioting in Tbilisi. Not being himself a Georgian, he takes the traditional Russian view that all Georgians are thieves and vagabonds, and better behind bars . . ."

Whitehall agreed not to press.

Merlin had suddenly drawn nearer. Was it only the acquisition of a London house that gave Smiley this new sense of Merlin's physical proximity? From the remote stillness of a Moscow winter, Merlin seemed suddenly to be sitting here before him in the tattered room; in the street outside his window, waiting in the rain, where now and then, he knew, Mendel kept his solitary guard. Here out of the blue was a Merlin who talked and answered back and gratuitously offered his opinions, a Merlin who had time to be met. Met here in London? Fed, entertained, debriefed in a sixty-thousand-pound house while he threw his weight about and made jokes about Georgians? What was this circle of knowledge that had now formed itself even within the wider circle of those initiated into the secrets of the Witchcraft operation?

At this point, an improbable figure flitted across the stage: one J.P.R., a new recruit to Whitehall's growing band of Witchcraft evaluators. Consulting the indoctrination list, Smiley established that his full name was Ribble, and that he was a member of Foreign Office Research Department. J. P. Ribble was puzzled.

J.P.R. to the Adriatic Working Party (A.W.P.): "May I respectfully draw your attention to an apparent discrepancy concerning dates? Witchcraft No. 104 (Soviet-French discussions on joint aircraft production) is dated April 21st. According to your covering minute, Merlin had this information directly from General Markov on the day after the negotiating parties agreed to a secret exchange of notes. But on that day, April 21st, according to our Paris Embassy, Markov was still in Paris, and Merlin, as witness your Report No. 109, was himself visiting a missile research establishment outside Leningrad . . ."

The minute cited no fewer than four similar "discrepancies," which, put together, suggested a degree of mobility in Merlin that would have done credit to his miraculous namesake.

J. P. Ribble was told in as many words to mind his own business. But in a separate minute to the Minister, Alleline made an extraordinary admission that shed an entirely new light on the nature of the Witchcraft operation.

"Extremely secret and personal. We spoke. Merlin, as you have known for some time, is not one source but several. While we have done our best for security reasons to disguise this fact from your readers, the sheer volume of material makes it increasingly difficult to continue with this fiction. Might it not be time to come clean, at least on a limited basis? By the same token it would do the Treasury no harm to learn that Merlin's ten thousand Swiss francs a month in salary, and a similar figure for expenses and running costs, are scarcely excessive when the cloth has to be cut so many ways."

But the minute ended on a harsher note: "Nevertheless, even if we agree to open the door this far, I regard it as paramount that knowledge of the existence of the London house, and the purpose for which it is used, remain absolutely at a minimum. Indeed, once Merlin's plurality is published among our readers, the delicacy of the London operation is increased."

Totally mystified, Smiley read this correspondence several times. Then, as if struck by a sudden thought, he looked up, his face a picture of confusion. So far away were his thoughts, indeed, so intense and complex, that the telephone rang several times inside the room before he responded to the summons. Lifting the receiver, he glanced at his watch; it was six in the evening; he had been reading barely an hour.

"Mr. Barraclough? This is Lofthouse from finance, sir."

Peter Guillam, using the emergency procedure, was asking by means of the agreed phrases for a crash meeting, and he sounded shaken.

20

The Circus Archives were not accessible from the main entrance. They rambled through a warren of dingy rooms and half-landings at the back of the building, more like one of the second-hand bookshops that proliferate round there than the organised memory of a large department. They were reached by a dull doorway in the Charing Cross Road, jammed between a picture-framer and an all-day café that was out of bounds to staff. A plate on the door read, "Town and Country Language School, Staff Only," and another, "C & L Distribution, Ltd." To enter, you pressed one or other bell and waited for Alwyn, an effeminate Marine who spoke only of weekends. Till Wednesday or so, he spoke of the weekend past; after that he spoke of the weekend to come. This morning, a Tuesday, he was in a mood of indignant unrest.

"Here, what about that storm, then?" he demanded as he pushed the book across the counter for Guillam to sign. "Might as well live in a lighthouse. All Saturday, all Sunday. I said to my friend: 'Here we are in the middle of London and listen to it.' Want me to look after that for you?"

"You should have been where I was," said Guillam, consigning the brown canvas grip into Alwyn's waiting hands. "Talk about listen to it, you could hardly stand upright."

Don't be over-friendly, he thought, talking to himself.

"Still, I do like the country," Alwyn confided, stowing the grip in one of the open lockers behind the counter. "Want a number, then? I'm supposed to give you one—the Dolphin would kill me if she knew."

"I'll trust you," said Guillam. Climbing the four steps, he pushed open the swing doors to the reading-room. The place was like a makeshift lecture hall: a dozen desks all facing the same way, a raised area where the archivist sat. Guillam took a desk near the back. It was still early—ten-ten by his watch—and the only other reader was Ben Thruxton, of research, who spent most of his time here. Long ago, masquerading as a Latvian dissident, Ben had run with revolutionaries through the streets of Moscow calling death to the oppressors. Now he crouched over his papers like an old priest, white-haired and perfectly still.

Seeing Guillam standing at her desk, the archivist smiled. Quite often, when Brixton was dead, Guillam would spend a day here searching through old cases for one that could stand refiring. She was Sal, a plump, sporting girl who ran a youth club in Chiswick and was a judo black-belt.

"Break any good necks this weekend?" he asked, helping himself to a bunch of green requisition slips.

Sal handed him the notes she kept for him in her steel cupboard.

"Couple. How about you?"

"Visiting aunts in Shropshire, thank you."

"Some aunts," said Sal.

Still at her desk, he filled in slips for the next two references on his list. He watched her stamp them, tear off the flimsies, and post them through a slot on her desk.

"D corridor," she murmured, handing back the top copies. "The two-eights are halfway on your right, the three-ones are next alcove down."

Pushing open the far door, he entered the main hall. At the centre an old lift like a miner's cage carried files into the body of the Circus. Two bleary juniors were feeding it; a third stood by to operate the winch. Guillam moved slowly along the shelves reading the fluorescent number cards.

"Lacon swears he holds no file on Testify at all," Smiley had explained in his usual worried way. "He has a few re-settlement papers on Prideaux and nothing else." And, in the same lugubrious tone: "So I'm afraid we'll have to find a way of getting hold of whatever there is in Circus Registry."

For "getting hold," in Smiley's dictionary, read "steal."

One girl stood on a ladder. Oscar Allitson, the collator, was filling a laundry basket with wrangler files; Astrid, the maintenance man, was mending a radiator. The shelves were wooden, deep as bunks, and divided into pigeon-holes by panels of ply. He knew already that the Testify reference was 4482E which meant alcove 44, where he now stood. "E" stood for "extinct" and was used for dead operations only. Guillam counted to the eighth pigeon-hole from the left. Testify should be second from the left, but there was no way of making certain because the spines were unmarked. His reconnaissance complete, he drew the two files he had requested, leaving the green slips in the steel brackets provided for them.

"There won't be much, I'm sure," Smiley had said, as if thinner files were easier. "But there ought to be something, if only for appearances." That was another thing about him that Guillam didn't like just then: he spoke as if you followed his reasoning, as if you were inside his mind all the time.

Sitting down, he pretended to read but passed the time thinking of Camilla. What was he supposed to make of her? Early this morning as she lay in his arms, she told him she had once been married. Sometimes she spoke like that, as if she'd lived about twenty lives. It was a mistake, so they packed it in.

"What went wrong?"

"Nothing. We weren't right for each other."

Guillam didn't believe her.

"Did you get a divorce?"

"I expect so."

"Don't be damn silly; you must know whether you're divorced or not!"

His parents handled it, she said; he was foreign.

"Does he send you money?"

"Why should he? He doesn't owe me anything."

Then the flute again, in the spare room, long questioning notes in the half-light while Guillam made coffee. Is she a fake or an angel? He'd half a mind to pass her name across the records. She had a lesson with Sand in an hour.

Armed with a green slip with a 43 reference, he returned the two files to their places and positioned himself at the alcove next to Testify.

Dry run uneventful, he thought.

The girl was still up her ladder. Allitson had vanished but the laundry basket was still there. The radiator had already exhausted Astrid and he was sitting beside it reading the *Sun*. The green slip read "4343," and he found the file at once because he had already marked it down. It had a pink jacket like Testify. Like Testify, it was reasonably thumbed. He fitted the green slip into the bracket. He moved back across the aisle, again checked Allitson and the girls, then reached for the Testify file and replaced it very fast with the file he had in his hand.

"I think the vital thing, Peter"—Smiley speaking—"is not to leave a gap. So what I suggest is, you requisition a comparable file—*physically* comparable, I mean—and pop it into the gap which is left by—"

"I get you," Guillam said.

Holding the Testify file casually in his right hand, title inward to his body, Guillam returned to the reading-room and again sat at his desk. Sal raised her eyebrows and mouthed something. Guillam nodded that all was well, thinking that was what she was asking, but she beckoned him over. Momentary panic. Take the file with me or leave it? What do I usually do? He left it on the desk.

"Juliet's going for coffee," Sal whispered. "Want some?"

Guillam laid a shilling on the counter.

He glanced at the clock, then at his watch. Christ, stop looking at your damn watch! Think of Camilla, think of her starting her lesson, think of those aunts you didn't spend the weekend with, think of Alwyn not looking in your bag. Think of anything but the time. Eighteen minutes to wait. "Peter, if you have the smallest reservation, you really mustn't go ahead with it. Nothing is as important as that." Great, so how do you spot a reservation when thirty teenage butterflies are mating in your stomach and the sweat is like a secret rain inside your shirt? Never, he swore, never had he had it this bad.

Opening the Testify file, he tried to read it.

It wasn't all that thin, but it wasn't fat, either. It looked pretty much like a token volume, as Smiley had said: the first serial was taken up with a description of what wasn't there. "Annexes 1 to 8 held London Station, cross-refer to P.F.s

ELLIS Jim, PRIDEAUX Jim, HAJEK Vladimir, COLLINS Sam, HABOLT Max . . ." and a whole football team besides. "For these files, consult H/London Station or C.C.," standing for Chief of Circus and his appointed mothers. Don't look at your watch; look at the clock and do the arithmetic, you idiot. Eight minutes. Odd to be pinching files about one's predecessor. Odd to have Jim as a predecessor, come to think of it, and a secretary who held a wake over him without ever mentioning his name. The only living trace Guillam had ever found of him, apart from his workname on the files, was his squash racket jammed behind the safe in his room, with "J.P." hand-done in pokerwork on the handle. He showed it to Ellen, a tough old biddy who could make Cy Vanhofer quail like a schoolboy, and she broke into floods of tears, wrapped it, and sent it to the housekeepers by the next shuttle, with a personal note to the Dolphin insisting that it be returned to him "if humanly possible." How's your game these days, Jim, with a couple of Czech bullets in your shoulder-bone?

Still eight minutes.

"Now, if you could contrive," said Smiley, "I mean if it wouldn't be too much bother, to take your car in for a service at your local garage. Using your home phone to make the appointment, of course, in the *hope* that Toby is listening . . ."

In the hope. Mother of Pearl. And all his cosy chats with Camilla? Still eight minutes.

The rest of the file seemed to be Foreign Office telegrams, Czech press cuttings, monitoring reports on Prague radio, extracts from a policy file on the resettlement and rehabilitation of blown agents, draft submissions to the Treasury, and a post-mortem by Alleline that blamed Control for the fiasco. Sooner you than me, George.

In his mind, Guillam began measuring the distance from his desk to the rear door, where Alwyn dozed at the reception counter. He reckoned it was five paces and he decided to make a tactical staging post. Two paces from the door stood a chart chest like a big yellow piano. It was filled with oddments of reference: large-scale maps, back copies of *Who's Who*, old Baedekers. Putting a pencil between his teeth, he picked up the Testify file, wandered to the chest, selected a telephone directory of Warsaw, and began writing names on a sheet of paper. My hand! a voice screamed inside him: my hand is shaking all over the page; look at those figures—I might be drunk! Why has no one noticed? . . . The girl Juliet came in with a tray and put a cup on his desk. He blew her a distracted kiss. He selected another directory—he thought for Poznan—and laid it beside the first. When Alwyn came through the door, he didn't even look up.

"Telephone, sir," he murmured.

"Oh, to hell," said Guillam, deep in the directory. "Who is it?"

"Outside line, sir. Someone rough. The garage, I think, regarding your car. Said he'd got some bad news for you," said Alwyn, very pleased.

Guillam was holding the Testify file in both hands, apparently cross-referring with the directory. He had his back to Sal and he could feel his knees shaking against his trouser legs. The pencil was still jammed in his mouth. Alwyn went ahead and held the swing door for him, and he passed through it reading the file. Like a damned choirboy, he thought. He waited for lightning to strike him, Sal to call murder, old Ben the superspy to leap suddenly to life, but it didn't happen. He felt much better: Alwyn is my ally, I trust him, we are united against the Dolphin, I can move. The swing doors closed; he went down the four steps and there was Alwyn again, holding open the door to the telephone cubicle. The lower part was panelled, the upper part glass. Lifting the receiver, he laid the file at his feet and heard Mendel tell him he needed a new gear-box; the job could cost anything up to a hundred quid. They'd worked this up for the benefit of the housekeepers or whoever read the transcripts, and Guillam kept it going nicely to and fro till Alwyn was safely behind his counter, listening like an eagle. It's working, he thought; I'm flying, it's working after all. He heard himself say, "Well, at least get on to the main agents first and find out how long they'll take to supply the damn thing. Have you got their number?" And irritably: "Hang on."

He half-opened the door and he kept the mouthpiece jammed against his backside because he was very concerned that this part should not go on tape. "Alwyn, chuck me that bag a minute, will you?"

Alwyn brought it over keenly, like the first-aid man at a football match. "All right, Mr. Guillam, sir? Open it for you, sir?"

"Just dump it there, thanks."

The bag was on the floor outside the cubicle. Now he stooped, dragged it inside, and unzipped it. At the middle, among his shirts and a lot of newspaper, were three dummy files, one buff, one green, one pink. He took out the pink dummy and his address book and replaced them with the Testify file. He closed the zip, and stood up and read Mendel a telephone number—actually the right one. He rang off, handed Alwyn the bag, and returned to the reading-room with the dummy file. He dawdled at the chart chest, fiddled with a couple more directories, then sauntered to the archive carrying the dummy file. Allitson was going through a comedy routine, first pulling then pushing the laundry basket.

"Peter, give us a hand, will you—I'm stuck."

"Half a sec."

Recovering the 43 file from the Testify pigeon-hole, he replaced it with the dummy, restored it to its rightful place in the 43 alcove, and removed the green slip from the bracket. God is in His heaven and the first night was a wow. He could have sung out loud: God is in His heaven and I can still fly.

He took the slip to Sal, who signed it and put it on a spike as she always did. Later today she would check. If the file was in its place, she would destroy both the green slip and the flimsy from the box, and not even clever Sal would remember that he had been alongside the 44 alcove. He was about to return to the archive to give old Allitson a hand when he found himself looking straight into the brown, unfriendly eyes of Toby Esterhase.

"Peter," said Toby, in his not quite perfect English. "I am so sorry to disturb you but we have a tiny crisis and Percy Alleline would like quite an urgent word with you. Can you come now? That would be very kind." And at the door, as Alwyn let them out: "Your opinion he wants, actually," he remarked with the officiousness of a small but rising man. "He wishes to consult you for an opinion."

In a desperately inspired moment, Guillam turned to Alwyn and said, "There's a midday shuttle to Brixton. You might just give transport a buzz and ask them to take that thing over for me, will you?"

"Will do, sir," said Alwyn. "Will do. Mind the step, sir."

And you pray for me, thought Guillam.

21

"Our Shadow Foreign Secretary," Haydon called him. The janitors called him "Snow White" because of his hair. Toby Esterhase dressed like a male model, but the moment he dropped his shoulders or closed his tiny fists he was unmistakably a fighter. Following him down the fourth-floor corridor—noting the coffee machine again, and Lauder Strickland's voice explaining that he was unobtainable—Guillam thought, Christ, we're back in Berne and on the run.

He'd half a mind to call this out to Toby, but decided the comparison was unwise.

Whenever he thought of Toby, that was what he thought of: Switzerland eight years ago, when Toby was just a humdrum watcher with a growing reputation for informal listening on the side. Guillam was kicking his heels after North Africa, so the Circus packed them both off to Berne on a one-time operation to spike a pair of Belgian arms dealers who were using the Swiss to spread their wares in unpopular directions. They rented a villa next door to the target house, and the following night Toby opened up a junction box and rearranged things so that they overheard the Belgians' conversations on their own phone. Guillam was boss and legman, and twice a day he dropped the tapes on the Berne residency, using a parked car as a letter-box. With the same ease, Toby bribed the local postman to give him a first sight of the Belgians' mail before he delivered it, and the cleaning lady to plant a radio mike in the drawing room where they held most of their discussions. For diversion, they went to the Chikito and Toby danced with the youngest girls. Now and then he brought one home, but by morning she was always gone and Toby had the windows open to get rid of the smell.

They lived this way for three months and Guillam knew him no better at the end than he had on the first day. He didn't even know his country of origin. Toby was a snob, and knew the places to eat and be seen. He washed his own clothes and at night he wore a net over his snow white hair, and on the day the police hit the villa and Guillam had to hop over the back wall, he found Toby at the Bellevue Hotel munching *pâtisseries* and watching the *thé dansant*. He listened to what Guillam had to say, paid his bill, tipped first the bandleader, then Franz, the head porter, and then led the way along a succession of corridors and staircases to the underground garage where he had cached the escape car and passports. There also, punctiliously, he asked for his bill. Guillam thought, If you ever want to get out of Switzerland in a hurry, you pay your bills first. The corridors were endless, with mirror walls and Versailles chandeliers, so that Guillam was following not just one Esterhase but a whole delegation of them.

It was this vision that came back to him now, though the narrow wooden staircase to Alleline's rooms was painted mud-green and only a battered parchment lampshade recalled the chandeliers.

"To see the Chief," Toby announced portentously to the young janitor who beckoned them through with an insolent nod. In the anteroom at four grey typewriters sat the four grey mothers, in pearls and twin-sets. They nodded to Guillam and ignored Toby. A sign over Alleline's door said "Engaged." Beside it, a six-foot wardrobe safe, new. Guillam wondered how on earth the floor took the strain. On its top, bottles of South African sherry; glasses, plates. Tuesday, he remembered: London Station's informal lunch meeting.

"I'll have no phone calls, tell them," Alleline shouted as Toby opened the door.

"The Chief will take no calls, please, ladies," said Toby elaborately, holding back the door for Guillam. "We are having a conference."

One of the mothers said, "We heard."

It was a war party.

Alleline sat at the head of the table in the megalomaniac's throne, reading a two-page document, and he didn't stir when Guillam came in. He just growled, "Down there with you. By Paul. Below the salt," and went on reading with heavy concentration.

The chair to Alleline's right was empty, and Guillam knew it was Haydon's by the posture-curve cushion tied to it with string. To Alleline's left sat Roy Bland, also reading, but he looked up as Guillam passed, and said "Wotcher, Peter," then followed him all the way down the table with his bulging eyes. Next to Bill's empty chair sat Mo Delaware, London Station's token woman, in bobbed hair and a brown tweed suit. Across from her, Phil Porteous, the head housekeeper, a rich servile man with a big house in suburbia. When he saw

Guillam, he stopped his reading altogether, ostentatiously closed the folder, laid his sleek hands over it, and smirked.

" 'Below the salt' means next to Paul Skordeno," said Phil, still smirking.

"Thanks. I can see it."

Across from Porteous came Bill's Russians, last seen in the fourth-floor men's room, Nick de Silsky and his boyfriend Kaspar. They couldn't smile, and for all Guillam knew they couldn't read, either, because they had no papers in front of them; they were the only ones who hadn't. They sat with their four thick hands on the table as if somebody were holding a gun behind them, and they just watched him with their four brown eyes.

Downhill from Porteous sat Paul Skordeno, now reputedly Roy Bland's fieldman on the satellite networks, though others said he ran between wickets for Bill. Paul was thin and mean and forty, with a pitted brown face and long arms. Guillam had once paired with him on a tough-guy course at the Nursery and they all but killed each other.

Guillam moved the chair away from him and sat down, so Toby sat next along like the other half of a bodyguard. Guillam thought, What the hell do they expect me to do—make a mad dash for freedom? Everyone was watching Alleline fill his pipe when Bill Haydon upstaged him. The door opened and at first no one came in. Then a slow shuffle and Bill appeared, clutching a cup of coffee in both hands, the saucer on top. He had a striped folder jammed under his arm and his glasses were over his nose, for a change, so he must have done his reading elsewhere. They've all been reading it except me, thought Guillam, and I don't know what it is. He wondered whether it was the same document that Esterhase and Roy were reading yesterday, and decided on no evidence at all that it was; that yesterday it had just come in, that Toby had brought it to Roy, and that he had disturbed them in their first excitement—if excitement was the word.

Alleline had still not looked up. Down the table Guillam

had only his rich black hair to look at, and a pair of broad tweedy shoulders. Mo Delaware was pulling at her fringe while she read. Percy had two wives, Guillam remembered, as Camilla once more flitted through his teeming mind, and both were alcoholics, which must mean something. He had met only the London edition. Percy was forming his supporters' club and gave a drinks party at his sprawling panelled flat in Buckingham Palace Mansions. Guillam arrived late and he was taking off his coat in the lobby when a pale blond woman loomed timidly towards him holding out her hands. He took her for the maid wanting his coat.

"I'm Joy," she said, in a theatrical voice, like "I'm Virtue" or "I'm Continence." It wasn't his coat she wanted but a kiss. Yielding to it, Guillam inhaled the joint pleasures of Je Reviens and a high concentration of inexpensive sherry.

"Well, now, young Peter Guillam"—Alleline speaking—"are you ready for me finally or have you other calls to make about my house?" He half looked up and Guillam noticed two tiny triangles of fur on each weathered cheek. "What are you getting up to out there in the sticks these days"—turning a page—"apart from chasing the local virgins, if there are any in Brixton, which I severely doubt—if you'll pardon my freedom, Mo—and wasting public money on expensive lunches?"

This banter was Alleline's one instrument of communication; it could be friendly or hostile, reproachful or congratulatory, but in the end it was like a constant tapping on the same spot.

"Couple of Arab ploys look quite promising. Cy Vanhofer's got a lead to a German diplomat. That's about it."

"Arabs," Alleline repeated, pushing aside the folder and dragging a rough pipe from his pocket. "Any bloody fool can burn an Arab—can't he, Bill? Buy a whole damn Arab Cabinet for half a crown, if you've a mind to." From another pocket Alleline took a tobacco pouch, which he tossed easily onto the table. "I hear you've been hobnobbing with our late-lamented Brother Tarr. How is he these days?"

A lot of things went through Guillam's mind as he heard himself answer. That the surveillance on his flat did not begin till last night—he was sure of it. That over the weekend he was in the clear unless Fawn, the captive baby-sitter, had doubled, which would have been hard for him. That Roy Bland bore a close resemblance to the late Dylan Thomas: Roy had always reminded him of someone and till this moment he'd never been able to pin down the connection; and that Mo Delaware had only passed muster as a woman because of her brownie mannishness. He wondered whether Dylan Thomas had had Roy's extraordinary blue eyes. That Toby Esterhase was helping himself to a cigarette from his gold case, and that Alleline didn't as a rule allow cigarettes but only pipes, so Toby must stand pretty well with Alleline just now. That Bill Haydon was looking strangely young and that Circus rumours about his love-life were not after all so laughable: they said he went both ways. That Paul Skordeno had one brown palm flat on the table and the thumb slightly lifted in a way that hardened the hitting surface on the outside of the hand. He thought also of his canvas case: had Alwyn put it on the shuttle? Or had he gone off for his lunch leaving it in Registry, waiting to be inspected by one of the new young janitors busting for promotion? And Guillam wondered—not for the first time—just how long Toby had been hanging around Registry before Guillam noticed him.

He selected a facetious tone: "That's right, Chief. Tarr and I have tea at Fortnum's every afternoon."

Alleline was sucking at his empty pipe, testing the packing of the tobacco.

"Peter Guillam," he said deliberately, in his pert brogue. "You may not be aware of this, but I am of an extremely forgiving nature. I am positively seething with goodwill, in fact. All I require is the matter of your discussion with Tarr. I do not ask for his head, nor any other part of his damned anatomy, and I will restrain my impulse personally to strangle him. Or you." He struck a match and lit his pipe, making a monstrous flame. "I would even go so far as to consider hanging a gold chain about your neck and bringing you into the palace from hateful Brixton."

"In that case, I can't wait for him to turn up," said Guillam.

"And there's a free pardon for Tarr till I get my hands on him."

"I'll tell him. He'll be thrilled."

A great cloud of smoke rolled out over the table.

"I'm very disappointed with you, young Peter. Giving ear to gross slanders of a divisive and insidious nature. I pay you honest money and you stab me in the back. I consider that extremely poor reward for keeping you alive. Against the entreaties of my advisers, I may tell you."

Alleline had a new mannerism, one that Guillam had noticed often in vain men of middle age: it involved taking hold of a tuck of flesh under the chin and massaging it between finger and thumb in the hope of reducing it.

"Tell us some more about Tarr's circumstances just now," said Alleline. "Tell us about his emotional state. He has a daughter, has he not? A wee daughter name of Danny. Does he talk of her at all?"

"He used to."

"Regale us with some anecdotes about her."

"I don't know any. He was very fond of her, that's all I know."

"Obsessively fond?" His voice rose suddenly in anger. "What's that shrug for? What the hell are you shrugging at me like that for? I'm talking to you about a defector from your own damn section; I'm accusing you of playing hookey with him behind my back, of taking part in damn-fool parlour games when you don't know the stakes involved, and all you do is shrug at me down the table. There's a *law*, Peter Guillam, against consorting with enemy agents. Maybe you didn't know that. I've a good mind to throw the book at you!"

"But I haven't been seeing him," said Guillam as anger

came also to his rescue. "It's not me who's playing parlour games. It's you. So get off my back."

In the same moment he sensed the relaxation round the table, like a tiny descent into boredom, like a general recognition that Alleline had shot off all his ammunition and the target was unmarked. Skordeno was fidgeting with a bit of ivory, some lucky charm he carried round with him. Bland was reading again and Bill Haydon was drinking his coffee and finding it terrible, for he made a sour face at Mo Delaware and put down the cup. Toby Esterhase, chin in hand, had raised his eyebrows and was gazing at the red cellophane that filled the Victorian grate. Only the Russians continued to watch him unblinkingly, like a pair of terriers not wanting to believe that the hunt was over.

"So he used to chat to you about Danny, eh? And he told you he loved her," said Alleline, back at the document before him. "Who's Danny's mother?"

"A Eurasian girl."

Now Haydon spoke for the first time. "Unmistakably Eurasian, or could she pass for something nearer home?"

"Tarr seems to think she looks full European. He thinks the kid does, too."

Alleline read aloud: "Twelve years old, long blond hair, brown eyes, slim. Is that Danny?"

"I should think it could be. It sounds like her."

There was a long silence and not even Haydon seemed inclined to break it.

"So if I told you," Alleline resumed, choosing his words extremely carefully: "if I told you that Danny and her mother were due to arrive three days ago at London Airport on the direct flight from Singapore, I may take it you would share our perplexity."

"Yes, I would."

"You would also keep your mouth shut when you got out of here. You'd tell no one but your twelve best friends?"

From not far away came Phil Porteous's purr: "The source

is extremely secret, Peter. It may sound to you like ordinary flight information but it isn't that at all. It's ultra, *ultra* sensitive."

"Ah, well, in that case I'll try to keep my mouth *ultra* shut," said Guillam to Porteous, and while Porteous coloured Bill Haydon gave another schoolboy grin.

Alleline came back. "So what would you make of this information? Come on, Peter—" the banter again—"Come on, you were his boss, his guide, philosopher, and his friend. Where's your psychology, for God's sake? Why is Tarr coming to England?"

"That's not what you said at all. You said Tarr's girl and her daughter Danny were expected in London three days ago. Perhaps she's visiting relations. Perhaps she's got a new boy-friend. How should I know?"

"Don't be obtuse, man. Doesn't it occur to you that where little Danny is, Tarr himself is unlikely to be far behind? If he's not here already, which I'm inclined to believe he is, that being the manner of men to come first and bring their impedimenta later. Pardon me, Mo Delaware, a lapse."

For the second time, Guillam allowed himself a little temperament. "Till now it had not occurred to me, no. Till now Tarr was a defector. Housekeepers' ruling as of seven months ago. Right or wrong, Phil? Tarr was sitting in Moscow and everything he knew should be regarded as blown. Right, Phil? That was also held to be a good enough reason for turning the lights out in Brixton and giving one chunk of our workload to London Station and another to Toby's lamp-lighters. What's Tarr supposed to be doing now, redefecting to us?"

"Redefecting would be a damned charitable way of putting it, I'll tell you that for nothing," Alleline retorted, back at the paper before him. "Listen to me. Listen exactly, and remember. Because I've no doubt that, like the rest of my staff, you've a memory like a sieve—all you prima donnas are the same. Danny and her mother are travelling on fake British passports in the name of Poole, like the harbour. The passports are Russian fakes. A third went to Tarr himself, the well-known *Mr.* Poole. Tarr is already in England but we don't know where. He left ahead of Danny and her mother and came here by a different route; our investigations suggest a black one. He instructed his wife or mistress or whatever"—he said this as if he had neither—"pardon again, Mo, to follow him in one week, which they have not yet done, apparently. This information only reached us yesterday, so we've a lot of footwork to do yet. Tarr instructed them, Danny and her mother, that if by any chance he failed to make contact with them, they should throw themselves on the mercy of one Peter Guillam. That's you, I believe."

"If they were due three days ago, what's happened to them?"

"Delayed. Missed their plane. Changed their plans. Lost their tickets. How the hell do I know?"

"Or else the information's wrong," Guillam suggested.

"It isn't," Alleline snapped.

Resentment, mystification: Guillam clung to them both. "All right. The Russians have turned Tarr round. They've sent his family over—God knows why; I'd have thought they'd put them in the bank—and they've sent him, too. Why's it all so hot? What sort of plant can he be when we don't believe a word he says?"

This time, he noticed with exhilaration, his audience was watching Alleline, who seemed to Guillam to be torn between giving a satisfactory but indiscreet answer or making a fool of himself.

"Never mind what sort of plant! Muddying pools. Poisoning wells, maybe. That damn sort. Pulling the rug out when we're all but home and dry." His circulars read that way, too, thought Guillam. Metaphors chasing each other off the page. "But just you remember this. At the first peep, before the first peep, at the first whisper of him or his lady or his wee daughter, young Peter Guillam, you come to one of us grown-ups. Anyone you see at this table. But not another damn soul.

Do you follow that injunction perfectly? Because there are more damn wheels within wheels here than you can possibly guess or have any right to know . . ."

It became suddenly a conversation in movement. Bland had plugged his hands into his pockets and slouched across the room to lean against the far door. Alleline had relit his pipe and was putting out the match with a long movement of his arm while he glowered at Guillam through the smoke. "Who are you courting these days, Peter—who's the lucky wee lady?" Porteous was sliding a sheet of paper down the table for Guillam's signature. "For you, Peter, if you please." Paul Skordeno was whispering something into the ear of one of the Russians, and Esterhase was at the door giving unpopular orders to the mothers. Only Mo Delaware's brown, unassuming eyes still held Guillam in their gaze.

"Read it first, won't you," Porteous advised silkily.

Guillam was halfway through the form already: "I certify that I have today been advised of the contents of Witchcraft Report No. 308, Source Merlin," ran the first paragraph. "I undertake not to divulge any part of this report to other members of the service, nor will I divulge the existence of Source Merlin. I also undertake to report at once any matter which comes to my notice which appears to bear on this material."

The door had stayed open and, as Guillam signed, the second echelon of London Station filed in, led by the mothers with trays of sandwiches. Diana Dolphin, Lauder Strickland looking taut enough to blow up, the girls from distribution, and a sour-faced old war-horse called Haggard, who was Ben Thruxton's overlord. Guillam left slowly, counting heads because he knew Smiley would want to know who was there. At the door, to his surprise, he found himself joined by Haydon, who seemed to have decided that the remaining festivities were not for him.

"Stupid bloody cabaret," Bill remarked, waving vaguely at the mothers. "Percy's getting more insufferable every day."

"He does seem to," said Guillam heartily.

"How's Smiley these days? Seen much of him? You used to be quite a chum of his, didn't you?"

Guillam's world, which was showing signs till then of steadying to a sensible pace, plunged violently. "Afraid not," he said; "he's out of bounds."

"Don't tell me you take any notice of that nonsense," Bill said, snorting. They had reached the stairs. Haydon went ahead.

"How about you?" Guillam called. "Have you seen much of him?"

"And Ann's flown the coop," said Bill, ignoring the question. "Pushed off with a sailor-boy or a waiter or something." The door to his room was wide open, the desk heaped with secret files. "Is that right?"

"I didn't know," said Guillam. "Poor old George."

"Coffee?"

"I think I'll get back, thanks."

"For tea with Brother Tarr?"

"That's right. At Fortnum's. So long."

In Archives Section, Alwyn was back from lunch. "Bag's all gone, sir," he said gaily. "Should be over in Brixton by now."

"Oh, damn," said Guillam, firing his last shot. "There was something in it I needed."

A sickening notion had struck him: it seemed so neat and so horribly obvious that he could only wonder why it had come to him so late. Sand was Camilla's husband. She was living a double life. Now whole new vistas of deceit opened before him. His friends, his loves, even the Circus itself; joined and re-formed in endless patterns of intrigue. A line of Mendel's came back to him, dropped two nights ago as they drank beer in some glum suburban pub: "Cheer up, Peter, old son. Jesus Christ only had twelve, you know, and one of them was a double."

Tarr, he thought. That bastard Ricki Tarr.

22

The bedroom was long and low, once a maid's room, built into the attic. Guillam was standing at the door; Tarr sat on the bed motionless, his head tilted back against the sloped ceiling, hands to either side of him, fingers wide. There was a dormer window above him, and from where Guillam stood he could see long reaches of black Suffolk countryside and a line of black trees traced against the sky. The wallpaper was brown with large red flowers. The one light hung from a black oak truss, lighting their two faces in strange geometric patterns, and when either one of them moved, Tarr on the bed or Smiley on the wooden kitchen chair, they seemed by their movement to take the light with them a distance before it resettled.

Left to himself, Guillam would have been very rough with Tarr, he had no doubt of it. His nerves were all over the place, and on the drive down he had touched ninety before Smiley sharply told him to go steady. Left to himself, he would have been tempted to beat the daylights out of Tarr, and if necessary he would have brought Fawn in to lend a hand; driving, he had a very clear picture of opening the front door of wherever Tarr lived and hitting him in the face several times, with love from Camilla and her ex-husband, the distinguished doctor of the flute. And perhaps in the shared tension of the journey Smiley had received the same picture telepathically, for the little he said was clearly directed to talking Guillam down. "Tarr has not lied to us, Peter. Not in any material way. He has simply done what agents do the world over: he has failed to tell us the whole story. On the other hand, he has been rather clever." Far from sharing

Guillam's bewilderment, he seemed curiously confident—
even complacent—to the extent of allowing himself a senten-
tious aphorism from Steed-Asprey on the arts of double-
cross; something about not looking for perfection, but for
advantage, which again had Guillam thinking about Camilla.
"Karla has admitted us to the inner circle," Smiley announced,
and Guillam made a bad joke about changing at Charing Cross.
After that Smiley contented himself with giving directions and
watching the wing mirror.

They had met at Crystal Palace, a van pick-up with Mendel
driving. They drove to Barnsbury, straight into a car-body
repair shop at the end of a cobbled alley full of children.
There they were received with discreet rapture by an old
German and his son, who had stripped the plates off the van
almost before they got out of it and led them to a souped-up
Vauxhall ready to drive out of the far end of the workshop.
Mendel stayed behind with the Testify file, which Guillam
had brought from Brixton in his night-bag; Smiley said, "Find
the A12." There was very little traffic but short of Colchester
they hit a cluster of lorries and Guillam suddenly lost patience. Smiley had to order him to pull in. Once they met an
old man driving at twenty in the fast lane. As they overtook
him on the inside, he veered wildly towards them, drunk or
ill, or just terrified. And once, with no warning, they hit a
fog wall; it seemed to fall on them from above. Guillam drove
clean through it, afraid to brake because of black ice. Past
Colchester they took small lanes. On the signposts were names
like Little Horkesley, Wormingford, and Bures Green; then
the signposts stopped and Guillam had a feeling of being
nowhere at all.

"Left here and left again at the dower house. Go as far as
you can but park short of the gates."

They reached what seemed to be a hamlet but there were
no lights, no people, and no moon. As they got out, the cold
hit them and Guillam smelt a cricket field and wood-smoke
and Christmas all at once; he thought he had never been any-

where so quiet or so cold or so remote. A church tower rose ahead of them, a white fence ran to one side, and up on the slope stood what he took to be the rectory, a low rambling house, part thatched; he could make out the fringe of gable against the sky. Fawn was waiting for them; he came to the car as they parked, and climbed silently into the back.

"Ricki's been that much better today, sir," he reported. He had evidently done a lot of reporting to Smiley in the last few days. He was a steady, soft-spoken boy with a great will to please, but the rest of the Brixton pack seemed to be afraid of him, Guillam didn't know why. "Not so nervy—more relaxed, I'd say. Did his pools this morning—loves the pools, Ricki does—this afternoon we dug up fir trees for Miss Ailsa, so's she could drive them into market. This evening we had a nice game of cards and early bed."

"Has he been out alone?" asked Smiley.

"No, sir."

"Has he used the telephone?"

"Gracious, no, sir, not while I'm around, and I'm sure not while Miss Ailsa was, either."

Their breath had misted the windows of the car, but Smiley would not have the engine on, so there was no heater and no de-mister.

"Has he mentioned his daughter Danny?"

"Over the weekend he did a lot. Now he's sort of cooled off about them. I think he's shut them out of his mind, in view of the emotional side."

"He hasn't talked about seeing them again?"

"No, sir."

"Nothing about arrangements for meeting when all this is over?"

"No, sir."

"Or bringing them to England?"

"No, sir."

"Nor about providing them with documents?"

"No, sir."

Guillam chimed in irritably: "So what has he talked about, for heaven's sake?"

"The Russian lady, sir. Irina. He likes to read her diary. He says when the mole's caught, he's going to make Centre swap him for Irina. Then we'll get her a nice place, sir—like Miss Ailsa's but up in Scotland where it's nicer. He says he'll see me right, too. Give me a big job in the Circus. He's been encouraging me to learn another language to increase my scope."

There was no telling, from the flat voice behind them in the dark, what Fawn made of this advice.

"Where is he now?"

"In bed, sir."

"Close the doors quietly."

Ailsa Brimley was waiting in the front porch for them: a grey-haired lady of sixty with a firm, intelligent face. She was old Circus, Smiley said, one of Lord Landsbury's coding ladies from the war, now in retirement but still formidable. She wore a trim brown suit. She shook Guillam by the hand and said "How do you do," bolted the door, and when he looked again she had gone. Smiley led the way upstairs. Fawn should wait on the lower landing in case he was needed.

"It's Smiley," he said knocking on Tarr's door. "I want a chat with you."

Tarr opened the door fast. He must have heard them coming, and been waiting just the other side. He opened it with his left hand, holding the gun in his right, and he was looking past Smiley down the corridor.

"It's only Guillam," said Smiley.

"That's what I mean," said Tarr. "Babies can bite."

They stepped inside. He wore slacks and some sort of cheap Malay wrap. Spelling cards lay spread over the floor and in the air hung a smell of curry that he had cooked for himself on a ring.

"I'm sorry to be pestering you," said Smiley with an air of sincere commiseration. "But I must ask you again what you did with those two Swiss escape passports you took with you to Hong Kong."

"Why?" said Tarr at last.

The jauntiness was all gone. He had a prison pallor; he had lost weight and as he sat on the bed with the gun on the pillow beside him, his eyes sought them out nervously, each in turn, trusting nothing.

Smiley said, "Listen. I want to believe your story. Nothing is altered. Once we know, we'll respect your privacy. But we have to know. It's terribly important. Your whole future stands by it."

And a lot more besides, thought Guillam, watching; a whole chunk of devious arithmetic was hanging by a thread, if Guillam knew Smiley at all.

"I told you I burned them. I didn't fancy the numbers. I reckoned they were blown. Might as well put a label round your neck 'Tarr, Ricki Tarr, Wanted' soon as use those passports."

Smiley's questions were terribly slow in coming. Even to Guillam it was painful waiting for them in the deep silence of the night.

"What did you burn them with?"

"What the hell does that matter?"

But Smiley apparently did not feel like giving reasons for his enquiries; he preferred to let the silence do its work, and he seemed confident that it would. Guillam had seen whole interrogations conducted that way: a laboured catechism swathed in deep coverings of routine; wearying pauses as each answer was written down in longhand and the suspect's brain besieged itself with a thousand questions to the interrogator's one; and his hold on his story weakened from day to day.

"When you bought your British passport in the name of Poole," Smiley asked, after another age, "did you buy any other passports from the same source?"

"Why should I?"

But Smiley did not feel like giving reasons.

"Why should I?" Tarr repeated. "I'm not a damn collector, for Christ's sake; all I wanted was to get out from under."

"And protect your child," Smiley suggested, with an understanding smile. "And protect her mother, too, if you could. I'm sure you gave a lot of thought to that," he said in a flattering tone. "After all, you could hardly leave them behind to the mercy of that inquisitive Frenchman, could you?"

Waiting, Smiley appeared to examine the lexicon cards, reading off the words longways and sideways. There was nothing to them: they were random words. One was misspelt; Guillam noticed "epistle" with the last two letters back to front. What's he been doing up there, Guillam wondered, in that stinking flea-pit of a hotel? What furtive little tracks has his mind been following, locked away with the sauce bottles and the commercial travellers?

"All right," said Tarr sullenly, "so I got passports for Danny and her mother. Mrs. Poole, Miss Danny Poole. What do we do now, cry out in ecstasy?"

Again it was the silence that accused.

"Now why didn't you tell us that before?" Smiley asked in the tone of a disappointed father. "We're not monsters. We don't wish them harm. Why didn't you tell us? Perhaps we could even have helped you," and went back to his examination of the cards. Tarr must have used two or three packs; they lay in rivers over the coconut carpet. "Why didn't you tell us?" he repeated. "There's no crime in looking after the people one loves."

If they'll let you, thought Guillam, with Camilla in mind.

To help Tarr answer, Smiley was making helpful suggestions: "Was it because you dipped into your operational expenses to buy these British passports? Was that the reason you didn't tell us? Good heavens, no one here is worried about money. You've brought us a vital piece of information. Why should we quarrel about a couple of thousand dollars?" And the time ticked away again without anyone using it.

"Or was it," Smiley suggested, "that you were ashamed?"

Guillam stiffened, his own problems forgotten.

"Rightly ashamed in a way, I suppose. It wasn't a very gallant act, after all, to leave Danny and her mother with blown passports, at the mercy of that so-called Frenchman who was looking so hard for Mr. Poole? While you yourself escaped to all this V.I.P. treatment? It is horrible to think of," Smiley agreed, as if Tarr, not he, had made the point. "It is horrible to contemplate the lengths Karla would go to in order to obtain your silence. Or your services."

The sweat on Tarr's face was suddenly unbearable. There was too much of it; it was like tears all over. The cards no longer interested Smiley; his eye had settled on a different game. It was a toy, made of two steel rods like the shafts of a pair of tongs. The trick was to roll a steel ball along them. The further you rolled it, the more points you won when it fell into one of the holes underneath.

"The other reason you might not have told us, I suppose, is that you burnt them. You burnt the *British* passports, I mean, not the Swiss ones."

Go easy, George, thought Guillam, and softly moved a pace nearer to cover the gap between them. Just go easy.

"You knew that Poole was blown, so you burnt the Poole passports you had bought for Danny and her mother, but you kept your own because there was no alternative. Then you made travel bookings for the two of them in the name of Poole in order to convince everybody that you still believed in the Poole passports. By everybody, I think I mean Karla's footpads, don't I? You doctored the Swiss escapes, one for Danny, one for her mother, took a chance that the numbers wouldn't be noticed, and you made a different set of arrangements which you didn't advertise. Arrangements which matured earlier than those you made for the Pooles. How would that be? Such as staying out East, but somewhere else, like Djakarta: somewhere you have friends."

Even from where he stood, Guillam was too slow. Tarr's hands were at Smiley's throat; the chair toppled and Tarr fell with him. From the heap, Guillam selected Tarr's right arm and flung it into a lock against his back, bringing it very near to breaking as he did so. From nowhere Fawn appeared, took the gun from the pillow, and walked back to Tarr as if to give him a hand. Then Smiley was straightening his suit and Tarr was back on the bed, dabbing the corner of his mouth with a handkerchief.

Smiley said, "I don't know where they are. As far as I know, no harm has come to them. You believe that, do you?"

Tarr was staring at him, waiting. His eyes were furious, but over Smiley a kind of calm had settled, and Guillam guessed it was the reassurance he had been hoping for.

"Maybe you should keep a better eye on your own damn woman and leave mine alone," Tarr whispered, his hand across his mouth. With an exclamation, Guillam sprang forward but Smiley restrained him.

"As long as you don't try to communicate with them," Smiley continued, "it's probably better that I shouldn't know. Unless you want me to do something about them. Money or protection or comfort of some sort?"

Tarr shook his head. There was blood in his mouth, a lot of it, and Guillam realised Fawn must have hit him but he couldn't work out when.

"It won't be long now," Smiley said. "Perhaps a week. Less, if I can manage it. Try not to think too much."

By the time they left, Tarr was grinning again, so Guillam guessed that the visit, or the insult to Smiley or the smash in the face, had done him good.

"Those football-pool coupons," Smiley said quietly to Fawn as they climbed into the car: "You don't post them anywhere, do you?"

"No, sir."

"Well, let's hope to God he doesn't have a win," Smiley remarked in a most unusual fit of jocularity, and there was laughter all round.

The memory plays strange tricks on an exhausted, overladen brain. As Guillam drove, one part of his conscious mind upon the road and another still wretchedly grappling with even more gothic suspicions of Camilla, odd images of this and other long days drifted freely through his memory. Days of plain terror in Morocco as one by one his agent lines went dead on him, and every footfall on the stair had him scurrying to the window to check the street; days of idleness in Brixton when he watched that poor world slip by and wondered how long before he joined it. And suddenly the written report was there before him on his desk: duplicated on blue flimsy because it was traded, source unknown, and probably unreliable, and every word of it came back to him in letters a foot high:

> According to a recently released prisoner from Lubianka, Moscow Centre held a secret execution in the punishment block in July. The victims were three of its own functionaries. One was a woman. All three were shot in the back of the neck.

"It was stamped 'internal,' " Guillam said dully. They had parked in a layby beside a roadhouse hung with fairy lights. "Somebody from London Station had scribbled on it: 'Can anyone identify the bodies?' "

By the coloured glow of the lights, Guillam watched Smiley's face pucker in disgust.

"Yes," he agreed at last. "Yes, well now, the woman was Irina, wasn't she? Then there was Ivlov and then there was Boris, her husband, I suppose." His voice remained extremely matter-of-fact. "Tarr mustn't know," he continued, as if shaking off lassitude. "It is vital that he should have no wind of this. God knows what he would do, or not do, if he knew that Irina was dead." For some moments neither moved; perhaps for their different reasons neither had the strength just then, or the heart.

"I ought to telephone," said Smiley, but he made no attempt to leave the car.

"George?"

"I have a phone call to make," Smiley muttered. "Lacon."
"Then make it."

Reaching across him, Guillam pushed open the door.
Smiley clambered, walked a distance over the tarmac, then
seemed to change his mind and came back.

"Come and eat something," he said through the window, in
the same preoccupied tone. "I don't think even Toby's people
would follow us in here."

It was once a restaurant, now a transport café with trap-
pings of old grandeur. The menu was bound in red leather
and stained with grease. The boy who brought it was half
asleep.

"I hear the *coq au vin* is always reliable," said Smiley, with
a poor effort at humour as he returned from the telephone
booth in the corner. And in a quieter voice, that fell short and
echoed nowhere: "Tell me, how much do you know about
Karla?"

"About as much as I know about Witchcraft and Source
Merlin, and whatever else it said on the paper I signed for
Porteous."

"Ah, well, now, that's a very good answer, as it happens.
You meant it as a rebuke, I expect, but as it happens, the
analogy was most apt." The boy reappeared, swinging a
bottle of Burgundy like an Indian club. "Would you please
let it breathe a little?"

The boy stared at Smiley as if he were mad.

"Open it and leave it on the table," said Guillam curtly.

It was not the whole story Smiley told. Afterwards Guillam did notice several gaps. But it was enough to lift his spirits
from the doldrums where they had strayed.

23

"It is the business of agent runners to turn themselves into legends," Smiley began, rather as if he were delivering a trainee lecture at the Nursery. "They do this first to impress their agents. Later they try it out on their colleagues and, in my personal experience, make rare asses of themselves in consequence. A few go so far as to try it on themselves. Those are the charlatans and they must be got rid of quickly, there's no other way."

Yet legends were made and Karla was one of them. Even his age was a mystery. Most likely Karla was not his real name. Decades of his life were not accounted for, and probably never would be, since the people he worked with had a way of dying off or keeping their mouths shut.

"There's a story that his father was in the Okhrana and later reappeared in the Cheka. I don't think it's true but it may be. There's another that he worked as a kitchen boy on an armoured train against Japanese Occupation troops in the East. He is said to have learnt his tradecraft from Berg—to have been his ewe lamb, in fact—which is a bit like being taught music by . . . oh, name a great composer. So far as I am concerned, his career began in Spain in 1936, because that at least is documented. He posed as a White Russian journalist in the Franco cause and recruited a stable of German agents. It was a most intricate operation, and for a young man remarkable. He popped up next in the Soviet counter-offensive against Smolensk in the autumn of 1941 as an intelligence officer under Konev. He had the job of running networks of partisans behind the German lines. Along the way he discovered that his radio operator had been turned round and was transmitting radio messages to the enemy. He turned him back and from then on played a radio game which had them going in all directions."

That was another part of the legend, said Smiley: at Yelnya, thanks to Karla, the Germans shelled their own forward line.

"And between these two sightings," he continued, "in 1936 and 1941, Karla visited Britain; we think he was here six months. But even today we don't know—that's to say, *I* don't know—under what name or cover. Which isn't to say Gerald doesn't. But Gerald isn't likely to tell us, at least not on purpose."

Smiley had never talked to Guillam this way. He was not given to confidences or long lectures; Guillam knew him as a shy man, for all his vanities, and one who expected very little of communication.

"In '48-odd, having served his country loyally, Karla did a spell in prison and later in Siberia. There was nothing personal about it. He simply happened to be in one of those sections of Red army intelligence which, in some purge or other, ceased to exist."

And certainly, Smiley went on, after his post-Stalin reinstatement, he went to America; because when the Indian authorities in the summer of '55 arrested him in Delhi on vague immigration charges, he had just flown in from California. Circus gossip later linked him with the big treason scandals in Britain and the States.

Smiley knew better: "Karla was in disgrace again. Moscow was out for his blood, and we thought we might persuade him to defect. That was why I flew to Delhi. To have a chat with him."

There was a pause while the weary boy slouched over and enquired whether everything was to their satisfaction. Smiley, with great solicitude, assured him that it was.

"The story of my meeting with Karla," he resumed, "belonged very much to the mood of the period. In the mid-fifties, Moscow Centre was in pieces on the floor. Senior officers were being shot or purged wholesale and its lower ranks were seized with a collective paranoia. As a first result, there was a crop of defections among Centre officers stationed overseas. All over the place—Singapore, Nairobi, Stockholm, Canberra, Washington, I don't know where—we got this same steady trickle from the residencies: not just the big fish, but the legmen, drivers, cypher clerks, typists. Somehow we had to respond—I don't think it's ever realised how much the industry stimulates its own inflation—and in no time I became a kind of commercial traveller, flying off one day to a capital city, the next to a dingy border outpost—once even to a ship at sea—to sign up defecting Russians. To seed, to stream, to fix the terms, to attend to debriefing and eventual disposal."

Guillam was watching him all the while, but even in that cruel neon glow Smiley's expression revealed nothing but a slightly anxious concentration.

"We evolved, you might say, three kinds of contract for those whose stories held together. If the client's access wasn't interesting, we might trade him to another country and forget him. Buy him for stock, as you would say, much as the scalphunters do today. Or we might play him back into Russia—that's assuming his defection had not already been noticed there. Or, if he was lucky, we took him; cleaned him of whatever he knew and resettled him in the West. London decided, usually. Not me. But remember this. At that time Karla—or Gerstmann, as he called himself—was just another client. I've told his story back to front; I didn't want to be coy with you, but you have to bear in mind now, through anything that happened between us—or didn't happen, which is more to the point—that all I or anyone in the Circus knew when I flew to Delhi was that a man calling himself Gerstmann had been setting up a radio link between Rudnev, head of illegal networks at Moscow Centre, and a Centre-run apparatus in California that was lying fallow for want of a means of communication. That's all. Gerstmann had smuggled a transmitter across the Canadian border and lain up for three weeks in San Francisco breaking in the new operator. That was the assumption, and there was a batch of test transmissions to back it up."

For these test transmissions between Moscow and California, Smiley explained, a book code was used: "Then, one day, Moscow signalled a straight order—"

"Still on the book code?"

"Precisely. That is the point. Owing to a temporary inattention on the part of Rudnev's cryptographers, we were ahead of the game. The wranglers broke the code and that's how we got our information. Gerstmann was to leave San Francisco at once and head for Delhi for a rendezvous with the Tass correspondent, a talent-spotter who had stumbled on a hot Chinese lead and needed immediate direction. Why they dragged him all the way from San Francisco to Delhi, why it had to be Karla and no one else—well, that's a story for another day. The only material point is that when Gerstmann kept the rendezvous in Delhi, the Tass man handed him an aeroplane ticket and told him to go straight home to Moscow. No questions. The order came from Rudnev personally. It was signed with Rudnev's workname and it was brusque even by Russian standards."

Whereupon the Tass man fled, leaving Gerstmann standing on the pavement with a lot of questions and twenty-eight hours until take-off.

"He hadn't been standing there long when the Indian authorities arrested him at our request and carted him off to Delhi jail. As far as I remember, we had promised the Indians a piece of the product. I *think* that was the deal," he remarked and, like someone suddenly shocked by the faultiness of his own memory, fell silent and looked distractedly down the steamy room. "Or perhaps we said they could have him when we'd done with him. Dear, oh dear."

"It doesn't really matter," Guillam said.

"For once in Karla's life, as I say, the Circus was ahead of him," Smiley resumed, having taken a sip of wine and made a face. "He couldn't know it but the San Francisco network which he had just serviced had been rolled up hide and hair the day he left for Delhi. As soon as Control had the story from the wranglers, he traded it to the Americans on the understanding that they missed Gerstmann but hit the rest of the Rudnev network in California. Gerstmann flew on to Delhi unaware, and he was still unaware when I arrived at Delhi jail to sell him a piece of insurance, as Control called it. His choice was very simple. There could not be the slightest doubt, on present form, that Gerstmann's head was on the block in Moscow, where to save his own neck Rudnev was busy denouncing him for blowing the San Francisco network. The affair had made a great splash in the States, and Moscow was very angry at the publicity. I had with me the American press photographs of the arrest, even of the radio set Karla had imported and the signal plans he had cached before he left. You know how prickly we all become when things get into the papers."

Guillam did; and with a jolt remembered the Testify file, which he had left with Mendel earlier that evening.

"To sum it up, Karla was the proverbial cold-war orphan. He had left home to do a job abroad. The job had blown up in his face, but he couldn't go back: home was more hostile than abroad. We had no powers of permanent arrest, so it was up to Karla to ask us for protection. I don't think I had ever come across a clearer case for defection. I had only to convince him of the arrest of the San Francisco network—wave the press photographs and cuttings from my briefcase at him—talk to him a little about the unfriendly conspiracies of Brother Rudnev in Moscow, and cable the somewhat overworked inquisitors in Sarratt, and with any luck I'd make London by the weekend. I rather think I had tickets for Sadler's Wells. It was Ann's great year for ballet."

Yes, Guillam had heard about that, too: a twenty-year-old

Welsh Apollo, the season's wonder boy. They had been burning up London for months.

The heat in the jail was appalling, Smiley continued. The cell had an iron table at the centre and iron cattle rings let into the wall. "They brought him manacled, which seemed silly because he was so slight. I asked them to free his hands and when they did, he put them on the table in front of him and watched the blood come back. It must have been painful but he didn't comment on it. He'd been there a week and he was wearing a calico tunic. Red. I forget what red meant. Some piece of prison ethic." Taking a sip of wine, he again pulled a face, then slowly corrected the gesture as the memories once more bore in upon him.

"Well, at first sight, he made little impression on me. I would have been hard put to it to recognise in the little fellow before me the master of cunning we have heard about in Irina's diary, poor woman. I suppose it's also true that my nerve-ends had been a good deal blunted by so many similar encounters in the last few months, by travel, and well by— well, by things at home."

In all the time Guillam had known him, it was the nearest Smiley had ever come to acknowledging Ann's infidelities.

"For some reason, it hurt an awful lot." His eyes were still open but his gaze had fixed upon an inner world. The skin of his brow and cheeks was drawn smooth as if by the exertion of his memory; but nothing could conceal from Guillam the loneliness evoked by this one admission. "I have a theory which I suspect is rather immoral," Smiley went on, more lightly. "Each of us has only a quantum of compassion. That if we lavish our concern on every stray cat, we never get to the centre of things. What do you think of it?"

"What did Karla look like?" Guillam asked, treating the question as rhetorical.

"Avuncular. Modest, and avuncular. He would have looked very well as a priest: the shabby, gnomic variety one sees in small Italian towns. Little wiry chap, with silvery hair and bright brown eyes and plenty of wrinkles. Or a school-master, he could have been a schoolmaster: tough—whatever that means—and sagacious within the limits of his experience; but the small canvas, all the same. He made no other initial impression, except that his gaze was straight and it fixed on me from early in our talk. If you can call it a talk, seeing that he never uttered a word. Not one, the whole time we were together; not a syllable. Also it was stinking hot and I was travelled to death."

Out of a sense of manners rather than appetite, Smiley set to work on his food, eating several mouthfuls joylessly before resuming his narrative. "There," he muttered, "that shouldn't offend the cook. The truth is, I was slightly predisposed against Mr. Gerstmann. We all have our prejudices and radio men are mine. They're a thoroughly tiresome lot, in my experience, bad fieldmen and overstrung, and disgracefully unreliable when it comes down to doing the job. Gerstmann, it seemed to me, was just another of the clan. Perhaps I'm looking for excuses for going to work on him with less"—he hesitated—"less care, less caution, than in retrospect would seem appropriate." He grew suddenly stronger. "Though I'm not at all sure I need make any excuses," he said.

Here Guillam sensed a wave of unusual anger, imparted by a ghostly smile that crossed Smiley's pale lips. "To hell with it," Smiley muttered.

Guillam waited, mystified.

"I also remember thinking that prison seemed to have taken him over very fast in seven days. He had that white dust in the skin and he wasn't sweating. I was, profusely. I trotted out my piece, as I had a dozen times that year already, except that there was obviously no question of his being played back into Russia as our agent. 'You have the alternative. It's no one else's business but your own. Come to the West and we can give you, within reason, a decent life. After questioning, at which you are expected to co-operate, we can help you to a new start, a new name, seclusion, a certain amount of money.

On the other hand, you can go home and I suppose they'll shoot you or send you to a camp. Last month they sent Bykov, Shur, and Muranov. Now why don't you tell me your real name?' Something like that. Then I sat back and wiped away the sweat and waited for him to say, 'Yes, thank you.' He did nothing. He didn't speak. He simply sat there stiff and tiny under the big fan that didn't work, looking at me with his brown, rather jolly eyes. Hands out in front of him. They were very calloused. I remember thinking I must ask him where he had been doing so much manual labour. He held them—like this—resting on the table, palms upward and fingers a little bent, as if he were still manacled."

The boy, thinking that by this gesture Smiley was indicating some want, came lumbering over, and Smiley again assured him that all was doubly well, and the wine in particular was exquisite—he really wondered where they had it from; till the boy left grinning with secret amusement and flapped his cloth at an adjoining table.

"It was then, I think, that an extraordinary feeling of unease began to creep over me. The heat was really getting to me. The stench was terrible and I remember listening to the *pat-pat* of my own sweat falling onto the iron table. It wasn't just his silence; his physical stillness began to get under my skin. Oh, I had known defectors who took time to speak. It can be a great wrench for somebody trained to secrecy even towards his closest friends suddenly to open his mouth and spill secrets to his enemies. It also crossed my mind that the prison authorities might have thought it a courtesy to soften him up before they brought him to me. They assured me they hadn't, but of course one can never tell. So at first, I put his silence down to shock. But this stillness—this intense, watchful stillness—was a different matter. Specially when everything inside me was so much in motion: Ann, my own heartbeats, the effects of heat and travel . . ."

"I can understand," said Guillam quietly.

"Can you? Sitting is an eloquent business; any actor will

tell you that. We sit according to our natures. We sprawl and straddle, we rest like boxers between rounds, we fidget, perch, cross and uncross our legs, lose patience, lose endurance. Gerstmann did none of those things. His posture was finite and irreducible, his little jagged body was like a promontory of rock; he could have sat that way all day, without stirring a muscle. Whereas I—" Breaking out in an awkward, embarrassed laugh, Smiley tasted the wine again, but it was no better than before. "Whereas I longed to have something before me—papers, a book, a report. I think I am a restless person, fussy, variable. I thought so then, anyway. I felt I lacked philosophic repose. Lacked philosophy, if you like. My work had been oppressing me much more than I realised; till now. But in that foul cell I really felt aggrieved. I felt that the entire responsibility for fighting the cold war had landed on my shoulders. Which was tripe, of course; I was just exhausted and a little bit ill." He drank again.

"I tell you," he insisted, once more quite angry with himself. "No one has any business to apologise for what I did."

"What did you do?" Guillam asked, with a laugh.

"So anyway there came this gap," Smiley resumed, disregarding the question. "Hardly of Gerstmann's making, since he was all gap; so of mine, then. I had said my piece; I had flourished the photographs, which he ignored—I may say, he appeared quite ready to take my word for it that the San Francisco network was blown. I restated this part, that part, talked a few variations, and finally I dried up. Or, rather, sat there sweating like a pig. Well, any fool knows that if ever that happens, you get up and walk out. 'Take it or leave it,' you say. 'See you in the morning'; anything. 'Go away and think for an hour.'

"As it was, the next thing I knew, I was talking about Ann." He left no time for Guillam's muffled exclamation. "Oh, not about *my* Ann, not in as many words. About *his* Ann. I assumed he had one. I had asked myself—lazily, no doubt—what would a man think of in such a situation, what would I? And my mind came up with a subjective answer: his woman. Is it called 'projection' or 'substitution'? I detest those terms but I'm sure one of them applies. I exchanged my predicament for his, that is the point, and as I now realise I began to conduct an interrogation with myself—he didn't speak, can you imagine? There were certain externals, it is true, to which I pinned the approach. He *looked* connubial; he *looked* like half a union; he *looked* too complete to be alone in all his life. Then there was his passport, describing Gerstmann as married; and it is a habit in all of us to make our cover stories, our assumed personae, at least parallel with the reality." He lapsed again into a moment of reflection. "I often thought that. I even put it to Control: we should take the opposition's cover stories more seriously, I said. The more identities a man has, the more they express the person they conceal. The fifty-year-old who knocks five years off his age. The married man who calls himself a bachelor; the fatherless man who gives himself two children . . . Or the interrogator who projects himself into the life of a man who does not speak. Few men can resist expressing their appetites when they are making a fantasy about themselves."

He was lost again, and Guillam waited patiently for him to come back. For while Smiley might have fixed his concentration upon Karla, Guillam had fixed his on Smiley; and just then would have gone anywhere with him, turned any corner, in order to remain beside him and hear the story out.

"I also knew from the American observation reports that Gerstmann was a chain-smoker: Camels. I sent out for several packs of them—'packs' is the American word?—and I remember feeling very strange as I handed money to a guard. I had the impression, you see, that Gerstmann saw something symbolic in the transaction of money between myself and the Indian. I wore a money belt in those days. I had to grope and peel off a note from a bundle. Gerstmann's gaze made me feel like a fifth-rate imperialist oppressor." He smiled. "And that I assuredly am *not*. Bill, if you like. Percy. But not I." He

called to the boy, in order to send him away: "May we have
some water, please? A jug and two glasses? Thank you."
Again he picked up the story: "So I asked him about Mrs.
Gerstmann. I asked him: where was she? It was a question I
would dearly have wished answered about Ann. No reply but
the eyes unwavering. To either side of him, the two guards,
and their eyes seemed so light by comparison. She must make a
new life, I said; there was no other way. Had he no friend he
could count on to look after her? Perhaps we could find methods of getting in touch with her secretly? I put it to him that
his going back to Moscow would do nothing for her at all.
I was listening to myself, I ran on, I couldn't stop. Perhaps I
didn't want to. I was really thinking of leaving Ann, you see; I
thought the time had come. To go back would be a quixotic
act, I told him, of no material value to his wife or anyone—
quite the reverse. She would be ostracised; at best, she would
be allowed to see him briefly before he was shot. On the other
hand, if he threw in his lot with us, we might be able to trade
her; we had a lot of stock in those days, remember, and some
of it was going back to Russia as barter; though why in God's
name we should have used it up for that purpose is beyond
me. Surely, I said, she would prefer to know him safe and well
in the West, with a fair chance that she herself would join
him, than shot or starving to death in Siberia? I really harped
upon her: his expression encouraged me. I could have sworn I
was getting through to him, that I had found the chink in his
armour; when of course all I was doing—all I was doing was
showing him the chink in mine. And when I mentioned
Siberia, I touched something. I could feel it, like a lump in my
own throat; I could feel in Gerstmann a shiver of revulsion.
Well, naturally I did," Smiley commented sourly; "since it
was only recently that he had been made an inmate. Finally,
back came the guard with the cigarettes, armfuls of them, and
dumped them with a clatter on the iron table. I counted the
change, tipped him, and in doing so again caught the expression
in Gerstmann's eyes; I fancied I read amusement there, but

really I was no longer in a state to tell. I noticed that the boy refused my tip; I suppose he disliked the English. I tore open a packet and offered Gerstmann a cigarette. 'Come,' I said, 'you're a chain-smoker, everyone knows that. And this is your favourite brand.' My voice sounded strained and silly, and there was nothing I could do about it. Gerstmann stood up and politely indicated to the warders that he would like to return to his cell."

Taking his time, Smiley pushed aside his half-eaten food, over which white flakes of fat had formed like seasonable frost.

"As he left the cell, he changed his mind and helped himself to a packet of cigarettes and the lighter from the table—my lighter, a gift from Ann. 'To George from Ann with all my love.' I would never have dreamed of letting him take it in the ordinary way; but this was not the ordinary way. Indeed I thought it thoroughly appropriate that he should take her lighter; I thought it—Lord help me—expressive of the bond between us. He dropped the lighter and the cigarettes into the pouch of his red tunic, then put out his hand for handcuffs. I said, 'Light one now, if you want.' I told the guards, 'Let him light a cigarette, please.' But he didn't make a movement. 'The intention is to put you on tomorrow's plane to Moscow unless we come to terms,' I added. He might not have heard me. I watched the guards lead him out, then returned to my hotel; someone drove me—to this day I couldn't tell you who. I no longer knew what I felt. I was more confused and more ill than I would admit, even to myself. I ate a poor dinner, drank too much, and ran a soaring temperature. I lay on my bed sweating, dreaming about Gerstmann. I wanted him terribly to stay. Lightheaded as I was, I had really set myself to keep him, to remake his life—if possible to set him up again with his wife in idyllic circumstances. To make him free; to get him out of the war for good. I wanted him desperately not to go back." He glanced up with an expression of self-irony.

"What I am saying, Peter, is it was Smiley, not Gerstmann, who was stepping out of the conflict that night."

"You were ill," Guillam insisted.

"Let us say tired. Ill or tired; all night, between aspirin and quinine and treacly visions of the Gerstmann marriage resurrected, I had a recurring image. It was of Gerstmann, poised on the sill, staring down into the street with those fixed brown eyes, and myself talking to him, on and on, 'Stay, don't jump, stay.' Not realising, of course, that I was dreaming of my own insecurity, not his. In the early morning a doctor gave me injections to bring down the fever. I should have dropped the case, cabled for a replacement. I should have waited before going to the prison, but I had nothing but Gerstmann in mind; I needed to hear his decision. By eight o'clock I was already having myself escorted to the accommodation cells. He was sitting stiff as a ramrod on a trestle bench; for the first time, I guessed the soldier in him, and I knew that, like me, he hadn't slept all night. He hadn't shaved and there was a silver down on his jaw which gave him an old man's face. On other benches Indians were sleeping, and with his red tunic and this silvery colouring he looked very white among them. He was holding Ann's lighter in his hands; the packet of cigarettes lay beside him on the bench, untouched. I concluded that he had been using the night, and the forsworn cigarettes, to decide whether he could face prison and interrogation, and death. One look at his expression told me that he had decided he could. I didn't beseech him," Smiley said, going straight on. "He would never have been swayed by histrionics. His plane left in the midmorning; I still had two hours. I am the worst advocate in the world, but in those two hours I tried to summon all the reasons I knew for his not flying to Moscow. I believed, you see, that I had seen something in his face that was superior to mere dogma, not realising that it was my own reflection. I had convinced myself that Gerstmann ultimately was accessible to ordinary human arguments coming from a man of his own age and profession and—well, durability. I didn't promise him wealth and women and Cadillacs and cheap butter; I accepted that he had no use for those things. I had the wit by then, at least, to steer clear of the topic of his wife. I didn't make speeches to him about freedom—whatever that means—or the essential good-will of the West; besides, they were not favourable days for selling that story, and I was in no clear ideological state myself. I took the line of kinship. 'Look,' I said, 'we're getting to be old men, and we've spent our lives looking for the weaknesses in one another's systems. I can see through East-ern values just as you can see through our Western ones. Both of us, I am sure, have experienced *ad nauseam* the technical satisfactions of this wretched war. But now your own side is going to shoot you. Don't you think it's time to recognise that there is as little worth on your side as there is on mine? Look,' I said, 'in our trade we have only negative vision. In that sense, neither of us has anywhere to go. Both of us when we were young subscribed to *great* visions—' Again I felt an impulse in him—Siberia—I had touched a nerve. 'But not any more. Surely?' I urged him just to answer me this: did it not occur to him that he and I by different routes might well have reached the same conclusions about life? Even if my conclu-sions were what he would call unliberated, surely our work-ings were identical? Did he not believe, for example, that the political generality was meaningless? That only the particular in life had value for him now? That in the hands of politicians grand designs achieve nothing but new forms of the old misery? And that therefore his life, the saving of it from yet another meaningless firing squad, was more important—morally, ethically more important—than the sense of duty, or obligation, or commitment, or whatever it was that kept him on this present path of self-destruction? Did it not occur to him to question—after all the travels of his life—to question the integrity of a system that proposed cold-bloodedly to shoot him down for misdemeanours he had never committed? I begged him—yes, I did beseech him, I'm afraid; we were on the way to the airport and he still had not addressed a word to me—I begged him to consider whether he really believed; whether faith in the system he had served was honestly possible to him at this moment."

For a while now, Smiley sat silent.

"I had thrown psychology to the winds, such as I possess; tradecraft, too. You can imagine what Control said. My story amused him, all the same; he loved to hear of people's weakness. Mine especially, for some reason." He had resumed his factual manner. "So there we are. When the plane arrived, I climbed aboard with him and flew part of the distance: in those days it wasn't all jet. He was slipping away from me and I couldn't do anything to stop him. I'd given up talking but I was there if he wanted to change his mind. He didn't. He would rather die than give me what I wanted; he would rather die than disown the political system to which he was committed. The last I saw of him, so far as I know, was his expressionless face framed in the cabin window of the aeroplane, watching me walk down the gangway. A couple of very Russian-looking thugs had joined us and were sitting in the seats behind him, and there was really no point in my staying. I flew home, and Control said: 'Well, I hope to God they do shoot him,' and restored me with a cup of tea. That filthy China stuff he drinks, lemon jasmine or whatever; he sends out for it to that grocer's round the corner. I mean he used to. Then he sent me on three months' leave without the option. 'I like you to have doubts,' he said. 'It tells me where you stand. But don't make a cult of them or you'll be a bore.' It was a warning. I heeded it. And he told me to stop thinking about the Americans so much; he assured me that he barely gave them a thought."

Guillam gazed at him, waiting for the resolution. "But what do *you* make of it?" he demanded, in a tone that suggested he had been cheated of the end. "Did Karla ever really think of staying?"

"I'm sure it never crossed his mind," said Smiley with disgust. "I behaved like a soft fool. The very archetype of a flabby Western liberal. But I would rather be my kind of fool than his, for all that. I am sure," he repeated vigorously, "that neither my arguments nor his own predicament at Moscow Centre would ultimately have swayed him in the least. I expect he spent the night working out how he would outgun Rudnev when he got home. Rudnev was shot a month later, incidentally. Karla got Rudnev's job and set to work reactivating his old agents. Among them Gerald, no doubt. It's odd to reflect that all the time he was looking at me, he could have been thinking of Gerald. I expect they've had a good laugh about it since."

The episode had one other result, said Smiley. Since his San Francisco experience, Karla had never once touched illegal radio. He cut it right out of his handwriting. "Embassy links are a different matter. But in the field his agents aren't allowed to go near it. And he still has Ann's cigarette lighter."

"Yours," Guillam corrected him.

"Yes. Yes, mine. Of course. Tell me," he continued, as the waiter took away his money, "was Tarr referring to anyone in particular when he made that unpleasant reference to Ann?"

"I'm afraid he was. Yes."

"The rumour is as precise as that?" Smiley enquired. "And it goes that far down the line? Even to Tarr?"

"Yes."

"And what does it say, precisely?"

"That Bill Haydon was Ann Smiley's lover," said Guillam, feeling that coldness coming over him which was his protection when he broke bad news such as: you're blown; you're sacked; you're dying.

"Ah. I see. Yes. Thank you."

There was a very awkward silence.

"And was there—is there a Mrs. Gerstmann?" Guillam asked.

"Karla once made a marriage with a girl in Leningrad, a student. She killed herself when he was sent to Siberia."

"So Karla is fireproof," Guillam asked finally. "He can't be bought and he can't be beaten?"

They returned to the car.

"I must say that was rather expensive for what we had," Smiley confessed. "Do you think the waiter robbed me?"

But Guillam was not disposed to chat about the cost of bad meals in England. Driving again, the day once more became a nightmare to him, a milling confusion of half-perceived dangers, and suspicions.

"So who's Source Merlin?" he demanded. "Where could Alleline have had that information from, if not from the Russians themselves?"

"Oh, he had it from the Russians all right."

"But for God's sake, if the Russians sent Tarr—"

"They didn't. Nor did Tarr use the British passports, did he? The Russians got it wrong. What Alleline had was the proof that Tarr had fooled them. That is the vital message we have learned from that whole storm in a teacup."

"So what the hell did Percy mean about 'muddying pools'? He must have been talking about Irina, for heaven's sake."

"And Gerald," Smiley agreed.

Again they drove in silence, and the gap between them seemed suddenly unbridgeable.

"Look, I'm not quite there myself, Peter," Smiley said quietly. "But nearly I am. Karla's pulled the Circus inside out; that much I understand, so do you. But there's a last clever knot, and I can't undo it. Though I mean to. And if you want a sermon, Karla is not fireproof, because he's a fanatic. And one day, if I have anything to do with it, that lack of moderation will be his downfall."

It was raining as they reached Stratford tube station; a bunch of pedestrians was huddled under the canopy.

"Peter, I want you to take it easy from now on."

"Three months without the option?"

"Rest on your oars a bit."

Closing the passenger door after him, Guillam had a sudden urge to wish Smiley good night or even good luck, so he leaned across the seat and lowered the window and drew in his breath to call. But Smiley was gone. He had never known anyone who could disappear so quickly in a crowd.

Through the remainder of that same night, the light in the dormer window of Mr. Barraclough's attic room at the Islay Hotel burned uninterrupted. Unchanged, unshaven, George Smiley remained bowed at the Major's card table, reading, comparing, annotating, cross-referring—all with an intensity that, had he been his own observer, would surely have recalled for him the last days of Control on the fifth floor at Cambridge Circus. Shaking the pieces, he consulted Guillam's leave rosters and sick-lists going back over the last year, and set these beside the overt travel pattern of Cultural Attaché Aleksey Aleksandrovich Polyakov, his trips to Moscow, his trips out of London, as reported to the Foreign Office by Special Branch and the immigration authorities. He compared these again with the dates when Merlin apparently supplied his information and, without quite knowing why he was doing it, broke down the Witchcraft reports into those which were demonstrably topical at the time they were received and those which could have been banked a month, two months before, either by Merlin or his controllers, in order to bridge empty periods: such as think pieces, character studies of prominent members of the administration, and scraps of Kremlin tittle-tattle which could have been picked up any time and saved for a rainless day. Having listed the topical reports, he set down their dates in a single column and threw out the rest. At this point, his mood could be best compared with that of a scientist who senses by instinct that he is on the brink of a discovery and is awaiting any minute the logical connection. Later, in conversation with Mendel, he called it "shoving everything into a test-tube and seeing if it exploded." What fascinated him most, he said, was the very point that Guillam had made regarding Alleline's grim warnings about muddied pools: he was looking, in other terms, for the "last clever knot" that Karla had tied in order to explain away the precise suspicions to which Irina's diary had given shape.

He came up with some curious preliminary findings. First, that on the nine occasions when Merlin had produced a topical report, either Polyakov had been in London or Toby Esterhase had taken a quick trip abroad. Second, that over the crucial period following Tarr's adventure in Hong Kong this year, Polyakov was in Moscow for urgent cultural consultations; and that soon afterwards Merlin came through with some of his most spectacular and topical material on the "ideological penetration" of the United States, including an appreciation of Centre's coverage of the major American intelligence targets.

Backtracking again, he established that the converse was also true: that the reports he had discarded on the grounds that they had no close attachment to recent events were those which most generally went into distribution while Polyakov was in Moscow or on leave.

And then he had it.

No explosive revelation, no flash of light, no cry of "Eureka," phone calls to Guillam, Lacon, "Smiley is a world champion." Merely that here before him, in the records he had examined and the notes he had compiled, was the corroboration of a theory which Smiley and Guillam and Ricki Tarr had that day from their separate points of view seen demonstrated: that between the mole Gerald and the Source Merlin there was an interplay which could no longer be denied; that Merlin's proverbial versatility allowed him to function as Karla's instrument as well as Alleline's. Or should he rather say, Smiley reflected—tossing a towel over his shoulder and hopping blithely into the corridor for a celebratory bath —as Karla's agent? And that at the heart of this plot lay a device so simple that it left him genuinely elated by its symmetry. It had even a physical presence: here in London, a house, paid for by the Treasury, all sixty thousand pounds of it; and often coveted, no doubt, by the many luckless tax-payers who daily passed it by, confident they could never afford it and not knowing that they had already paid for it.

It was with a lighter heart than he had known for many months that he took up the stolen file on Operation Testify.

24

To her credit, Matron had been worried about Roach all week, ever since she had spotted him alone in the washroom, ten minutes after the rest of his dormitory had gone down to breakfast, still in his pyjama trousers, hunched over a basin while he doggedly scrubbed his teeth. When she questioned him, he avoided her eye. "It's that wretched father of his," she told Thursgood. "He's getting him down again." And by the Friday: "You *must* write to the mother and tell her he's having a spell."

But not even Matron, for all her motherly perception, would have hit on plain terror as the diagnosis.

Whatever could he do—he, a child? That was his guilt. That was the threat that led directly back to the misfortune of his parents. That was the predicament that threw upon his hunched shoulders the responsibility night and day for preserving the world's peace. Roach, the watcher—"best watcher in the whole damn unit," to use Jim Prideaux's treasured words—had finally watched too well. He would have sacrificed everything he possessed—his money, his leather photograph case of his parents, whatever gave him value in the world—if it would buy him release from the knowledge that had consumed him since Sunday evening.

He had put out signals. On Sunday night, an hour after lights out, he had gone noisily to the lavatory, probed his throat, gagged, and finally vomited. But the dormitory monitor, who was supposed to wake and raise the alarm— "Matron, Roach's been sick"—slept stubbornly through the whole charade. Roach clambered miserably back to bed. From the call-box outside the staffroom next afternoon, he had dialled the menu for the day and whispered strangely into the mouthpiece, hoping to be overheard by a master and taken for mad. No one paid him any attention. He had tried mixing up reality with dreams, in the hope that the event would be converted into something he had imagined; but each morning as he passed the Dip he saw again Jim's crooked figure stooping over the spade in the moonlight; he saw the black shadow of his face under the brim of his old hat, and heard the grunt of effort as he dug.

Roach should never have been there. That also was his guilt: that the knowledge was acquired by sin. After a cello lesson on the far side of the village, he had returned to school with deliberate slowness in order to be too late for evensong, and Mrs. Thursgood's disapproving eye. The whole school was worshipping, all but himself and Jim: he heard them sing the *Te Deum* as he passed the church, taking the long route so that he could skirt the Dip, where Jim's light was glowing. Standing in his usual place, Roach watched Jim's shadow move slowly across the curtained window. He's turning in early, he decided with approval as the light suddenly went out; for Jim had recently been too absent for his taste, driving off in the Alvis after rugger and not returning till Roach was asleep. Then the trailer door opened and closed, and Jim was standing at the vegetable patch with a spade in his hand and Roach in great perplexity was wondering what on earth he should be wanting to dig for in the dark. Vegetables for his supper? For a moment Jim stood very still, listening to the *Te Deum*; then glared slowly round and straight at Roach, though he was out of sight against the blackness of the hummocks. Roach even thought of calling to him, but felt too sinful on account of missing chapel.

Finally Jim began measuring. That, at least, was how it

seemed to Roach. Instead of digging, he had knelt at one corner of the patch and laid the spade on the earth, as if aligning it with something that was out of sight to Roach: for instance, the church spire. This done, Jim strode quickly to where the blade lay, marked the spot with a thud of his heel, took up the spade, and dug fast—Roach counted twelve times—then stood back, taking stock again. From the church, silence; then prayers. Quickly stooping, Jim drew a package from the ground, which he at once smothered in the folds of his duffel coat. Seconds later, and much faster than seemed possible, the trailer door slammed, the light went on again, and in the boldest moment of his life Bill Roach tiptoed down the Dip to within three feet of the poorly curtained window, using the slope to give himself the height he needed to look in.

Jim stood at the table. On the bunk behind him lay a heap of exercise books, a vodka bottle, and an empty glass. He must have dumped them there to make space. He had a pen-knife ready but he wasn't using it. Jim would never have cut string if he could avoid it. The package was a foot long and made of yellowy stuff like a tobacco pouch. Pulling it open, he drew out what seemed to be a monkey wrench wrapped in sacking. But who would bury a monkey wrench, even for the best car England ever made? The screws or bolts were in a separate yellow envelope; he spilled them on to the table and examined each in turn. Not screws: pen-tops. Not pen-tops, either; but they had sunk out of sight.

And not a monkey wrench, not a spanner—nothing, but absolutely nothing, for the car.

Roach had blundered wildly to the brow. He was running between the hummocks, making for the drive, but running slower than he had ever run before; running through sand and deep water and dragging grass, gulping the night air, sobbing it out again, running lopsidedly like Jim, pushing now with this leg, now with the other, flailing with his head for extra speed. He had no thought for where he was heading.

All his awareness was behind him, fixed on the black revolver and the bands of chamois leather; on the pen-tops that turned to bullets as Jim threaded them methodically into the chamber, his lined face tipped towards the lamplight, pale and slightly squinting in the dazzle.

25

"I won't be quoted, George," the Minister warned, in his lounging drawl. "No minutes, no pack-drill. I got voters to deal with. You don't. Nor does Oliver Lacon, do you, Oliver?"

He had also, thought Smiley, the American violence with auxiliary verbs. "Yes, I'm sorry about that," he said.

"You'd be sorrier still if you had my constituency," the Minister retorted.

Predictably, the mere question of where they should meet had sparked a silly quarrel. Smiley had pointed out to Lacon that it would be unwise to meet at his room in Whitehall, since it was under constant attack by Circus personnel, whether janitors delivering dispatch boxes or Percy Alleline dropping in to discuss Ireland. Whereas the Minister declined both the Islay Hotel and Bywater Street, on the arbitrary grounds that they were insecure. He had recently appeared on television and was proud of being recognised. After several more calls back and forth, they settled for Mendel's semi-detached Tudor residence in Mitcham, where the Minister and his shiny car stuck out like a sore thumb. There they now sat, Lacon, Smiley, and the Minister, in the trim front room with net curtains and fresh salmon sandwiches, while their host stood upstairs watching the approaches. In the lane, children tried to make the chauffeur tell them whom he worked for.

Behind the Minister's head ran a row of books on bees. They were Mendel's passion, Smiley remembered: he used the word "exotic" for bees that did not come from Surrey. The Minister was a young man still, with a dark jowl that looked as though it had been knocked off-true in some unseemly fracas. His head was bald on top, which gave him an unwarranted air of maturity, and a terrible Eton drawl. "All right, so what are the decisions?" He also had the bully's art of dialogue.

"Well first, I suppose, you should damp down whatever recent negotiations you've been having with the Americans. I was thinking of the untitled secret annexe which you keep in your safe," said Smiley, "the one that discusses the further exploitation of Witchcraft material."

"Never heard of it," said the Minister.

"I quite understand the incentives, of course; it's always tempting to get one's hands on the cream of that enormous American service, and I can see the argument for trading them Witchcraft in return."

"So what are the arguments *against?*" the Minister enquired as if he were talking to his stockbroker.

"If the mole Gerald exists," Smiley began. Of all her cousins, Ann had once said proudly, only Miles Sercombe was without a single redeeming feature. For the first time, Smiley really believed she was right. He felt not only idiotic but incoherent. "If the mole exists, which I assume is common ground among us . . ." He waited, but no one said it wasn't. "If the mole exists," he repeated, "it's not only the Circus that will double its profits by the American deal. Moscow Centre will, too, because they'll get from the mole whatever you buy from the Americans."

In a gesture of frustration, the Minister slapped his hand on Mendel's table, leaving a moist imprint on the polish.

"God damn it, I do *not* understand," he declared. "That

Witchcraft stuff is bloody marvellous! A month ago it was buying us the moon. Now we're disappearing up our orifices and saying the Russians are cooking it for us. What the hell's happening?"

"Well, I don't think that's quite as illogical as it sounds, as a matter of fact. After all, we've run the odd Russian network from time to time, and though I say it myself we ran them rather well. We gave them the best material we could afford. Rocketry, war planning. You were in on that yourself"—this to Lacon, who threw a jerky nod of agreement. "We tossed them agents we could do without; we gave them good communications, safed their courier links, cleared the air for their signals so that we could listen to them. That was the price we paid for running the opposition—what was your expression? —'for knowing how they briefed their commissars.' I'm sure Karla would do as much for us if he was running our networks. He'd do more, wouldn't he, if he had his eye on the American market, too?" He broke off and glanced at Lacon. "Much, much more. An American connection—a big American dividend, I mean—would put the mole Gerald *right* at the top table. The Circus, too, by proxy of course. As a Russian, one would give almost anything to the English if . . . well, if one could buy the Americans in return."

"Thank you," said Lacon quickly.

The Minister left, taking a couple of sandwiches with him to eat in the car and failing to say goodbye to Mendel, presumably because he was not a constituent.

Lacon stayed behind.

"You asked me to look out for anything on Prideaux," he announced at last. "Well, I find that we do have a few papers on him, after all."

He had happened to be going through some files on the internal security of the Circus, he explained, "Simply to clear my decks." Doing so, he had stumbled on some old positive vetting reports. One of them related to Prideaux.

"He was cleared absolutely, you understand. Not a

shadow. However"—an odd inflexion of his voice caused Smiley to glance at him—"I think it might interest you, all the same. Some tiny murmur about his time at Oxford. We're all entitled to be a bit pink at that age."

"Indeed, yes."

The silence returned, broken only by the soft tread of Mendel upstairs.

"Prideaux and Haydon were really very close indeed, you know," Lacon confessed. "I hadn't realised."

He was suddenly in a great hurry to leave. Delving in his briefcase, he hauled out a large plain envelope, thrust it into Smiley's hand, and went off to the prouder world of White-hall; and Mr. Barraclough to the Islay Hotel, where he returned to his reading of Operation Testify.

26

It was lunchtime next day. Smiley had read and slept a little, read again and bathed, and as he climbed the steps to that pretty London house he felt pleased, because he liked Sam.

The house was brown brick and Georgian, just off Grosvenor Square. There were five steps and a brass doorbell in a scalloped recess. The door was black, with pillars either side. He pushed the bell and he might as well have pushed the door; it opened at once. He entered a circular hallway with another door the other end, and two large men in black suits who might have been ushers at Westminster Abbey. Over a marble chimney-piece, horses pranced and they might have been Stubbs. One man stood close while he took off his coat; the second led him to a Bible desk to sign the book.

"Hebden," Smiley murmured as he wrote, giving a work-name Sam could remember. "Adrian Hebden."

The man who had his coat repeated the name into a house telephone: "Mr. Hebden—Mr. Adrian Hebden."

"If you wouldn't mind waiting one second, sir," said the man by the Bible desk. There was no music, and Smiley had the feeling there should have been; also a fountain.

"I'm a friend of Mr. Collins's, as a matter of fact," said Smiley. "If Mr. Collins is available. I think he may even be expecting me."

The man at the telephone murmured, "Thank you," and hung it on the hook. He led Smiley to the inner door and pushed it open. It made no sound at all, not even a rustle on the silk carpet.

"Mr. Collins is over there, sir," he murmured respectfully. "Drinks are with the courtesy of the house."

The three reception rooms had been run together, with pillars and arches to divide them optically, and mahogany panelling. In each room was one table, the third was sixty feet away. The lights shone on meaningless pictures of fruit in colossal gold frames, and on the green baize tablecloths. The curtains were drawn, the tables about one third occupied, four or five players to each, all men, but the only sounds were the click of the ball in the wheel, the click of the chips as they were redistributed, and the very low murmur of the croupiers.

"Adrian Hebden," said Sam Collins, with a twinkle in his voice. "Long time no see."

"Hullo, Sam," said Smiley, and they shook hands.

"Come down to my lair," said Sam, and nodded to the only other man in the room who was standing, a very big man with blood pressure and a chipped face. The big man nodded, too.

"Care for it?" Sam enquired as they crossed a corridor draped in red silk.

"It's very impressive," said Smiley politely.

"That's the word," said Sam. "Impressive. That's what it is." He was wearing a dinner jacket. His office was done in Edwardian plush, his desk had a marble top and ball-and-claw feet, but the room itself was very small and not at all well ventilated—more like the back room of a theatre, Smiley thought, furnished with leftover props.

"They might even let me put in a few pennies of my own later, give it another year. They're toughish boys, but very go-ahead, you know."

"I'm sure," said Smiley.

"Like we were in the old days."

"That's right."

He was trim and lighthearted in his manner and he had a trim black moustache. Smiley couldn't imagine him without it. He was probably fifty. He had spent a lot of time out East, where they had once worked together on a catch-and-carry job against a Chinese radio operator. His complexion and hair were greying but he still looked thirty-five. His smile was warm and he had a confiding, messroom friendliness. He kept both hands on the table as if he were at cards, and he looked at Smiley with a possessive fondness that was paternal or filial or both.

"If chummy goes over five," he said, still smiling, "give me a buzz, Harry, will you? Otherwise keep your big mouth shut; I'm chatting up an oil king." He was talking into a box on his desk. "Where is he now?"

"Three up," said a gravel voice. Smiley guessed it belonged to the chipped man with blood pressure.

"Then he's got eight to lose," said Sam blandly. "Keep him at the table, that's all. Make a hero of him." He switched off and grinned. Smiley grinned back.

"Really, it's a great life," Sam assured him. "Better than selling washing machines, anyway. Bit odd, of course, putting on the dinner jacket at ten in the morning. Reminds one of diplomatic cover." Smiley laughed. "Straight, too, believe it or not," Sam added with no change to his expression. "We get all the help we need from the arithmetic."

"I'm sure you do," said Smiley, once more with great politeness.

"Care for some music?"

It was canned and came out of the ceiling. Sam turned it up as loud as they could bear.

"So what can I do you for?" Sam asked, the smile broadening.

"I want to talk to you about the night Jim Prideaux was shot. You were duty officer."

Sam smoked brown cigarettes that smelt of cigar. Lighting one, he let the end catch fire, then watched it die to an ember. "Writing your memoirs, old boy?" he enquired.

"We're reopening the case."

"What's this *we*, old boy?"

"I, myself, and me, with Lacon pushing and the Minister pulling."

"All power corrupts but some must govern, and in that case Brother Lacon will reluctantly scramble to the top of the heap."

"It hasn't changed," said Smiley.

Sam drew ruminatively on his cigarette. The music switched to phrases of Noël Coward.

"It's a dream of mine, actually," said Sam Collins through the smoke. "One of these days Percy Alleline walks through that door with a shabby brown suitcase and asks for a flutter. He puts the whole of the secret vote on red and loses."

"The record's been filleted," said Smiley. "It's a matter of going to people and asking what they remember. There's almost nothing on file at all."

"I'm not surprised," said Sam. Over the phone he ordered sandwiches. "Live on them," he explained. "Sandwiches and canapés. One of the perks."

He was pouring coffee when the red pinlight glowed between them on the desk.

"Chummy's even," said the gravel voice.

"Then start counting," said Sam, and closed the switch.

He told it plainly but precisely, the way a good soldier recalls a battle, not to win or lose any more, but simply to remember. He had just come back from abroad, he said; a three-year stint in Vientiane. He'd checked in with personnel and cleared himself with the Dolphin; no one seemed to have any plans for him, so he was thinking of taking off for the South of France for a month's leave when MacFadean, that old janitor who was practically Control's valet, scooped him up in the corridor and marched him to Control's room.

"This was which day, exactly?" said Smiley.

"October 19th."

"The Thursday."

"The Thursday. I was thinking of flying to Nice on Monday. You were in Berlin. I wanted to buy you a drink but the mothers said you were *occupé*, and when I checked with Movements they told me you'd gone to Berlin."

"Yes, that's true," Smiley said simply. "Control sent me there."

To get me out of the way, he might have added; it was a feeling he had had even at the time.

"I hunted round for Bill but Bill was also in baulk. Control had packed him up-country somewhere," said Sam, avoiding Smiley's eye.

"On a wild goose chase," Smiley murmured. "But he came back."

Here Sam tipped a sharp, quizzical glance in Smiley's direction, but he added nothing on the subject of Bill Haydon's journey.

"The whole place seemed dead. Damn nearly caught the first plane back to Vientiane."

"It pretty much *was* dead," Smiley confessed, and thought, Except for Witchcraft.

And Control, said Sam, looked as though he'd had a five-day fever. He was surrounded by a sea of files, his skin was yellow, and as he talked he kept breaking off to wipe his forehead with a handkerchief. He scarcely bothered with the usual fan-dance at all, said Sam. He didn't congratulate him on three good years in the field, or make some snide reference to his private life, which was at that time messy; he simply said he wanted Sam to do weekend duty instead of Mary Masterman; could Sam swing it?

" 'Sure I can swing it,' I said. 'If you want me to do duty officer, I'll do it.' He said he'd give me the rest of the story on Saturday. Meanwhile I must tell no one. I mustn't give a hint anywhere in the building, even that he'd asked me this one thing. He needed someone good to man the switchboard in case there was a crisis, but it had to be someone from an outstation or someone like me who'd been away from head office for a long time. And it had to be an old hand."

So Sam went to Mary Masterman and sold her a hard-luck story about not being able to get the tenant out of his flat before he went on leave on Monday; how would it be if he did her duty for her and saved himself the hotel? He took over at nine on Saturday morning with his toothbrush and six cans of beer in a briefcase, which still had palm-tree stickers on the side. Geoff Agate was slated to relieve him on Sunday evening.

Once again Sam dwelt on how dead the place was. Back in the old days, Saturdays were much like any other day, he said. Most regional sections had a deskman working weekends, some even had night staff, and when you took a tour of the building you had the feeling that, warts and all, this was an outfit that had a lot going. But that Saturday morning the building might have been evacuated, said Sam; which in a way, from what he heard later, it had been—on orders from Control. A couple of wranglers toiled on the second floor; the radio and code rooms were going strong, but those boys worked all the hours anyway. Otherwise, said Sam, it was the big silence. He sat around waiting for Control to ring but nothing happened. He fleshed out another hour teasing the janitors, whom he reckoned the idlest lot of so-and-so's in the Circus. He checked their attendance lists and found two typists and one desk officer marked in but absent, so he put the head janitor, a new boy called Mellows, on report. Finally he went upstairs to see if Control was in.

"He was sitting all alone, except for MacFadean. No mothers, no you—just old Mac peeking around with jasmine tea and sympathy. Too much?"

"No, just go on, please. As much detail as you can remember."

"So then Control peeled off another veil. Half a veil. Someone was doing a special job for him, he said. It was of great importance to the service. He kept saying that: to the service. Not Whitehall or sterling or the price of fish, but us. Even when it was all over, I must never breathe a word about it. Not even to you. Or Bill or Bland or anyone."

"Nor Alleline?"

"He never mentioned Percy once."

"No," Smiley agreed. "He scarcely could at the end."

"I should regard him, for the night, as Director of Operations. I should see myself as cut-out between Control and whatever was going on in the rest of the building. If anything came in—a signal, a phone call, however trivial it seemed—I should wait till the coast was clear, then whip upstairs and hand it to Control. No one was to know, now or later, that Control was the man behind the gun. In no case should I phone him or minute him; even the internal lines were taboo. Truth, George," said Sam, helping himself to a sandwich.

"Oh, I do believe you," said Smiley with feeling.

If outgoing telegrams had to be sent, Sam should once more act as Control's cut-out. He need not expect much to happen till this evening; even then it was most unlikely anything would happen. As to the janitors and people like that, as Control put it, Sam should do his damnedest to act natural and look busy.

The séance over, Sam returned to the duty room, sent out for an evening paper, opened a can of beer, selected an outside telephone line, and set about losing his shirt. There was steeplechasing at Kempton, which he hadn't watched for years. Early evening, he took another walk around the lines and tested the alarm pads on the floor of the general registry.

Three out of fifteen didn't work, and by this time the janitors were really loving him. He cooked himself an egg, and when he'd eaten it he trotted upstairs to take a pound off old Mac and give him a beer.

"He'd asked me to put him a quid on some nag with three left feet. I chatted with him for ten minutes, went back to my post, wrote some letters, watched a rotten movie on the telly, then turned in. The first call came just as I was getting to sleep. Eleven-twenty, exactly. The phones didn't stop ringing for the next ten hours. I thought the switchboard was going to blow up in my face."

"Arcadi's five down," said a voice over the box.

"Excuse me," said Sam, with his habitual grin and, leaving Smiley to the music, slipped upstairs to cope.

Sitting alone, Smiley watched Sam's brown cigarette slowly burning away in the ashtray. He waited, Sam didn't return, and he wondered whether he should stub it out. Not allowed to smoke on duty, he thought; house rules.

"All done," said Sam.

The first call came from the Foreign Office resident clerk on the direct line, said Sam. In the Whitehall stakes, you might say, the Foreign Office won by a curled lip.

"The Reuters headman in London had just called him with a story of a shooting in Prague. A British spy had been shot dead by Russian security forces, there was a hunt out for his accomplices, and was the F.O. interested? The duty clerk was passing it to us for information. I said it sounded bunkum, and rang off just as Mike Meakin, of wranglers, came through to say that all hell had broken out on the Czech air: half of it was coded, but the other half was *en clair*. He kept getting garbled accounts of a shooting near Brno. Prague or Brno? I asked. Or both? Just Brno. I said keep listening, and by then all five buzzers were going. Just as I was leaving the room, the resident clerk came back on the direct. The Reuters man had corrected his story, he said: for Prague read Brno. I closed the door and it was like leaving a wasps' nest in your drawing-room. Control was standing at his desk as I came in. He'd heard me coming up the stairs. Has Alleline put a carpet on those stairs, by the way?"

"No," said Smiley. He was quite impassive. "George is like a swift," Ann had once told Haydon in his hearing. "He cuts down his body temperature till it's the same as the environment. Then he doesn't lose energy adjusting."

"You know how quick he was when he looked at you. He checked my hands to see whether I had a telegram for him, and I wished I'd been carrying something but they were empty. 'I'm afraid there's a bit of a panic,' I said. I gave him the gist, he looked at his watch; I suppose he was trying to work out what should have been happening if everything had been plain sailing. I said, 'Can I have a brief, please?' He sat down; I couldn't see him too well—he had that low green light on his desk. I said again, 'I'll need a brief. Do you want me to deny it? Why don't I get someone in?' No answer. Mind you, there wasn't anyone to get, but I didn't know that yet. 'I must have a brief.' We could hear footsteps downstairs and I knew the radio boys were trying to find me. 'Do you want to come down and handle it yourself?' I said. I went round to the other side of the desk, stepping over these files, all open at different places; you'd think he was compiling an encyclopaedia. Some of them must have been pre-war. He was sitting like this."

Sam bunched the fingers of one hand, put the tips to his forehead, and stared at the desk. His other hand was laid flat, holding Control's imaginary fob watch. " 'Tell MacFadean to get me a cab, then find Smiley.' 'What about the operation?' I asked. I had to wait all night for an answer. 'It's deniable,' he says. 'Both men had foreign documents. No one could know they were British at this stage.' 'They're only talking about one man,' I said. Then I said, 'Smiley's in Berlin.' That's what I think I said, anyway. So we have another two-minute silence. 'Anyone will do. It makes no difference.' I should have been sorry for him, I suppose, but just then I couldn't raise much sympathy. I was having to hold the baby and I didn't know a damn thing. MacFadean wasn't around so I reckoned Control could find his own cab, and by the time I got to the bottom of the steps I must have looked like Gordon at Khartoum. The duty harridan from monitoring was waving bulletins at me like flags, a couple of janitors were yelling at me, the radio boy was clutching a bunch of signals, the phones were going—not just my own, but half a dozen of the direct lines on the fourth floor. I went straight to the duty room and switched off all the lines while I tried to get my bearings. The monitor—what's that woman's name, for God's sake, used to play bridge with the Dolphin?"

"Purcell. Molly Purcell."

"That's the one. Her story was at least straightforward. Prague radio was promising an emergency bulletin in half an hour's time. That was quarter of an hour ago. The bulletin would concern an act of gross provocation by a Western power, an infringement of Czechoslovakia's sovereignty, and an outrage against freedom-loving people of all nations. Apart from that," said Sam dryly, "it was going to be laughs all the way. I rang Bywater Street, of course; then I made a signal to Berlin telling them to find you and fly you back by yesterday. I gave Mellows the main phone numbers and sent him off to find an outside line and get hold of whoever was around of the top brass. Percy was in Scotland for the weekend and out to dinner. His cook gave Mellows a number; he rang it, spoke to his host. Percy had just left."

"I'm sorry," Smiley interrupted. "Rang Bywater Street, what for?" He was holding his upper lip between his finger and thumb, pulling it out like a deformity, while he stared into the middle distance.

"In case you'd come back early from Berlin," said Sam.

"And had I?"

"No."

"So who did you speak to?"

"Ann."

Smiley said, "Ann's away just now. Could you remind me how it went, that conversation?"

"I asked for you and she said you were in Berlin."

"And that was all?"

"It was a crisis, George," Sam said, in a warning tone.

"So?"

"I asked her whether by any chance she knew where Bill Haydon was. It was urgent. I gathered he was on leave but might be around. Somebody once told me they were cousins." He added: "Besides, he's a friend of the family, I understood."

"Yes. He is. What did she say?"

"Gave me a shirty '*no*' and rang off. Sorry about that, George. War's war."

"How did she sound?" Smiley asked, after letting the aphorism lie between them for some while.

"I told you: shirty."

Roy Bland was at Leeds University talent-spotting, said Sam, and not available.

Between calls, Sam was getting the whole book thrown at him. He might as well have invaded Cuba. The military were yelling about Czech tank movements along the Austrian border; the wranglers couldn't hear themselves think for the radio traffic round Brno; and as for the Foreign Office, the resident clerk was having the vapours and yellow fever all in one. "First Lacon, then the Minister were baying at the doors, and at half past twelve we had the promised Czech news bulletin, twenty minutes late but none the worse for that. A British spy named Jim Ellis, travelling on false Czech papers and assisted by Czech counter-revolutionaries, had attempted to kidnap an unnamed Czech general in the forests near Brno and smuggle him over the Austrian border. Ellis had been shot but they didn't say killed; other arrests were imminent. I looked Ellis up in the workname index and found

Jim Prideaux. And I thought, just as Control must have thought, If Jim is shot and has Czech papers, how the hell do they know his workname, and how do they know he's British? Then Bill Haydon arrived, white as a sheet. Picked up the story on the ticker-tape at his club. He turned straight round and came to the Circus."

"At what time was that, exactly?" Smiley asked, with a vague frown. "It must have been rather late."

Sam looked as if he wished he could make it easier. "One-fifteen," he said.

"Which is late, isn't it, for reading club ticker-tapes."

"Not my world, old boy."

"Bill's the Savile, isn't he?"

"Don't know," said Sam doggedly. He drank some coffee. "He was a treat to watch, that's all I can tell you. I used to think of him as an erratic sort of devil. Not that night, believe me. All right, he was shaken. Who wouldn't be? He arrived knowing there'd been a God-awful shooting party and that was about all. But when I told him that it was Jim who'd been shot, he looked at me like a madman. Thought he was going to go for me. 'Shot. Shot how? Shot dead?' I shoved the bulletins into his hand and he tore through them one by one—"

"Wouldn't he have known already from the ticker-tape?" Smiley asked, in a small voice. "I thought the news was every-where by then: Ellis shot. That was the lead story, wasn't it?"

"Depends which news bulletin he saw, I suppose," Sam shrugged it off. "Anyway, he took over the switchboard and by morning he'd picked up what few pieces there were and introduced something pretty close to calm. He told the For-eign Office to sit tight and hold its water; he got hold of Toby Esterhase and sent him off to pull in a brace of Czech agents, students at the London School of Economics. Bill had been letting them hatch till then; he was planning to turn them round and play them back into Czecho. Toby's lamplighters sandbagged the pair of them and locked them up in Sarratt. Then Bill rang the Czech head resident in London and spoke to him like a sergeant major: threatened to strip him so bare he'd be the laughing-stock of the profession if a hair of Jim Prideaux's head was hurt. He invited him to pass that on to his masters. I felt I was watching a street accident and Bill was the only doctor. He rang a press contact and told him in strict confidence that Ellis was a Czech mercenary with an American contract; he could use the story unattributably. It actually made the late editions. Soon as he could, he slid off to Jim's rooms to make sure he'd left nothing around that a journalist might pick on if a journalist were clever enough to make the connection, Ellis to Prideaux. I guess he did a thorough cleaning-up job. Dependents, everything."

"There weren't any dependents," Smiley said. "Apart from Bill, I suppose," he added, half under his breath.

Sam wound it up: "At eight o'clock Percy Alleline arrived; he'd cadged a special plane off the Air Force. He was grinning all over. I didn't think that was very clever of him, considering Bill's feelings, but there you are. He wanted to know why I was doing duty, so I gave him the same story I'd given to Mary Masterman: no flat. He used my phone to make a date with the Minister, and was still talking when Roy Bland came in, hopping mad and half plastered, wanting to know who the hell had been messing on his patch and practically accusing me. I said, 'Christ, man, what about old Jim? You could pity him while you were about it,' but Roy's a hungry boy and likes the living better than the dead. I gave him the switchboard with my love, went down to the Savoy for breakfast, and read the Sundays. The most any of them did was run the Prague radio reports and a pooh-pooh denial from the Foreign Office."

Finally Smiley said, "After that you went to the South of France?"

"For two lovely months."

"Did anyone question you again—about Control, for instance?"

"Not till I got back. You were out on your ear by then; Control was ill in hospital." Sam's voice deepened a little. "He didn't do anything *silly*, did he?"

"He just died. What happened?"

"Percy was acting head boy. He called for me and wanted to know why I'd done duty for Masterman and what communication I'd had with Control. I stuck to my story and Percy called me a liar."

"So that's what they sacked you for: lying?"

"Alcoholism. The janitors got a bit of their own back. They'd counted five beer cans in the waste-basket in the duty officer's lair and reported it to the housekeepers. There's a standing order: no booze on the premises. In the due process of time, a disciplinary body found me guilty of setting fire to the Queen's dockyards so I joined the bookies. What happened to you?"

"Oh, much the same. I didn't seem to be able to convince them I wasn't involved."

"Well, if you want anyone's throat cut," said Sam as he saw him quietly out through a side door into a pretty mews, "give me a buzz." Smiley was sunk in thought. "And if you ever want a flutter," Sam went on, "bring along some of Ann's smart friends."

"Sam, listen. Bill was making love to Ann that night. No, listen. You phoned her, she told you Bill wasn't there. As soon as she'd rung off, she pushed Bill out of bed and he turned up at the Circus an hour later knowing that there had been a shooting in Czecho. If you were giving me the story from the shoulder—on a postcard—that's what you'd say?"

"Broadly."

"But you didn't tell Ann about Czecho when you phoned her—"

"He stopped at his club on the way to the Circus."

"If it was open. Very well: then why didn't he know that Jim Prideaux had been shot?"

In the daylight, Sam looked briefly old, though the grin had not left his face. He seemed about to say something, then changed his mind. He seemed angry, then thwarted, then blank again. "Cheeribye," he said. "Mind how you go," and withdrew to the permanent night-time of his elected trade.

27

When Smiley had left the Islay for Grosvenor Square that morning, the streets had been bathed in harsh sunshine and the sky was blue. Now as he drove the hired Rover past the unlovable façades of the Edgware Road, the wind had dropped, the sky was black with waiting rain, and all that remained of the sun was a lingering redness on the tarmac. He parked in St. John's Wood Road, in the forecourt of a new tower block with a glass porch, but he did not enter by the porch. Passing a large sculpture describing, as it seemed to him, nothing but a sort of cosmic muddle, he made his way through icy drizzle to a descending outside staircase marked "Exit Only." The first flight was of terrazzo tile and had a bannister of African teak. Below that, the contractor's generosity ceased. Rough-rendered plaster replaced the earlier luxury and a stench of uncollected refuse crammed the air. His manner was cautious rather than furtive, but when he reached the iron door he paused before putting both hands to the long handle and drew himself together as if for an ordeal. The door opened a foot and stopped with a thud, to be answered by a shout of fury, which echoed many times like a shout in a swimming pool.

"Hey, why you don't look out once?"

Smiley edged through the gap. The door had stopped against the bumper of a very shiny car, but Smiley wasn't looking at the car. Across the garage two men in overalls were hosing down a Rolls-Royce in a cage. Both were looking in his direction.

"Why you don't come other way?" the same angry voice demanded. "You tenant here? Why you don't use tenant lift? This stair for fire."

It was not possible to tell which of them was speaking, but whichever it was, he spoke in a heavy Slav accent. The light in the cage was behind them. The shorter man held the hose.

Smiley walked forward, taking care to keep his hands clear of his pockets. The man with the hose went back to work, but the taller stayed watching him through the gloom. He wore white overalls and he had turned the collar-points upwards, which gave him a rakish air. His black hair was swept back and full.

"I'm not a tenant, I'm afraid," Smiley conceded. "But I wonder if I might just speak to someone about renting a space. My name's *Carmichael*," he explained, in a louder voice. "I've bought a flat up the road."

He made a gesture as if to produce a card, as if his documents would speak better for him than his insignificant appearance. "I'll pay in advance," he promised. "I could sign a contract or whatever is necessary, I'm sure. I'd want it to be above-board, naturally. I can give references, pay a deposit, anything within reason. As long as it's above-board. It's a Rover. A new one. I won't go behind the company's back, because I don't believe in it. But I'll do anything else within reason. I'd have brought it down, but I didn't want to presume. And—well, I know it sounds silly but I didn't like the look of the ramp. It's so new, you see."

Throughout this protracted statement of intent, which he delivered with an air of fussy concern, Smiley had remained in the downbeam of a bright light strung from the rafter: a supplicant, rather abject figure, one might have thought, and easily visible across the open space. The attitude had its effect. Leaving the cage, the white figure strode towards a glazed kiosk, built between two iron pillars, and with his fine head beckoned Smiley to follow. As he went, he pulled the gloves off his hands. They were leather gloves, hand-stitched and quite expensive.

"Well, you want mind out how you open door," he warned in the same loud voice. "You want use lift, see, or maybe you pay couple pounds. Use lift you don't make no trouble."

"Max, I want to talk to you," said Smiley once they were inside the kiosk. "Alone. Away from here."

Max was broad and powerful with a pale boy's face, but the skin of it was lined like an old man's. He was handsome and his brown eyes were very still. He had altogether a rather deadly stillness.

"Now? You want talk now?"

"In the car. I've got one outside. If you walk to the top of the ramp, you can get straight into it."

Putting his hand to his mouth, Max yelled across the garage. He was half a head taller than Smiley and had a roar like a drum major's. Smiley couldn't catch the words. Possibly they were Czech. There was no answer, but Max was already unbuttoning his overall.

"It's about Jim Prideaux," Smiley said.

"Sure," said Max.

They drove up to Hampstead and sat in the shiny Rover, watching the kids breaking the ice on the pond. Real rain had held off, after all; perhaps because it was so cold.

Above ground Max wore a blue suit and a blue shirt. His tie was blue but carefully differentiated from the other blues: he had taken a lot of trouble to get the shade. He wore several rings and flying boots with zips at the side.

"I'm not in it any more. Did they tell you?" Smiley asked. Max shrugged. "I thought they would have told you," Smiley said.

Max was sitting straight; he didn't use the seat to lean on;

he was too proud. He did not look at Smiley. His eyes were turned fixedly to the pool and the kids fooling and skidding in the reeds.

"They don't tell me nothing," he said.

"I was sacked," said Smiley. "I guess at about the same time as you."

Max seemed to stretch slightly, then settle again. "Too bad, George. What you do, steal money?"

"I don't want them to know, Max."

"You private—I private, too," said Max, and from a gold case offered Smiley a cigarette, which he declined.

"I want to hear what happened," Smiley went on. "I wanted to find out before they sacked me but there wasn't time."

"That why they sack you?"

"Maybe."

"You don't know so much, huh?" said Max, his gaze nonchalantly on the kids.

Smiley spoke very simply, watching all the while in case Max didn't understand. They could have spoken German but Max wouldn't have that, he knew. So he spoke English and watched Max's face.

"I don't know anything, Max. I had no part in it at all. I was in Berlin when it happened; I knew nothing of the planning or the background. They cabled me, but when I arrived in London it was too late."

"Planning," Max repeated. "That was some planning." His jaw and cheeks became suddenly a mass of lines and his eyes turned narrow, making a grimace or a smile. "So now you got plenty time, eh, George? Jesus, that was some planning."

"Jim had a special job to do. He asked for you."

"Sure. Jim ask for Max to baby-sit."

"How did he get you? Did he turn up in Acton and speak to Toby Esterhase, and say, 'Toby, I want Max?' How did he get you?"

Max's hands were resting on his knees. They were groomed

and slender—all but the knuckles, which were very broad. Now, at the mention of Esterhase, he turned the palms slightly inwards and made a light cage of them as if he had caught a butterfly.

"What the hell?" Max asked.

"So what did happen?"

"Was private," said Max. "Jim private, I private. Like now."

"Come," said Smiley. "Please."

Max spoke as if it were any mess: family or business or love. It was a Monday evening in mid-October—yes, the sixteenth. It was a slack time, he hadn't been abroad for weeks, and he was fed up. He had spent all day making a reconnaissance of a house in Bloomsbury where a pair of Chinese students was supposed to live; the lamplighters were thinking of mounting a burglary against their rooms. He was on the point of returning to the Laundry in Acton to write his report when Jim picked him up in the street with a chance-encounter routine and drove him up to Crystal Palace, where they sat in the car and talked, like now, except they spoke Czech. Jim said there was a special job going, something so big, so secret that no one else in the Circus, not even Toby Esterhase, was allowed to know that it was taking place. It came from the very top of the tree and it was hairy. Was Max interested?

"I say, 'Sure, Jim. Max interested.' Then he ask me: 'Take leave. You go to Toby, you say, Toby, my mother sick, I got to take some leave.' I don't got no mother. 'Sure,' I say, 'I take leave. How long for, please, Jim?' "

The whole job shouldn't last more than the weekend, said Jim. They should be in on Saturday and out on Sunday. Then he asked Max whether he had any current identities running for him: best would be Austrian, small trade, with driving licence to match. If Max had none handy at Acton, Jim would get something put together in Brixton.

"Sure, I say. I have Hartmann, Rudi, from Linz, Sudeten émigré."

So Max gave Toby a story about girl trouble up in Brad-ford and Toby gave Max a ten-minute lecture on the sexual mores of the English; and on the Thursday, Jim and Max met in a safe house that the scalp-hunters ran in those days, a rackety old place in Lambeth. Jim had brought the keys. A three-day hit, Jim repeated; a clandestine conference outside Brno. Jim had a big map and they studied it. Jim would travel Czech, Max would go Austrian. They would make their separate ways as far as Brno. Jim would fly from Paris to Prague, then train from Prague. He didn't say what papers he would be carrying himself, but Max presumed Czech because Czech was Jim's other side; Max had seen him use it before. Max was Hartmann Rudi, trading in glass and ovenware. He was to cross the Austrian border by van near Mikulov, then head north to Brno, giving himself plenty of time to make a six-thirty rendezvous on Saturday evening in a side street near the football ground. There was a big match that evening start-ing at seven. Jim would walk with the crowd as far as the side street, then climb into the van. They agreed times, fallbacks, and the usual contingencies; and besides, said Max, they knew each other's handwriting by heart.

Once out of Brno, they were to drive together along the Bilovice road as far as Krtiny, then turn east towards Racice. Somewhere along the Racice road they would pass on the left side a parked black car, most likely a Fiat. The first two figures of the registration would be 99. The driver would be reading a newspaper. They would pull up; Max would go over and ask whether he was all right. The man would reply that his doctor had forbidden him to drive more than three hours at a stretch. Max would say it was true that long journeys were a strain on the heart. The driver would then show them where to park the van and take them to the rendezvous in his own car.

"Who were you meeting, Max? Did Jim tell you that as well?"

No, that was all Jim told him.

As far as Brno, said Max, things went pretty much as planned. Driving from Mikulov, he was followed for a while by a couple of civilian motorcyclists who interchanged every ten minutes, but he put that down to his Austrian number plates and it didn't bother him. He made Brno comfortably by mid-afternoon, and to keep things shipshape he booked into the hotel and drank a couple of coffees in the restaurant. Some stooge picked him up and Max talked to him about the vicissitudes of the glass trade and about his girl in Linz who'd gone off with an American. Jim missed the first rendezvous but he made the fallback an hour later. Max supposed at first the train was late, but Jim just said, "Drive slowly," and he knew then that there was trouble.

This was how it was going to work, said Jim. There'd been a change of plan. Max was to stay right out of it. He should drop Jim short of the rendezvous, then lie up in Brno till Monday morning. He was not to make contact with any of the Circus's trade routes: no one from Aggravate, no one from Plato, least of all with the Prague residency. If Jim didn't surface at the hotel by eight on Monday morning, Max should get out any way he could. If Jim did surface, Max's job would be to carry Jim's message to Control: the message could be very simple; it might be no more than one word. When he got to London, he should go to Control personally, make an appointment through old MacFadean, and give him the message—was that clear? If Jim didn't show up, Max should take up life where he left off and deny everything, inside the Circus as well as out.

"Did Jim say why the plan had changed?"

"Jim worried."

"So something had happened to him on his way to meet you?"

"Maybe. I say Jim: 'Listen, Jim, I come with. You worried, I be baby-sitter. I drive for you, shoot for you, what the hell?' Jim get damn angry, okay?"

"Okay," said Smiley.

They drove to the Racice road and found the car parked without lights facing a track over a field, a Fiat, 99 on the number plates, black. Max stopped the van and let Jim out. As Jim walked towards the Fiat, the driver opened the door an inch in order to work the courtesy light. He had a newspaper opened over the steering wheel.

"Could you see his face?"

"Was in shadow."

Max waited; presumably they exchanged word codes, Jim got in, and the car drove away over the track, still without lights. Max returned to Brno. He was sitting over a schnapps in the restaurant when the whole town started rumbling. He thought at first the sound came from the football stadium; then he realised it was lorries, a convoy racing down the road. He asked the waitress what was going on, and she said there had been a shooting in the woods—counter-revolutionaries were responsible. He went out to the van, turned on the radio, and caught the bulletin from Prague. That was the first he had heard of a general. He guessed there were cordons everywhere, and anyway he had Jim's instructions to lie up in the hotel till Monday morning.

"Maybe Jim send me message. Maybe some guy from resistance come to me."

"With this one word," said Smiley quietly.

"Sure."

"He didn't say what sort of word it was?"

"You crazy," said Max. It was either a statement or a question.

"A Czech word or an English word or a German word?"

No one came, said Max, not bothering to answer craziness.

On Monday he burned his entry passport, changed the plates on his van, and used his West German escape. Rather than head south he drove south west, ditched the van, and crossed the border by bus to Freistadt, which was the softest route he knew. In Freistadt he had a drink and spent the night with a girl because he felt puzzled and angry and he needed to catch his breath. He got to London on Tuesday night, and despite Jim's orders he thought he'd better try and contact Control. "That was quite damn difficult," he commented.

He tried to telephone but only got as far as the mothers. MacFadean wasn't around. He thought of writing but he remembered Jim, and how no one else in the Circus was allowed to know. He decided that writing was too dangerous. The rumour at the Acton Laundry said that Control was ill. He tried to find out what hospital, but couldn't.

"Did people at the Laundry seem to know where you'd been?"

"I wonder."

He was still wondering when the housekeepers sent for him and asked to look at his Rudi Hartmann passport. Max said he had lost it, which was after all pretty near true. Why hadn't he reported the loss? He didn't know. When had the loss occurred? He didn't know. When did he last see Jim Prideaux? He couldn't remember. He was sent down to the Nursery at Sarratt but Max felt fit and angry, and after two or three days the inquisitors got tired of him or somebody called them off.

"I go back Acton Laundry; Toby Esterhase give me hundred pound, tell me go to hell."

A scream of applause went up round the pond. Two boys had sunk a great slab of ice and now the water was bubbling through the hole.

"Max, what happened to Jim?"

"What the hell?"

"You hear these things. It gets around among the émigrés. What happened to him? Who mended him, how did Bill Haydon buy him back?"

"Emigrés don't speak Max no more."

"But you have heard, haven't you?"

This time it was the white hands that told him. Smiley saw the spread of fingers, five on one hand, four on the other and already he felt the sickness before Max spoke.

"So they shoot Jim from behind. Maybe Jim was running away, what the hell? They put Jim in prison. That's not so good for Jim. For my friends also. Not good." He started counting: "Pribyl," he began, touching his thumb. "Bukova Mirek, from Pribyl's wife the brother," he took a finger. "Also Pribyl's wife," a second finger. A third: "Kolin Jiri. Also his sister, mainly dead. This was network Aggravate." He changed hands. "After network Aggravate come network Plato. Come lawyer Rapotin, come Colonel Landkron, and typists Eva Krieglova and Hanka Bilova. Also mainly dead. That's damn big price, George"—holding the clean fingers close to Smiley's face—"that's damn big price for one Englishman with bullet-hole." He was losing his temper. "Why you bother, George? Circus don't be no good for Czecho. Allies don't be no good for Czecho. No rich guy don't get no poor guy out of prison! You want know some history? How you say '*Märchen*,' please, George?"

"Fairy tale," said Smiley.

"Okay, so don't tell me no more damn fairy tale how English got to save Czecho no more!"

"Perhaps it wasn't Jim," said Smiley after a long silence. "Perhaps it was someone else who blew the networks. Not Jim."

Max was already opening the door. "What the hell?" he asked.

"Max," said Smiley.

"Don't worry, George. I don't got no one to sell you to. Okay?"

"Okay."

Sitting in the car still, Smiley watched him hail a taxi. He did it with a flick of the hand, as if he were summoning a waiter. He gave the address without bothering to look at the driver. Then rode off sitting very upright again, staring straight ahead of him, like royalty ignoring the crowd.

As the taxi disappeared, Inspector Mendel rose slowly from

a bench, folded together his newspaper, walked over to the Rover.

"You're clean," he said. "Nothing on your back, nothing on your conscience."

Not so sure of that, Smiley handed him the keys to the car, then walked to the bus stop, first crossing the road in order to head west.

28

His destination was in Fleet Street, a ground-floor cellar full of wine barrels. In other areas, three-thirty might be considered a little late for a pre-luncheon apéritif, but as Smiley gently pushed open the door a dozen shadowy figures turned to eye him from the bar. And at a corner table, as unremarked as the plastic prison arches or the fake muskets on the wall, sat Jerry Westerby with a very large pink gin.

"Old boy," said Jerry Westerby shyly, in a voice that seemed to come out of the ground. "Well, I'll be damned. Hey, Jimmy!" His hand, which he laid on Smiley's arm while he signalled for refreshment with the other, was enormous and cushioned with muscle, for Jerry had once been wicket-keeper for a county cricket team. In contrast to other wicketkeepers he was a big man, but his shoulders were still hunched from keeping his hands low. He had a mop of sandy grey hair and a red face and he wore a famous sporting tie over a cream silk shirt. The sight of Smiley clearly gave him great joy, for he was beaming with pleasure.

"Well, I'll be damned," he repeated. "Of all the amazing things. Hey, what are you doing these days," dragging him forcibly into the seat beside him. "Sunning your fanny, spitting at the ceiling? Hey—" a most urgent question—"what'll it be?"

Smiley ordered a Bloody Mary.

"It isn't *complete* coincidence, Jerry," Smiley confessed. There was a slight pause between them, which Jerry was suddenly concerned to fill.

"Listen, how's the demon wife? All well? That's the stuff. One of the great marriages, that one—always said so."

Jerry Westerby himself had made several marriages but few that had given him pleasure.

"Do a deal with you, George," he proposed, rolling one great shoulder towards him. "I'll shack up with Ann and spit at the ceiling, you take my job and write up the women's Ping-Pong. How's that? God bless."

"Cheers," said Smiley good-humouredly.

"Haven't seen many of the boys and girls for a while, matter of fact," Jerry confessed awkwardly with an unaccountable blush. "Christmas card from old Toby last year, that's about my lot. Guess they've put me on the shelf as well. Can't blame them." He flicked the rim of his glass. "Too much of this stuff, that's what it is. They think I'll blab. Crack up."

"I'm sure they don't," said Smiley, and the silence reclaimed them both.

"Too much firewater not good for braves," Jerry intoned solemnly. For years they had had this Red Indian joke running, Smiley remembered with a sinking heart.

"*How*," said Smiley.

"*How*," said Jerry, and they drank.

"I burnt your letter as soon as I'd read it," Smiley went on in a quiet, unbothered voice. "In case you wondered. I didn't tell anyone about it at all. It came too late, anyway. It was all over."

At this, Jerry's lively complexion turned a deep scarlet.

"So it wasn't the letter you wrote me that put them off you," Smiley continued in the same very gentle voice, "if that's what you were thinking. And, after all, you did drop it in to me by hand."

"Very decent of you," Jerry muttered. "Thanks. Shouldn't have written it. Talking out of school."

"Nonsense," said Smiley as he ordered two more. "You did it for the good of the service."

To himself, saying this, Smiley sounded like Lacon. But the only way to talk to Jerry was to talk like Jerry's newspaper: short sentences; facile opinions.

Jerry expelled some breath and a lot of cigarette smoke. "Last job—oh, year ago," he recalled with a new airiness. "More. Dumping some little packet in Budapest. Nothing to it, really. Phone box. Ledge at the top. Put my hand up. Left it there. Kid's play. Don't think I muffed it or anything. Did my sums first—all that. Safety signals. 'Box ready for emptying. Help yourself.' The way they taught us, you know. Still, you lads know best, don't you? You're the owls. Do one's bit, that's the thing. Can't do more. All part of a pattern. Design."

"They'll be beating the doors down for you soon," said Smiley consolingly. "I expect they're resting you up for a season. They do that, you know."

"Hope so," said Jerry with a loyal, very diffident smile. His glass shook slightly as he drank.

"Was that the trip you made just before you wrote to me?" Smiley asked.

"Sure. Same trip, actually; Budapest, then Prague."

"And it was in Prague that you heard this story? The story you referred to in your letter to me?"

At the bar a florid man in a black suit was predicting the imminent collapse of the nation. He gave it three months, he said, then curtains.

"Rum chap, Toby Esterhase," said Jerry.

"But good," said Smiley.

"Oh, my God, old boy, first rate. Brilliant, my view. But rum, you know. *How.*" They drank again, and Jerry Westerby loosely poked a finger behind his head, in imitation of an Apache feather.

"Trouble is," the florid man at the bar was saying over the top of his drink, "we won't even know it's happened."

They decided to lunch straight away, because Jerry had a story to file for tomorrow's edition about some top footballer who'd been caught shoplifting. They went to a curry house where the management was content to serve beer at teatime, and they agreed that if anyone bumped into them Jerry would introduce George as his bank manager, a notion that tickled him repeatedly throughout his hearty meal. There was background music, which Jerry called the connubial flight of the mosquito, and at times it threatened to drown the fainter notes of his husky voice. Which was probably just as well, for while Smiley made a brave show of enthusiasm for the curry, Jerry was launched, after his initial reluctance, upon quite a different story, concerning one Jim Ellis: the story that dear old Toby Esterhase had refused to let him print.

Jerry Westerby was that extremely rare person, the perfect witness. He had no fantasy, no malice, no personal opinion. Merely, the thing was rum. He couldn't get it off his mind and, come to think of it, he hadn't spoken to Toby since.

"Just this card, you see, 'Happy Christmas, Toby'—picture of Leadenhall Street in the snow." He gazed in great perplexity at the electric fan. "Nothing *special* about Leadenhall Street, is there, old boy? Not a spy-house or a meeting place or something, is it?"

"Not that I know of," said Smiley, with a laugh.

"Couldn't think why he chose Leadenhall Street for a Christmas card. Damned odd, don't you think?"

Perhaps he just wanted a snowy picture of London, Smiley suggested; Toby, after all, was quite foreign in lots of ways.

"Rum way to keep in touch, I must say. Used to send me a crate of Scotch regular as clockwork." Jerry frowned and drank from his krug. "It's not the Scotch I mind," he explained with that puzzlement that often clouded the greater visions of his life; "buy my own Scotch any time. It's just that when you're on the outside, you think everything has a meaning, so presents are important—see what I'm getting at?"

It was a year ago—well, December. The Restaurant Sport in Prague, said Jerry Westerby, was a bit off the track of your average Western journalist. Most of them hung around the Cosmo or the International, talking in low murmurs and keeping together because they were jumpy. But Jerry's local was the Sport, and ever since he had taken Holotek, the goalie, along after the winning match against the Tartars, Jerry had had the big hand from the barman, whose name was Stanislaus or Stan.

"Stan's a perfect prince. Does just what he damn well pleases. Makes you suddenly think Czecho's a free country."

Restaurant, he explained, meant bar. Whereas bar in Czecho meant nightclub, which was rum. Smiley agreed that it must be confusing.

All the same, Jerry always kept an ear to the ground when he went there; after all, it was Czecho, and once or twice he'd been able to bring back the odd snippet for Toby or put him onto the track of someone.

"Even if it was just currency-dealing, black-market stuff. All grist to the mill, according to Tobe. These little scraps add up—that's what Tobe said, anyway."

Quite right, Smiley agreed. That was the way it worked.

"Tobe was the owl, what?"

"Sure."

"I used to work straight to Roy Bland, you see. Then Roy got kicked upstairs, so Tobe took me over. Bit unsettling, actually, changes. Cheers."

"How long had you been working to Toby when this trip took place?"

"Couple of years, not more."

There was a pause while food came and krugs were refilled and Jerry Westerby with his enormous hands shattered a popadam onto the hottest curry on the menu, then spread a crimson sauce over the top. The sauce, he said, was to give it bite. "Old Khan runs it up for me specially," he explained, aside. "Keeps it in a deep shelter."

So anyway, he resumed, that night in Stan's bar there was this young boy with the pudding-bowl haircut and the pretty girl on his arm.

"And I thought, Watch out, Jerry, boy; that's an army haircut. Right?"

"Right," Smiley echoed, thinking that in some ways Jerry was a bit of an owl himself.

It turned out the boy was Stan's nephew, and very proud of his English. "Amazing what people will tell you if it gives them a chance of showing off their languages." He was on leave from the army and he'd fallen in love with this girl; he'd eight days to go and the whole world was his friend, Jerry included. Jerry particularly, in fact, because Jerry was paying for the booze.

"So we're all sitting hugger-mugger at the big table in the corner—students, pretty girls, all sorts. Old Stan had come round from behind the bar and some laddie was doing a fair job with a squeeze-box. Bags of *Gemütlichkeit*, bags of booze, bags of noise."

The noise was specially important, Jerry explained, because it let him chat to the boy without anyone else paying attention. The boy was sitting next to Jerry; he'd taken a shine to him from the start. He had one arm slung round the girl and one arm round Jerry.

"One of those kids who can touch you without giving you the creeps. Don't like being touched, as a rule. Greeks do it. Hate it, personally."

Smiley said he hated it, too.

"Come to think of it, the girl looked a bit like Ann," Jerry reflected. "Foxy—know what I mean? Garbo eyes, lots of oomph."

So while everyone was carrying on, singing and drinking and playing kiss-in-the-ring, this lad asked Jerry whether he would like to know the truth about Jim Ellis.

"Pretended I'd never heard of him," Jerry explained to

Smiley. " 'Love to,' I said. 'Who's Jim Ellis when he's at home?' And the boy looks at me as if I'm daft and says, 'A British spy.' Only no one else heard, you see; they were all yelling and singing saucy songs. He had the girl's head on his shoulder, but she was half cut and in her seventh heaven, so he just went on talking to me, proud of his English, you see."

"I get it," said Smiley.

" 'British spy.' Yells straight into my ear-hole. 'Fought with Czech partisans in the war. Came here calling himself Hajek and was shot by the Russian secret police.' So I just shrugged and said, 'News to me, old boy.' Not pushing, you see. Mustn't be pushy, ever. Scares them off."

"You're absolutely right," said Smiley wholeheartedly, and for an interlude patiently parried further questions about Ann, and what it was like to love—really to love—the other person all your life.

"I am a conscript," the boy began, according to Jerry Westerby. "I have to serve in the army or I can't go to university." In October he had been on basic-training manoeuvres in the forests near Brno. There was always a lot of military in the woods there; in summer the whole area was closed to the public for a month at a time. He was on a boring infantry exercise that was supposed to last two weeks, but on the third day it was called off for no reason and the troops were ordered back to town. That was the order: pack now and get back to barracks. The whole forest was to be cleared by dusk.

"Within hours, every sort of daft rumour was flying around," Jerry went on. "Some fellow said the ballistics research station at Tisnov had blown up. Somebody else said the training battalions had mutinied and were shooting up the Russian soldiers. Fresh uprising in Prague, Russians taken over the government, the Germans had attacked—God knows what hadn't happened. You know what soldiers are. Same everywhere, soldiers. Gossip till the cows come home."

The reference to the army moved Jerry Westerby to ask after certain acquaintances from his military days, people Smiley had dimly known, and forgotten. Finally they resumed.

"They broke camp, packed the lorries, and sat about waiting for the convoy to get moving. They'd gone half a mile when everything stopped again and the convoy was ordered off the road. Lorries had to duckshuffle into the trees. Got stuck in the mud, ditches, every damn thing. Chaos, apparently."

It was the Russians, said Westerby. They were coming from the direction of Brno, and they were in a very big hurry and everything that was Czech had to get out of the light or take the consequences.

"First came a bunch of motorcycles tearing down the track with lights flashing and the drivers screaming at them. Then a staff car and civilians—the boy reckoned six civilians altogether. Then two lorryloads of special troops armed to the eyebrows and wearing combat paint. Finally a truck full of tracker dogs. All making a most God-awful row. Not boring you am I, old boy?"

Westerby dabbed the sweat from his face with a handkerchief and blinked like someone coming round. The sweat had come through his silk shirt as well; he looked as if he had been under a shower. Curry not being a food he cared for, Smiley ordered two more krugs to wash away the taste.

"So that was the first part of the story. Czech troops out, Russian troops in. Got it?"

Smiley said yes, he thought he had his mind round it so far.

Back in Brno, however, the boy quickly learned that his unit's part in the proceedings was nowhere near done. Their convoy was joined up with another, and the next night for eight or ten hours they tore round the countryside with no apparent destination. They drove west to Trebic, stopped and waited while the signals section made a long transmission; then they cut back south east nearly as far as Znojmo on the Austrian border, signalling like mad as they went. No one knew who had ordered the route; no one would explain a thing. At one point they were ordered to fix bayonets; at another they pitched camp, then packed up all their kit again and pushed off. Here and there they met up with other units: near Breclav marshalling-yards, tanks going round in circles, once a pair of self-propelled guns on pre-laid track. Everywhere the story was the same: chaotic, pointless activity. The older hands said it was a Russian punishment for being Czech. Back in Brno again, the boy heard a different explanation. The Russians were after a British spy called Hajek. He'd been spying on the research station and tried to kidnap a general and the Russians had shot him.

"So the boy asked, you see," said Jerry. "Sassy little devil asked his sergeant, 'If Hajek is already shot, why do we have to tear round the countryside creating an uproar?' And the sergeant told him, 'Because it's the army.' Sergeants all over the world, what?"

Very quietly Smiley asked, "We're talking about two nights, Jerry. Which night did the Russians move into the forest?"

Jerry Westerby screwed up his face in perplexity. "That's what the boy wanted to tell me, you see, George. That's what he was trying to put over in Stan's bar. What all the rumours were about. The Russians moved in on Friday. They didn't shoot Hajek till Saturday. So the wise lads were saying: there you are, Russians were waiting for Hajek to turn up. Knew he was coming. Knew the lot. Lay in wait. Bad story, you see. Bad for our reputation—see what I mean? Bad for big chief. Bad for tribe. *How*."

"*How*," said Smiley, into his beer.

"That's what Toby felt, too, mind. We saw it the same way; we just reacted differently."

"So you told all to Toby," said Smiley lightly, as he passed Jerry a large dish of dal. "You had to see him anyway to tell him you'd dropped the package for him in Budapest, so you told him the Hajek story, too."

Well, that was just it, said Jerry. That was the thing that had bothered him, the thing that was rum, the thing that made him write to George, actually. "Old Tobe said it was tripe. Got all regimental and nasty. First he was keen as mustard, clapping me on the back, and Westerby for mayor. He went back to the shop, and next morning he threw the book at me. Emergency meeting, drove me round and round the park in a car, yelling blue murder. Said I was so plastered these days I didn't know fact from fiction. All that stuff. Made me a bit shirty, actually."

"I expect you wondered who he'd been talking to in between," said Smiley sympathetically. "What did he say *exactly*," he asked, not in any intense way but as if he just wanted to get it all crystal clear in his mind.

"Told me it was most likely a put-up ploy. Boy was a provocateur. Disruption job to make the Circus chase its own tail. Tore my ears off for disseminating half-baked rumours. I said to him, George: 'Old boy,' I said. 'Tobe, I was only reporting, old boy. No need to get hot under the collar. Yesterday you thought I was the cat's whiskers. No point in turning round and shooting the messenger. If you've decided you don't like the story, that's your business.' Wouldn't sort of listen any more—know what I mean? Illogical, I thought it was. Bloke like that. Hot one minute and cold the next. Not his best performance—know what I mean?"

With his left hand Jerry rubbed the side of his head, like a schoolboy pretending to think. " 'Okie-dokie,' I said, 'forget it. I'll write it up for the rag. Not the part about the Russians getting there first. The other part. "Dirty work in the forest," that sort of tripe.' I said to him, 'If it isn't good enough for the Circus, it'll do for the rag.' Then he went up the wall again. Next day some owl rings the old man. Keep that baboon

Westerby off the Ellis story. Rub his nose in the D notice:
formal warning. 'All further references to Jim Ellis alias Hajek
against the national interest, so put 'em on the spike.' Back to
women's Ping-Pong. Cheers."

"But by then you'd written to me," Smiley reminded him.

Jerry Westerby blushed terribly. "Sorry about that," he
said. "Got all xenophobe and suspicious. Comes from being
on the outside: you don't trust your best friends. Trust
them—well, less than strangers." He tried again: "Just that I
thought old Tobe was going a bit haywire. Shouldn't have
done it, should I? Against the rules." Through his embarrassment he managed a painful grin. "Then I heard on the
grapevine that the firm had given you the heave-ho, so I felt
an even bigger damn fool. Not hunting alone, are you, old
boy? Not . . ." He left the question unasked; but not, perhaps, unanswered.

As they parted, Smiley took him gently by the arm.

"If Toby should get in touch with you, I think it better if
you don't tell him we met today. He's a good fellow but he
does tend to think people are ganging up on him."

"Wouldn't dream of it, old boy."

"And if he *does* get in touch in the next few days," Smiley
went on—in that remote contingency, his tone suggested—
"you could even warn me, actually. Then I can back you up.
Don't ring *me*, come to think of it, ring this number."

Suddenly Jerry Westerby was in a hurry; that story about
the shoplifting footballer couldn't wait. But as he accepted
Smiley's card he did ask with a queer, embarrassed glance
away from him, "Nothing untoward going on is there, old
boy? No dirty work at the crossroads?" The grin was quite
terrible. "Tribe hasn't gone on the rampage or anything?"

Smiley laughed and lightly laid a hand on Jerry's enormous,
slightly hunched shoulder.

"Any time," said Westerby.

"I'll remember."

"I thought it was you, you see: you who telephoned the
old man."

"It wasn't."

"Maybe it was Alleline."

"I expect so."

"Any time," said Westerby again. "Sorry, you know. Love to Ann." He hesitated.

"Come on, Jerry, out with it," said Smiley.

"Toby had some bad story about her and Bill the Brain. I told him to stuff it up his shirt-front. Nothing to it, is there?"

"Thanks, Jerry. So long. *How.*"

" I knew there wasn't," said Jerry, very pleased, and lifting his finger to denote the feather, padded off into his own reserves.

29

Waiting that night, alone in bed at the Islay but not yet able to sleep, Smiley once more took up the file that Lacon had given him in Mendel's house. It dated from the late fifties, when the Circus, like other Whitehall departments, was being pressed by the competition to take a hard look at the loyalty of its staff. Most of the entries were routine: telephone intercepts, surveillance reports, endless interviews with dons, friends, and nominated referees. But one document held Smiley like a magnet; he could not get enough of it. It was a letter, entered baldly on the index as "Haydon to Fanshawe, February 3, 1937." More precisely it was a handwritten letter, from the undergraduate Bill Haydon to his tutor Fanshawe, a Circus talent-spotter, introducing the young Jim Prideaux as a suitable candidate for recruitment to British intelligence. It was prefaced by a wry *explication de texte*. The Optimates were "an upper-class Christ Church Club, mainly old Etonian," wrote the unknown author. Fanshawe (P.R. de T.

Fanshawe, Légion d'Honneur, O.B.E., Personal File so-and-so) was its founder; Haydon (countless cross-references) was in that year its leading light. The political complexion of the Optimates, to whom Haydon's father had also in his day belonged, was unashamedly conservative. Fanshawe, now long dead, was a passionate Empire man and "the Optimates were his private selection tank for The Great Game," ran the preface. Curiously enough, Smiley dimly remembered Fanshawe from his own day: a thin eager man with rimless spectacles, a Neville Chamberlain umbrella, and an unnatural flush to his cheeks as if he were still teething. Steed-Asprey called him the fairy godfather.

"My dear Fan, I suggest you stir yourself to make a few enquiries about the young gentleman whose name is appended on the attached fragment of human skin." [Inquisitors' superfluous note: Prideaux] "You probably know Jim—if you know him at all—as an *athleticus* of some accomplishment. What you do not know but ought to is that he is no mean linguist nor yet a total idiot either . . ." [Here followed a biographical summary of surprising accuracy: . . . Lycée Lakanal in Paris, put down for Eton, never went there, Jesuit day-school Prague, two semesters Strasbourg, parents in European banking, small aristo, live apart . . .]

"Hence our Jim's wide familiarity with parts foreign, and his rather parentless look, which I find irresistible. By the way: though he is made up of all different bits of Europe, make no mistake: the completed version is devoutly our own. At present, he is a bit of a striver and a puzzler, for he has just noticed that there is a World Beyond the Touchline and that world is me.

"But you must first hear how I met him.

"As you know, it is my habit (and your command) now and then to put on Arab costume and go down to the bazaars, there to sit among the great unwashed and give ear to the word of their prophets, that I may in due course better confound them. The juju man *en vogue* that evening came from the bosom of Mother Russia herself: one Academician Khleb-nikov, presently attached to the Soviet Embassy in London, a jolly, rather infectious little fellow, who managed some quite witty things among the usual nonsense. The bazaar in question was a debating club called the Populars—our rival, dear Fan, and well known to you from other forays I have occasionally made. After the sermon a wildly proletarian coffee was served, to the accompaniment of a dreadfully democratic bun, and I noticed this large fellow sitting alone at the back of the room, apparently too shy to mingle. His face was familiar from the cricket field; it turns out we both played in some silly scratch team without exchanging a word. I don't quite know how to describe him. He has it, Fan. I am serious now."

Here the handwriting, till now ill-at-ease, spread out as the writer got into his stride:

"He has that heavy quiet that commands. Hard-headed, quite literally. One of those shrewd quiet ones that lead the team without anyone noticing. Fan, you know how hard it is for me to *act*. You have to remind me all the time, intellectually remind me, that unless I sample life's dangers I shall never know its mysteries. But Jim acts from instinct . . . he is functional . . . He's my other half; between us we'd make one marvellous man, except that neither of us can sing. And, Fan, you know that feeling when you just have to go out and find someone new or the world will die on you?"

The writing steadied again.

" 'Yavas Lagloo,' says I, which I understand is Russian for meet me in the woodshed or something similar, and he says 'Oh, hullo,' which I think he would have said to the Archangel Gabriel if he'd happened to be passing.

" 'What is your dilemma?' says I.

" 'I haven't got one,' says he, after about an hour's thought.

" 'Then what are you doing here? If you haven't a dilemma, how did you get in?'

"So he gives a big placid grin and we saunter over to the great Khlebnikov, shake his tiny paw for a while, then toddle back to my rooms. Where we drink. And drink. And, Fan, he drank everything in sight. Or perhaps I did, I forget. And come the dawn, do you know what we did? I will tell you, Fan. We walked solemnly down to the Parks, I sit on a bench with a stop-watch, and big Jim gets into his running kit and lopes twenty circuits. Twenty. I was quite exhausted.

"We can come to you any time; he asks nothing better than to be in my company or that of my wicked, divine friends. In short, he has appointed me his Mephistopheles and I am vastly tickled by the compliment. By the by, he is virgin, about eight feet tall, and built by the same firm that did Stonehenge. Do not be alarmed."

The file died again. Sitting up, Smiley turned the yellowed pages impatiently, looking for stronger meat. The tutors of both men aver (twenty years later) that it is inconceivable that the relationship between the two was "more than purely friendly" . . . Haydon's evidence was never called . . . Jim's tutor speaks of him as "intellectually omnivorous after long starvation"—dismisses any suggestion that he was "pink." The confrontation, which takes place at Sarratt, begins with long apologies, particularly in view of Jim's superb war record. Jim's answers breathe a pleasing straight-forwardness after the extravagance of Haydon's letter. One representative of the competition present, but his voice is seldom heard. No, Jim never again met Khlebnikov or anyone representing himself as his emissary . . . No, he never spoke to him but on that one occasion. No, he had no other contact with Communists or Russians at that time; he could not remember the name of a single member of the Populars . . .

> Q: (*Alleline*) Shouldn't think that keeps you awake, does it?
> A: As a matter of fact, no. (*Laughter*)

Yes, he had been a member of the Populars just as he had been a member of his college drama club, the philatelic society, the modern language society, the Union and the historical society, the ethical society and the Rudolf Steiner study group . . . It was a way of getting to hear interesting lectures, and of meeting people, particularly the second. No, he had never distributed left-wing literature, though he did for a while take *Soviet Weekly* . . . No, he had never paid dues to any political party, at Oxford or later; as a matter of fact, he had never even used his vote . . . One reason why he joined so many clubs at Oxford was that after a messy education abroad he had no natural English contemporaries from school . . .

By now the inquisitors are one and all on Jim's side; everyone is on the same side against the competition and its bureaucratic meddling.

> Q: (*Alleline*) As a matter of interest, since you were overseas so much, do you mind telling us where you learned your off-drive? (*Laughter*)
> A: Oh, I had an uncle, actually, with a place outside Paris. He was cricket mad. Had a net and all the equipment. When I went there for holidays, he bowled at me non-stop.

[Inquisitors' note: Comte Henri de Sainte-Yvonne, dec. 1942, P.F. AF64-7.] End of interview. Competition representative would like to call Haydon as a witness but Haydon is abroad and not available. Fixture postponed *sine die* . . .

Smiley was nearly asleep as he read the last entry on the file, tossed in haphazard long after Jim's formal clearance had come through from the competition. It was a cutting from an Oxford newspaper of the day giving a review of Haydon's one-man exhibition in June, 1938, headed "Real or Surreal? An Oxford Eye."

Having torn the exhibition to shreds, the critic ended on this gleeful note: "We understand that the distinguished Mr. James Prideaux took time off from his cricket in order to help hang the canvases. He would have done better, in our opinion, to remain in the Banbury Road. However, since his role of Dobbin to the arts was the only heartfelt thing about the whole occasion, perhaps we had better not sneer too loud . . ."

He dozed, his mind a controlled clutter of doubts, suspicions, and certainties. He thought of Ann, and in his tiredness cherished her profoundly, longing to protect her frailty with his own. Like a young man, he whispered her name aloud and imagined her beautiful face bowing over him in the half-light, while Mrs. Pope Graham yelled prohibition through the keyhole. He thought of Tarr and Irina, and pondered uselessly on love and loyalty; he thought of Jim Prideaux and what tomorrow held. He was aware of a modest sense of approaching conquest. He had been driven a long way; he had sailed backwards and forwards. Tomorrow, if he was lucky, he might spot land: a peaceful little desert island, for instance. Somewhere Karla had never heard of. Just for himself and Ann. He fell asleep.

PART III

30

In Jim Prideaux's world, Thursday had gone along like any other, except that some time in the small hours of the morning the wounds in his shoulder-bone started leaking, he supposed because of the inter-house run on Wednesday afternoon. He was woken by the pain, and by the draught on the wet of his back where the discharge flowed. The other time this happened he had driven himself to Taunton General, but the nurses took one look at him and slapped him into emergency to wait for doctor somebody and an X-ray, so he filched his clothes and left. He'd done with hospitals and he'd done with medicos. English hospitals, other hospitals—Jim had done with them. They called the discharge a "track."

He couldn't reach the wound to treat it, but after last time he had hacked himself triangles of lint and stitched strings to the corners. Having put these handy on the draining board and prepared the hibitane, he heated hot water, added half a packet of salt, and gave himself an improvised shower, crouching to get his back under the jet. He soaked the lint in the hibitane, flung it across his back, strapped it from the front, and lay face down on the bunk with a vodka handy. The pain eased and a drowsiness came over him, but he knew if he gave way to it he would sleep all day, so he took the vodka bottle to the window and sat at the table correcting Five B French while Thursday's dawn slipped into the Dip and the rooks started their clatter in the elms.

Sometimes he thought of the wound as a memory he couldn't keep down. He tried his damnedest to patch it over and forget, but even his damnedest wasn't always enough.

He took the correcting slowly because he liked it, and because correcting kept his mind in the right places. At six-thirty, seven, he was done so he put on some old flannel bags and a sports coat and walked quietly down to the church, which was never locked. There he knelt a moment in the centre aisle of the Curtois antechapel, which was a family monument to the dead from two wars, and seldom visited by anyone. The cross on the little altar had been carved by sappers at Verdun. Still kneeling, Jim groped cautiously under the pew until his fingertips discovered the line of several pieces of adhesive tape, and following these, a casing of cold metal. His devotions over, he bashed up Combe Lane to the hilltop, jogging a bit to get a sweat running, because the warm did him wonders while it lasted, and rhythm soothed his vigilance.

After his sleepless night and the early-morning vodka, he was feeling a bit light-headed, so when he saw the ponies down the combe, gawping at him with their fool faces, he yelled at them in bad Somerset—"Git 'an there! Damned old fools, take your silly eyes off me!"—before pounding down the lane again for coffee, and a change of bandage.

First lesson after prayers was Five B French, and there Jim all but lost his temper: doled out a silly punishment to damn-fool Clements, draper's son; had to take it back at the end of class. In the common-room he went through another routine, of the sort he had followed in the church: quickly, mindlessly, no fumble and out. It was a simple enough notion, the mail check, but it worked. He'd never heard of anyone else who used it, among the pros, but then pros don't talk about their game. "See it this way," he would have said. "If the opposition is watching you, it's certain to be watching your mail, because mail's the easiest watch in the game—easier still if the opposition is the home side and has the co-operation of the postal service. So what do you do? Every week, from the same post-box, at the same time, at the same rate, you post one envelope to yourself and a second to an innocent party at the same address. Shove in a bit of trash—charity Christmas-card literature, come-on from local supermarket—be sure to seal envelope, stand back and compare times of arrival. If your letter turns up later than the other feller's, you've just felt someone's hot breath on you—in this case, Toby's."

Jim called it, in his odd, chipped vocabulary, water-testing, and once again the temperature was unobjectionable. The two letters clocked in together, but Jim arrived too late to pinch back the one addressed to Marjoribanks, whose turn it was to act as unwitting running mate. So, having pocketed his own, Jim snorted at the *Daily Telegraph* while Marjoribanks, with an irritable "Oh, to hell," tore up a printed invitation to join the Bible Reading Fellowship. From there, school routine carried him again till junior rugger versus St. Ermin's, which he was billed to referee. It was a fast game and when it was over his back acted up again, so he drank vodka till first bell, which he'd promised to take for young Elwes. He couldn't remember why he'd promised, but the younger staff and specially the married ones relied on him a lot for odd jobs and he let it happen. The bell was an old ship's tocsin, something Thursgood's father had dug up and now part of the tradition. As Jim rang it, he was aware of little Bill Roach standing right beside him, peering up at him with a white smile, wanting his attention, as he wanted it half a dozen times each day.

"Hullo, there, Jumbo, what's your headache this time?"

"Sir, please, sir."

"Come on, Jumbo, out with it."

"Sir, there's someone asking where you live, sir," said Roach.

Jim put down the bell.

"What sort of someone, Jumbo? Come on, I won't bite you, come on, hey . . . hey! What sort of someone? Man someone? Woman? Juju man? Hey! Come on, old feller," he said softly, crouching to Roach's height. "No need to cry. What's the matter, then? Got a temperature?" He pulled a handkerchief from his sleeve. "What sort of someone?" he repeated in the same low voice.

"He asked at Mrs. McCullum's. He said he was a friend.

Then he got back into his car; it's parked in the churchyard, sir." A fresh gust of tears. "He's just sitting in it."

"Get the hell away, damn you!" Jim called to a bunch of seniors grinning in a doorway. "Get the hell!" He went back to Roach. "Tall friend?" he asked softly. "Sloppy tall kind of fellow, Jumbo? Eyebrows and a stoop? Thin feller? Bradbury, come here and stop gawping! Stand by to take Jumbo up to Matron! Thin feller?" he asked again, very steady.

But Roach had run out of words. He had no memory any more, no sense of size or perspective; his faculty of selection in the adult world had gone. Big men, small men, old, young, crooked, straight—they were a single army of indistinguishable dangers. To say no to Jim was more than he could bear; to say yes was to shoulder the whole awful responsibility of disappointing him. He saw Jim's eyes on him; he saw the smile go out and he felt the merciful touch of a big hand upon his arm.

"Attaboy, Jumbo. Nobody ever watched like you, did they?"

Laying his head hopelessly against Bradbury's shoulder, Bill Roach closed his eyes. When he opened them, he saw through his tears that Jim was already halfway up the staircase.

Jim felt calm; almost easy. For days he had known there was someone. That also was part of his routine: to watch the places where the watchers asked. The church, where the ebb and flow of the local population is a ready topic; county hall, register of electors; tradesmen, if they kept customer accounts; pubs, if the quarry didn't use them. In England, he knew these were the natural traps that watchers automatically patrolled before they closed on you. And, sure enough, in Taunton two days ago, chatting pleasantly with the assistant librarian, Jim had come across the footprint he was looking for. A stranger, apparently down from London, had been interested in village wards; yes, a political gentleman—well, more in the line of political research, he was—profes-

sional, you could tell—and one of the things he had wanted—
fancy that, now—was the up-to-date record of Jim's very
village—yes, the voters' list—as they were thinking of making
a door-to-door survey of a really out-of-the-way community,
specially new immigrants . . . Yes, fancy that, Jim agreed,
and, from then on, made his dispositions. He bought railway
tickets to places—Taunton to Exeter, Taunton to London,
Taunton to Swindon, valid one month—because he knew that
if he were on the run again, tickets would be hard to come by.
He had uncached his old identities and his gun, and hid them
handily above ground; he dumped a suitcase full of clothes in
the boot of the Alvis, and kept the tank full. These precautions
eased his fears a little, made sleep a possibility; or would have
done, before his back.

"Sir, who won, sir?"

Prebble, a new boy, in dressing gown and toothpaste, on his
way to surgery. Sometimes boys spoke to Jim for no reason;
his size and crookedness were a challenge.

"Sir, the match, sir, versus Saint Ermin's."

"Saint *Vermin's*," another boy piped. "Yes, sir, who won,
actually?"

"Sir, *they* did, sir," Jim barked. "As you'd have known, *sir*,
if you'd been watching, *sir*," and swinging an enormous fist at
them in a slow feinted punch, he propelled both boys across
the corridor to Matron's dispensary.

"Night, sir."

"Night, you toads," Jim sang, and stepped the other way
into the sick-bay for a view of the church and the cemetery.
The sick-bay was unlit; it had a look and a stink he hated.
Twelve boys lay in the gloom, dozing between supper and
temperatures.

"Who's that?" asked a hoarse voice.

"Rhino," said another. "Hey, Rhino, who won against
Saint Vermin's?"

To call Jim by his nickname was insubordinate, but boys in sick-bay feel free from discipline.

"Rhino? Who the hell's *Rhino?* Don't know him. Not a name to me," Jim snorted, squeezing between two beds. "Put that torch away—not allowed. Damn walk-over, that's who won. Eighteen to nothing for Vermin's." That window went down almost to the floor. An old fireguard protected it from boys. "Too much damn fumble in the three-quarter line," he muttered, peering down.

"I hate rugger," said a boy called Stephen.

The blue Ford was parked in the shadow of the church, close in under the elms. From the ground floor it would have been out of sight but it didn't look hidden. Jim stood very still, a little back from the window, studying it for telltale signs. The light was fading fast, but his eyesight was good and he knew what to look for: discreet aerial, second inside mirror for the legman, burn marks under the exhaust. Sensing the tension in him, the boys became facetious.

"Sir, is it a bird, sir? Is she any good, sir?"

"Sir, are we on fire?"

"Sir, what are her legs like?"

"Gosh, sir, don't say it's Miss *Aaronson?*" At this everyone started giggling, because Miss Aaronson was old and ugly.

"Shut up," Jim snapped, quite angry. "Rude pigs, shut up." Downstairs in assembly, Thursgood was calling senior roll before prep.

Abercrombie? Sir. Astor? Sir. Blakeney? Sick, sir.

Still watching, Jim saw the car door open and George Smiley climb cautiously out, wearing a heavy overcoat.

Matron's footsteps sounded in the corridor. He heard the squeak of her rubber heels and the rattle of thermometers in a paste pot.

"My good Rhino, whatever are you doing in my sick-bay? And close that curtain, you bad boy—you'll have the whole lot of them dying of pneumonia. William Merridew, sit up at once."

Smiley was locking the car door. He was alone and he carried nothing, not even a briefcase.

"They're screaming for you in Grenville, Rhino."

"Going, gone," Jim retorted briskly and with a jerky "Night, all," he humped his way to Grenville dormitory, where he was pledged to finish a story by John Buchan. Reading aloud, he noticed that there were certain sounds he had trouble pronouncing; they caught somewhere in his throat. He knew he was sweating, he guessed his back was seeping, and by the time he had finished there was a stiffness round his jaw that was not just from reading aloud. But all these things were small symptoms beside the rage that was mounting in him as he plunged into the freezing night air. For a moment, on the overgrown terrace, he hesitated, staring at the church. It would take him three minutes, less, to untape the gun from underneath the pew, shove it into the waistband of his trousers, left side, butt inward to the groin . . .

But instinct advised him "no," so he set course directly for the trailer, singing "Hey, diddle-diddle" as loud as his tuneless voice would carry.

31

Inside the motel room, the state of restlessness was constant. Even when the traffic outside went through one of its rare lulls, the windows continued vibrating. In the bathroom the tooth glasses also vibrated, while from either wall and above them they could hear music, thumps, and bits of conversation or laughter. When a car arrived in the forecourt, the slam of the door seemed to happen inside the room, and the footsteps too. Of the furnishings, everything matched. The yellow chairs matched the yellow pictures and the yellow carpet. The candlewick bedspreads matched the orange paintwork on the doors, and by coincidence the label on the vodka bottle. Smiley had arranged things properly. He had spaced the chairs and put the vodka on the low table, and now as Jim sat glaring at him he extracted a plate of smoked salmon from the tiny refrigerator, and brown bread already buttered. His mood in contrast to Jim's was noticeably bright, his movements swift and purposeful.

"I thought we should at least be comfortable," he said, with a short smile, setting things busily on the table. "When do you have to be at school again? Is there a particular time?" Receiving no answer, he sat down. "How do you like teaching? I seem to remember you had a spell of it after the war—is that right? Before they hauled you back? Was that also a prep school? I don't think I knew."

"Look at the file," Jim barked. "Don't you come here playing cat-and-mouse with me, George Smiley. If you want to know things, read my file."

Reaching across the table, Smiley poured two drinks and handed one to Jim.

"Your personal file at the Circus?"

"Get it from housekeepers. Get it from Control."

"I suppose I should," said Smiley doubtfully. "The trouble is Control's dead and I was thrown out long before you came back. Didn't anyone bother to tell you that when they got you home?"

A softening came over Jim's face at this, and he made in slow motion one of those gestures which so amused the boys at Thursgood's. "Dear God," he muttered, "so Control's gone," and passed his left hand over the fangs of his moustache, then upward to his moth-eaten hair. "Poor old devil," he muttered. "What did he die of, George? Heart? Heart kill him?"

"They didn't even tell you this at the debriefing?" Smiley asked.

At the mention of a debriefing, Jim stiffened and his glare returned.

"Yes," said Smiley. "It was his heart."

"Who got the job?"

Smiley laughed. "My goodness, Jim, what *did* you all talk about at Sarratt, if they didn't even tell you that?"

"God damn it, who got the job? Wasn't you, was it— threw you out! Who got the job, George?"

"Alleline got it," said Smiley, watching Jim very carefully, noting how the right forearm rested motionless across the knees. "Who did you want to get it? Have a candidate, did you, Jim?" And after a long pause: "And they didn't tell you what happened to the Aggravate network, by any chance? To Pribyl, to his wife, and brother-in-law? Or the Plato network? Landkron, Eva Krieglova, Hanka Bilova? You recruited some of those, didn't you, in the old days before Roy Bland? Old Landkron even worked for you in the war."

There was something terrible just then about the way Jim would not move forward and could not move back. His red face was twisted with the strain of indecision and the sweat had gathered in studs over his shaggy ginger eyebrows.

"God damn you, George, what the devil do you want? I've drawn a line. That's what they told me to do. Draw a line, make a new life, forget the whole thing."

"Which *they* is this, Jim? Roy? Bill, Percy?" He waited. "Did they tell you what happened to Max, whoever they were? Max is all right, by the way." Rising, he briskly refreshed Jim's drink, then sat again.

"All right, come on, so what's happened to the networks?"

"They're blown. The story is you blew them to save your own skin. I don't believe it. But I have to know what happened." He went on, "I know Control made you promise by all that's holy, but that's finished. I know you've been questioned to death and I know you've pushed some things so far down you can hardly find them any more or tell the difference between truth and cover. I know you've tried to draw a line under it and say it didn't happen. I've tried that, too. Well, after tonight you can draw your line. I've brought a letter from Lacon and if you want to ring him he's standing by. I don't want to silence you. I'd rather you talked. Why didn't you come and see me at home when you got back? You could have done. You tried to see me before you left, so why not when you got back? Wasn't just the rules that kept you away."

"Didn't anyone get out?" Jim said.

"No. They seem to have been shot."

They had telephoned Lacon and now Smiley sat alone sipping his drink. From the bathroom he could hear the sound of running taps and grunts as Jim sluiced water in his face.

"For God's sake, let's get somewhere we can breathe," Jim whispered when he came back, as if it were a condition of his talking. Smiley picked up the bottle and walked beside him as they crossed the tarmac to the car.

They drove for twenty minutes, Jim at the wheel. When they parked, they were on the plateau, this morning's hilltop free of fog, and a long view down the valley. Scattered lights reached into the distance. Jim sat as still as iron, right shoulder high and hands hung down, gazing through the misted windscreen at the shadow of the hills. The sky was light and Jim's face was cut sharp against it. Smiley kept his first questions short. The anger had left Jim's voice and little by little he spoke with greater ease. Once, discussing Control's tradecraft, he even laughed, but Smiley never relaxed; he was as cautious as if he were leading a child across the street. When Jim ran on, or bridled, or showed a flash of temper, Smiley gently drew him back until they were level again, moving at the same pace and in the same direction. When Jim hesitated, Smiley coaxed him forward over the obstacle. At first, by a mixture of instinct and deduction, Smiley actually fed Jim his own story.

For Jim's first briefing by Control, Smiley suggested, they had made a rendezvous outside the Circus? They had. Where? At a service flat in St. James's, a place proposed by Control. Was anyone else present? No one. And to get in touch with Jim in the first place, Control had used Mac-Fadean, his personal janitor? Yes, old Mac came over on the Brixton shuttle with a note asking Jim for a meeting that night. Jim was to tell Mac yes or no and give him back the note. He was on no account to use the telephone, even the internal line, to discuss the arrangement. Jim had told Mac yes and arrived at seven.

"First, I suppose, Control cautioned you?"

"Told me not to trust anyone."

"Did he name particular people?"

"Later," said Jim. "Not at first. At first, he just said trust nobody. Specially nobody in the mainstream. George?"

"Yes."

"They were shot all right, were they? Landkron, Krieglova, Bilova, the Pribyls? Straight shooting?"

"The secret police rolled up both networks the same night. After that no one knows, but next of kin were told they were dead. That usually means they are."

To their left, a line of pine trees like a motionless army climbed out of the valley.

"And then, I suppose, Control asked you what Czech identities you had running for you," Smiley resumed. "Is that right?"

He had to repeat the question.

"I told him Hajek," said Jim finally. "Vladimir Hajek, Czech journalist based on Paris. Control asked me how much longer the papers were good for. 'You never know,' I said. 'Sometimes they're blown after one trip.'" His voice went suddenly louder, as if he had lost his hold on it. "Deaf as an adder, Control was, when he wanted to be."

"So then he told you what he wanted you to do," Smiley suggested.

"First, we discussed deniability. He said if I was caught, I should keep Control out of it. A scalp-hunter ploy, bit of private enterprise. Even at the time I thought, Who the hell will ever believe that? Every word he spoke was letting blood," said Jim. "All through the briefing, I could feel his resistance to telling me anything. He didn't want me to know but he wanted me well briefed. 'I've had an offer of service,' Control says. 'Highly placed official, cover name Testify.' 'Czech official?' I ask. 'On the military side,' he says. 'You're a military minded man, Jim, you two should hit it off pretty well.' That's how it went, the whole damn way. I thought, If you don't want to tell me, don't, but stop dithering."

After more circling, said Jim, Control announced that Testify was a Czech general of artillery. His name was Stevcek; he was known as a pro-Soviet hawk in the Prague defence hierarchy, whatever that was worth; he had worked in Moscow on liaison and was one of the very few Czechs the Russians trusted. Stevcek had conveyed to Control, through an intermediary whom Control had personally interviewed in Austria, his desire to talk to a ranking officer of the Circus on matters of mutual interest. The emissary must be a Czech speaker, somebody able to take decisions. On Friday, October 20th, Stevcek would be inspecting the weapon research station at Tisnov, near Brno, about a hundred miles north of the Austrian border. From there he would be visiting a hunting-lodge for the weekend, alone. It was a place high up in the forests not far from Racice. He would be willing to receive an emissary there on the evening of Saturday, the twenty-first. He would also supply an escort to and from Brno.

Smiley asked, "Did Control have any suggestions about Stevcek's motive?"

"A girlfriend," Jim said. "Student he was going with, having a last spring, Control said; twenty years' age difference between them. She was shot during the uprising of summer '68. Till then, Stevcek had managed to bury his anti-Russian feelings in favour of his career. The girl's death put an end to all that: he was out for their blood. For four years he'd lain low acting friendly and salting away information that would really hurt them. Soon as we gave him assurances and fixed the trade routes, he was ready to sell."

"Had Control checked any of this?"

"What he could. Stevcek was well enough documented. Hungry desk general with a long list of staff appointments. Technocrat. When he wasn't on courses, he was sharpening his teeth abroad: Warsaw, Moscow, Peking for a year, spell of military attaché in Africa, Moscow again. Young for his rank."

"Did Control tell you what you were to expect in the way of information?"

"Defence material. Rocketry. Ballistics."

"Anything else?" said Smiley, passing the bottle.

"Bit of politics."

"Anything else?"

Not for the first time, Smiley had the distinct sense of stumbling not on Jim's ignorance but on the relic of a willed determination not to remember. In the dark, Jim Prideaux's breathing became suddenly deep and greedy. He had lifted his hands to the top of the wheel and was resting his chin on them, peering blankly at the frosted windscreen.

"How long were they in the bag before being shot?" Jim demanded to know.

"I'm afraid, a lot longer than you were," Smiley confessed.

"Holy God," said Jim. With a handkerchief taken from his sleeve, he wiped away the perspiration and whatever else was glistening on his face.

"The intelligence Control was hoping to get out of Stevcek," Smiley prompted, ever so softly.

"That's what they asked me at the interrogation."

"At Sarratt?"

Jim shook his head. "Over there." He nodded his untidy head towards the hills. "They knew it was Control's operation from the start. There was nothing I could say to persuade them it was mine. They laughed."

Once again Smiley waited patiently till Jim was ready to go on.

"Stevcek," said Jim. "Control had this bee in his bonnet: Stevcek would provide the answer, Stevcek would provide the key. 'What key?' I asked. 'What key?' Had his bag, that old brown music case. Pulled out charts, annoted all in his own handwriting. Charts in coloured inks, crayons. 'Your visual aid,' he says. 'This is the fellow you'll be meeting.' Stevcek's career plotted year by year: took me right through it. Military academies, medals, wives. 'He's fond of horses,' he says. 'You used to ride yourself, Jim. Something else in common—remember it.' I thought, That'll be fun, sitting in Czecho with the dogs after me, talking about breaking thoroughbred mares." He laughed a little strangely, so Smiley laughed, too.

"The appointments in red were for Stevcek's Soviet liaison work. Green were his intelligence work. Stevcek had had a finger in everything. Fourth man in Czech army intelligence, chief boffin on weaponry, secretary to the national internal security committee, military counsellor of some sort to the Praesidium, Anglo-American desk in the Czech military intelligence set-up. Then Control comes to this patch in the mid-sixties, Stevcek's second spell in Moscow, and it's marked green and red fifty-fifty. Ostensibly, Stevcek was attached to the Warsaw Pact Liaison staff as a colonel general, says Control, but that was just cover. 'He'd nothing to do with the Warsaw Pact Liaison staff. His real job was in Moscow Centre's England section. He operated under the workname of Minin,' he says. 'His job was dovetailing Czech efforts with Centre's. This is the treasure,' Control says. 'What Stevcek really wants to sell us is the name of Moscow Centre's mole inside the Circus.' "

It might be only one word, Smiley thought, remembering Max, and felt again that sudden wave of apprehension. In the end, he knew, that was all it would be: a name for the mole Gerald, a scream in the dark.

" 'There's a rotten apple, Jim,' Control said, 'and he's infecting all the others.' " Jim was going straight on. His voice had stiffened, his manner also. "Kept talking about elimination, how he'd backtracked and researched and was nearly there. There were five possibilities, he said. Don't ask me how he dug them up. 'It's one of the top five,' he says. 'Five fingers to a hand.' He gave me a drink and we sat there like a pair of schoolboys making up a code, me and Control. We used Tinker, Tailor. We sat there in the flat putting it together, drinking that cheap Cyprus sherry he always gave. If I couldn't get out, if there was any fumble after I'd met Stevcek, if I had to go underground, I must get the one word to him, even if I had to go to Prague and chalk it on the Embassy door or ring the Prague resident and yell it at him down the phone. Tinker, Tailor, Soldier, Sailor. Alleline was Tinker, Haydon was Tailor, Bland was Soldier, and Toby Esterhase was Poorman. We dropped Sailor because it rhymed with Tailor. You were Beggarman," Jim said.

"Was I, now? And how did you take to it, Jim, to Control's theory? How did the idea strike you, over-all?"

"Damn silly. Poppycock."

"Why?"

"Just damn silly," he repeated in a tone of military stubbornness. "Think of any one of you—mole—*mad!*"

"But did you believe it?"

"No! Lord alive, man, why do you—"

"Why not? Rationally we always accepted that sooner or later it would happen. We always warned one another: be on your guard. We've turned up enough members of other outfits: Russians, Poles, Czechs, French. Even the odd American. What's so special about the British, all of a sudden?"

Sensing Jim's antagonism, Smiley opened his door and let the cold air pour in.

"How about a stroll?" he said. "No point in being cooped up when we can walk around."

With movement, as Smiley had anticipated, Jim found a new fluency of speech.

They were on the western rim of the plateau, with only a

few trees standing and several lying felled. A frosted bench was offered, but they ignored it. There was no wind, the stars were very clear, and as Jim took up his story they went on walking side by side, Jim adjusting always to Smiley's pace, now away from the car, now back again. Occasionally they drew up, shoulder to shoulder, facing down the valley.

First Jim described his recruitment of Max and the manoeuvres he went through in order to disguise his mission from the rest of the Circus. He let it leak that he had a tentative lead to a high-stepping Soviet cypher clerk in Stockholm, and booked himself to Copenhagen in his old workname Ellis. Instead, he flew to Paris, switched to his Hajek papers, and landed by scheduled flight at Prague airport at ten on Saturday morning. He went through the barriers like a song, confirmed the time of his train at the terminus, then took a walk because he had a couple of hours to kill and thought he might watch his back a little before he left for Brno. That autumn there had been freak bad weather. There was snow on the ground and more falling.

In Czecho, said Jim, surveillance was not usually a problem. The security services knew next to nothing about streetwatching, probably because no administration in living memory had ever had to feel shy about it. The tendency, said Jim, was still to throw cars and pavement artists around like Al Capone, and that was what Jim was looking for: black Skodas and trios of squat men in trilbies. In the cold, spotting these things is marginally harder because the traffic is slow, the people walk faster, and everyone is muffled to the nose. All the same, till he reached Masaryk Station—or Central, as they're pleased to call it these days—he had no worries. But at Masaryk, said Jim, he got a whisper, more instinct than fact, about two women who'd bought tickets ahead of him.

Here, with the dispassionate ease of a professional, Jim went back over the ground. In a covered shopping arcade beside Wenceslaus Square he had been overtaken by three women, of whom the one in the middle was pushing a pram.

The woman nearest the curb carried a red plastic handbag and the woman on the inside was walking a dog on a lead. Ten minutes later two other women came towards him, arm in arm, both in a hurry, and it crossed his mind that if Toby Esterhase had had the running of the job, an arrangement like this would be his handwriting; quick profile changes from the pram, backup cars standing off with short-wave radio or bleep, with a second team lying back in case the forward party overran. At Masaryk, looking at the two women ahead of him in the ticket queue, Jim was faced with the knowledge that it was happening now. There is one garment that a watcher has neither time nor inclination to change, least of all in sub-Arctic weather, and that is his shoes. Of the two pairs offered for his inspection in the ticket queue, Jim recognised one: fur-lined plastic, black, with zips on the outside and soles of a thick brown composition that sang slightly in the snow. He had seen them once already that morning, in the Sterba passage, worn with different top clothes by the woman who had pushed past him with the pram. From then on, Jim didn't suspect. He knew, just as Smiley would have known.

At the station bookstall, Jim bought himself a *Rude Pravo* and boarded the Brno train. If they had wanted to arrest him, they would have done so by now. They must be after the branch lines: they were following Jim in order to house his contacts. There was no point in looking for reasons, but Jim guessed that the Hajek identity was blown and they'd primed the trap the moment he booked himself on the plane. As long as they didn't know he had flushed them, he still had the edge, said Jim; and for a moment Smiley was back in occupied Germany, in his own time as a field agent, living with terror in his mouth, naked to every stranger's glance.

He was supposed to catch the thirteen-eight arriving Brno sixteen-twenty-seven. It was cancelled, so he took some wonderful stopping train, a special for the football match, which called at every other lamp-post, and each time Jim reckoned he could pick out the hoods. The quality was variable. At

Chocen, a one-horse place if ever he saw one, he got out and bought himself a sausage, and there were no fewer than five, all men, spread down the tiny platform with their hands in their pockets, pretending to chat to one another and making damn fools of themselves.

"If there's one thing that distinguishes a good watcher from a bad one," said Jim, "it's the gentle art of doing damn all convincingly."

At Svitavy two men and a woman entered his carriage and talked about the big match. After a while Jim joined the conversation; he had been reading up the form in his newspaper. It was a club replay, and everyone was going crazy about it. By Brno, nothing more had happened, so he got out and sauntered through shops and crowded areas where they had to stay close for fear of losing him.

He wanted to lull them, demonstrate to them that he suspected nothing. He knew now that he was the target of what Toby would call a grand-slam operation. On foot they were working teams of seven. The cars changed so often he couldn't count them. The over-all direction came from a scruffy green van driven by a thug. The van had a loop aerial and a chalk star scrawled high on the back where no child could reach. The cars, where he picked them out, were declared to one another by a woman's handbag on the gloveboard and a passenger sun visor turned down. He guessed there were other signs but those two were good enough for him. He knew from what Toby had told him that jobs like this could cost a hundred people and were unwieldy if the quarry bolted. Toby hated them for that reason.

There is one store in Brno main square that sells everything, said Jim. Shopping in Czecho is usually a bore because there are so few retail outlets for each state industry, but this place was new and quite impressive. He bought children's toys, a scarf, some cigarettes, and tried on shoes. He guessed his watchers were still waiting for his clandestine contact. He stole a fur hat and a white plastic raincoat and a carrier bag to put them in. He loitered at the men's department long enough to confirm that two women who formed the forward pair were still behind him but reluctant to come too close. He guessed they had signalled for men to take over, and were waiting. In the men's lavatory he moved very fast. He pulled the white raincoat over his overcoat, stuffed the carrier bag into the pocket, and put on the fur hat. He abandoned his remaining parcels, then ran like a madman down the emergency staircase, smashed open a fire door, pelted down an alley, strolled up another, which was one-way, stuffed the white raincoat into the carrier bag, sauntered into another store, which was just closing, and there bought a black raincoat to replace the white one. Using the departing shoppers for cover, he squeezed into a crowded tram, stayed aboard till the last stop but one, walked for an hour, and made the fall-back with Max to the minute.

Here he described his dialogue with Max and said they nearly had a standing fight.

Smiley asked, "It never crossed your mind to drop the job?"

"No. It did not," Jim snapped, his voice rising in a threat.

"Although, right from the start, you thought the idea was poppycock?" There was nothing but deference in Smiley's tone. No edge, no wish to score: only a wish to have the truth, clear under the night sky. "You just kept marching. You'd seen what was on your back, you thought the mission absurd, but you still went on, deeper and deeper into the jungle."

"I did."

"Had you perhaps changed your mind about the mission? Did curiosity draw you, after all—was that it? You wanted passionately to know who the mole was, for instance? I'm only speculating, Jim."

"What's the difference? What the hell does my motive matter in a damn mess like this?"

The half-moon was free of cloud and seemed very close.

Jim sat on the bench. It was bedded in loose gravel, and while he spoke he occasionally picked up a pebble and flicked it backhand into the bracken. Smiley sat beside him, looking nowhere but at Jim. Once, to keep him company, he took a pull of vodka and thought of Tarr and Irina drinking on their hilltop in Hong Kong. It must be a habit of the trade, he decided: we talk better when there's a view.

Through the window of the parked Fiat, said Jim, the word code passed off without a hitch. The driver was one of those stiff, muscle-bound Czech Magyars with an Edwardian moustache and a mouthful of garlic. Jim didn't like him but he hadn't expected to. The two back doors were locked and there was a row about where he should sit. The Magyar said it was insecure for Jim to be in the back. It was also undemocratic. Jim told him to go to hell. He asked Jim whether he had a gun, and Jim said no, which was not true, but if the Magyar didn't believe him he didn't dare say so. He asked whether Jim had brought instructions for the General. Jim said he had brought nothing. He had come to listen.

Jim felt a bit nervy, he said. They drove and the Magyar said his piece. When they reached the lodge, there would be no lights and no sign of life. The General would be inside. If there was any sign of life—a bicycle, a car, a light, a dog—if there was any sign that the hut was occupied, then the Magyar would go in first and Jim would wait in the car. Otherwise Jim should go in alone and the Slav would do the waiting. Was that clear?

Why didn't they just go in together? Jim asked. Because the General didn't want them to, said the Slav.

They drove for half an hour by Jim's watch, heading north east at an average of thirty kilometres an hour. The track was winding and steep and tree-lined. There was no moon and he could see very little except occasionally against the skyline more forest, more hilltops. The snow had come from the north, he noticed; it was a point that was useful later. The track was clear but rutted by heavy lorries. They drove without lights. The Magyar had begun telling a dirty story and Jim guessed it was his way of being nervous. The smell of garlic was awful. He seemed to chew it all the time. Without warning, he cut the engine. They were running downhill, but more slowly. They had not quite stopped when the Magyar reached for the handbrake and Jim smashed his head against the window-post and took his gun. They were at the opening to a side-path. Thirty yards down this path lay a low wooden hut. There was no sign of life.

Jim told the Magyar what he would like him to do. He would like him to wear Jim's fur hat and Jim's coat and take the walk for him. He should take it slowly, keeping his hands linked behind his back, and walking at the centre of the path. If he failed to do either of those things, Jim would shoot him. When he reached the hut, he should go inside and explain to the General that Jim was indulging in an elementary precaution. Then he should walk back slowly, report to Jim that all was well, and that the General was ready to receive him. Or not, as the case might be.

The Magyar didn't seem very happy about this but he didn't have much choice. Before he got out, Jim made him turn the car round and face it down the path. If there was any monkey business, Jim explained, he would put on the headlights and shoot him along the beam, not once but several times, and not in the legs. The Magyar began his walk. He had nearly reached the hut when the whole area was floodlit: the hut, the path, and a large space around. Then a number of things happened at once. Jim didn't see everything, because he was busy turning the car. He saw four men fall out of the trees, and so far as he could work out, one of them had sandbagged the Magyar. Shooting started but none of the four paid it any attention; they were standing back while somebody took photographs. The shooting seemed to be directed at the clear sky behind the floodlights. It was very theatrical. Flares exploded, Very lights went up, even tracers, and as Jim raced the Fiat down the track, he had the impression of leaving a military tattoo at its climax. He was almost clear—he really felt he *was* clear—when from the woods to his right someone opened up with a machine-gun at close quarters. The first burst shot off a back wheel and turned the car over. He saw the wheel fly over the bonnet as the car took to the ditch on the left. The ditch might have been ten feet deep but the snow let him down kindly. The car didn't burn so he lay behind it and waited, facing across the track hoping to get a shot at the machine-gunner. The next burst came from behind him and threw him up against the car. The woods must have been crawling with troops. He knew that he had been hit twice. Both shots caught him in the right shoulder and it seemed amazing to him, as he lay there watching the tattoo, that they hadn't taken off the arm. A klaxon sounded, maybe two or three. An ambulance rolled down the track and there was still enough shooting to frighten the game for years. The ambulance reminded him of those old Hollywood fire engines, it was so upright. A whole mock battle was taking place, yet the ambulance boys stood gazing at him without a care in the world. He was losing consciousness as he heard a second car arrive, and men's voices, and more photographs were taken, this time of the right man. Someone gave orders, but he couldn't tell what they were because they were given in Russian. His one thought, as they dumped him on the stretcher and the lights went out, concerned going back to London. He imagined himself in the St. James's flat, with the coloured charts and the sheaf of notes, sitting in the armchair and explaining to Control how in their old age the two of them had walked into the biggest sucker's punch in the history of the trade. His only consolation was that they had sandbagged the Magyar, but looking back Jim wished very much he'd broken his neck for him: it was a thing he could have managed very easily, and without compunction.

32

The describing of pain was to Jim an indulgence to be dispensed with. To Smiley, his stoicism had something awesome about it, the more so because he seemed unaware of it. The gaps in his story came mainly where he passed out, he explained. The ambulance drove him, so far as he could fathom, further north. He guessed this from the trees when they opened the door to let the doctor in: the snow was heaviest when he looked back. The surface was good and he guessed they were on the road to Hradec. The doctor gave him an injection; he came round in a prison hospital with barred windows high up, and three men watching him. He came round again after the operation, in a different cell with no windows at all, and he thought probably the first questioning took place there, about seventy-two hours after they'd patched him up, but time was already a problem and of course they'd taken away his watch.

They moved him a lot. Either to different rooms, depending on what they were going to do with him, or to other prisons, depending on who was questioning him. Sometimes they just moved to keep him awake, walking him down cell corridors at night. He was also moved in lorries, and once by a Czech transport plane, but he was trussed for the flight and hooded, and passed out soon after they took off. The interrogation which followed this flight was very long. Otherwise he had little sense of progression from one questioning to another and thinking didn't get it any straighter for him—rather the reverse. The thing that was still strongest in his memory was the plan of campaign he formed while he waited for the first interrogation to begin. He knew silence would be impossible and that for his own sanity, or survival, there had to be a dialogue, and at the end of it they had to think he had told them what he knew, all he knew. Lying in hospital, he prepared his mind into lines of defence behind which, if he was lucky, he could fall back stage by stage until he had given the impression of total defeat. His forward line, he reckoned, and his most expendable, was the bare bones of Operation Testify. It was anyone's guess whether Stevcek was a plant, or had been betrayed. But whichever was the case, one thing was certain: the Czechs knew more about Stevcek than Jim did. His first concession, therefore, would be the Stevcek story, since they had it already; but he would make them work for it. First he would deny everything and stick to his cover. After a fight, he would admit to being a British spy and give his workname Ellis, so that if they published it, the Circus would at least know he was alive and trying. He had little doubt that the elaborate trap and the photographs augured a lot of ballyhoo. After that, in accordance with his understanding with Control, he would describe the operation as his own show, mounted without the consent of his superiors, and calculated to win him favour. And he would bury, as deep as they could go and deeper, all thoughts of a spy inside the Circus.

"No mole," said Jim, to the black outlines of the Quantocks. "No meeting with Control, no service flat in St. James's."

"No Tinker, Tailor."

His second line of defence would be Max. He proposed at first to deny that he had brought a legman at all. Then he might say he had brought one but didn't know his name. Then, because everyone likes a name, he would give them one: the wrong one first, then the right one. By that time Max must be clear, or underground, or caught.

Now came in Jim's imagination a succession of less strongly held positions: recent scalp-hunter operations, Circus tittle-tattle—anything to make his interrogators think he was broken and talking free and that this was all he had, they had passed the last trench. He would rack his memory for back scalp-hunter cases, and if necessary he would give them the names of one or two Soviet and satellite officials who had recently been turned or burned; of others who in the past had made a one-time sale of assets and, since they had not defected, might now be considered to be in line for burning or a second bite. He would throw them any bone he could think of—sell them, if necessary, the entire Brixton stable. And all of this would be the smokescreen to disguise what seemed to Jim to be his most vulnerable intelligence, since they would certainly expect him to possess it: the identity of members of the Czech end of the Aggravate and Plato networks.

"Landkron, Krieglova, Bilova, the Pribyls," said Jim.

Why did he choose the same order for their names? Smiley wondered.

For a long time Jim had had no responsibility for these networks. Years earlier, before he took over Brixton, he had helped establish them, recruited some of the founder members; since then, a lot had happened to them in the hands of Bland and Haydon of which he knew nothing. But he was certain that he still knew enough to blow them both sky high. And what worried him most was the fear that Control, or Bill, or Percy Alleline, or whoever had the final say these days, would be too greedy, or too slow, to evacuate the networks by the time Jim, under forms of duress he could only guess at, had no alternative but to break completely.

"So that's the joke," said Jim, with no humour whatever. "They couldn't have cared less about the networks. They asked me half a dozen questions about Aggravate, then lost interest. They knew damn well that Testify wasn't my private brain-child and they knew all about Control buying the Stevcek pass in Vienna. They began exactly where I wanted to end: with the briefing in St. James's. They didn't ask me about a legman; they weren't interested in who had driven me to the rendezvous with the Magyar. All they wanted to talk about was Control's rotten-apple theory."

One word, thought Smiley again, it might be just one word. He said, "Did they actually know the St. James's address?"

"They knew the brand of the bloody sherry, man."

"And the charts?" asked Smiley quickly. "The music case?"

"No." He added, "Not at first. No."

Thinking inside out, Steed-Asprey used to call it. They knew because the mole Gerald had told them, thought Smiley. The mole knew what the housekeepers had succeeded in getting out of old MacFadean. The Circus conducts its post-mortem: Karla has the benefit of its findings in time to use them on Jim.

"So I suppose by now you were beginning to think Control was right: there *was* a mole," said Smiley.

Jim and Smiley were leaning on a wooden gate. The ground sloped sharply away from them in a long sweep of bracken and fields. Below them lay another village, a bay, and a thin ribbon of moonlit sea.

"They went straight to the heart of it. 'Why did Control go it alone? What did he hope to achieve?' 'His come-back,' I said. So they laugh: 'With tinpot information about military emplacements in the area of Brno? That wouldn't even buy him a square meal in his club.' 'Maybe he was losing his grip,' I said. If Control was losing his grip, they said, who was stamping on his fingers? Alleline, I said, that was the buzz; Alleline and Control were in competition to provide intelligence. But in Brixton we only got the rumours, I said. 'And what is Alleline producing that Control is *not* producing?' 'I don't know.' 'But you just said that Alleline and Control are in competition to provide intelligence.' 'It's rumour. I don't know.' Back to the cooler."

Time, said Jim, at this stage lost him completely. He lived either in the darkness of the hood, or in the white light of the cells. There was no night or day, and to make it even more weird they kept the noises going most of the time.

They were working him on the production-line principle, he explained: no sleep, relays of questions, a lot of disorientation, a lot of muscle, till the interrogation became to him a slow race between going a bit dotty, as he called it, and breaking completely. Naturally, he hoped he'd go dotty but that wasn't something you could decide for yourself, because they had a way of bringing you back. A lot of the muscle was done electrically.

"So we start again. New tack. 'Stevcek was an important general. If he asked for a senior British officer, he could expect him to be properly informed about all aspects of his career. Are you telling us you did not inform yourself?' 'I'm saying I got my information from Control.' 'Did you read Stevcek's dossier at the Circus?' 'No.' 'Did Control?' 'I don't know.' 'What conclusions did Control draw from Stevcek's second appointment in Moscow? Did Control speak to you about Stevcek's role in the Warsaw Pact Liaison Committee?' 'No.' They stuck to that question and I suppose I stuck to my answer, because after a few more 'no's they got a bit crazy. They seemed to lose patience. When I passed out, they hosed me down and had another crack."

Movement, said Jim. His narrative had become oddly jerky. Cells, corridors, car . . . at the airport V.I.P. treatment and a mauling before the aeroplane . . . on the flight, dropped off to sleep and was punished for it. "Came round in a cell again, smaller, no paint on the walls. Sometimes I thought I was in Russia. I worked out by the stars that we had flown east. Sometimes I was in Sarratt, back on the interrogation resistance course."

For a couple of days they let him alone. Head was muzzy. He kept hearing the shooting in the forest and he saw the tattoo again, and when finally the big session started—the one he remembered as the marathon—he had the disadvantage of feeling half defeated when he went in.

"Matter of health, much as anything," he explained, very tense now.

"We could take a break if you want," Smiley said, but

where Jim was, there were no breaks, and what he wanted was irrelevant.

That was the long one, Jim said. Sometime in the course of it, he told them about Control's notes and his charts and the coloured inks and crayons. They were going at him like the devil and he remembered an all-male audience, at one end of the room, peering like a lot of damn medicos and muttering to one another, and he told them about the crayons just to keep the talk alive, to make them stop and listen. They listened but they didn't stop.

"Once they had the colours, they wanted to know what the colours meant. 'What did blue mean?' 'Control didn't have blue.' 'What did red mean? What did red stand for? Give us an example of red on the chart. What did red mean? What did red mean? What did red mean?' Then everybody clears out except a couple of guards and one cold little fellow, stiff back, seemed to be head boy. The guards take me over to a table, and this little fellow sits beside me like a bloody gnome with his hands folded. He's got two crayons in front of him, red and green, and a chart of Stevcek's career."

It wasn't that Jim broke exactly; he just ran out of invention. He couldn't think up any more stories. The truths that he had locked away so deeply were the only things that suggested themselves.

"So you told him about the rotten apple," Smiley suggested. "And you told him about Tinker, Tailor."

Yes, Jim agreed, he did. He told him that Control believed Stevcek could identify a mole inside the Circus. He told him about the Tinker, Tailor code and who each of them was, name by name.

"What was his reaction?"

"Thought for a bit, then offered me a cigarette. Hated the damn thing."

"Why?"

"Tasted American. Camel, one of those."

"Did he smoke one himself?"

Jim gave a short nod. "Bloody chimney," he said.

Time, after that, began once more to flow, said Jim. He was taken to a camp, he guessed outside a town, and lived in a compound of huts with a double perimeter of wire. With the help of a guard, he was soon able to walk; one day they even went for a stroll in the forest. The camp was very big; his own compound was only a part of it. At night he could see the glow of a city to the east. The guards wore denims and didn't speak, so he still had no way of telling whether he was in Czecho or in Russia, but his money was heavily on Russia, and when the surgeon came to take a look at his back he used a Russian-English interpreter to express his contempt for his predecessor's handiwork. The interrogation continued sporadically, but without hostility. They put a fresh team on him but it was a leisurely crowd by comparison with the first eleven. One night he was taken to a military airport and flown by R.A.F. fighter to Inverness. From there he went by small plane to Elstree, then by van to Sarratt; both were night journeys.

Jim was winding up fast. He was already launched on his experiences at the Nursery, in fact, when Smiley asked, "And the headman, the little cold one: you never saw him again?"

Once, Jim conceded; just before he left.

"What for?"

"Gossip." Much louder. "Lot of damned tripe about Circus personalities, matter of fact."

"Which personalities?"

Jim ducked that question. Tripe about who was on the up staircase, he said, who was on the down. Who was next in line for Chief: " 'How should I know,' I said. 'Bloody janitors hear it before Brixton does.' "

"So who came in for the tripe, precisely?"

Mainly Roy Bland, said Jim sullenly. How did Bland reconcile his left-wing leanings with his work at the Circus? He hasn't got any left-wing leanings, said Jim, that's how. What was Bland's standing with Esterhase and Alleline?

What did Bland think of Bill's paintings? Then how much Roy drank and what would become of him if Bill ever withdrew his support for him? Jim gave meagre answers to these questions.

"Was anyone else mentioned?"

"Esterhase," Jim snapped, in the same taut tone. "Bloody man wanted to know how anyone could trust a Hungarian."

Smiley's next question seemed, even to himself, to cast an absolute silence over the whole black valley.

"And what did he say about me?" He repeated: "What did he say about me?"

"Showed me a cigarette lighter. Said it was yours. Present from Ann. 'With all my love.' Her signature. Engraved."

"Did he mention how he came by it? What did he say, Jim? Come on, I'm not going to weaken at the knees just because some Russian hood made a bad joke about me."

Jim's answer came out like an army order. "He reckoned that after Bill Haydon's fling with her, she might care to redraft the inscription." He swung away towards the car. "I told him," he shouted furiously. "Told him to his wrinkled little face. You can't judge Bill by things like that. Artists have totally different standards. See things we can't see. Feel things that are beyond us. Bloody little man just laughed. 'Didn't know his pictures were that good,' he said. I told him, George. 'Go to hell. Go to bloody hell. If you had one Bill Haydon in your damned outfit, you could call it set and match.' I said to him: 'Christ Almighty,' I said, 'what are you running over here? A service or the bloody Salvation Army?' "

"That was well said," Smiley remarked at last, as if commenting on some distant debate. "And you'd never seen him before?"

"Who?"

"The little frosty chap. He wasn't familiar to you—from long ago, for instance? Well, you know how we are. We're trained, we see a lot of faces, photographs of Centre personalities, and sometimes they stick. Even if we can't put a name to them any more. This one didn't, anyway. I just wondered. It occurred to me you had a lot of time to think," he went on, conversationally. "You lay there recovering, waiting to come home, and what else had you to do, but think?" He waited. "So what did you think of, I wonder? The mission. Your mission, I suppose."

"Off and on."

"With what conclusions? Anything useful? Any suspicions, insights, any hints for me to take away?"

"Damn all, thank you," Jim snapped, very hard. "You know me, George Smiley. I'm not a juju man, I'm a—"

"You're a plain fieldman who lets the other chaps do his thinking. Nevertheless, when you know you have been led into a king-sized trap, betrayed, shot in the back, and have nothing to do for months but lie or sit on a bunk, or pace a Russian cell, I would guess that even the most dedicated man of action"—his voice had lost none of its friendliness—"might put his mind to wondering how he landed in such a scrape. Let's take Operation Testify a minute," Smiley suggested to the motionless figure before him. "Testify ended Control's career. He was disgraced and he couldn't pursue his mole, assuming there was one. The Circus passed into other hands. With a sense of timeliness, Control died. Testify did something else, too. It revealed to the Russians—through you, actually—the exact reach of Control's suspicions. That he'd narrowed the field to five, but apparently no further. I'm not suggesting you should have fathomed all that for yourself in your cell, waiting. After all, you had no idea, sitting in the pen, that Control had been thrown out—though it might have occurred to you that the Russians laid on that mock battle in the forest in order to raise a wind. Did it?"

"You've forgotten the networks," said Jim dully.

"Oh, the Czechs had the networks marked down long before you came on the scene. They only rolled them up in order to compound Control's failure."

The discursive, almost chatty tone with which Smiley

threw out these theories found no resonance in Jim. Having waited in vain for him to volunteer some word, Smiley let the matter drop. "Well, let's just go over your reception at Sarratt, shall we? To wrap it up?"

In a rare moment of forgetfulness, he helped himself to the vodka bottle before passing it to Jim.

To judge by his voice, Jim had had enough. He spoke fast and angrily, with that same military shortness which was his refuge from intellectual incursions.

For four days Sarratt was limbo, he said: "Ate a lot, drank a lot, slept a lot. Walked round the cricket ground." He'd have swum, but the pool was under repair, as it had been six months before: damned inefficient. He had a medical, watched television in his hut, and played a bit of chess with Cranko, who was running reception.

Meanwhile he waited for Control to show up, but he didn't. The first person from the Circus to visit him was the resettlement officer, talking about a friendly teaching agency; next came some pay wallah to discuss his pension entitlement; then the doctor again to assess him for a gratuity. He waited for the inquisitors to appear but they never did, which was a relief because he didn't know what he would have told them until he had the green light from Control and he'd had enough of questions. He guessed Control was holding them off. It seemed mad that he should keep from the inquisitors what he had already told the Russians and the Czechs, but until he heard from Control, what else could he do? When Control still sent no word, he formed notions of presenting himself to Lacon and telling his story. Then he decided that Control was waiting for him to get clear of the Nursery before he contacted him. He had a relapse for a few days, and when it was over Toby Esterhase turned up in a new suit, apparently to shake him by the hand and wish him luck. But in fact to tell him how things stood.

"Bloody odd fellow to send, but he seemed to have come up in the world. Then I remembered what Control said about only using chaps from outstations."

Esterhase told him that the Circus had very nearly gone under as a result of Testify and that Jim was currently the Circus's Number One leper. Control was out of the game and a reorganisation was going on in order to appease Whitehall.

"Then he told me not to worry," said Jim.

"In what way not worry?"

"About my special brief. He said a few people knew the real story, and I needn't worry because it was being taken care of. All the facts were known. Then he gave me a thousand quid in cash to add to my gratuity."

"Who from?"

"He didn't say."

"Did he mention Control's theory about Stevcek? Centre's spy inside the Circus?"

"The facts were known," Jim repeated, glaring. "He *ordered* me not to approach anyone or try to get my story heard, because it was all being taken care of at the highest level and anything I did might spoil the kill. The Circus was back on the road. I could forget Tinker, Tailor and the whole damn game—moles, everything. 'Drop out,' he said. 'You're a lucky man, Jim,' he kept saying. 'You've been ordered to become a lotus-eater.' I could forget it. Right? Forget it. Just behave as if it had never happened." He was shouting. "And that's what I've been doing: obeying orders and forgetting!"

The night landscape seemed to Smiley suddenly innocent; it was like a great canvas on which nothing bad or cruel had ever been painted. Side by side, they stared down the valley over the clusters of lights to a tor raised against the horizon. A single tower stood at its top and for a moment it marked for Smiley the end of the journey.

"Yes," he said. "I did a bit of forgetting, too. So Toby actually mentioned Tinker, Tailor to you. However did he get hold of *that* story, unless . . . And no word from Bill?" he went on. "Not even a postcard."

"Bill was abroad," said Jim shortly.

"Who told you that?"

"Toby."

"So you never saw Bill; since Testify, your oldest, closest friend, he disappeared."

"You heard what Toby said. I was out of bounds. Quarantine."

"Bill was never much of a one for regulations, though, was he?" said Smiley, in a reminiscent tone.

"And you were never one to see him straight," Jim barked.

"Sorry I wasn't there when you called on me, before you left for Czecho," Smiley remarked after a small pause. "Control had pushed me over to Germany to get me out of the light and when I came back—what was it that you wanted, exactly?"

"Nothing. Thought Czecho might be a bit hairy. Thought I'd give you the nod, say goodbye."

"Before a mission?" cried Smiley in mild surprise. "Before such a *special* mission?" Jim showed no sign that he had heard. "Did you give anyone else the nod? I suppose we were all away. Toby, Roy—Bill; did he get one?"

"No one."

"Bill was on leave, wasn't he? But I gather he was around, all the same."

"No one," Jim insisted, as a spasm of pain caused him to lift his right shoulder and rotate his head. "All out," he said.

"That's very unlike you, Jim," said Smiley in the same mild tone, "to go round shaking hands with people before you go on vital missions. You must have been getting sentimental in your old age. It wasn't . . ." he hesitated. "It wasn't advice or anything that you wanted, was it? After all, you did think the mission was poppycock, didn't you? And that Control was losing his grip. Perhaps you felt you should take your problem to a third party? It all had rather a mad air, I agree."

Learn the facts, Steed-Asprey used to say, then try on the stories like clothes.

With Jim still locked in a furious silence, they returned to the car.

.   .   .

At the motel Smiley drew twenty postcard-sized photographs from the recesses of his coat and laid them out in two lines across the ceramic table. Some were snaps, some portraits; all were of men and none of them looked English. With a grimace Jim picked out two and handed them to Smiley. He was sure of the first, he muttered, less sure of the second. The first was the headman, the cool little man. The second was one of the swine who watched from the shadows while the thugs took Jim to pieces. Smiley returned the photographs to his pocket. As he topped up their glasses for a nightcap, a less tortured observer than Jim might have noticed a sense not of triumph but of ceremony about him; as though the drink were putting a seal on something.

"So when was the last time you saw Bill, actually? To talk to," Smiley asked, just as one might about any old friend. He had evidently disturbed Jim in other thoughts, for he took a moment to lift his head and catch the question.

"Oh, round about," he said carelessly. "Bumped into him in the corridors, I suppose."

"And to talk to? Never mind." For Jim had returned to his other thoughts.

Jim would not be driven all the way to school. Smiley had to drop him short, at the top of the tarmac path that led through the graveyard to the church. He had left some workbooks in the antechapel, he said. Momentarily, Smiley felt disposed to disbelieve him, but could not understand why. Perhaps because he had come to the opinion that after thirty years in the trade, Jim was still a rather poor liar. The last Smiley saw of him was that lop-sided shadow striding towards the Norman porch as his heels cracked like gunshot between the tombs.

Smiley drove to Taunton and from the Castle Hotel made a string of telephone calls. Though exhausted, he slept fitfully between visions of Karla sitting at Jim's table with two crayons, and Cultural Attaché Polyakov alias Viktorov, fired by concern for the safety of his mole Gerald, waiting impatiently in the interrogation cell for Jim to break. Lastly of Toby Esterhase bobbing into Sarratt in place of the absent Haydon, cheerfully advising Jim to forget all about Tinker, Tailor, and his dead inventor, Control.

The same night, Peter Guillam drove west, clean across England to Liverpool, with Ricki Tarr as his only passenger. It was a tedious journey in beastly conditions. For most of it, Tarr boasted about the rewards he would claim, and the promotion, once he had carried out his mission. From there he talked about his women: Danny, her mother, Irina. He seemed to envisage a *ménage à quatre* in which the two women would jointly care for Danny, and for himself.

"There's a lot of the mother in Irina. That's what frustrates her, naturally." Boris, he said, could get lost; he would tell Karla to keep him. As their destination approached, his mood changed again and he fell silent. The dawn was cold and foggy. In the suburbs they had to drop to a crawl and cyclists overtook them. A reek of soot and steel filled the car.

"Don't hang about in Dublin, either," said Guillam suddenly. "They expect you to work the soft routes, so keep your head down. Take the first plane out."

"We've been through all that."

"Well, I'm going through it all again," Guillam retorted. "What's Mackelvore's workname?"

"For Christ's sake," Tarr breathed, and gave it.

It was still dark when the Irish ferry sailed. There were soldiers and police everywhere: this war, the last, the one before. A fierce wind was blowing off the sea and the going looked rough. At the dockside, a sense of fellowship briefly touched the small crowd as the ship's lights bobbed quickly into the gloom. Somewhere a woman was crying, somewhere a drunk was celebrating his release.

He drove back slowly, trying to work himself out: the new Guillam who starts at sudden noises, has nightmares, and not only can't keep his girl but makes up crazy reasons for distrusting her. He had challenged Camilla about Sand, and the hours she kept, and about her secrecy in general. After listening with her grave brown eyes fixed on him, she told him he was a fool, and left. "I am what you think I am," she said, and fetched her things from the bedroom. From his empty flat he telephoned Toby Esterhase, inviting him for a friendly chat later that day.

33

Smiley sat in the Minister's Rolls, with Lacon beside him. In Ann's family the car was called the black bed-pan, and hated for its flashiness. The chauffeur had been sent to find himself breakfast. The Minister sat in the front and everyone looked forward down the long bonnet, across the river to the foggy towers of Battersea Power Station. The Minister's hair was full at the back, and licked into small black horns around the ears.

"If you're right," the Minister declared, after a funereal silence. "I'm not saying you're not, but if you are, how much porcelain will he break at the end of the day?"

Smiley did not quite understand.

"I'm talking about scandal. Gerald gets to Moscow. Right, so then what happens? Does he leap on a soap-box and laugh his head off in public about all the people he's made fools of over here? I mean, Christ, we're all in this together, aren't we? I don't see why we should let him go just so's he can pull the bloody roof down over our heads and the competition sweep the bloody pool."

He tried a different tack. "I mean to say, just because the Russians know our secrets, doesn't mean everyone else has to. We got plenty of other fish to fry apart from them, don't we? What about all the black men: are they going to be reading the gory details in the Walla Walla *News* in a week's time?"

Or his constituents, Smiley thought.

"I think that's always been a point the Russians accept," said Lacon. "After all, if you make your enemy look a fool, you lose the justification for engaging him." He added, "They've never made use of their opportunities so far, have they?"

"Well, make sure they toe the line. Get it in writing. No, don't. But you tell them what's sauce for the goose is sauce for the gander. We don't go round publishing the batting order at Moscow Centre, so they can bloody well play ball, too, for once."

Declining a lift, Smiley said the walk would do him good.

It was Thursgood's day for duty and he felt it badly. Headmasters, in his opinion, should be above the menial tasks; they should keep their minds clear for policy and leadership. The flourish of his Cambridge gown did not console him, and as he stood in the gymnasium watching the boys file in for morning line-up, his eye fixed on them balefully, if not with downright hostility. It was Marjoribanks, though, who dealt the death-blow.

"He said it was his mother," he explained, in a low murmur to Thursgood's left ear. "He'd had a telegram and proposed to leave at once. He wouldn't even stay for a cup of tea. I promised to pass on the message."

"It's monstrous, absolutely monstrous," said Thursgood.

"I'll take his French, if you like. We can double up Five and Six."

"I'm furious," said Thursgood. "I can't think, I'm so furious."

"And Irving says he'll take the rugger final."

"Reports to be written, exams, rugger finals to play off. What's supposed to be the matter with the woman? Just a flu, I suppose, a seasonal flu. Well, we've all got that, so have our mothers. Where does she live?"

"I rather gathered from what he said to Sue that she was dying."

"Well, that's *one* excuse he won't be able to use again," said Thursgood, quite unmollified, and with a sharp bark quelled the noise and read the roll.

"Roach?"

"Sick, sir."

That was all he needed to fill his cup. The school's richest boy having a nervous breakdown about his wretched parents, and the father threatening to remove him.

34

It was almost four o'clock on the afternoon of the same day. Safe houses I have known, thought Guillam, looking round the gloomy flat. He could write of them the way a commercial traveller could write about hotels: from your five-star hall of mirrors in Belgravia, with Wedgwood pilasters and gilded oak leaves, to this two-room scalp-hunters' shakedown in Lexham Gardens, smelling of dust and drains, with a three-foot fire extinguisher in the pitch-dark hall. Over the fireplace, cavaliers drinking out of pewter. On the nest of tables, sea-shells for ashtrays; and in the grey kitchen, anonymous instructions to "Be Sure and Turn Off the Gas Both Cocks." He was crossing the hall when the house bell rang, exactly on time. He lifted the phone and heard Toby's distorted voice howling in the earpiece. He pressed the button and heard the clunk of the electric lock echoing in the stairwell. He opened the front door but left it on the chain till he was sure Toby was alone.

"How are we?" said Guillam cheerfully, letting him in.

"Fine, actually, Peter," said Toby, pulling off his coat and gloves.

There was tea on a tray: Guillam had prepared it, two cups. To safe houses belongs a certain standard of catering. Either you are pretending that you live there or that you are adept anywhere; or simply that you think of everything. In the trade, naturalness is an art, Guillam decided. That was something Camilla could not appreciate.

"Actually, it's quite strange weather," Esterhase announced, as if he had really been analysing its qualities. Safe-house small-talk was never much better. "One walks a few steps and is completely exhausted already. So we are expecting a Pole?" he said, sitting down. "A Pole in the fur trade who you think might run courier for us."

"Due here any minute."

"Do we know him? I had my people look up the name but they found no trace."

My people, thought Guillam: I must remember to use that one. "The Free Poles made a pass at him a few months back and he ran a mile," he said. "Then Karl Stack spotted him round the warehouses and thought he might be useful to the scalp-hunters." He shrugged. "I liked him but what's the point? We can't even keep our own people busy."

"Peter, you are very generous," said Esterhase reverently, and Guillam had the ridiculous feeling he had just tipped him. To his relief, the front doorbell rang and Fawn took up his place in the doorway.

"Sorry about this, Toby," Smiley said, a little out of breath from the stairs. "Peter, where shall I hang my coat?"

Turning him to the wall, Guillam lifted Toby's unresisting hands and put them against it, then searched him for a gun, taking his time. Toby had none.

"Did he come alone?" Guillam asked. "Or is there some little friend waiting in the road?"

"Looked all clear to me," said Fawn.

Smiley was at the window, gazing down into the street. "Put the light out a minute, will you?" he said.

"Wait in the hall," Guillam ordered, and Fawn withdrew, carrying Smiley's coat. "Seen something?" he asked Smiley, joining him at the window.

Already the London afternoon had taken on the misty pinks and yellows of evening. The square was Victorian residential; at the centre, a caged garden, already dark. "Just a shadow, I suppose," said Smiley with a grunt, and turned back to Esterhase. The clock on the mantelpiece chimed four. Fawn must have wound it up.

"I want to put a thesis to you, Toby. A notion about what's going on. May I?"

Esterhase didn't move an eyelash. His little hands rested on the wooden arms of his chair. He sat quite comfortably, but slightly to attention, toes and heels of his polished shoes together.

"You don't have to speak at all. There's no risk to listening, is there?"

"Maybe."

"It's two years ago. Percy Alleline wants Control's job, but he has no standing in the Circus. Control has made sure of that. Control is sick and past his prime but Percy can't dislodge him. Remember the time?"

Esterhase gave a neat nod.

"One of those silly seasons," said Smiley, in his reasonable voice. "There isn't enough work outside so we start intriguing around the service, spying on one another. Percy's sitting in his room one morning with nothing to do. He has a paper appointment as Operational Director, but in practice he's a rubber stamp between the regional sections and Control, if that. Percy's door opens and somebody walks in. We'll call him Gerald—it's just a name. 'Percy,' he says, 'I've stumbled on a major Russian source. It could be a gold-mine.' Or perhaps he doesn't say anything till they're outside the building, because Gerald is very much a fieldman; he doesn't like to talk with walls and telephones around. Perhaps they take a walk in the park or a drive in a car. Perhaps they eat a meal somewhere, and at this stage there isn't much Percy can do but listen. Percy's had very little experience of the European scene, remember, least of all Czecho or the Balkans. He cut his teeth in South America and after that he worked the old possessions: India, the Middle East. He doesn't know a lot about Russians or Czechs or what you will; he's inclined to see red as red and leave it at that. Unfair?"

Esterhase pursed his lips and frowned a little, as if to say he never discussed a superior.

"Whereas Gerald is an expert on those things. His operational life has been spent weaving and ducking round the Eastern markets. Percy's out of his depth but keen. Gerald's on his home ground. This Russian source, says Gerald, could be the richest the Circus has had for years. Gerald doesn't want to say too much but he expects to be getting some trade samples in a day or two, and when he does, he'd like Percy to run his eye over them just to get a notion of the quality. They can go into source details later. 'But why me?' says Percy. 'What's it all about?' So Gerald tells him. 'Percy,' he says, 'some of us in the regional sections are worried sick by the level of operational losses. There seems to be a jinx around. Too much loose talk inside the Circus and out. Too many people being cut in on distribution. Out in the field, our agents are going to the wall, our networks are being rolled up or worse, and every new ploy ends up a street accident. We want you to help us put that right.' Gerald is not mutinous, and he's careful not to suggest that there's a traitor inside the Circus who's blowing all the operations, because you and I know that once talk like that gets around the machinery grinds to a halt. Anyway the last thing Gerald wants is a witch-hunt. But he does say that the place is leaking at the joints, and that slovenliness at the top is leading to failures lower down. All balm to Percy's ear. He lists the recent scandals and he's careful to lean on Alleline's own Middle East adventure, which went so wrong and nearly cost Percy his career. Then he makes his proposal. This is what he says. In my thesis, you understand—it's just a thesis."

"Sure, George," said Toby, and licked his lips.

"Another thesis would be that Alleline was his own Gerald, you see. It just happens that I don't believe it; I don't believe Percy is capable of going out and buying himself a top Russian spy and manning his own boat from then on. I think he'd mess it up."

"Sure," said Esterhase, with absolute confidence.

"So this, in my thesis, is what Gerald says to Percy next. 'We—that is, myself and those like-minded souls who are associated with this project—would like you to act as our father figure, Percy. We're not political men, we're operators. We don't understand the Whitehall jungle. But you do. You handle the committees, we'll handle Merlin. If you act as our cut-out, and protect us from the rot that's set in, which means in effect limiting knowledge of the operation to the absolute minimum, we'll supply the goods.' They talk over ways and means in which this might be done; then Gerald leaves Percy to fret for a bit. A week, a month, I don't know. Long enough for Percy to have done his thinking. One day Gerald produces the first sample. And of course it's very good. Very, very good. Naval stuff, as it happens, which couldn't suit Percy better, because he's very well in at the Admiralty; it's his supporters' club. So Percy gives his naval friends a sneak preview and they water at the mouth. 'Where does it come from? Will there be more?' There's plenty more. As to the identity of the source—well, that's a big big mystery at this stage, but so it should be. Forgive me if I'm a little wide of the mark here and there, but I've only the file to go by."

The mention of a file, the first indication that Smiley might be acting in some official capacity, produced in Esterhase a discernible response. The habitual licking of the lips was accompanied by a forward movement of the head and an expression of shrewd familiarity, as if Toby by all these signals was trying to indicate that he, too, had read the file, whatever file it was, and entirely shared Smiley's conclusions. Smiley had broken off to drink some tea.

"More for you, Toby?" he asked over his cup.

"I'll get it," said Guillam with more firmness than hospitality. "Tea, Fawn," he called through the door. It opened at once and Fawn appeared on the threshold, cup in hand.

Smiley was back at the window. He had parted the curtain an inch, and was staring into the square.

"Toby?"

"Yes, George?"

"Did you bring a baby-sitter?"

"No."

"No one?"

"George, why should I bring baby-sitters if I am just going to meet Peter and a poor Pole?"

Smiley returned to his chair. "Merlin as a source," he resumed. "Where was I? Yes, well, conveniently Merlin wasn't just one source, was he, as little by little Gerald explained to Percy and the two others he had by now drawn into the magic circle. Merlin was a Soviet agent, all right, but, rather like Alleline, he was also the spokesman of a dissident group. We love to see ourselves in other people's situations, and I'm sure Percy warmed to Merlin from the start. This group, this caucus of which Merlin was the leader, was made up of, say, half a dozen like-minded Soviet officials, each in his way well-placed. With time, I suspect, Gerald gave his lieutenants, and Percy, a pretty close picture of these sub-sources, but I don't know. Merlin's job was to collate their intelligence and get it to the West, and over the next few months he showed remarkable versatility in doing just that. He used all manner of methods, and the Circus was only too willing to feed him the equipment. Secret writing, microdots stuck over full stops on innocent-looking letters, dead letter-boxes in

Western capitals, filled by God knows what brave Russian, and dutifully cleared by Toby Esterhase's brave lamplighters. Live meetings, even, arranged and watched over by Toby's baby-sitters"—a minute pause as Smiley glanced again towards the window—"a couple of drops in Moscow that had to be fielded by the local residency, though they were never allowed to know their benefactor. But no clandestine radio; Merlin doesn't care for it. There was a proposal once—it even got as far as the Treasury—to set up a permanent long-arm radio station in Finland, just to service him, but it all foundered when Merlin said, 'Not on your nelly.' He must have been taking lessons from Karla, mustn't he? You know how Karla hates radio. The great thing is, Merlin has mobility: that's his biggest talent. Perhaps he's in the Moscow Trade Ministry and can use the travelling salesmen. Anyway, he has the resources and he has the leads out of Russia. And that's why his fellow conspirators look to him to deal with Gerald and agree to the terms, the financial terms. Because they do want money. Lots of money. I should have mentioned that. In that respect, secret services and their customers are like anyone else, I'm afraid. They value most what costs most, and Merlin costs a fortune. Ever bought a fake picture?"

"I sold a couple once," said Toby with a flashy, nervous smile, but no one laughed.

"The more you pay for it, the less inclined you are to doubt it. Silly, but there we are. It's also comforting for everyone to know that Merlin is venal. That's a motive we all understand—right, Toby? Specially in the Treasury. Twenty thousand francs a month into a Swiss bank: well, there's no knowing who wouldn't bend a few egalitarian principles for money like that. So Whitehall pays him a fortune, and calls his intelligence priceless. And some of it *is* good," Smiley conceded. "Very good, I do think, and so it should be. Then, one day, Gerald admits Percy to the greatest secret of all. The Merlin caucus has a London end. It's the start, I should tell you now, of a very, very clever knot."

Toby put down his cup and with his handkerchief primly dabbed the corners of his mouth.

"According to Gerald, a member of the Soviet Embassy here in London is actually ready and able to act as Merlin's London representative. He is even in the extraordinary position of being able to use, on rare occasions, the Embassy facilities to talk to Merlin in Moscow, to send and receive messages. And if every imaginable precaution is taken, it is even possible now and then for Gerald to arrange clandestine meetings with this wonder-man, to brief and debrief him, to put follow-up questions and receive answers from Merlin almost by return of post. We'll call this Soviet official Aleksey Aleksandrovich Polyakov, and we'll pretend he's a member of the cultural section of the Soviet Embassy. Are you with me?"

"I didn't hear anything," said Esterhase. "I gone deaf."

"The story is, he's been a member of the London Embassy quite a while—nine years, to be precise—but Merlin's only recently added him to the flock. While Polyakov was on leave in Moscow, perhaps?"

"I'm not hearing nothing."

"Very quickly Polyakov becomes important, because before long Gerald appoints him linchpin of the Witchcraft operation and a lot more besides. The dead drops in Amsterdam and Paris, the secret inks, the microdots—they all go on, all right, but at less of a pitch. The convenience of having Polyakov right on the doorstep is too good to miss. Some of Merlin's best material is smuggled to London by diplomatic bag; all Polyakov has to do is slit open the envelopes and pass them to his counterpart in the Circus—Gerald or whomever Gerald nominates. But we must never forget that this part of the Merlin operation is deathly, deathly secret. The Witchcraft committee itself is, of course, secret, too, but large. That's inevitable. The operation is large, the take is large; processing and distribution alone require a mass of clerical supervision—transcribers, translators, codists, typists, evaluators, and God knows what. None of that worries Gerald at all, of course: he likes it, in fact, because the art of being Gerald is to be one of a crowd. Is the Witchcraft committee led from below? From the middle or from the top? I rather like Karla's description of committees, don't you? Is it Chinese? A committee is an animal with four back legs.

"But the London end—Polyakov's leg—that part is confined to the original magic circle. Skordeno, de Silsky, all the pack: they can tear off abroad and devil like mad for Merlin away from home. But here in London, the operation involving Brother Polyakov, the way that knot is tied—that's a very special secret, for very special reasons. You, Percy, Bill Haydon, and Roy Bland. You four are the magic circle. Right? Now let's just speculate about how it works, in detail. There's a house, we know that. All the same, meetings there are very elaborately arranged; we can be sure of that, can't we? Who meets him, Toby? Who has the handling of Polyakov? You? Roy? Bill?"

Taking the fat end of his tie, Smiley turned the silk lining outwards and polished his glasses. "Everyone does," he said, answering his own question. "How's that? Sometimes Percy meets him. I would guess Percy represents the authoritarian side with him: 'Isn't it time you took a holiday? Have you heard from your wife this week?' Percy would be good at that. But the Witchcraft committee uses Percy sparingly. Percy's the big gun and he must have rarity value. Then there's Bill Haydon; Bill meets him. That would happen more often, I think. Bill's impressive on Russia and he has entertainment value. I have a feeling that he and Polyakov would hit it off pretty well. I would think Bill shone when it came to the briefing and the follow-up questions, wouldn't you? Making certain that the right messages went to Moscow? Sometimes he takes Roy Bland with him, sometimes he sends Roy on his own. I expect that's something they work out between themselves. And Roy, of course, is an economic expert, as well as top man on satellites, so there'll be lots to talk about in that department also. And sometimes—I imagine birthdays, Toby, or a Christmas, or special presentations of thanks and money —there's a small fortune written down to entertainment, I notice, let alone bounties. Sometimes, to make the party go, you all four trot along, and raise your glasses to the king across the water: to Merlin, through his envoy, Polyakov. Finally, I suppose, Toby himself has things to talk to friend Polyakov about. There's tradecraft to discuss; there are the useful snippets about goings on inside the Embassy, which are so handy to the lamplighters in their bread-and-butter surveillance operations against the residency. So Toby also has his solo sessions. After all, we shouldn't overlook Polyakov's local potential, quite apart from his role as Merlin's London representative. It's not every day we have a tame Soviet diplomat in London eating out of our hands. A little training with a camera and Polyakov could be very useful just at the straight domestic level. Provided we all remember our priorities."

His gaze had not left Toby's face. "I can imagine that Polyakov might run to quite a few reels of film, can't you? And that one of the jobs of whoever was seeing him might be to replenish his stock: take him little sealed packets. Packets of film. Unexposed film, of course, since it came from the Circus. Tell me, Toby—could you, please—is the name Lapin familiar to you?"

A lick, a frown, a smile, a forward movement of the head: "Sure, George, I know Lapin."

"Who ordered the lamplighter reports on Lapin destroyed?"

"I did, George."

"On your own initiative?"

The smile broadened a fraction. "Listen, George, I made some rungs up the ladder these days."

"Who said Connie Sachs had to be pushed downhill?"

"Look, I think it was Percy—okay? Say it was Percy, maybe Bill. You know how it is in a big operation. Shoes to mend, pots to clean, always a thing going." He shrugged. "Maybe it was Roy, huh?"

"So you take orders from all of them," said Smiley lightly. "That's very indiscriminate of you, Toby. You should know better."

Esterhase didn't like that at all.

"Who told you to cool off Max, Toby? Was it the same three people? Only I have to report all this to Lacon, you see. He's being awfully pressing just at the moment. He seems to have the Minister on his back. Who was it?"

"George, you been talking to the wrong guys."

"One of us has," Smiley agreed pleasantly. "That's for sure. They also want to know about Westerby: just who put the muzzle on him. Was it the same person who sent you down to Sarratt with a thousand quid in cash and a brief to put Jim Prideaux's mind at rest? It's only facts I'm after, Toby, not scalps. You know me—I'm not the vindictive sort. Anyway, what's to say you're not a very loyal fellow? It's just a question of who to." He added, "Only they do badly want to know, you see. There's even some ugly talk of calling in the competition. Nobody wants that, do they? It's like going to solicitors when you've had a row with your wife: an irrevocable step. Who gave you the message for Jim about Tinker, Tailor? Did you know what it meant? Did you have it straight from Polyakov, was that it?"

"For God's sake," Guillam whispered, "let me sweat the bastard."

Smiley ignored him. "Let's keep talking about Lapin. What was his job over here?"

"He worked for Polyakov."

"His secretary in the cultural department?"

"His legman."

"But, my dear Toby, what on earth is a cultural attaché doing with his own legman?"

Esterhase's eyes were on Smiley all the time. He's like a dog, thought Guillam; he doesn't know whether to expect a kick or a bone. They flickered from Smiley's face to his hands, then back to his face, constantly checking the telltale places.

"Don't be damn silly, George," Toby said carelessly. "Polyakov is working for Moscow Centre. You know that as well as I do." He crossed his little legs and, with a resurgence of all his former insolence, sat back in his chair and took a sip of cold tea.

Whereas Smiley, to Guillam's eye, appeared momentarily set back; from which Guillam in his confusion dryly inferred that he was doubtless very pleased with himself. Perhaps because Toby was at last doing the talking.

"Come on, George," Toby said. "You're not a child. Think how many operations we ran this way. We buy Polyakov, okay? Polyakov's a Moscow hood but he's our Joe. But he's got to pretend to his own people that he's spying on us. How else does he get away with it? How does he walk in and out of that house all day, no gorillas, no baby-sitters, everything so easy? He comes down to our shop, so he got to take home the goodies. So we give him goodies. Chicken-feed, so he can pass it home and everyone in Moscow claps him on the back and tells him he's a big guy—happens every day."

If Guillam's head by now was reeling with a kind of furious awe, Smiley's seemed remarkably clear.

"And that's pretty much the standard story, is it, among the four initiated?"

"Well, standard I wouldn't know," said Esterhase, with a very Hungarian movement of the hand, a spreading of the palm and a tilting either way.

"So who is Polyakov's agent?"

The question, Guillam saw, mattered very much to Smiley: he had played the whole long hand in order to arrive at it. As Guillam waited, his eyes now on Esterhase, who was by no means so confident any more, now on Smiley's mandarin face, he realised that he, too, was beginning to understand the shape of Karla's last clever knot, as Smiley had called it—and of his own gruelling interview with Alleline.

"What I'm asking you is very simple," Smiley insisted. "Notionally, who is Polyakov's agent inside the Circus? Good heavens, Toby, don't be obtuse. If Polyakov's cover for meeting you people is that he is spying on the Circus, then he must have a Circus spy, mustn't he? So who is he? He can't come back to the Embassy after a meeting with you people, loaded with reels of Circus chicken-feed, and say, 'I got this from the boys.' There has to be a story—and a good one, at that: a whole history of courtship, recruitment, clandestine meetings, money, and motive. Doesn't there? Heavens, this isn't just Polyakov's cover story: it's his life-line. It's got to be thorough. It's got to be convincing; I'd say it was a very big issue in the game. So who is he?" Smiley enquired pleasantly. "You? Toby Esterhase masquerades as a Circus traitor in order to keep Polyakov in business? My hat, Toby, that's worth a whole handful of medals."

They waited while Toby thought.

"You're on a damn long road, George," Toby said at last. "What happens you don't reach the other end?"

"Even with Lacon behind me?"

"You bring Lacon here. Percy, too; Bill. Why you come to the little guy? Go to the big ones, pick on them."

"I thought you *were* a big guy these days. You'd be a good choice for the part, Toby. Hungarian ancestry, resentment about promotion, reasonable access but not too much . . . quick-witted, likes money . . . With you as his agent, Polyakov would have a cover story that really sits up and works. The big three give you the chicken-feed, you hand it to Polyakov, Centre thinks Toby is all theirs, everyone's served, everyone's content. The only problem arises when it transpires that you've been handing Polyakov the crown jewels and getting Russian chicken-feed in return. If that *should* turn out to be the case, you're going to need pretty good friends. Like us. That's how my thesis runs—just to complete it. That Gerald is a Russian mole, run by Karla. And he's pulled the Circus inside out."

Esterhase looked slightly ill. "George, listen. If you're wrong, I don't want to be wrong too, get me?"

"But if he's right, you want to be right," Guillam suggested, in a rare interruption. "And the sooner you're right, the happier you'll be."

"Sure," said Toby, quite unaware of any irony. "Sure. I mean George got a nice idea, but Jesus, there's two sides to everyone, George, agents specially, and maybe it's you who got the wrong one. Listen: who ever called Witchcraft chicken-feed? No one. Never. It's the best. You get one guy with a big mouth starts shouting the dirt, and you dug up half London already. Get me? Look, I do what they tell me. Okay? They say act the stooge for Polyakov, I act him. Pass him this film, I pass it. I'm in a very dangerous situation," he explained. "For me, very dangerous indeed."

"I'm sorry about that," said Smiley at the window, where through a chink in the curtain he was once more studying the square. "Must be worrying for you."

"Extremely," Toby agreed. "I get ulcers, can't eat. Very bad predicament."

For a moment, to Guillam's fury, they were all three joined in a sympathetic silence over Toby Esterhase's bad predicament.

"Toby, you wouldn't be lying about those baby-sitters, would you?" Smiley enquired, still from the window.

"George, I cross my heart, I swear you."

"What would you use for a job like this? Cars?"

"Pavement artists. Put a bus back by the air terminal, walk them through, turn 'em over."

"How many?"

"Eight, ten. This time of year—six, maybe. We get a lot ill. Christmas," he said morosely.

"And one man alone?"

"Never. You crazy. One man! You think I run a toffee shop these days?"

Leaving the window, Smiley sat down again.

"Listen, George, that's a terrible idea you got there, you know that? I'm a patriotic fellow. Jesus," Toby repeated.

"What is Polyakov's job in the London residency?" Smiley asked.

"Polly works solo."

"Running his master spy inside the Circus?"

"Sure. They take him off regular work, give him a free hand so's he can handle Toby, master spy. We work it all out; hours on end I sit with him. 'Listen,' I say. 'Bill is suspecting me, my wife is suspecting me, my kid got measles, and I can't pay the doctor.' All the crap that agents give you, I give it to Polly so's he can pass it home for real."

"And who's Merlin?"

Esterhase shook his head.

"But at least you've heard he's based in Moscow," Smiley said. "And a member of the Soviet intelligence establishment, whatever else he isn't?"

"That much they tell me," Esterhase agreed.

"Which is how Polyakov can communicate with him. In the Circus's interest, of course. Secretly, without his own people becoming suspicious?"

"Sure." Toby resumed his lament, but Smiley seemed to be listening to sounds that were not in the room.

"And Tinker, Tailor?"

"I don't know what the hell it is. I do what Percy tells me."

"And Percy told you to square Jim Prideaux?"

"Sure. Maybe it was Bill. Or Roy, maybe. Listen, it was Roy. I got to eat, George, understand? I don't cut my throat two ways, follow me?"

"It is the perfect fix; you see that, don't you, Toby, really?" Smiley remarked in a quiet, rather distant way. "Assuming it *is* a fix. It makes everyone wrong who's right: Connie Sachs, Jerry Westerby . . . Jim Prideaux . . . even Control. Silences the doubters before they've even spoken out . . . The permutations are infinite, once you've brought off the basic lie. Moscow Centre must be allowed to think she has an important Circus source; Whitehall on no account must get wind of the same notion. Take it to its logical conclusion and Gerald would have us strangling our own children in their beds. It would be beautiful in another context," he remarked almost dreamily. "Poor Toby; yes, I do see. What a time you must have been having, running between them all."

Toby had his next speech ready: "Naturally, if there is anything I can do of a practical nature, you know me, George, I am always pleased to help—no trouble. My boys are pretty well trained; you want to borrow them, maybe we can work a deal. Naturally, I have to speak to Lacon first. All I want, I want to get this thing cleared up. For the sake of the Circus, you know. That's all I want. The good of the firm. I'm a modest man; I don't want anything for myself—okay?"

"Where's this safe house you keep exclusively for Polyakov?"

"Five Lock Gardens, Camden Town."

"With a caretaker?"

"Mrs. McCraig."

"Lately a listener?"

"Sure."

"Is there built-in audio?"

"What do you think?"

"So Millie McCraig keeps house and mans the recording instruments."

She did, said Toby, ducking his head with great alertness.

"In a minute, I want you to telephone her and tell her I'm staying the night and I'll want to use the equipment. Tell her I've been called in on a special job and she's to do whatever I ask. I'll be round about nine. What's the procedure for contacting Polyakov if you want a crash meeting?"

"My boys have a room on Haverstock Hill. Polly drives past the window each morning on the way to the Embassy, each night going home. If they put up a yellow poster protesting against traffic, that's the signal."

"And at night? At weekends?"

"Wrong-number phone call. But nobody likes that."

"Has it ever been used?"

"I don't know."

"You mean you don't listen to his phone?"

No answer.

"I want you to take the weekend off. Would that raise eyebrows at the Circus?" Enthusiastically, Esterhase shook his head. "I'm sure you'd prefer to be out of it, anyway, wouldn't you?" Esterhase nodded. "Say you're having girl trouble or whatever sort of trouble you're in these days. You'll be spending the night here, possibly two. Fawn will look after you; there's food in the kitchen. What about your wife?"

While Guillam and Smiley looked on, Esterhase dialled the Circus and asked for Phil Porteous. He said his lines perfectly: a little self-pity, a little conspiracy, a little joke. Some girl who was passionate about him up north, Phil, and threatening wild things if he didn't go and hold her hand.

"Don't tell me, I know it happens to you every day, Phil. Hey, how's that gorgeous new secretary of yours? And listen, Phil, if Mara phones from home, tell her Toby's on a big job, okay? Blowing up the Kremlin, back on Monday. Make it nice and heavy, huh? Cheers, Phil."

He rang off and dialled a number in north London. "Mrs. M., hullo, this is your favourite boyfriend—recognise the voice? Good. Listen, I'm sending you a visitor tonight—an old, old friend, you'll be surprised. She hates me," he explained to them, his hand over the mouthpiece. "He wants to check the wiring," he went on. "Look it all over, make sure it's working okay, no bad leaks—all right?"

"If he's any trouble," Guillam said to Fawn with real venom as they left, "bind him hand and foot."

In the stairwell, Smiley lightly touched his arm. "Peter, I

want you to watch my back. Will you do that for me? Give me a couple of minutes, then pick me up on the corner of Marloes Road, heading north. Stick to the west pavement."

Guillam waited, then stepped into the street. A thin drizzle lay on the air, which had an eerie warmness like a thaw. Where lights shone, the moisture shifted in fine clouds, but in shadow he neither saw nor felt it: simply, a mist blurred his vision, making him half close his eyes. He completed one round of the gardens, then entered a pretty mews well south of the pick-up point. Reaching Marloes Road, he crossed to the west pavement, bought an evening paper, and began walking at a leisurely rate past villas set in deep gardens. He was counting off pedestrians, cyclists, cars, while out ahead of him, steadily plodding the far pavement, he picked out George Smiley, the very prototype of the homegoing Londoner. "Is it a team?" Guillam had asked. Smiley could not be specific. "Short of Abingdon Villas, I'll cross over," he said. "Look for a solo. But look!"

As Guillam watched Smiley pulled up abruptly, as if he had just remembered something, stepped perilously into the road, and scuttled between the angry traffic to disappear at once through the doors of a liquor store. As he did so, Guillam saw, or thought he saw, a tall crooked figure in a dark coat step out after him, but at that moment a bus drew up, screening both Smiley and his pursuer; and when it pulled away, it must have taken his pursuer with it, for the only survivor on that strip of pavement was an older man in a black plastic raincoat and cloth cap lolling at the bus stop while he read his evening paper; and when Smiley emerged from the store with his brown bag, the man did not so much as lift his head from the sporting pages. For a short while longer, Guillam trailed Smiley through the smarter reaches of Victorian Kensington as he slipped from one quiet square to another, sauntered into a mews and out again by the same route. Only once, when

Guillam forgot Smiley and out of instinct turned upon his own tracks, did he have a suspicion of a third figure walking with them: a fanged shadow thrown against the broadloom brickwork of an empty street, but when he started forward, it was gone.

The night had its own madness after that; events ran too quickly for him to fasten on them singly. Not till days afterwards did he realise that the figure, or the shadow of it, had struck a chord of familiarity in his memory. Even then, for some time, he could not place it. Then one early morning, waking abruptly, he had it clear in his mind: a barking, military voice, a gentleness of manner heavily concealed, a squash racket jammed behind the safe of his room in Brixton, which brought tears to the eyes of his unemotional secretary.

35

Probably the only thing which Steve Mackelvore did wrong that same evening, in terms of classic tradecraft, was blame himself for leaving the passenger door of his car unlocked. Climbing in from the driver's side, he put it down to his own negligence that the other lock was up. Survival, as Jim Prideaux liked to recall, is an infinite capacity for suspicion. By that purist standard, Mackelvore should have suspected that in the middle of a particularly vile rush-hour, on a particularly vile evening, in one of those blaring side streets that feed into the lower end of the Elysées, Ricki Tarr would unlock the passenger door and hold him up at gunpoint. But life in the Paris residency these days did little to keep a man's wits sharp, and most of Mackelvore's working day had been taken up with filing his weekly expenses and completing his weekly returns of staff for the housekeepers. Only lunch, a longish affair with an insincere anglophile in the French security labyrinth, had broken the monotony of that Friday.

His car, parked under a lime tree that was dying of exhaust fumes, had an extraterritorial registration and "C.C." plastered on the back, for the residency cover was consular, though no one took it seriously. Mackelvore was a Circus elder, a squat, white-haired Yorkshireman with a long record of consular appointments which in the eyes of the world had brought him no advancement. Paris was the last of them. He did not care particularly for Paris, and he knew from an operational lifetime in the Far East that the French were not for him. But as a prelude to retirement it could not be bettered. The allowances were good, the billet was comfortable, and the most that had been asked of him in the ten months he had been here was to welfare the occasional agent in transit, put up a chalk-mark here and there, play postman to some ploy by London Station, and show a time to the visiting firemen.

Until now, that was, as he sat in his own car with Tarr's gun jammed against his rib-cage, and Tarr's hand resting affectionately on his right shoulder, ready to wrench his head off if he tried any monkey business. A couple of feet away, girls hurried past on their way to the Metro, and six feet beyond that the traffic had come to a standstill; it could stay that way for an hour. None was faintly stirred by the sight of two men having a cosy chat in a parked car.

Tarr had been talking ever since Mackelvore sat down. He needed to send a message to Alleline, he said. It would be personal and decypher yourself, and Tarr would like Steve to work the machine for him while Tarr stood off with the gun.

"What the hell have you been up to, Ricki?" Mackelvore complained, as they walked arm in arm back to the residency. "The whole service is looking for you—you know that, don't you? They'll skin you alive if they find you. We're supposed to do blood-curdling things to you on sight."

He thought of turning into the hold and smacking Tarr's

neck, but he knew he hadn't the speed and Tarr would kill him.

The message would run to about two hundred groups, said Tarr, as Mackelvore unlocked the front door and put on the lights. When Steve had transmitted them, they would sit on the machine and wait for Percy's answer. By tomorrow, if Tarr's instinct was correct, Percy would be coming over to Paris hotfoot to have a conference with Ricki. This conference would also take place in the residency, because Tarr reckoned it was marginally less likely that the Russians would try to kill him on British consular premises.

"You're berserk, Ricki. It's not the Russians who want to kill you. It's us."

The front room was called Reception; it was what remained of the cover. It had an old wooden counter and out-of-date "Notices to British Subjects" hanging on the grimy wall. Here, with his left hand, Tarr searched Mackelvore for a weapon but found none. It was a courtyard house and most of the sensitive stuff was across the yard: the cypher-room, the strong-room, and the machines.

"You're out of your mind, Ricki," Mackelvore warned monotonously, as he led the way through a couple of empty offices and pressed the bell to the cypher-room. "You always thought you were Napoleon Bonaparte and now it's got you completely. You'd too much religion from your dad."

The steel message hatch slid back and a mystified, slightly silly face appeared in the opening. "You can go home, Ben, boy. Go home to your missus but stay close to your phone in case I need you, there's a lad. Leave the books where they are and put the keys in the machines. I'll be talking to London presently, under my own steam."

The face withdrew and they waited while the boy unlocked the door from inside: one key, two keys, a spring lock.

"This gentleman's from out East, Ben," Mackelvore explained as the door opened. "He's one of my most distinguished connections."

"Hullo, sir," said Ben. He was a tall, mathematical-looking boy with spectacles and an unblinking gaze.

"Get along with you, Ben. I'll not dock it against your duty pay. You've the weekend free on full rates, and you'll not owe me time, either. Off you go, then."

"Ben stays here," said Tarr.

In Cambridge Circus the lighting was quite yellow and from where Mendel stood, on the third floor of the clothes shop, the wet tarmac glistened like cheap gold. It was nearly midnight and he had been standing three hours. He stood between a net curtain and a clothes-horse. He stood the way coppers stand the world over: weight on both feet equally, legs straight, leaning slightly backward over the line of balance. He had pulled his hat low and turned up his collar to keep the white of his face from the street, but his eyes as they watched the front entrance below him glittered like a cat's eyes in a coal-hole. He would wait another three hours or another six: Mendel was back on the beat; the scent of the hunt was in his nostrils. Better still, he was a night bird; the darkness of that fitting room woke him wonderfully. Such light as reached him from the street lay upside down in pale pieces on the ceiling. All the rest—the cutting-benches, the bolts of cloth, the draped machines, the steam iron, the signed photographs of princes of the blood—these were there because he had seen them on his reconnaissance that afternoon; the light did not reach them and even now he could barely make them out.

From his window he covered most of the approaches: eight or nine unequal roads and alleys that for no good reason had chosen Cambridge Circus as their meeting point. Between them, the buildings were gimcrack, cheaply fitted out with bits of Empire: a Roman bank, a theatre like a vast desecrated mosque. Behind them, high-rise blocks advanced like an army of robots. Above, a pink sky was slowly filling with fog.

Why was it so quiet? he wondered. The theatre had long emptied but why didn't the pleasure trade of Soho, only a stone's throw from his window, fill the place with taxis, groups of loiterers? Not a single fruit lorry had rumbled down Shaftesbury Avenue on its way to Covent Garden.

Through his binoculars Mendel once more studied the building straight across the road from him. It seemed to sleep even more soundly than its neighbours. The twin doors of the portico were closed and no light was visible in the ground-floor windows. Only on the fourth floor, out of the second window from the left, a pale glow issued, and Mendel knew it was the duty officer's room; Smiley had told him. Briefly he raised the glasses to the roof, where a plantation of aerials made wild patterns against the sky, then down a floor to the four blackened windows of the radio section.

"At night everyone uses the front door," Guillam had said. "It's an economy measure to cut down on janitors."

In those three hours, only three events had rewarded Mendel's vigil; one an hour is not much. At half past nine a blue Ford Transit delivered two men carrying what looked like an ammunition box. They unlocked the door for themselves and closed it as soon as they were inside, while Mendel murmured his commentary into the telephone. At ten o'clock the shuttle arrived; Guillam had warned him of this, too. The shuttle collected hot documents from the outstations and stored them for safekeeping at the Circus over the weekend. It called at Brixton, Acton, and Sarratt, in that order, said Guillam, lastly at the Admiralty, and it made the Circus by about ten. In the event, it arrived on the dot of ten, and this time two men from inside the building came out to help unload; Mendel reported that, too, and Smiley acknowledged with a patient "Thank you."

Was Smiley sitting down? Was he in the darkness like Mendel? Mendel had a notion he was. Of all the odd coves he had known, Smiley was the oddest. You thought, to look at him, that he couldn't cross the road alone, but you might as well have offered protection to a hedgehog. Funnies, Mendel mused. A lifetime of chasing villains and how do I end up? Breaking and entering, standing in the dark and spying on the Funnies. He'd never held with Funnies till he met Smiley. Thought they were an interfering lot of amateurs and college boys; thought they were unconstitutional; thought the best thing the Special Branch could do, for its own sake and the public's, was say "Yes, sir," "No, sir" and lose the correspondence. Come to think of it, with the notable exception of Smiley and Guillam, that's exactly what he thought tonight.

Shortly before eleven, just an hour ago, a cab arrived. A plain licensed London hackney cab, and it drew up at the theatre. Even that was something Smiley had warned him about: it was the habit within the service not to take taxis to the door. Some stopped at Foyle's, some in Old Compton Street or at one of the shops; most people had a favourite cover destination and Alleline's was the theatre. Mendel had never seen Alleline, but he had their description of him and as he watched him through the glasses he recognised him without a doubt, a big lumbering fellow in a dark coat; he even noticed how the cabby pulled a bad face at his tip and called something after him as Alleline delved for his keys.

The front door is not secured, Guillam had explained; it is only locked. The security begins inside, once you have turned left at the end of the corridor. Alleline lives on the fifth floor. You won't see his windows light up but there's a skylight and the glow should catch the chimney-stack. Sure enough, as he watched, a patch of yellow appeared on the grimy bricks of the chimney: Alleline had entered his room.

And young Guillam needs a holiday, thought Mendel. He'd seen *that* happen before, too: the tough ones who crack at forty. They lock it away, pretend it isn't there, lean on grown-ups who turn out not to be so grown up after all; then one day it's all over them, and their heroes come tumbling down and they're sitting at their desks with the tears pouring onto the blotter.

He had laid the receiver on the floor. Picking it up, he said, "Looks like Tinker's clocked in."

He gave the number of the cab, then went back to waiting.

"How did he look?" Smiley murmured.

"Busy," said Mendel.

"So he should be."

That one won't crack, though, Mendel decided with approval; one of your flabby oak trees, Smiley was. Think you could blow him over with one puff, but when it comes to the storm he's the only one left standing at the end of it. At this point in his reflections a second cab drew up, squarely at the front entrance, and a tall slow figure cautiously climbed the steps one at a time, like a man who takes care of his heart.

"Here's your Tailor," Mendel murmured into the telephone. "Hold on, here's Soldier-boy, too. Proper gathering of the clans, by the look of it. I say, take it easy."

An old Mercedes 190 shot out of Earlham Street, swung directly beneath his window, and held the curve with difficulty as far as the northern outlet of the Charing Cross Road, where it parked. A young heavy fellow with ginger hair clambered out, slammed the door, and clumped across the street to the entrance without even taking the key out of the dash. A moment later another light went up on the fourth floor as Roy Bland joined the party.

All we need to know now is who comes out, thought Mendel.

36

Lock Gardens, which presumably drew its name from the Camden and Hampstead Road Locks nearby, was a terrace of four flat-fronted nineteenth-century houses built at the centre of a crescent, each with three floors and a basement and a strip of walled back garden running down to the Regent's Canal. The numbers ran 2 to 5: number 1 had either fallen down or never been built. Number 5 made up the north end, and as a safe house it could not have been improved, for there were three approaches in thirty yards and the canal towpath offered two more. To the north lay Camden High Street for joining traffic; south and west lay the parks and Primrose Hill. Better still, the neighbourhood possessed no social identity and demanded none. Some of the houses had been turned into one-room flats, and had ten doorbells laid out like a typewriter. Some were got up grandly and had only one. Number 5 had two: one for Millie McCraig and one for her lodger, Mr. Jefferson.

Mrs. McCraig was churchy and collected for everything, which was incidentally an excellent way of keeping an eye on the locals, though that was scarcely how they viewed her zeal. Jefferson, her lodger, was known vaguely to be foreign and in oil and away a lot. Lock Gardens was his *pied-à-terre*. The neighbours, when they bothered to notice him, found him shy and respectable. They would have formed the same impression of George Smiley if they had happened to spot him in the dim light of the porch at nine that evening, as Millie McCraig admitted him to her front room and drew the pious curtains. She was a wiry Scottish widow with brown stockings and bobbed hair and the polished, wrinkled skin of an old man. In the interest of God and the Circus, she had run Bible schools in Mozambique and a seaman's mission in Hamburg, and though she had been a professional eavesdropper for twenty years since then, she was still inclined to treat all menfolk as transgressors. Smiley had no way of telling what she thought. Her manner, from the moment he arrived, had a deep and lonely stillness; she showed him round the house like a chatelaine whose guests had long since died.

First the semi-basement, where she lived herself, full of plants and that medley of old postcards, brass table-tops, and carved black furniture which seems to attach itself to travelled British ladies of a certain age and class. Yes, if the Circus wanted her at night they rang her on the basement phone. Yes, there was a separate line upstairs, but it was only for outgoing calls. The basement phone had an extension in the upstairs dining-room. Then up to the ground floor, a veritable shrine to the costly bad taste of the housekeepers: loud Regency stripes, gilded reproduction chairs, plush sofas with roped corners. The kitchen was untouched and squalid. Beyond it lay a glass outhouse, half conservatory, half scullery, which looked down to the rough garden and the canal. Strewn over the tiled floor: an old mangle, a copper tub, and crates of tonic water.

"Where are the mikes, Millie?" Smiley had returned to the drawing-room.

They were in pairs, Millie murmured, bedded behind the wallpaper: two pairs to each room on the ground floor, one to each room upstairs. Each pair was connected with a separate recorder. He followed her up the steep stairs. The top floor was unfurnished save for an attic bedroom that contained a grey steel frame with eight tape machines, four up, four down.

"And Jefferson knows all about this?"

"Mr. Jefferson," said Millie primly, "is run on a basis of trust." That was the nearest she came to expressing her disapproval of Smiley, or her devotion to Christian ethics.

Downstairs again, she showed him the switches that controlled the system. An extra switch was fitted in each finger panel. Any time Jefferson or one of the boys, as she put it, wanted to go over to record, he had only to get up and turn down the left-hand light switch. From then on, the system was voice-activated; that is to say, the tape deck did not turn unless somebody was speaking.

"And where are you while all this goes on, Millie?"

She remained downstairs, she said, as if that were a woman's place.

Smiley was pulling open cupboards, lockers, walking from room to room. Then back to the scullery again, with its view to the canal. Taking out a pocket torch, he signalled one flash into the darkness of the garden.

"What are the safety procedures?" Smiley asked as he thoughtfully fingered the end light switch by the drawing-room door.

Her reply came in a liturgical monotone. "Two full milk bottles on the doorstep, you may come in and all's well. No milk bottles and you're not to enter."

From the direction of the sunroom came a faint tapping. Returning to the scullery, Smiley opened the glazed door and after a hastily murmured conversation reappeared with Guillam.

"You know Peter, don't you, Millie?"

Millie might, she might not; her little hard eyes had fixed on him with scorn. He was studying the switch panel, feeling in his pocket as he did so.

"What's he doing? He's not to do that. Stop him."

If she was worried, said Smiley, she should ring Lacon on the basement phone. Millie McCraig didn't stir, but two red bruises had appeared on her leathery cheeks and she was snapping her fingers in anger. With a small screwdriver Guillam had cautiously removed the screws from either side of the plastic panel, and was peering at the wiring behind. Now, very carefully, he turned the end switch upside down, twisting it on its wires, then screwed the plate back in position, leaving the remaining switches undisturbed.

"We'll just try it," said Guillam, and while Smiley went upstairs to check the tape deck, Guillam sang "Old Man River," in a low Paul Robeson growl.

"Thank you," said Smiley with a shudder, coming down again. "That's more than enough."

Millie had gone to the basement to ring Lacon. Quietly, Smiley set the stage. He put the telephone beside an armchair in the drawing-room, then cleared his line of retreat to the scullery. He fetched two full bottles of milk from the icebox and placed them on the doorstep to signify, in the eclectic language of Millie McCraig, that you may come in and all's well. He removed his shoes and took them to the scullery, and having put out all the lights, took up his post in the armchair just as Mendel made his connecting call.

On the canal towpath, meanwhile, Guillam had resumed his vigil of the house. The footpath is closed to the public one hour before dark: after that it can be anything from a trysting place for lovers to a haven for down-and-outs; both, for different reasons, are attracted by the darkness of the bridges. That cold night Guillam saw neither. Occasionally an empty train raced past, leaving a still greater emptiness behind. His nerves were so taut, his expectations so varied, that for a moment he saw the whole architecture of that night in apocalyptic terms: the signals on the railway bridge turned to gallows; the Victorian warehouses to gigantic prisons, their windows barred and arched against the misty sky. Closer at hand, the ripple of rats and the stink of still water. Then the drawing-room lights went out; the house stood in darkness except for the chinks of yellow to either side of Millie's basement window. From the scullery a pin of light winked at him down the unkempt garden. Taking a pen torch from his pocket, he slipped out the silver hood, sighted it with shaking fingers at the point from which the light had come, and signalled back. From now on, they could only wait.

Tarr tossed the incoming telegram back to Ben, together with the one-time pad from the safe.

"Come on," he said, "earn your pay. Unbutton it."

"It's personal for you," Ben objected. "Look. 'Personal from Alleline decypher yourself.' I'm not allowed to touch it. It's the tops."

"Do as he asks, Ben," said Mackelvore, watching Tarr.

For ten minutes, no word passed between the three men.

Tarr was standing across the room from them, very nervous from the waiting. He had jammed the gun in his waistband. His jacket lay over a chair. The sweat had stuck his shirt to his back all the way down. Ben was using a ruler to read off the number groups, then carefully writing his findings on the block of graph paper before him. To concentrate, he put his tongue against his teeth, and now he made a small click as he withdrew it. Putting aside his pencil, he offered Tarr the tearsheet.

"Read it aloud," Tarr said.

Ben's voice was kindly, and a little fervent. " 'Personal for Tarr from Alleline decypher yourself. I positively require clarification and/or trade samples before meeting your request. Quote information vital to safeguarding of the service unquote does not qualify. Let me remind you of your bad position here following your disgraceful disappearance stop urge you confide Mackelvore immediately repeat immediately stop Chief.' "

Ben had not quite finished before Tarr began laughing in a strange, excited way.

"That's the way, Percy boy!" he cried. "Yes repeat no! Know why he's stalling, Ben, darling? He's sizing up to shoot me in the bloody back! That's how he got my Russki girl. He's playing the same tune, the bastard." He was ruffling Ben's hair, shouting at him, laughing. "I warn you, Ben: there's some damn lousy people in this outfit, so don't you trust the one of them, I'm telling you, or you'll never grow up strong!"

Alone in the darkness of the drawing-room, Smiley also waited, sitting in the housekeeper's uncomfortable chair, his head propped awkwardly against the earpiece of the telephone. Occasionally he would mutter something and Mendel would mutter back; most of the time they shared the silence. His mood was subdued, even a little glum. Like an actor, he had a sense of approaching anti-climax before the curtain went up, a sense of great things dwindling to a small, mean end; as death itself seemed small and mean to him after the struggles of his life. He had no sense of conquest that he knew of. His thoughts, as often when he was afraid, concerned people. He had no theories or judgements in particular. He simply wondered how everyone would be affected; and he felt responsible. He thought of Jim and Sam and Max and Connie and Jerry Westerby, and personal loyalties all broken; in a separate category he thought of Ann and the hopeless dislocation of their talk on the Cornish cliffs; he wondered whether there was any love between human beings that did not rest upon some sort of self-delusion; he wished he could just get up and walk out before it happened, but he couldn't. He worried, in a quite paternal way, about Guillam, and wondered how he would take the late strains of growing up. He thought again of the day he buried Control. He thought about treason and wondered whether there was mindless treason in the same way, supposedly, as there was mindless violence. It worried him that he felt so bankrupt; that whatever intellectual or philosophical precepts he clung to broke down entirely now that he was faced with the human situation.

"Anything?" he asked Mendel, into the telephone.

"A couple of drunks," said Mendel, "singing 'See the jungle when it's wet with rain.'"

"Never heard of it."

Changing the telephone to his left side, he drew the gun from the wallet pocket of his jacket, where it had already ruined the excellent silk lining. He discovered the safety catch, and for a moment played with the idea that he didn't know which way was on and which way off. He snapped out the magazine and put it back, and remembered doing this hundreds of times on the trot, in the night range at Sarratt before the war; he remembered how you always shot with two hands, sir, one to hold the gun and one the magazine, sir;

and how there was a piece of Circus folklore which demanded that he should lay his index finger along the barrel and pull the trigger with his second. But when he tried it the sensation was ridiculous and he forgot about it.

"Just taking a walk," he murmured, and Mendel said "Righty-ho."

The gun still in his hand, he returned to the scullery, listening for a creak in the floorboards that might give him away, but the floor must have been concrete under the tatty carpet; he could have jumped and caused not even a vibration. With his torch he signalled two short flashes, a long delay, then two more. At once Guillam replied with three short.

"Back again."

"Got you," said Mendel.

He settled, thinking glumly of Ann: to dream the impossible dream. He put the gun in his pocket. From the canal side, the moan of a hooter. At night? Boats moving at night? Must be a car. What if Gerald has a whole emergency procedure that we know nothing about? A call-box to call-box, a car pick-up? What if Polyakov has after all a legman, a helper whom Connie never identified? He'd been through that already. This system was built to be watertight, to accommodate meetings in all contingencies. When it comes to tradecraft, Karla is a pedant.

And his fancy that he was being followed? What of that? What of the shadow he never saw, only felt, till his back seemed to tingle with the intensity of his watcher's gaze; he saw nothing, heard nothing, only felt. He was too old not to heed the warning. The creak of a stair that had not creaked before; the rustle of a shutter when no wind was blowing; the car with a different number plate but the same scratch on the offside wing: the face on the Metro that you know you have seen somewhere before: for years at a time these were signs he had lived by; any one of them was reason enough to move, change towns, identities. For in that profession there is no such thing as coincidence.

"One gone," said Mendel suddenly. "Hullo?"

"I'm here."

Somebody had just come out of the Circus, said Mendel. Front door, but he couldn't be certain of the identification. Mackintosh and hat. Bulky and moving fast. He must have ordered a cab to the door and stepped straight into it.

"Heading north, your way."

Smiley looked at his watch. Give him ten minutes, he thought. Give him twelve; he'll have to stop and phone Polyakov on the way. Then he thought, Don't be silly, he's done that already from the Circus.

"I'm ringing off," said Smiley.

"Cheers," said Mendel.

On the footpath, Guillam read three long flashes. The mole is on his way.

In the scullery Smiley had once more checked his thoroughfare, shoved some deck-chairs aside, and pinned a string to the mangle to guide him because he saw badly in the dark. The string led to the open kitchen door, and the kitchen led to the drawing-room and dining-room both; it had the two doors side by side. The kitchen was a long room, actually an annexe to the house before the glass scullery was added. He had thought of using the dining-room but it was too risky, and besides from the dining-room he couldn't signal to Guillam. So he waited in the scullery, feeling absurd in his stockinged feet, polishing his spectacles because the heat of his face kept misting them. It was much colder in the scullery. The drawing-room was close and overheated but the scullery had these outside walls, and this glass and this concrete floor beneath the matting, which made his feet feel wet. The mole arrives first, he thought; the mole plays host: that is protocol, part of the pretence that Polyakov is Gerald's agent.

A London taxi is a flying bomb.

The comparison rose in him slowly, from deep in his

unconscious memory. The clatter as it barges into the crescent, the metric *tick-tick* as the bass notes die. The cut-off: where has it stopped, which house—when all of us on the street are waiting in the dark, crouching under tables or clutching at pieces of string—which house? Then the slam of the door, the explosive anti-climax: if you can hear it, it's not for you.

But Smiley heard it, and it was for him.

He heard the tread of one pair of feet on the gravel, brisk and vigorous. They stopped. It's the wrong door, Smiley thought absurdly; go away. He had the gun in his hand; he had dropped the catch. Still he listened, heard nothing. You're suspicious, Gerald, he thought. You're an old mole, you can sniff there's something wrong. Millie, he thought; Millie has taken away the milk bottles, put up a warning, headed him off. Millie's spoilt the kill. Then he heard the latch turn, one turn, two; it's a Banham lock, he remembered—my God, we must keep Banham's in business. Of course: the mole had been patting his pockets, looking for his key. A nervous man would have it in his hand already, would have been clutching it, cosseting it in his pocket all the way in the taxi; but not the mole. The mole might be worried but he was not nervous. At the same moment the latch turned, the bell chimed—housekeepers' taste again: high tone, low tone, high tone. That will mean it's one of us, Millie had said; one of the boys, her boys, Connie's boys, Karla's boys. The front door opened, someone stepped into the house, he heard the shuffle of the mat, he heard the door close, he heard the light switches snap and saw a pale line appear under the kitchen door. He put the gun in his pocket and wiped the palm of his hand on his jacket, then took it out again and in the same moment he heard a second flying bomb, a second taxi pulling up, and footsteps fast. Polyakov didn't just have the key ready, he had his taxi money ready, too: do Russians tip, he wondered, or is tipping undemocratic? Again the bell rang, the front door opened and closed, and Smiley heard the double chink as two milk bottles were put on the hall table in the interest of good order and sound tradecraft.

Lord save me, thought Smiley in horror as he stared at the old icebox beside him; it never crossed my mind: suppose he had wanted to put them back in the fridge?

The strip of light under the kitchen door grew suddenly brighter as the drawing-room lights were switched on. An extraordinary silence descended over the house. Holding the string, Smiley edged forward over the icy floor. Then he heard voices. At first they were indistinct. They must still be at the far end of the room, he thought. Or perhaps they always begin in a low tone. Now Polyakov came nearer: he was at the trolley, pouring drinks.

"What is our cover story in case we are disturbed?" he asked in good English.

"Lovely voice," Smiley remembered; "mellow like yours. I often used to play the tapes twice, just to listen to him speaking." Connie, you should hear him now.

From the further end of the room still, a muffled murmur answered each question. Smiley could make nothing of it. "Where shall we regroup?" "What is our fallback?" "Have you anything on you that you would prefer me to be carrying during our talk, bearing in mind I have diplomatic immunity?"

It must be a catechism, Smiley thought; part of Karla's school routine.

"Is the switch down? Will you please check? Thank you. What will you drink?"

"Scotch," said Haydon, "a bloody great big one."

With a feeling of utter disbelief, Smiley listened to the familiar voice reading aloud the very telegram that Smiley himself had drafted for Tarr's use only forty-eight hours ago.

Then, for a moment, one part of Smiley broke into open revolt against the other. The wave of angry doubt that had swept over him in Lacon's garden, and that ever since had pulled against his progress like a worrying tide, drove him now on to the rocks of despair, and then to mutiny: I refuse. Nothing is worth the destruction of another human being. Somewhere the path of pain and betrayal must end. Until that happened, there was no future; there was only a continued slide into still more terrifying versions of the present. This man was my friend and Ann's lover, Jim's friend and—for all I know—Jim's lover, too; it was the treason, not the man, that belonged to the public domain.

Haydon had betrayed. As a lover, a colleague, a friend; as a patriot; as a member of that inestimable body that Ann loosely called the Set: in every capacity, Haydon had overtly pursued one aim and secretly achieved its opposite. Smiley knew very well that even now he did not grasp the scope of that appalling duplicity; yet there was a part of him that rose already in Haydon's defence. Was not Bill also betrayed? Connie's lament rang in his ears: "Poor loves. Trained to Empire, trained to rule the waves . . . You're the last, George, you and Bill." He saw with painful clarity an ambitious man born to the big canvas, brought up to rule, divide and conquer, whose visions and vanities all were fixed, like Percy's, upon the world's game; for whom the reality was a poor island with scarcely a voice that would carry across the water. Thus Smiley felt not only disgust, but, despite all that the moment meant to him, a surge of resentment against the institutions he was supposed to be protecting: "The social contract cuts both ways, you know," said Lacon. The Minister's lolling mendacity, Lacon's tight-lipped moral complacency, the bludgeoning greed of Percy Alleline: such men invalidated any contract—why should anyone be loyal to them?

He knew, of course. He had always known it was Bill. Just as Control had known, and Lacon in Mendel's house. Just as Connie and Jim had known, and Alleline and Esterhase; all of them had tacitly shared that unexpressed half-knowledge which like an illness they hoped would go away if it was never owned to, never diagnosed.

And Ann? Did Ann know? Was that the shadow that fell over them that day on the Cornish cliffs?

For a space, that was how Smiley stood: a fat, barefooted spy, as Ann would say, deceived in love and impotent in hate, clutching a gun in one hand, a bit of string in the other, as he waited in the darkness. Then, gun still in hand, he tiptoed backward as far as the window, from which he signalled five short flashes in quick succession. Having waited long enough to read the acknowledgement, he returned to his listening post.

Guillam raced down the canal towpath, the torch jolting wildly in his hand, till he reached a low arched bridge and a steel stairway that led upward in zigzags to Gloucester Avenue. The gate was closed and he had to climb it, ripping one sleeve to the elbow. Lacon was standing at the corner of Princess Road, wearing an old country coat and carrying a briefcase.

"He's there. He's arrived," Guillam whispered. "He's got Gerald."

"I won't have bloodshed," Lacon warned. "I want absolute calm."

Guillam didn't bother to reply. Thirty yards down the road Mendel was waiting in a tame cab. They drove for two minutes, not so much, and stopped the cab short of the crescent. Guillam was holding Esterhase's door key. Reaching number 5, Mendel and Guillam stepped over the gate, rather than risk the noise of it, and kept to the grass verge. As they went, Guillam glanced back and thought for a moment he saw a figure watching them—man or woman, he couldn't tell—from the shadow of a doorway across the road; but when he drew Mendel's attention to the spot there was nothing there, and Mendel ordered him quite roughly to calm down. The porch light was out. Guillam went ahead; Mendel waited under an apple tree. Guillam inserted the key, felt the lock ease as he turned it. Damn fool, he thought triumphantly, why didn't you drop the latch? He pushed open the door an inch and hesitated. He was breathing slowly, filling his lungs for action. Mendel moved forward another bound. In the street two young boys went by, laughing loudly because they were nervous of the night. Once more Guillam looked back but the crescent was clear. He stepped into the hall. He was wearing suède shoes and they squeaked on the parquet; there was no carpet. At the drawing-room door he listened long enough for the fury to break in him at last.

His butchered agents in Morocco, his exile to Brixton, the daily frustration of his efforts as daily he grew older and youth slipped through his fingers; the drabness that was closing round him; the truncation of his power to love, enjoy, and laugh; the constant erosion of the standards he wished to live by; the checks and stops he had imposed on himself in the name of tacit dedication—he could fling them all in Haydon's sneering face. Haydon, once his confessor; Haydon, always good for a laugh, a chat, and a cup of burnt coffee; Haydon, a model on which he built his life.

And more. Now that he saw, he knew. Haydon was more than his model, he was his inspiration, the torch-bearer of a certain kind of antiquated romanticism, a notion of English calling which—for the very reason that it was vague and understated and elusive—had made sense of Guillam's life till now. In that moment, Guillam felt not merely betrayed but orphaned. His suspicions, his resentments for so long turned outward on the real world—on his women, his attempted loves—now swung upon the Circus and the failed magic that had formed his faith. With all his force he shoved open the door and sprang inside, gun in hand. Haydon and a heavy man with black hair were seated either side of a small table. Polyakov—Guillam recognised him from the photographs— was smoking a very English pipe. He wore a grey cardigan with a zip down the front, like the top half of a track suit. He had not even taken the pipe from his mouth before

Guillam had Haydon by the collar. With a single heave he lifted him straight out of his chair. He had thrown away his gun and was hurling Haydon from side to side, shaking him, and shouting. Then suddenly there seemed no point. After all, it was only Bill and they had done a lot together. Guillam had drawn back long before Mendel took his arm, and he heard Smiley, politely as ever, inviting "Bill and Colonel Viktorov," as he called them, to raise their hands and place them on their heads till Percy Alleline arrived.

"There was no one out there, was there, that you noticed?" Smiley asked of Guillam, while they waited.

"Quiet as the grave," said Mendel, answering for both of them.

37

There are moments that are made up of too much stuff for them to be lived at the time they occur. For Guillam and all those present, this was one. Smiley's continued distraction and Haydon's indifference; his frequent cautious glances from the window; Polyakov's predictable fit of indignation, his demands to be treated as became a member of the Diplomatic Corps—demands that Guillam from his place on the sofa tersely threatened to meet; the flustered arrival of Alleline and Bland; more protestations and the pilgrimage upstairs, where Smiley played the tapes; the long glum silence that followed their return to the drawing-room; the arrival of Lacon and finally of Esterhase and Fawn; Millie McCraig's silent ministrations with the teapot: all these events and cameos unrolled with a theatrical unreality that, much like the trip to Ascot an age before, was intensified by the unreality of

the hour of day. It was also true that these incidents, which
included at an early point the physical constraint of Polyakov
—and a stream of Russian abuse directed at Fawn for hitting
him, heaven knows where, despite Mendel's vigilance—were
like a silly subplot against Smiley's only purpose in convening
the assembly: to persuade Alleline that Haydon offered
Smiley's one chance to treat with Karla, and to save, in
humanitarian if not professional terms, whatever was left of
the networks that Haydon had betrayed. Smiley was not
empowered to conduct these transactions, nor did he seem to
want to; perhaps he reckoned that between them Esterhase
and Bland and Alleline were better placed to know what
agents were still theoretically in being. In any event he soon
took himself upstairs, where Guillam heard him once more
restlessly padding from one room to the other as he continued
his vigil from the windows.

So while Alleline and his lieutenants withdrew with Polyakov to the dining-room to conduct their business alone, the
rest of them sat in silence in the drawing-room, either looking
at Haydon or deliberately away from him. He seemed unaware that they were there. Chin in hand, he sat apart from
them in a corner, watched over by Fawn, and he looked
rather bored. The conference ended, they all trooped out of
the dining-room and Alleline announced to Lacon, who insisted on not being present at the discussions, that an appointment had been made three days hence at this address, by
which time "the Colonel will have had a chance to consult his
superiors." Lacon nodded. It might have been a board
meeting.

The departures were even stranger than the arrivals. Between Esterhase and Polyakov in particular, there was a
curiously poignant farewell. Esterhase, who would always
rather have been a gentleman than a spy, seemed determined
to make a gallant occasion of it, and offered his hand, which
Polyakov struck petulantly aside. Esterhase looked round
forlornly for Smiley, perhaps in the hope of ingratiating

himself further with him, then shrugged and flung an arm across Bland's broad shoulder. Soon afterwards they left together. They didn't say goodbye to anybody, but Bland looked dreadfully shaken and Esterhase seemed to be consoling him, though his own future at that moment could hardly have struck him as rosy. Soon afterwards a radio cab arrived for Polyakov and he, too, left without a nod to anyone. By now, the conversation had died entirely; without the Russian present, the show became wretchedly parochial. Haydon remained in his familiar bored pose, still watched by Fawn and Mendel, and stared at in mute embarrassment by Lacon and Alleline. More telephone calls were made, mainly for cars. At some point Smiley reappeared from upstairs and mentioned Tarr. Alleline phoned the Circus and dictated one telegram to Paris saying that he could return to England with honour, whatever that meant; and a second to Mackelvore saying that Tarr was an acceptable person, which again seemed to Guillam a matter of opinion.

Finally, to the general relief, a windowless van arrived from the Nursery, and two men got out whom Guillam had never seen before, one tall and limping, the other doughy and fair-haired. With a shudder Guillam realised they were inquisitors. Fawn fetched Haydon's coat from the hall, went through the pockets, and respectfully helped him into it. At this point, Smiley gently interposed himself and insisted that Haydon's walk from the front door to the van should take place without the hall light on, and that the escort should be large. Guillam, Fawn, even Alleline, were pressed into service, and finally, with Haydon at its centre, the whole motley group shuffled through the garden to the van.

"It's simply a precaution," Smiley insisted. No one was disposed to argue with him. Haydon climbed in, and the inquisitors followed, locking the grille from inside. As the doors closed, Haydon lifted one hand in an amiable, if dismissive, gesture directed at Alleline.

So it was only afterwards that separate things came back to

Guillam and single people came forward for his recollection: the unqualified hatred, for instance, which Polyakov directed against everyone present, from poor little Millie McCraig upwards, and which actually distorted him; his mouth curved in a savage, uncontrollable sneer, he turned white and trembled, but not from fear and not from anger. It was just plain hatred, of the sort that Guillam could not visit on Haydon, but then Haydon was of his own kind.

For Alleline, in the moment of his defeat, Guillam discovered a sneaking admiration: Alleline at least had shown a certain bearing. But later Guillam was not so sure whether Percy realised, on that first presentation of the facts, quite what the facts were: after all, he was still Chief, and Haydon was still his Iago.

But the strangest thing to Guillam, the insight that he took away with him and thought over much more deeply than was commonly his policy, was that despite his banked-up anger at the moment of breaking into the room, it required an act of will on his own part—and quite a violent one, at that—to regard Bill Haydon with much other than affection. Perhaps, as Bill would say, he had finally grown up. Best of all, on the same evening he climbed the steps to his flat and heard the familiar notes of Camilla's flute echoing in the well. And if Camilla that night lost something of her mystery, at least by morning he had succeeded in freeing her from the toils of double-cross to which he had latterly consigned her.

In other ways also, over the next few days, his life took on a brighter look. Percy Alleline had been dispatched on indefinite leave; Smiley had been asked to come back for a while and help sweep up what was left. For Guillam himself there was talk of being rescued from Brixton. It was not till much, much later that he learned that there had been a final act; and he put a name and a purpose to that familiar shadow which had followed Smiley through the night streets of Kensington.

38

For the next two days George Smiley lived in limbo. To his neighbours, when they noticed him, he seemed to have lapsed into a wasting grief. He rose late and pottered round the house in his dressing gown, cleaning things, dusting, cooking himself meals and not eating them. In the afternoon, quite against the local by-laws, he lit a coal fire and sat before it reading among his German poets or writing letters to Ann, which he seldom completed and never posted. When the telephone rang, he went to it quickly, only to be disappointed. Outside the window the weather continued foul, and the few passers-by—Smiley studied them continuously—were huddled in Balkan misery. Once Lacon called with a request from the Minister that Smiley should "stand by to help clear up the mess at Cambridge Circus, were he called upon to do so"—in effect, to act as night watchman till a replacement for Percy Alleline could be found. Replying vaguely, Smiley prevailed on Lacon to take extreme care of Haydon's physical safety while he was at Sarratt.

"Aren't you being a little dramatic?" Lacon retorted. "The only place he can go is Russia, and we're sending him there anyway."

"When? How soon?"

The details would take several more days to arrange. Smiley disdained, in his state of anti-climactic reaction, to ask how the interrogation was progressing meanwhile, but Lacon's manner suggested that the answer would have been "badly." Mendel brought him more solid fare.

"Immingham railway station's shut," he said. "You'll have to get out at Grimsby and hoof it or take a bus."

More often, Mendel simply sat and watched him, as one might an invalid. "Waiting won't make her come, you know," he said once. "Time the mountain went to Mohammed. Faint heart never won fair lady, if I may say so."

On the morning of the third day, the doorbell rang and Smiley answered it so fast that it might have been Ann, having mislaid her key as usual. It was Lacon. Smiley was required at Sarratt, he said; Haydon insisted on seeing him. The inquisitors had got nowhere and time was running out. The understanding was that if Smiley would act as confessor, Haydon would give a limited account of himself.

"I'm assured there has been no coercion," Lacon said.

Sarratt was a sorry place after the grandeur that Smiley remembered. Most of the elms had gone with the disease; pylons burgeoned over the old cricket field. The house itself, a sprawling brick mansion, had also come down a lot since the heyday of the cold war in Europe, and most of the better furniture seemed to have disappeared, he supposed into one of Alleline's houses. He found Haydon in a Nissen hut hidden among the trees.

Inside, it had the stink of an army guardhouse, black-painted walls and high-barred windows. Guards manned the rooms to either side and they received Smiley respectfully, calling him "sir." The word, it seemed, had got around. Haydon was dressed in denims, he was trembling, and he complained of dizziness. Several times he had to lie on his bed to stop the nosebleeds he was having. He had grown a half-hearted beard: apparently there was a dispute about whether he was allowed a razor.

"Cheer up," said Smiley. "You'll be out of here soon."

He had tried, on the journey down, to remember Prideaux, and Irina, and the Czech networks, and he even entered Haydon's room with a vague notion of public duty: somehow, he thought, he ought to censure him on behalf of right-thinking men. He felt instead rather shy; he felt he had never known Haydon at all, and now it was too late. He was also angry at Haydon's physical condition, but when he taxed the guards they professed mystification. He was angrier still to learn that the additional security precautions he had insisted on had been relaxed after the first day. When he demanded to see Craddox, head of Nursery, Craddox was unavailable and his assistant acted dumb.

Their first conversation was halting and banal.

Would Smiley please forward the mail from his club, and tell Alleline to get a move on with the horse-trading with Karla? And he needed tissues, paper tissues for his nose. His habit of weeping, Haydon explained, had nothing to do with remorse or pain; it was a physical reaction to what he called the pettiness of the inquisitors, who had made up their minds that Haydon knew the names of other Karla recruits, and were determined to have them before he left. There was also a school of thought which held that Fanshawe, of the Christ Church Optimates, had been acting as a talent-spotter for Moscow Centre as well as for the Circus, Haydon explained. "Really, what can one do with asses like that?" He managed, despite his weakness, to convey that his was the only level head around. They walked in the grounds, and Smiley established with something close to despair that the perimeter was not even patrolled any more, either by night or by day. After one circuit, Haydon asked to go back to the hut, where he dug up a piece of floorboard and extracted some sheets of paper covered in hieroglyphics. They reminded Smiley forcibly of Irina's diary. Squatting on the bed, he sorted through them, and in that pose, in that dull light, with his long forelock dangling almost to the paper, he might have been lounging in Control's room, back in the sixties, propounding some wonderfully plausible and quite inoperable piece of skulduggery for England's greater glory. Smiley did not bother to write anything down, since it was common ground between them that their conversation was being recorded anyway. The statement began with a long apologia, of which he afterwards recalled only a few sentences.

"We live in an age where only fundamental issues matter . . .

"The United States is no longer capable of undertaking its own revolution . . .

"The political posture of the United Kingdom is without relevance or moral viability in world affairs . . ."

With much of it, Smiley might, in other circumstances, have agreed; it was the tone, rather than the music, that alienated him.

"In capitalist America economic repression of the masses is institutionalised to a point which not even Lenin could have foreseen . . .

"The cold war began in 1917 but the bitterest struggles lie ahead of us, as America's death-bed paranoia drives her to greater excesses abroad . . ."

He spoke not of the decline of the West, but of its death by greed and constipation. He hated America very deeply, he said, and Smiley supposed he did. Haydon also took it for granted that secret services were the only real measure of a nation's political health, the only real expression of its subconscious.

Finally he came to his own case. At Oxford, he said, he was genuinely of the right, and in the war it scarcely mattered where one stood as long as one was fighting the Germans. For a while, after '45, he said, he had remained content with Britain's part in the world, till gradually it dawned on him just how trivial this was. How and when was a mystery. In the historical mayhem of his own lifetime he could point to no one occasion; simply he knew that if England were out of the game, the price of fish would not be altered by a farthing. He had often wondered which side he would be on if the test ever came; after prolonged reflection he had finally to admit that if either monolith had to win the day, he would prefer it to be the East.

"It's an aesthetic judgement as much as anything," he explained, looking up. "Partly a moral one, of course."

"Of course," said Smiley politely.

From then on, he said, it was only a matter of time before he put his efforts where his convictions lay.

That was the first day's take. A white sediment had formed on Haydon's lips, and he had begun weeping again. They agreed to meet tomorrow at the same time.

"It would be nice to go into the detail a little, if we could, Bill," Smiley said as he left.

"Oh, and look—tell Jan, will you?" Haydon was lying on the bed, staunching his nose again. "Doesn't matter a hoot what you say, long as you make it final." Sitting up, he wrote out a cheque and put it in a brown envelope. "Give her that for the milk bill."

Realising, perhaps, that Smiley was not quite at ease with this brief, he added, "Well, I can't take her with me, can I? Even if they let her come, she'd be a bloody millstone."

The same evening, following Haydon's instructions, Smiley took a tube to Kentish Town and unearthed a cottage in an unconverted mews. A flat-faced fair girl in jeans opened the door to him; there was a smell of oil paint and baby. He could not remember whether he had met her at Bywater Street, so he opened with "I'm from Bill Haydon. He's quite all right but I've got various messages from him."

"Jesus," said the girl softly. "About bloody time and all."

The drawing-room was filthy. Through the kitchen door he saw a pile of dirty crockery and he knew she used everything until it ran out, then washed it all at once. The floorboards were bare except for long psychedelic patterns of snakes and flowers and insects painted over them.

"That's Bill's Michelangelo ceiling," she said conversationally. "Only he's not going to have Michelangelo's bad back. Are you government?" she asked, lighting a cigarette. "He works for government, he told me." Her hand was shaking and she had yellow smudges under her eyes.

"Oh, look, first I'm to give you that," said Smiley, reaching in an inside pocket, and handing her the envelope with the cheque.

"Bread," said the girl, and put the envelope beside her.

"Bread," said Smiley, answering her grin; then something in his expression, or the way he echoed that one word, made her take up the envelope and rip it open. There was no note, just the cheque, but the cheque was enough; even from where Smiley sat, he could see it had four figures.

Not knowing what she was doing, she walked across the room to the fireplace and put the cheque with the grocery bills in an old tin on the mantelpiece. She went into the kitchen and mixed two cups of Nescafé, but she came out with only one.

"Where is he?" she said. She stood facing him. "He's gone chasing after that snotty little sailor-boy again. Is that it? And this is the pay-off, is that it? Well, you bloody tell him from me—"

Smiley had had scenes like this before, and now absurdly the old words came back to him.

"Bill's been doing work of national importance. I'm afraid we can't talk about it, and nor must you. A few days ago he went abroad on a secret job. He'll be away some while. Even years. He wasn't allowed to tell anyone he was leaving. He wants you to forget him. I really am most awfully sorry."

He got that far before she burst out. He didn't hear all she said, because she was blurting and screaming, and when the baby heard her it started screaming, too, from upstairs. She was swearing—not at him, not even particularly at Bill, just swearing dry-eyed—and demanding to know who the hell, who the bloody bloody hell believed in government any more? Then her mood changed. Round the walls, Smiley noticed Bill's other paintings, mainly of the girl; few were finished, and they had a cramped, condemned quality by comparison with his earlier work.

"You don't like him, do you? I can tell," she said. "So why do you do his dirty work for him?"

To this question also there seemed no immediate answer. Returning to Bywater Street, he again had the impression of being followed, and tried to telephone Mendel with the number of a cab which had twice caught his eye, and to ask him to make immediate enquiries. For once, Mendel was out till after midnight: Smiley slept uneasily and woke at five. By eight he was back at Sarratt, to find Haydon in festive mood. The inquisitors had not bothered him; he had been told by Craddox that the exchanges had been agreed and he should expect to travel tomorrow or the next day. His requests had a valedictory ring: the balance of his salary and the proceeds of any odd sales made on his behalf should be forwarded to him care of the Moscow Narodny Bank, which would also handle his mail. The Arnolfini Gallery in Bristol had a few pictures of his, including some early water-colours of Damascus, which he coveted. Could Smiley please arrange? Then, the cover for his disappearance:

"Play it long," he advised. "Say I've been posted, lay on the mystery, give it a couple of years, then run me down . . ."

"Oh, I think we can manage something, thank you," Smiley said.

For the first time since Smiley had known him, Haydon was worried about clothes. He wanted to arrive *looking* like someone, he said; first impressions were so important. "Those Moscow tailors are unspeakable. Dress you up like a bloody beadle."

"Quite," said Smiley, whose opinion of London tailors was no better.

Oh, and there was a boy, he added carelessly, a sailor friend, lived in Notting Hill. "Better give him a couple of hundred to shut him up. Can you do that out of the reptile fund?"

"I'm sure."

He wrote out an address. In the same spirit of good fellowship, Haydon then entered into what Smiley had called the details.

He declined to discuss any part of his recruitment or of his lifelong relationship with Karla. "Lifelong?" Smiley repeated quickly. "When did you meet?" The assertions of yesterday appeared suddenly nonsensical; but Haydon would not elaborate.

From about 1950 onwards, if he was to be believed, Haydon had made Karla occasional selected gifts of intelligence. These early efforts were confined to what he hoped would directly advance the Russian cause over the American; he was "scrupulous not to give them anything harmful to ourselves," as he put it, or harmful to our agents in the field.

The Suez adventure in '56 finally persuaded him of the inanity of the British situation, and of the British capacity to spike the advance of history while not being able to offer anything by way of contribution. The sight of the Americans sabotaging the British action in Egypt was, paradoxically, an additional incentive. He would say therefore that from '56 on, he was a committed, full-time Soviet mole with no holds barred. In 1961 he formally received Soviet citizenship, and over the next ten years two Soviet medals—quaintly, he would not say which, though he insisted that they were "top stuff." Unfortunately, overseas postings during this period limited his access; and since he insisted on his information being acted upon wherever possible—"rather than being chucked into some daft Soviet archive"—his work was dangerous as well as uneven. With his return to London, Karla sent him Polly (which seemed to be the house name for Polyakov) as a helpmate, but Haydon found the constant pressure of clandestine meetings difficult to sustain, particularly in view of the quantity of stuff he was photographing.

He declined to discuss cameras, equipment, pay, or tradecraft during this pre-Merlin period in London, and Smiley was conscious all the while that even the little Haydon was telling him was selected with meticulous care from a greater, and perhaps somewhat different truth.

Meanwhile both Karla and Haydon were receiving signals that Control was smelling a rat. Control was ill, of course, but clearly he would never willingly give up the reins while there was a chance that he was making Karla a present of the service. It was a race between Control's researches and his health. Twice he had very nearly struck gold—again Haydon declined to say how—and if Karla had not been quick on his feet, the mole Gerald would have been trapped. It was out of this nervy situation that first Merlin and finally Operation Testify were born. Witchcraft was conceived primarily to take care of the succession: to put Alleline next to the throne, and hasten Control's demise. Secondly, of course, Witchcraft gave Centre absolute autonomy over the product flowing into Whitehall. Thirdly—and in the long run most important, Haydon insisted—it brought the Circus into position as a major weapon against the American target.

"How much of the material was genuine?" Smiley asked.

Obviously the standard varied according to what one wanted to achieve, said Haydon. In theory, fabrication was very easy: Haydon had only to advise Karla of Whitehall's areas of ignorance and the fabricators would write for them. Once or twice, for the hell of it, said Haydon, he had written the odd report himself. It was an amusing exercise to receive, evaluate, and distribute one's own work. The advantages of Witchcraft in terms of tradecraft were, of course, inestimable. It placed Haydon virtually out of Control's reach, and gave him a cast-iron cover story for meeting Polly whenever he wished. Often months would pass without their meeting at all. Haydon would photograph Circus documents in the seclusion of his room—under cover of preparing Polly's chicken-feed—hand it over to Esterhase with a lot of other rubbish, and let him cart it down to the safe house in Lock Gardens.

"It was a classic," Haydon said simply. "Percy made the running, I slipstreamed behind him, Roy and Toby did the legwork."

Here Smiley asked politely whether Karla had ever thought of having Haydon actually take over the Circus himself: why bother with a stalking-horse at all? Haydon stalled and it occurred to Smiley that Karla, like Control, might well have considered Haydon better cast as a subordinate.

Operation Testify, said Haydon, was rather a desperate

throw. Haydon was certain that Control was getting very warm indeed. An analysis of the files he was drawing produced an uncomfortably complete inventory of the operations that Haydon had blown, or otherwise caused to abort. He had also succeeded in narrowing the field to officers of a certain age and rank . . .

"Was Stevcek's original offer genuine, by the way?" Smiley asked.

"Good Lord, no," said Haydon, actually shocked. "It was a fix from the start. Stevcek existed, of course. He was a distinguished Czech general. But he never made an offer to anyone."

Here Smiley sensed Haydon falter. For the first time, he actually seemed uneasy about the morality of his behaviour. His manner became noticeably defensive.

"Obviously, we needed to be certain Control would rise, and how he would rise . . . and who he would send. We couldn't have him picking some half-arsed little pavement artist; it had to be a big gun to make the story stick. We knew he'd only settle for someone outside the mainstream and someone who wasn't Witchcraft-cleared. If we made it a Czech, he'd have to choose a Czech speaker, naturally."

"Naturally."

"We wanted old Circus: someone who could bring down the temple a bit."

"Yes," said Smiley, remembering that heaving, sweating figure on the hilltop. "Yes, I see the logic of that."

"Well, damn it, I got him back," Haydon snapped.

"Yes, that was good of you. Tell me, did Jim come to see you before he left on that Testify mission?"

"Yes, he did, as a matter of fact."

"To say what?"

For a long, long while Haydon hesitated, then did not answer. But the answer was written there, all the same: in the sudden emptying of his eyes, in the shadow of guilt that crossed his face. He came to warn you, Smiley thought; because he loved you. To warn you; just as he came to tell me that Control was mad, but couldn't find me because I was in Berlin. Jim was watching your back for you right till the end.

Also, Haydon resumed, it had to be a country with a recent history of counter-revolution: Czecho was honestly the only place.

Smiley appeared not quite to be listening.

"Why did you bring him back?" he asked. "For friendship's sake? Because he was harmless and you held all the cards?"

It wasn't just that, Haydon explained. As long as Jim was in a Czech prison (he didn't say Russian), people would agitate for him and see him as some sort of key. But once he was back, everyone in Whitehall would conspire to keep him quiet; that was the way of it with repatriations.

"I'm surprised Karla didn't just shoot him. Or did he hold back out of delicacy towards you?"

But Haydon had drifted away again into half-baked political assertions.

Then he began speaking about himself, and already, to Smiley's eye, he seemed visibly to be shrinking to something quite small and mean. He was touched to hear that Ionesco had recently promised us a play in which the hero kept silent and everyone round him spoke incessantly. When the psychologists and fashionable historians came to write their apologias for him, he hoped they would remember that that was how he saw himself. As an artist he had said all he had to say at the age of seventeen, and one had to do something with one's later years. He was awfully sorry he couldn't take some of his friends with him. He hoped Smiley would remember him with affection.

Smiley wanted at that point to tell him that he would not remember him in those terms at all, and a good deal more besides, but there seemed no point and Haydon was having another nosebleed.

"Oh, I'm to ask you to avoid publicity, by the way. Miles Sercombe made quite a thing of it."

Here Haydon managed a laugh. Having messed up the

Circus in private, he said, he had no wish to repeat the process in public.

Before he left, Smiley asked the one question he still cared about.

"I'll have to break it to Ann. Is there anything particular you want me to pass on to her?"

It required discussion for the implication of Smiley's question to get through to him. At first, he thought Smiley had said "Jan," and couldn't understand why he had not yet called on her.

"Oh, *your* Ann," he said, as if there were a lot of Ann's around.

It was Karla's idea, he explained. Karla had long recognised that Smiley represented the biggest threat to the mole Gerald. "He said you were quite good."

"Thank you."

"But you had this one price: Ann. The last illusion of the illusionless man. He reckoned that if I were known to be Ann's lover around the place you wouldn't see me very straight when it came to other things." His eyes, Smiley noticed, had become very fixed. Pewtery, Ann called them. "Not to strain it or anything but, if it was possible, join the queue. Point?"

"Point," said Smiley.

For instance, on the night of Testify, Karla was adamant that if possible Haydon should be dallying with Ann. As a form of insurance.

"And wasn't there in fact a small hitch that night?" Smiley asked, remembering Sam Collins and the matter of whether Ellis had been shot. Haydon agreed that there had been. If everything had gone according to plan, the first Czech bulletins should have broken at ten-thirty. Haydon would have had a chance to read his club ticker-tape after Sam Collins had rung Ann, and before he arrived at the Circus to take over. But because Jim had been shot, there was fumble at the Czech end and the bulletin was released after his club had closed.

"Lucky no one followed it up," he said, helping himself to another of Smiley's cigarettes. "Which one was I, by the way?" he asked conversationally. "I forget."

"Tailor. I was Beggarman."

By then Smiley had had enough, so he slipped out, not bothering to say goodbye. He got into his car and drove for an hour anywhere, till he found himself on a side road to Oxford doing eighty, so he stopped for lunch and headed back for London. He still couldn't face Bywater Street, so he went to a cinema, dined somewhere, and got home at midnight, slightly drunk, to find both Lacon and Miles Sercombe on the doorstep, and Sercombe's fatuous Rolls, the black bedpan, all fifty feet of it, shoved up on the curb in everyone's way.

They drove to Sarratt at a mad speed, and there, in the open night under a clear sky, lit by several hand torches and stared at by several white-faced inmates of the Nursery, sat Bill Haydon on a garden bench facing the moonlit cricket field. He was wearing striped pyjamas under his overcoat; they looked more like prison clothes. His eyes were open and his head was propped unnaturally to one side, like the head of a bird when its neck has been expertly broken.

There was no particular dispute about what had happened. At ten-thirty Haydon had complained to his guards of sleeplessness and nausea: he proposed to take some fresh air. His case being regarded as closed, no one thought to accompany him and he walked out into the darkness alone. One of the guards remembered him making a joke about "examining the state of the wicket." The other was too busy watching the television to remember anything. After half an hour they became apprehensive, so the senior guard went off to take a look while his assistant stayed behind in case Haydon should return. Haydon was found where he was now sitting; the guard thought at first that he had fallen asleep. Stooping over him, he caught the smell of alcohol—he guessed gin or vodka—and decided that Haydon was drunk, which surprised him since the

352

Nursery was officially dry. It wasn't till he tried to lift him that his head flopped over, and the rest of him followed as dead weight. Having vomited (the traces were over there by the tree), the guard propped him up again and sounded the alarm.

Had Haydon received any messages during the day? Smiley asked.

No. But his suit had come back from the cleaners and it was possible a message had been concealed in it—for instance inviting him to a rendezvous.

"So the Russians did it," the Minister announced with satisfaction to Haydon's unresponsive form. "To stop him peaching, I suppose. Bloody thugs."

"No," said Smiley. "They take pride in getting their people back."

"Then who the hell *did?*"

Everyone waited on Smiley's answer, but none came. The torches went out and the group moved uncertainly towards the car.

"Can we lose him just the same?" the Minister asked on the way back.

"He was a Soviet citizen. Let them have him," said Lacon.

They agreed it was a pity about the networks. Better see whether Karla would do the deal anyhow.

"He won't," said Smiley.

39

Recalling all this in the seclusion of his first-class compartment, Smiley had the curious sensation of watching Haydon through the wrong end of a telescope. He had eaten very little since last night, but the bar had been open for most of the journey.

Leaving King's Cross, he had had a wistful notion of liking Haydon and respecting him: Bill was a man, after all, who had had something to say and had said it. But his mental system rejected this convenient simplification. The more he puzzled over Haydon's rambling account of himself, the more conscious he was of the contradictions. He tried at first to see Haydon in the romantic newspaper terms of a thirties intellectual, for whom Moscow was the natural Mecca. "Moscow was Bill's discipline," he told himself. "He needed the symmetry of an historical and economic solution." This struck him as too sparse, so he added more of the man whom he was trying to like: "Bill was a romantic and a snob. He wanted to join an elitist vanguard and lead the masses out of darkness." Then he remembered the half-finished canvases in the girl's drawing room in Kentish Town: cramped, over-worked, and condemned. He remembered also the ghost of Bill's authoritarian father—Ann had called him simply the Monster—and he imagined Bill's Marxism making up for his inadequacy as an artist and for his loveless childhood. Later, of course, it hardly mattered if the doctrine wore thin. Bill was set on the road and Karla would know how to keep him there. Treason is very much a matter of habit, Smiley decided, seeing Bill again stretched out on the floor in Bywater Street, while Ann played him music on the gramophone.

Bill had loved it, too. Smiley didn't doubt that for a moment. Standing at the middle of a secret stage, playing world against world, hero and playwright in one: oh, Bill had loved that, all right.

Smiley shrugged it all aside, distrustful as ever of the standard shapes of human motive. He settled instead for a picture of one of those wooden Russian dolls that open up, revealing one person inside the other, and another inside him. Of all men living, only Karla had seen the last little doll inside Bill Haydon. When was Bill recruited, and how? Was his right-wing stand at Oxford a pose, or was it paradoxically the state of sin from which Karla summoned him to grace?

Ask Karla: pity I didn't.

Ask Jim: I never shall.

Over the flat East Anglian landscape as it slid slowly by, the unyielding face of Karla replaced Bill Haydon's crooked death mask. "But you had this one price: Ann. The last illusion of the illusionless man. He reckoned that if I were known to be Ann's lover around the place you wouldn't see me very straight when it came to other things."

Illusion? Was that really Karla's name for love? And Bill's?

"Here," said the guard very loudly, and perhaps for the second time. "Come on with it, you're for Grimsby, aren't you?"

"No, no—Immingham." Then he remembered Mendel's instructions and clambered onto the platform.

There was no cab in sight, so, having enquired at the ticket office, he made his way across the empty forecourt and stood beside a green sign marked "Queue." He had hoped she might collect him, but perhaps she hadn't received his wire. Ah well: the post office at Christmas: who could blame them? He wondered how she would take the news about Bill; till, remembering her frightened face on the cliffs in Cornwall, he realized that by then Bill was already dead for her. She had sensed the coldness of his touch, and somehow guessed what lay behind it.

Illusion? He repeated to himself. Illusionless?

It was bitterly cold. He hoped very much that her wretched lover had found her somewhere warm to live.

He wished he had brought her fur boots from the cupboard under the stairs.

He remembered the copy of Grimmelshausen, still uncollected at Martindale's club.

Then he saw her: her disreputable car shunting towards him down the lane marked "Buses Only" and Ann at the wheel staring the wrong way. Saw her get out, leaving the indicator winking, and walk into the station to enquire: tall and puckish, extraordinarily beautiful, essentially another man's woman.

. . .

For the rest of that term, Jim Prideaux behaved in the eyes of Roach much as his mother had behaved when his father went away. He spent a lot of time on little things, like fixing up the lighting for the school play and mending the soccer nets with string, and in French he took enormous pains over small inaccuracies. But big things, like his walks and solitary golf, he gave up altogether, and in the evenings stayed in and kept clear of the village. Worst of all was his staring empty look when Roach caught him unaware, and the way he forgot things in class, even red marks for merit. Roach had to remind him to hand them in each week.

To support him, Roach took the job of dimmer man on the lighting. Thus at rehearsals Jim had to give him a special signal—to Bill and no one else. He was to raise his arm and drop it to his side when he wanted the footlights to fade.

With time, Jim seemed to respond to treatment, however. His eye grew clearer and he became alert again, as the shadow of his mother's death withdrew. By the night of the play, he was more light-hearted than Roach had ever known him. "Hey, Jumbo, you silly toad, where's your mac—can't you see it's raining?" he called out as, tired but triumphant, they trailed back to the main building after the performance. "His real name is Bill," he heard him explain to a visiting parent. "We were new boys together."

The gun, Bill Roach had finally convinced himself, was, after all, a dream.

A Note on the Type

The text of this book was set on the Linotype in Janson, a re-cutting made direct from type cast from matrices long thought to have been made by the Dutchman Anton Janson, who was a practicing type founder in Leipzig during the years 1668–87. However, it has been conclusively demonstrated that these types are actually the work of Nicholas Kis (1650–1702), a Hungarian, who most probably learned his trade from the master Dutch type founder Dirk Voskens. The type is an excellent example of the influential and sturdy Dutch types that prevailed in England up to the time William Caslon developed his own incomparable designs from these Dutch faces.